W9-CBY-011

A Will of Her Own

BY

ANNE NICHOLS REYNOLDS

the Peppertree Press
Sarasota, Florida

 Graphic design by Rebecca Barbier.
Cover photography by Paula Sapp.

For information regarding permission,
call 941-922-2662 or contact us at our website:
www.peppertreepublishing.com or write to:
the Peppertree Press, LLC.
Attention: Publisher
1269 First Street, Suite 7
Sarasota, Florida 34236

ISBN: 978-1-61493-304-5
Library of Congress Number: 2014918575
Printed in the U.S.A.
Printed January 2015

Dedication

For Dan and Kathryn Durrance, special, lifelong friends,
who showed me a Florida the tourists rarely see.
Camping on Buck Island Ranch is one of my all-time
favorite memories, and the experience gave me
a greater appreciation of Florida's unique
environment and history.

Also by Anne Nichols Reynolds

Winter Harvest

Acknowledgments

Kudos go to the Avon Park Wordsmiths, a critique group and chapter of the Florida Writer's Association. They are truly "Writers helping writers." Thank you, Christine and Carl Yarbour, Dottie Rexford, Lynn Ullin, Lorna Keith, SuzannaCrean, Sunny Serafino, and our seasonal members.

Thank you, to the Lake Tsuga Artists who read my novel to check for flow. Special thanks to Catherine Cornelius, Sunny Serafino, Sue Dambrell, and Jennifer Goodson for helping edit, and to all of my wonderful friends and family, who encourage and inspire me. The expertise of Charles Reynolds, Gillie Russell, and Rita Youngman is greatly appreciated. Paula Sapp's photography and Paul and Candy Albritton's time are also appreciated.

The dedication of Florida archaeologists, who strive to study, document, and preserve remaining Native American sites, and landowners who volunteer and help in this endeavor are to be commended.

A big thank you to Kissimmee Valley Archaeological and Historical Conservancy, Gordon Davis and the archaeology students of Walker Memorial Academy, David Butler, Ph.D., and the volunteers at the Blueberry dig. Thank you all for the journey.

Although some of the Florida sites and events are real, A Will of Her Own is a work of fiction created in the author's mind. Any mistakes in this novel are the author's own.

CHAPTER ONE

Katie Mulholland sat ramrod straight as she gave herself a no nonsense lecture to keep her mind on driving. This was a futile exercise because, in truth, she felt as wretched as the weather. The gray sky darkened to a purple bruise. Strong gusts of wind buffeted the blue Taurus and strewed broken limbs and clumps of gray moss across the empty two-lane road. White hot shards of lightning fractured the darkness and burst in a macabre dance above the treetops.

Thoughts of Gunnar's insistence on living together without marriage went against the values her parents had instilled in their children. She heard again her mother's admonition, "If you don't respect yourself, how can you expect others to respect you?"

Gunnar had one more year of law school and was adamant about not being pressured into marriage until he took a position in his father's law firm. Katie had met his parents once. They broadly hinted that a live-in arrangement was more amenable to them than marriage at this point in Gunnar's career. They hadn't said she was socially unacceptable, but their body language fairly shouted their disappointment.

A cold splash hit Katie when his mother snidely remarked, "We understand hormones, dear. Just be careful. You comprehend what I mean, don't you, dear?" His mother nodded as if believing Katie got the message. "There now, we understand one another."

The embarrassing comments provoked Katie to respond.

Gunnar accurately read the rising storm and jumped into the breach. "Mother, you're out of line. Katie's a nice girl, and I want her to be treated as such."

Katie was grateful for his words and the arm he had placed protectively around her shoulders. She swallowed her retort.

His mother had shrugged eloquently, and the bemused expression she cast her immaculately groomed husband was far from apologetic. The evening had been disastrous, and Gunnar was moody for days. "They'll learn to love you, as I do," he told her. This was the only time he mentioned love.

At least Katie's family had been warm and friendly, making Gunnar feel at home. They trusted Katie's judgment. Katie knew her parents would be disappointed if she moved in with Gunnar.

Katie longed to be home. She would miss the little apartment her parents helped her find near school, so she wouldn't have the distraction of dorm life. Her little abode had once housed the horses of the Delacroix family. The stable had been restored and turned into an apartment. Two maiden ladies, heiresses of the Delacroix line, kept their eyes on her comings and goings across the courtyard. Katie loved the rustic rooms that displayed her romantic décor, and the French Provencal eclectic mix of furniture. Her upright piano was the focal point, by way of, taking up the most space. Katie's music lifted her spirits and relaxed her.

Gunnar's larger apartment, a condo on Beecher Street, had a view of the swimming pool two floors below. His taste ran to stark Danish blond furniture, angular lines, and neutral colors. The uncluttered, pristine atmosphere suited the sophisticated Gunnar Andre Lindgren. He was a modern Viking, a masterful, suave intellectual who teased her about her naïve idealism and her romance novels. He was a devotee of Dvorsak, she of Chopin, but they found common ground in jazz. Katie was churched, and Gunnar dismissed religion as a crutch. His unbelief bothered her the most. Her faith was the cornerstone of her existence. Her mental list of pros and cons to the relationship was lopsided because they were opposites in many ways. Gunnar was handsome and on track to a great future. Katie knew part of the attraction was pride. He had pursued *her*. Katie's problem was not being comfortable with the idea of living with Gunnar. Liking someone and living with them were two different things. Adjustments and compromises were involved. Gunnar dominated. His superior attitude might be a deterrent to her growth as an individual.

A visit to the home of her older sister, Myra, had only confirmed she and Gunnar were mismatched. Katie wanted a marriage like Myra's, a husband like Paul to cherish her, and a couple of children to complete their lives. She and Myra were close, and on this last visit, she shared with her the hopes for her future and her fears of losing Gunnar. Confiding in Myra had always been easy.

Gunnar had given her an ultimatum after she stopped him during a sexually charged moment. He shook his head frustrated by her denial. "We can't go on like this. I'm not made out of stone. Grow up, Katie." His nostrils flared with passion, his sculptured lips drew back in a cynical smile, and his grey eyes glinted. Gunnar reclined away from her, his elbow on the arm of the couch, his other arm extended across its back. "Katie, Katie," he laughed with a touch of scorn.

"I want you. I need you, sweetheart," not "I love you." *He's too proud to say it, to get what he wants.* He looked so handsome with his blond hair swept across a broad forehead. Katie had felt stinging humiliation and despair as she buttoned her blouse. *Why can't I give myself to Gunnar? Because I'm not sure, not ready? Will I ever be?*

"You're all grown up now. You can make your own choices." His hands cupped her face, his thumbs rhythmically rubbing her cheeks. This was his way of saying her upbringing shouldn't matter, and he made her feel like a child. "You want this as much as I do."

Only she didn't. His seduction didn't feel right. Would she ever be totally comfortable with him? She knew the answer. *Why beat myself up over it? Because of pride, fear of failure?*

"I think you have some reservations about building a life with Gunnar," Myra had said. "You aren't comfortable with his lifestyle, and you're afraid he isn't going to change. And he won't change," she said emphatically, "but *you* will ... if you want your marriage to succeed. Are you willing to compromise?"

Can I give up my beliefs, my identity for a future with Gunnar?

"You and Gunnar aren't in love. You're attracted to one another. There's a lot of territory between the two," Myra stated. "Real love doesn't demand compliance and issue ultimatums." Her sister's words had merit.

"If Gunnar loved you, he'd respect your feelings and understand your upbringing instead of making fun of it."

Katie's white-knuckled fingers gripped the steering wheel as one fat drop became ten, and a deluge followed. The wipers attempted to give her a glimpse of the road ahead but did little to facilitate the view. Chill bumps skated across her skin at the thought of driving alone in this wilderness. Darkness descended as the temperature dropped into the low 40s, unusual for early October in Louisiana. "Myra and her short cuts," Katie grumbled aloud. The interstate might have added eighteen miles, but at the moment, it would have been preferable. She wanted to pull over, but only a narrow strip of shrubbery separated the road from a canal.

A pickup truck pulled into her path from a hidden driveway causing her to swerve as she mashed her brakes in an effort not to collide. Katie's car lights illuminated the back of an older man at the wheel. Shaken, she fought to control her car. The tail lights of the truck dimmed. With miles of empty road, she couldn't believe he hadn't seen her lights. *And older people talk about young drivers!*

Tension drew Katie's neck and shoulders taut. She tried to concentrate on the faint red lights ahead, but they seemed to weave from one side of the road to the other. Katie blinked, wondering if her impaired vision played tricks. The lights vanished. She applied her brakes, and horrified, watched as the white body of the truck plunged down into the dark water of the canal. Katie pushed on the hazard lights and pulled two wheels onto the narrow shoulder. By the time she got out of her car, the front of the truck was below the surface.

She saw no one in the water. Several large bubbles rose to the surface followed by lines of smaller bubbles. Everything shifted into slow motion. Extricating herself from the confining jacket and jumping into the murky water seemed to take an interminable time instead of moments. The cold slap of the water brought her to the surface gasping. The icy reality of the situation fisted in her chest. Her water-soaked jeans and tennis shoes weighed her down. Holding her breath, she went under and removed them, a time-consuming task. *Don't panic,* she told herself repeatedly as she tried to wriggle out of her sodden pants. *Don't panic.*

You can do this. A man is in the truck. He hasn't surfaced. He must be hurt. Her energy focused on getting him out.

Submerging, she felt around the outline of the truck, found the door handle, and pulled. The door didn't budge. She couldn't see much, but she knew the truck was upright, the nose pointing downward, as it sank. Breaking the surface, she filled her burning lungs with air. Scrambling over the top of the truck, she tried the other side, fumbling again for a door handle. The passenger side opened a crack as water filled the cab. Adrenalin surged through Katie's system. With abnormal strength, she pried open the door. A rush of water pushed her into the cab and forced her against the dashboard, causing the truck to shift eerily. She felt a brief jab as her arm caught the edge of the open glove compartment.

Grabbing a hand that brushed her face, she tugged and the man's body moved. *He must not have been wearing a seat belt.* He wasn't struggling. Closing his nose and mouth with one hand and pulling on him with her other, she wrestled to free him from the cab. Her lungs burned. Bracing her feet on the open door and the cab, she levered herself away from the interior. With her remaining strength, she fought an upward battle, dragging the man's inert weight.

Breaking the surface, she gulped precious air greedily along with some water. Katie coughed and sputtered as she hauled his head above water and pulled him to the bank. She pushed him up as far as she could, until his chest was partially above water. She tried to gain purchase on solid ground. Her feet sank into a mucky area. Katie dug in her toes, pushing forward over submerged roots. *Help me, God.*

Two cars passed but didn't stop. *We're not visible because of the weeds.*

Katie clawed her way through brush lining the road, and at the same time, tried to keep the man from slipping back into the water. Sobs wracked her as she pulled herself free. She turned and grabbed the man under the arms and pulled him up the bank until his torso was flat on the road in front of her car.

She had a brief glimpse of his pallid face and thin white hair plastered to his skull as she rolled him onto his side to let any water escape. She tried to remember what to do. She had taken a course in CPR, but did it work on a drowning victim? He wasn't breathing. She checked to see if his mouth was clear.

Turning him onto his back, she pinched his nostrils closed and blew in two breaths. Then she put the heel of one hand in the center of his chest, clasped it with the other, and compressed, repeating the whole process a dozen times. Her body shook as she worked.

Breathe, she commanded silently at each compression. "Breathe. Please God, let him breathe," she prayed aloud.

A strangled sound answered, and she knew he was going to be sick. She pulled him over onto his side so he wouldn't choke and held his head while he vomited. She swallowed the bile of nausea that threatened to weaken her.

Shivering uncontrollably, Katie lay down. She felt drained but exultant. The rain had subsided to a drizzle, and the wind died to short gusts as chill bit her bare legs and seeped through her wet clothing. "Yes," she shouted. "Thank you, God. Thank you," she said over and over. They were alive, incredibly alive. "We're alive!" she shouted, easing her constricted throat.

The man opened his eyes and looked at her as if she were mad. "What the hell?" Bits and pieces of memory clicked into place as J.D. Stetson faced the girl who had just pulled him from the canal. She was young and not very big, her wet hair plastered to her head. *How did she do it?* His head hurt like it had been hit with a bat, and he felt sick. His wet clothing was glued to his limbs and his chilled body jerked uncontrollably. She didn't have on much clothing. Her feet were bare. *Why isn't she dressed?* His brain must be shutting down, his thoughts scrambled. *What happened?*

"We're going to freeze to death," Katie shouted above the pounding of her heart. He was not a big man, but her efforts to pull him upright were hampered by the weight of his wet clothing.

The man's fingers dug into the pavement. He moved and collapsed, a sodden heap.

She began to hiccup, the canal water leaving a bad taste. Becoming aware of their dire situation, Katie released a keening sound unfamiliar to her ears. "God," she implored, "we can't freeze to death now!" She took one of his frozen hands and rubbed vigorously. Surely, someone would stop and help, but when no cars passed, reality seeped into her consciousness. The road was little used because of the Interstate. She looked at the canal where just a blur of white remained visible. The fetid smell wrinkled Katie's nose and made her aware the taste of rotted vegetation lingered in her mouth. Visions of snakes, gators, and slimy things in those dark depths brought her to her feet, the insidious lethargy replaced by an urgent desire to leave.

"We have to get help," she urged as she pulled at his shoulders. He didn't move, but tortured breaths rattled in his chest, and he had a spasm of coughing. *Lord,* she prayed fervently, *what do we do now?* "Help us, God."

Several oaths and expletives in a hoarse voice widened her eyes. Drawing himself up on his hands and knees, the man half-crawled and half-staggered toward her car. He pulled himself up, using the fender for support, leaving her behind.

Katie managed to help him into the back seat and fastened his seat belt.

A car was coming. She tried to flag the driver down, but he didn't stop. *Couldn't he tell a half-naked woman was in trouble?*

Katie retrieved her jacket and put it over the injured man. The material was wet on the outside but dry inside. She noticed a lump on his forehead and a gash that bled down into his collar. She opened the trunk and got out some spare clothing to put over him. With trembling fingers, Katie wrapped the sleeve of a shirt over the wound, tied it, and piled the rest of the shirt over his head like a turban.

J.D.'s head throbbed. He reached up to pull the thing off.

"Leave it," she ordered. "This will help hold in your body heat." He dropped his hand, and she closed his door.

J.D. looked out the window where his truck had left the road. He rubbed his temple, trying to collect his thoughts. He remembered hitting a puddle and fishtailing. The truck lost traction and ditched in the canal. *I must have hit my head ... have to make calls before the press gets hold of the story.*

Judd was at Corazon. Aaron would have to call in a team and make arrangements. He tapped his pocket. The phone was gone.

Katie pulled a beach towel out of the trunk and wrapped it around her bare legs. After slamming the trunk shut, she got behind the wheel and started the engine. Shaking in short, violent spasms, Katie managed to turn up the heater and drive. She turned on the light and angled the rearview mirror to check on him.

The man leaned back, breathing noisily. Deep furrows gouged his face, and a predominant nose perched under startling black brows. "You believe there's a God, girl?" a raspy voice challenged her.

"Yes," she answered emphatically. "I'll never doubt Him again."

"Humph!" he grumbled. "God!" he barked. *She believes in the almighty, all-powerful … what do you expect? She's young and ignorant.*

Humph, indeed! Katie thought. *He probably doesn't have an appreciative bone in his body. I could have died back there, and so might he.*

"Why'd you do it?" the old man asked, his voice scratchy snd barely audible.

Katie didn't have an answer. "I don't know," she said, her teeth chattering and her lips numb. "I guess if I'd thought about it first, I wouldn't have."

"Do you know who I am, girl?" *Why bother to ask? She knows who I am.*

The gruffness of the man's voice surprised her. Katie looked in the rearview mirror.

He had straightened and leaned toward her shoulder as he spoke.

She glanced at him, startled by the glaring eyes that seemed to accuse her of some criminal act. She gasped and turned her attention back to the road. *He could be a convict, or insane, or both.* Fear crept into her mind, and she accelerated the car, dodging the larger puddles in the road.

"What do you want for saving my life?" he demanded. His voice had become stronger as each question pelted her.

Katie slowed and took a closer look at him.

His eyes gleamed expectantly, and a cynical smirk cracked his granite face. "Well, what do you want, girl?" He knew. *Money. A job. Fame.* The thoughts exhausted him. *It's always money. More money.* His chin dropped onto his chest, the aftertaste of bile and soreness in his throat, a reminder of his mortality. *I'm tired. So tired.*

Katie shivered at the venom of bitterness she detected. She shut off the light.

"Nothing," she answered shortly, turning her attention back to the road. "I want *nothing* from you." *The only thing I want is to get you out of my car.*

"Hah!" he snorted. "You'll change your tune soon enough." *They all do. Yes. They all do.*

Katie's head throbbed, and she sneezed several times in rapid succession. Wiggling in the seat, she shed the sodden towel and laid a dry blouse over her legs. They'd be lucky to escape pneumonia, and who knew what they had swallowed. The scummy water combined with bile left a bad taste.

The man had leaned back and closed his eyes. He was mercifully quiet except for a deep rattle when he breathed.

Several miles down the road, Katie spotted a mailbox and slowed. A narrow bridge over concrete culverts crossed the canal. The structure looked sturdy, but it took the last of her courage to cross to the other side. Down the driveway, she had seen a light. A single lit window glowed like a gem in the distance.

"What are you doing? Why aren't we on the road?" J.D. Stetson leaned forward and shook her shoulder. "Am I being kidnapped?" His voice rose as his situation cleared everything else from his mind. "You won't get any ransom for me. You hear me, girl? No money. That's policy."

Her answer was to accelerate down the dirt track.

A dog barked behind a wire fence as she brought the car to a stop. Another light came on, and a man stood silhouetted in the screened doorway.

Katie leaned her head against the cool steering wheel, exhausted.

CHAPTER TWO

Five Years Later

Katie's secretary, Mrs. DuPuis, beeped her phone line. "A Mr. Judd Stetson is here, and he insists on seeing you."

"I don't know him," Katie said as she arranged the designs on her desk. "Please tell him to make an appointment. I'll see him later today." *Stetson.* She closed her eyes. *J. D. Stetson? Why would he want to see her?* The extra time would give her a chance to calm down and gather her thoughts.

The door opened, and Katie raised her head to look into a pair of piercing blue eyes. They arrogantly appraised her beneath dark brows, their impact startling. *Not J.D. This man gets what he wants.* The evidence lay in his commanding stance, the expensive cut of his suit, and the hard implacable face which had arrested her attention when he barged into her office unannounced.

"I don't *know* J.D. Stetson," she told him. The intense sense of pleasure to see his startled expression strengthened her backbone.

"The name is Stetson. Judd Stetson," the man grated out between clenched teeth. He couldn't believe this slip of a girl wanted him to come back later. "You are the same Katie Mulholland who fished my grandfather out of that canal five years ago," his words scathing in tone.

"That's over and done with. I don't know the man."

Incredulous disbelief flickered briefly in his eyes and firmed his mouth. Clearly, her answer wasn't expected. Quickly looking down, she reshuffled the designs on her desk. "Now, if that's all Mr. ..." she started dismissively.

Two powerful hands slammed down on the desktop startling her, the papers scattering. He leaned over her desk. "Stetson, and no, that is not all, Ms. Mulholland, You knew him. You saved him from ..."

Katie's eyes widened at this unexpected outburst. "Well, I've certainly tried to forget the fact, Mr. Stetson!" she retorted just as emphatically.

"You've been thoroughly investigated, Ms. Mulholland," he continued as though he hadn't heard her.

Katie felt the heat rising to her neck. *Will that one incident hound me forever?* So much of her life had changed because of an act of fate. She saw and felt the raw anger emanating from the man. Pride ignited and flared. "Now, just a minute, Mr. Stetson," she said, stressing the name above all names she wished to forget, "I wouldn't care if you were J.D. Stetson himself. You are not welcome in this office." She rose from her chair and leaned forward, an indignant cat with fur rubbed the wrong way. "Take your sleazy investigation, and get out!" Katie's voice trebled in strength.

Mrs. Jeanne DuPuis, the self-effacing secretary, opened the door, sidled in, and hovered nearby. Her face and body reflected disapproval in every line. Katie could only imagine how this must have sounded in the outer office. Mrs. DuPuis coming to her rescue deflated her sails, and Katie sank back down in her chair. The last thing she wanted was a scene.

Judd Stetson drew himself up to his full height, which was considerable, and held up a placating hand. He had not expected to walk into a hornet's nest, and this was definitely not going as planned. *Who expected her to deny knowing J.D.?* His next thought more accurately described the problem nagging his mind. *What was the nature of your relationship with my grandfather?* His eyes narrowed as he remembered the pictures of her in J.D.'s office and of his grandfather speaking about her as if he knew her well. *How well?*

"Look, Ms. Mulholland," he began in a deeper, soothing voice, "I'm sorry, truly sorry. You took me by surprise." *And that's an understatement,* he thought wryly. "J.D. had a massive heart attack several days ago. He's dead."

Katie closed her eyes and prayed J.D. Stetson's death ended all the speculation. *Now what?*

Judd gauged her reaction as shock first, then disbelief, and finally, what? *Relief?* His eyes wandered over her impeccable figure. She was above medium height, slender, with a clear complexion, now devoid of color. Her black hair scraped into a ponytail made her look young and vulnerable, a far cry from the tigress of minutes before. He definitely felt uneasy about his reactions to her.

No, he didn't see relief. When she looked up at him, her large hazel eyes were full of dread, a bewildering revelation. Her long, slender fingers began to tremble, and he watched them clutch the desk as she fought for control.

Mrs. DuPuis cleared her throat.

Katie caught her eye, nodded a dismissal, and she slipped from the room quietly.

"What do you want?" Katie asked wearily as he sat down across from her. Before he could speak, she rose from the desk and walked to the window away from his disturbing presence. She briskly rubbed her arms to restore feeling. One of them still bore a scar, a daily reminder of the incident. Twenty-two stitches were needed to close a deep cut under her arm and above her right elbow. She hadn't been aware of the gash until later. Her stay in the emergency room had been brief. Mr. Stetson had not been so lucky. He contracted pneumonia and nearly died.

"What happened … happened in another lifetime. It's best forgotten. I wanted nothing from Mr. Stetson then, and his death hasn't changed that. I'm sorry you lost your grandfather."

Judd was impressed but not convinced. He knew time would confirm his suspicions. The family was going to get more than they bargained for, this time. Katie was an enigma, an unexpected surprise.

"You took a position with the firm." His pointed statement sounded incriminating.

Katie detected a hint of accusation which brought her attention squarely back to him. "What has joining Centaur International to do with J.D. Stetson?" She sat down abruptly, holding onto the desk to keep from falling.

She saw his flinty blue eyes follow her down. Their condemnation confirmed her uneasy thoughts.

Fear rose to her throat and threatened to paralyze her very breath. "No," she whispered finally. *Did J.D. use his influence to hire me? Was Centaur International part of his empire?*

"Yes," he affirmed, as he leaned back in the chair. The smile on his curled lips displayed unveiled contempt.

Katie felt like sinking into the carpet. *It can't be true.* Her mind traveled back four years to her graduation and the letter of recommendation from her professor, Dr. Barnett. He had referred her to Centaur International Advertising and several other agencies. He had told her to start at the top, confident her ability and creative talent would be an asset. She had indeed applied at Centaur and received a position with what she considered excellent salary, great benefits, and an opportunity to move up in the agency.

She was good. No, she was very good, as Evan Collins, a junior partner in the firm, had told her on numerous occasions. Some of her ideas and her imaginative presentations brought the firm clients, well-known clients. The agency grew, and she was a part of its expansion. She had received several raises and her own small office. She shared a secretary with two commercial ad directors. *Have I gotten too much too soon?* J.D. Stetson hadn't been mentioned. He couldn't have anything to do with Centaur.

One quelling look on Judd Stetson's arrogant face was threatening to crumble her hopes of a future. Katie straightened her back. *I might be ignorant, but I won't be badgered.* "Maybe you should spell it out for me, Mr. Stetson," her voice deceptively soft. "What is the connection you are bursting to tell me?" She refused to look down or anywhere but straight into those cold blue eyes.

Judd felt a brief stab of pain in the region of his heart as her unwavering gaze challenged him. He had watched those incredulous golden eyes as they narrowed and widened on their journey of discovery. The furrows between those dark, winged brows first deepened, and then her creamy, unblemished skin smoothed out. *Hell, she acts like she doesn't know. But of course she does. She has to know.* Something about her actions didn't add up. *What if she doesn't?* At the thought, Judd's anger ebbed. If she didn't know, he was a dream slayer. That's what he had seen reflected in her eyes. He remembered his own shattered dreams as a boy and later as a man. A feeling of protectiveness crept unwanted into a chink of his armor. She had courage, but he knew that. Five years ago seemed like a lifetime had passed since she had pulled J.D. out of a dark canal. She had only been nineteen. Several times he drove by the very spot and wondered at her courage.

She was a lovely young woman, and she was waiting. He didn't want to hurt her. He didn't want to say anything. He just wanted to get out of her life and never ... but of course, he couldn't. J. D. had seen to that. Settling back into the chair, he wondered what she had gleaned from the last few moments, if she had insight into the new feelings assailing him.

Katie felt vindicated. It was as if the wind had stopped, and he was becalmed. He no longer portrayed an arrogant ogre but a man who had known pain and retreated from it.

"Miss Mulholland," he began quietly, drawing her out of her reverie. He dropped the Ms. title. His deep, resonant voice soothed when it was in control. "I apologize for barging in here and acting like a belligerent schoolboy. There are things of which you are evidently unaware." He was uncomfortable with his apology.

It occurred to Katie he wasn't in the habit of admitting he was wrong. Her bemusement evaporated at his next words. They were edged in a smattering of anger she felt lingered just below the surface.

"You may wish you had never heard of J.D. Stetson, but you were irrevocably a part of his life and now his death. No amount of wishing can change the fact. I think it best to begin again, at another time, when we've both mastered our feelings of animosity. Over dinner tonight, we'll begin again, discuss the situation, and answer questions. Will seven be convenient?"

The gall of the man. Katie almost choked. She rose to her feet, ignoring her quaking knees. "You come in here accusing me of using J.D. Stetson, apologize, and expect me to be so grateful, I'll have dinner with you." She knew her voice was rising, but she couldn't stop it any more than she could stop shaking. "I don't have any questions. Please leave." Katie folded her arms across her chest and willed him to go.

Judd rose slowly to his feet and smiled.

Her heart plummeted to her feet. *This man meant trouble.*

"Seven then," he said pleasantly and left.

Katie was speechless. What was happening to her? Nothing seemed real any more. Scenarios bounced around in her head. She was about to explode with questions. The course of her life was about to change again. She sensed it. "Irrevocably," the word he used. The independent part of her itched to fight the tide. "Irrevocably" he had said.

CHAPTER THREE

The door to Evan's office pounded the wall as Katie swept in unannounced. Lyn Watkins, his secretary, reached in and closed the door behind her, the surprised "O" still pasted on her face.

Evan cringed ever so slightly, stood, and tugged on his collar. "What's wrong? I've never seen you like this." He tried to sound cheerfully concerned, but he was tense, and Katie observed his reticence. Evan Collins was about her height with blond hair thinning on top. The brown eyes that had always seemed sincere now evaded hers. He was definitely perspiring.

"Does the name J.D. Stetson mean anything to you?"

Evan punched the intercom, "Lyn, find Hershal, and tell him to come here, now."

Hershal Cleeland was the senior partner in the firm and Evan's immediate superior.

Katie was sure Lyn shared her own surprise at the demanding of his boss's immediate presence.

"Please sit down, Katie. I'm sure Hershal will be here any moment." Evan waved her to a chair, but she ignored him and walked to a window.

Katie wasn't seeing the city or hearing its familiar sounds. She was hearing her heart begin to hammer as she revisited the past.

After her "heroic action," as the press dubbed the rescue, she had been a reluctant celebrity. Reporters with flashbulbs flashing, college administrators, and lawyers courted her, wanting whatever they could get. But it was Gunnar who had disillusioned her, betrayed her. She thought she loved him. Now, he wanted to marry her quickly, greed, the great motivator. His fawning pleas had been nauseating. He envisioned a soaring career with the influence of J.D. Stetson, and he had pressed her to accept the money "Old" J.D. was offering.

Gunnar had been with her when Mr. Pickering of Pickering and Whitson handed her a check for a staggering amount of money. He was a stately gentleman, dignified and quiet. Mr. Pickering had handed her the check without ceremony or fuss, and she intuited his disapproval though he was careful to hide it.

Gunnar was ecstatic. He all but whooped with excitement.

Katie's eyes widened at the amount, and she had been tempted. Lord, had she been tempted. She heard again that raspy voice: "What do you want for saving my life?" She had responded, "Nothing," and he had answered, "You'll change your tune soon enough." Katie knew taking the money was wrong. How much was a life worth? He expected her to take it. He probably had reason to be the cynical, bitter man he had become. With trembling fingers she had torn up the check and handed the pieces back to an astonished Mr. Pickering before she could change her mind.

His eyes glistened with moisture, and he looked at her with such admiration, she knew her ethical decision was the right one. J.D. Stetson was about to find out that money did not buy everything.

Gunnar, on the other hand, was another matter. He apologized for her, and beside himself, made excuses for her.

She had backed out of the office. Resolutely, she marched down the hall with Gunnar circling her like a buzzard.

He pled with her to come to her senses, and when pleas didn't work, he bombarded her with his anger. "You're not woman enough for me. I need a woman with experience and a good business head, a woman who will help me, be ambitious for me. You're nothing but a stubborn fool. I can't believe I ever contemplated marrying you."

Katie thought of a reason. *Everything is about him.* When she slammed the taxi door in his incredulous face, she metaphorically slammed a door on her youth. Dreams are hard to give up.

A check in the amount of the reward was donated by J.D. Stetson to the college. As the Mulholland Graphics Design addition to the Arts Complex neared completion, she evaded the press and ignored the fawning attitude of the administration. Her parents were proud, but bewildered by all the "hoopla." They couldn't understand why she didn't go to the dedication. The ceremony was to honor her. Only Myra understood and supported her decision. Katie heard J.D. had skipped the ceremony, and the administration told the press she was unwell. She wondered if Judd Stetson attended.

Katie had spent several weeks with her family after graduation to bring balance back into her life.

Hershal Cleeland arrived in Evan's office. If he was surprised to see her, he didn't show it. He held a chair for her, and when she sat down, he followed suit.

She asked him the same question she had asked Evan.

"Yes, I've heard of J.D. Stetson," he answered without hesitation. "I believe he died." Hershal was a large man with a full black beard. He had always been friendly and encouraging. He offered both constructive criticism and praise. He helped her, and she respected his opinions. He treated her no differently than he treated his other employees. Indeed, why should he?

"Mr. Cleeland, I'm asking if J.D. Stetson has anything to do with this firm or with hiring me?"

Evan shifted uneasily in his chair.

Hershal Cleeland did not appear in the least nervous. "I know of your connection with Mr. Stetson, and I think I understand your question. Twenty-three years ago Centaur International was a fledgling ad agency," he explained. "A representative for Stetson Department Stores asked us to do an advertising campaign for them. We were one of a half dozen firms in the state asked to present an ad. I had an idea, and it seemed a good one. Mr. Stetson was so enthusiastic, he invited me to meet with him and personally show him my presentation. He was a shrewd businessman, and he had ideas of his own. We found we could work together, and our association with him has been lucrative. I've only met the man twice. Some of our clients sell their products in his stores." He paused and Evan nodded. "These accounts are ours because we earned them. They were not handed to us. Am I making myself clear?"

"Yes, sir," Katie answered. "I think so."

"I knew who you were when I interviewed you. Had you been less qualified, it might have swayed my decision, but it didn't come to that. I did, however, tell everyone on my staff J.D. Stetson was not to be discussed in your presence. I felt you were uncomfortable about the publicity."

Katie bit her lip and wondered if he would answer the second question.

"You were recommended by Dr. Barnett, an old codger who has never been corrupted by the powers that be." Hershal smiled at her as if his description told the story. "He was quite impressed by your creative imagination and illustrations. He brought some of your work to my office, something he had never done before or since." He leaned toward her and looked her straight in the eyes. "I hired Katie Mulholland because she had talent, because she would be an asset to Centaur International, and I was right."

Katie released the breath she had been holding. *He hired me because of my talent.*

Hershal Cleeland leaned back and regarded her thoughtfully beneath hooded eyelids. Bringing steepled fingers to his pursed lips, he contemplated the wisdom of his next words.

Katie wondered if he would continue.

Evan leaned forward expectantly.

"J.D. called me three years ago, a year after I hired you. He wanted to see me. The meeting was my last personal contact with him. He wanted to know about your work and said he knew everything else about you."

Katie felt her color rising, and Hershal seemed to be aware of it, even embarrassed. He asked Evan to give them some privacy and waited for him to exit before continuing.

"Mr. Stetson said he had seen your ads. He was proud of your work and wanted to know if you were happy here. He seemed quite fond of you."

Katie's head jerked up at that. "Fond?" The word seemed foreign in a non-existent relationship. "What do you mean, 'fond'? I only met the man once, and it wasn't an acquaintance I pursued."

"Yes, I know," he responded gently. "I was perplexed, myself. There were several pictures of you in his office."

"Pictures?" She felt like a parrot repeating everything he said. "What kind of pictures?"

"Yes, well, there was one of you with a dog, one of you with two children, a boy and a girl, I think, and one of you laughing. I thought it strange at the time."

Katie's mind whirled. *He had me watched.* "You've been investigated," Judd Stetson had said. *When? Where? How long?* The hair on the back of her neck prickled, and she put up a hand to smooth it.

"It was more than the pictures," Hershal emphasized when he sensed where her thoughts were leading her. Her hand arrested in midair. "Mr. Stetson spoke of you as a friend. He told me, 'Do you know she laughs when she hurts? I think she never cries, at least not in public.' That's what he said." Hershal sat back in his chair. "He wanted you to be happy with your work and asked if I thought you were happy.

"I told him, 'Yes, quite happy,' and he asked me why I thought so. His question was odd, but it was obvious that he cared and cared deeply."

Katie stood up in a daze. "I don't understand. I don't understand what any of this means."

Hershal Cleeland rose, took her fluttering hands into his own large ones, and squeezed them.

His support had a calming effect on her. *He hired me because I had talent.* He had been honest with her. She was grateful. Katie's eyes conveyed her appreciation to him, and he smiled in return.

She eased her hands from his grasp and walked back to her office to retrieve her purse.

Mrs. DuPuis watched her walk by, peering over the glasses hanging precipitously on the end of her nose. *Such a nice young woman. Too nice to get mixed up with that rude Judd Stetson. My, but he is a fine-looking man. Best stay clear of him though, Miss Katie. He's bad news with a capital B. And you best be quiet,* she reminded herself and shook her head. *It's none of my business.*

Katie didn't know Mrs. DuPuis was present or thinking about her. "Irrevocably," he had said. The walls closed in. She had to make a decision about tonight.

She took a long walk outside. Her feet ached. Several times she caught herself looking around to see if she was being followed. Katie told herself she was being foolish. J.D. was dead. He would have died five years ago if she hadn't pulled him from a watery grave.

"*What if …?* No, she couldn't allow herself the luxury of what ifs. They were not part of her life now. Her shoulders drooped with the tiredness burdening her.

Judd Stetson sat in the black BMW. He braced his elbows on the steering wheel and rubbed his forehead and temples as he watched Katie walk back to her apartment. The file in his possession listed her address, and he had waited for her return. With no spring in her steps, no smile or hint of exultation, Judd thought his assessment of the girl might need revision. The dejected slope of her shoulders and slow pace in a misty drizzle magnified her vulnerability. She didn't carry an umbrella, and he imagined she was soaked. He wanted to comfort her, tell her everything would be all right, and only a few hours ago, he wanted to throttle her. This was not someone elated over her good fortune. His mind did not compute her rejection of everything Stetson. Hershal Cleeland had answers, and Judd left to get them.

Katie didn't notice the BMW speed down the street as she entered her apartment building. The elevator was empty. She gazed at her reflection in the gleaming doors. A wan face framed by straggly hair peered back. *Stop feeling sorry for yourself. You were hired because of your talent, no matter what that high falutin'* …. Katie laughed. She couldn't think of a name to call him.

"Do you know she laughs when she hurts?" J.D.'s description rankled. The elevator doors slid open, but no one was there to see her brace herself against her door or hear her pathetic laughter.

CHAPTER FOUR

Katie decided she would go to dinner with Judd Stetson. He had spoken of animosity, and she was curious to know why. What did she need to know? She told herself his ruggedly handsome appearance had nothing to do with her decision. *Nothing! This isn't a date. Try and remember that. Not a date.*

She bypassed the baby grand piano, the focal point of the living area by virtue of taking over half the space. The instrument was a cherished possession and one she had saved over a number of years to buy. She turned on the CD player and allowed the haunting melodies of Zamphir's pan pipes flow through her as she prepared a warm bath and sank into the froth of bubbles. The liquid warmth was so relaxing; she drifted off and woke with the chill of cooled water and silence. Feeling revived, she turned on the shower and washed her hair.

Half of her closet lay across the bed as she tried to choose the outfit for her non-date. *This is not a major event. It shouldn't be this hard.* Katie settled on a deep-rose shirred blouse with smocked cuffs and a long black-and-rose paisley skirt. A wide, black belt accentuated her small waist. She added a black velvet vest and wore soft black half-boots. Katie examined the outfit in a full-length mirror and liked the results. She would wear her hair down around her shoulders.

Katie's complexion was good, so she rubbed in a moisturizer, added a touch of eye shadow, a little blush, and rose-tinted lipstick. Her thick eyelashes and winged black brows were *au naturelle*. She dabbed a touch of Xia Xiang behind her ears and left off the gold hoop earrings and bracelets. Katie looked just unconventional enough to bolster her courage.

She restarted the CD, looked around, and tried to see the room with the eyes of Judd Stetson. The antique cherry secretary had belonged to her grandmother. Cabbage-rose-patterned upholstery covered a loveseat, and a burgundy oriental rug softened the room's effect. The Bentley rocker had been a gift from her dad when she moved into the apartment, and the crystal lamp illuminated family pictures and some of the original paintings she had collected.

Judd knocked on Katie's door. He thought about what to say if she declined his offer of dinner and an explanation. *This is business.* The sealed letter Aaron had given him was tucked in his pocket, a backup if he failed in his mission. Its secret contents weighed on his mind. *Hell, she might not open the door.*

Hearing the rap, Katie glanced at her watch. He was punctual. She opened the door and was overwhelmed by an armful of red roses and baby's breath wrapped in green cellophane.

"A peace offering."

Astonished, Katie looked up into a pair of blue eyes that sparkled with mischief and turned to fire. A heated sensation followed. *How ridiculous! Judd Stetson isn't the devil. He's just a good looking man who knows how to charm a woman like me. Be careful.*

He grinned, his white teeth a contrast to his tanned face, and Katie was mesmerized by his sensuous mouth and the grooves bracketing it.

"May I come in?"

"Yes, yes, of course." She hoped she didn't look as confused as she felt. "I didn't expect, I mean you didn't have to, well, you know what I mean." She took the roses and hurried to the kitchen, her face burning. "A peace offering," he had said. She found a large glass vase on a shelf and wished for cut crystal. The roses reminded her of her grandmother's rose garden in Tennessee. She took out a crocheted doily and placed it and the vase of flowers on the piano.

"They're beautiful, thank you," she said a little breathlessly. She turned off the stereo. *Calm down. This is not a date. Don't make a fool of yourself, for heaven's sake.*

Judd studied the painting of a boy and girl in a meadow, and Katie said, "I bought the painting because the children reminded me of my niece and nephew, Karen and Hank."

He looked around the room appreciatively, his hands in his pockets, and she looked at him. Judd Stetson was handsome in a hard sort of way. The smile had thrown her off balance. She had not expected any softening in his attitude. He wore a gray suit that fit his broad shoulders perfectly. *Custom made, no doubt.*

"Nice," he commented. "Comfortable. You must play." His eyes moved over the piano and back to her.

"Yes," she managed to say as she gathered her purse and shawl. His intent eyes made her uneasy, and she wanted to escape their magnetic pull.

Don't be ridiculous. Katie swallowed, tried to think rationally and breathe at the same time. He affected her like no one else, not even Gunnar, and she had known Gunnar two years.

At the door, she looked back. Judd hadn't moved. He was looking at her with an expression she couldn't quite fathom. He looked as if seeing her for the first time and the speculation on his face arresting. *About what?*

Judd walked toward her, his eyes never leaving her own.

A dangerous man, an inner voice clamored. *Leave before it's too late.* Katie broke eye contact and hurried out to the elevator, leaving him to close the self-latching door. She pushed the button and touched her throat. A pulse raced against her fingers. She felt the warmth of his presence and smelled his masculine scent when he stepped in behind her. They rode down to the lobby in silence, and Judd took her elbow and steered her toward the entrance.

Electricity arced up her arm, and she shivered. He felt the quiver and stopped. Easing the shawl from Katie's arm, he placed the wrap around her shoulders and opened the door.

His actions revealed knowledge of good manners when he chose to use them.

The climate outside was cool but not cold. She did not look at his face again, even when he opened the door of the black BMW for her. He slid behind the wheel and started the car.

While the engine warmed, Judd studied her, and she turned to look out the window at the empty sidewalk, chewing her lip self-consciously.

"You look lovely tonight," he said, his voice soft velvet.

"Thank you."

Judd saw her take a breath and reach for the door handle. He turned the car out of the parking space before she changed her mind. *So the tigress is now a kitten.*

Katie felt like a fifteen-year-old on her first date instead of twenty-four. *Well, my girl, you have no one else to blame.* Katie hadn't actually had many dates since Gunnar. Several men had drifted in and out of her life, but the dates were uneventful. No one had time for a platonic friendship these days. The men at the firm treated her like a sister. Gunnar left her calloused to a meaningful relationship. Even her parents had given up on her finding the right man. She immersed herself in her work and her music.

"I spoke to Hershal Cleeland this afternoon."

She looked at Judd, but his features were hard to read in the dark. Flashes of light from passing cars highlighted his profile. A hawk-like nose jutted from a high forehead. His attention focused on the road, so she imagined sculpted lips above a cleft chin without actually seeing them.

"He was quite defensive of you" Judd continued. "Let me know you had asked questions, and he told you the truth. Then he set me straight. I'm glad we weren't in a dark alley. He's a bit larger than me and quite put out about my inquiries."

Somehow she knew that if Judd Stetson ever ended up in a dark alley, he would be the victor. Her estimation of him rose because he hadn't said so. She wondered how much Hershal Cleeland told him.

"Can you forgive me for barging in and acting like an idiot, earlier?"

"I think it can be arranged," she said and smiled, remembering his peace offering.

He laughed, but it was without mirth. "You're an easy woman to please, Katie Mulholland." A wealth of cynicism lined that comment.

Katie looked out the window thoughtfully. She didn't even know if he was married. He wasn't wearing a wedding band, but a lot of men didn't. How did a man with his attributes not get taken? *Think about something else,* she chided herself.

Judd was berating himself for being every kind of fool. What was Aaron Pickering thinking when he sent him unarmed to bring this child-woman to New Orleans? Yes, child-woman was the right label. He had run a gamut of emotions today. This afternoon he wanted to strangle her, and tonight … tonight a gypsy opened the door and bewitched him. A wave of possessiveness washed over him and took his breath. He'd had to put his hands in his pockets, for God's sake, to keep them from tangling in that incredible hair and molding her softness to the hardness of his body. He wanted to kiss off her lipstick and brand her mouth. The last woman who had made him feel that way, his wife, Rita, whose fire burned him beyond redemption. *Rita.* His eyes narrowed, and his lips settled into a grim line. *Don't resurrect the past. View these feelings as warnings.*

Clearly, Katie had sensed his attraction. She was as skittish as a doe in a hunter's sight. A woman running from him, he thought amused as he maneuvered the car through traffic, a novel experience. He had been pursued by some of the most beautiful and sophisticated women in the world. Money and power remained reliable aphrodisiacs.

She was twenty-four to his thirty-five, eleven years younger, but surely old enough to have tasted life several times. Aaron Pickering said she was engaged to some cad in college, so she wasn't going to pull an innocent act on him.

CHAPTER FIVE

The Blue Adagio, a rambling tin-roofed restaurant, perched on the banks of Bayou L'Etoile. The parking lot filled almost to capacity. People milled around on a patio and dock laughing, talking, and drinking as they waited. She wanted to join them, but Judd had a reservation, and they were deferentially ushered to a table on the second level. It overlooked moss-laden oaks, their limbs stretched out over the dark water. A red candle dripped wax over its predecessors, tiers of varying colors coating a wine bottle.

Judd pulled out Katie's chair, and when she was seated, a waiter approached and handed them the wine offerings. "Do you have a preference before dinner?" he asked.

"A water with lemon, please, and an unsweet tea." She smiled up at the waiter.

Judd ordered a bottle of Chardonnay.

"I've heard so much about The Blue Adagio, but it's the first time I've been here." *It's also too costly for my budget.* "You seem to know the area well."

"I enjoy eating, so becoming familiar with good restaurants is important. My grandmother shared the place with me. This restaurant was a favorite of hers." His voice softened and his momentary, wistful expression arrested Katie's attention. He loved his grandmother.

The waiter brought their drinks, recited the chef's specials, and retreated to give them time to decide.

Katie wasn't hungry. She was too nervous. Her eyes scanned the entrees looking for something light. She settled on the broiled red snapper.

Judd asked her what she had chosen and signaled the waiter they were ready. He ordered her choices and the blackened grouper for himself. He watched the candlelight flicker over the smooth planes of Katie's face, highlighting her hair, softening her delicate features. Thick lashes were smudges against her cheeks, and he wondered when he would see those golden eyes again.

"Are you married?" Katie asked, all the while stirring a sweetener in her tea and watching the ice cubes go round and round.

So that was what was bothering her. "No," he replied, reaching for his wine and smiling said, "Are you?"

His question brought her head up. "No. No, of course not." She looked shocked.

"Why of course not?" he asked, now her attention focused on him. Her eyes were wide and guileless.

"I wouldn't be here with you, if I were married," she said as if her answer explained it.

Add naïve to the list on the child side, Judd mentally tallied. He gave her a two-hundred watt smile and agreed. "Aaron said he tried to phone you, but you wouldn't speak with him."

"Aaron who?"

As if she didn't know. "Aaron Pickering, J.D.'s attorney."

"Oh."

He watched her mouth form a perfect circle, and he reached up and loosened his tie.

"Oh, what?" he said with more than a little frustration.

"I remember Mr. Pickering. I didn't know his first name was Aaron." She flushed, remembering the last time she had met Mr. Pickering. She wanted to forget. His secretary had called several times, but she refused to take his calls.

"Why wouldn't you speak with him?

The waiter brought their salads and hovered over them with a large pepper grinder. They both declined, and he faded away.

"I thought I made it clear enough. I want to forget the past. Forget J.D." Katie tasted the chilled salad. The tangy raspberry vinaigrette was the house special, and she ate several more bites. Katie wasn't going to volunteer information. She remembered this dinner was to help dispel animosity. "Why were you angry today?"

"I jumped to conclusions and ran with them. I'm not proud of my actions. You were not what I expected." *That cliché is an understatement.*

Katie smiled as if he said something wonderful.

He was forgiven. It was that simple. This girl ... and that's how he saw her now, as a girl not a woman, interested him but on an unfamiliar level. Judd realized fear kept him from going to that level. He was by nature predatory. He took what was offered. *Katie is too young.*

They ate the rest of their salads in silence. After a cup of rich fish gumbo, the waiter brought out a lemon ice sorbet to clear their palates.

Judd watched her raise the spoon to her mouth and suck off just a little at a time. He revised his earlier thoughts. *She is twenty-four, a desirable woman, not off limits.*

She looked up and blushed. The spoon chimed against the crystal as she dropped it.

Judd was intrigued. *Maybe she read my mind.* An honest to goodness blush would be hard to fake. "Aaron holds you in the highest regard," Judd said. "He phoned me yesterday."

The waiter cleared the sorbet dishes and refilled the water goblets.

The interruptions tried Judd's patience. *Maybe I should have taken her to the library.*

"Do we have to talk about Mr. Pickering?" Katie was tired of the subject.

"Yes, we do. This is important," Judd informed her. "He wants me to bring you to New Orleans on Thursday." The news startled her, and golden eyes watched him intently. "I'm sure you've already guessed that it has to do with the reading of J.D.'s Will." He held up his hand to indicate he wanted to finish. "Aaron said it is imperative that you be present on Friday. We'll have to leave Thursday afternoon. He's booked a room for you at The Royal Orleans." Judd held up his hand again when she started to speak. "The plane is scheduled to leave around three. Mr. Cleeland understands and has given you time off."

Katie closed her eyes and opened them again. *Irrevocably, irrevocably,* beat a tattoo at her temples, her fate a foregone conclusion. He said so, and she would do it. He assumed a lot. Putting her elbows on the table and lacing her fingers together, she rested her chin on them. "What if I don't want to go?"

He laughed. "You'll go." She was teasing him. He'd play along. "If you're stubborn, I'll have to dig out my cave man paraphernalia and manhandle you."

Katie half-believed him.

Judd thought briefly of the sealed envelope in the pocket of his jacket. It was to be given to Katie only if she balked at coming. The contents more than piqued his curiosity.

"I'm happy here," Katie said. "There isn't anything of J.D. Stetson's I want. You may not believe this, but I don't want my life to change. Mr. Pickering should believe it, even if you don't."

She was serious. Her voice had a sincere ring to it. *No, I don't believe it for a minute.* Judd was losing his patience. "Good," he said. "That settles it." He spoke as if the subject were closed, but there was a challenge in his voice.

"Settles what?" she forced herself to ask.

"I'll pick you up at two o'clock Thursday, and Friday you'll tell Aaron what you just told me."

She sighed. Apparently he didn't believe her. "I will!" Katie stressed each word. *Now, the subject is closed.*

Their meal arrived a few moments later, and she attacked it so vigorously, Judd was sure she confused him with the poor snapper. He watched as she put down her fork, and amused by her attempt to regain control poured her a glass of wine.

She sipped a little but hardly touched it.

"Don't you like the wine?"

"I don't know. I never acquired a taste for it." Her attention returned to the food.

She was certainly unaffected. *Refreshing.* The grouper was good, but Judd found the spicy morsels hard to swallow. He contemplated the evening ahead.

Katie knew Judd studied her. This whole day was beyond unreal. She put down her fork, her poor fish in little pieces all over the plate. She sipped her tea and giggled. Then her laughter bubbled up and spilled over, attracting attention. Katie covered her mouth with a napkin before she embarrassed them both.

Judd laughed with her, and it was liberating. *God, she's beautiful. Her uncommon beauty has nothing to do with artifice. She's unique, her laugh spontaneous, uninhibited.* Her joy touched Judd like a slice of life he remembered eons ago. He didn't want to examine the feeling too closely.

And he didn't like the question forming in his gut. *What was your relationship with my grandfather?* She claimed to have only met him once, but all the indicators pointed to some kind of relationship. The personal pictures he saw in J.D.'s office, the way his grandfather spoke of her, his tone of voice warm, accepting, so unlike the man he knew. J. D. had changed. He had made it a mission to make-up time with Judd in the last five years. He sought him out, talked to him about getting out more, appreciating life, feeling alive. When he started talking to Judd about going to church, he thought his grandfather had come unhinged, and in kinder words, he declined the invitation. J. D. backed off.

One day, J.D. had asked, "Have you ever really looked at a rose?"

Judd told him he had, thinking it a strange question.

"No, I mean have you ever noticed the perfection, the velvet richness of the petals, the way they fold and open to release a fragrance like no other?"

Judd remembered thinking his grandfather sounded like he was on drugs.

Katie laughed, and Judd had almost forgotten the tension. He wasn't alone. Everyone was jittery about J.D.'s Will. He may have left his entire fortune to charity. J.D. had spent the last five years trying to do just that. This woman was key. *How did you get to him, Katie?* Judd knew better than anyone how difficult it had been to see J.D. His grandfather had an army of people to run his businesses and protect his privacy. And Aaron had been emphatic about her early presence for the reading of the Will. Once again, the envelope weighed on his mind.

The waiter returned to clear away the dishes, and Katie excused herself to go to the Ladies Room before she began to laugh again.

Katie wasn't like any woman Judd had ever known. Rita was at the other end of the spectrum, and thinking of Rita, his wife, was enough to take permanence out of his vocabulary forever. He shifted his thoughts to pressing business matters.

Judd watched Katie wend her way back to the table, saw the appreciative looks that followed her, and again felt unwanted prickles of possessiveness. She attracted admiring glances but seemed unaware. The thrill of the chase excited his hunting instincts. The urge persisted even though he believed her naiveté and attraction to him made her easy prey.

A cup of *café au lait* awaited her return. Katie didn't disappoint. Her smile was reserved for him alone.

Judd's eyes hooded their predatory intent. He smiled benignly. *Best not to give away the game.* She enjoyed simple pleasures. *Refreshing.* Yes, the word suited her.

The French Quarter coffee infused with a hint of chicory enlivened the taste buds and was just what Katie needed. This man attracted her. All the feelings she thought dead were very much alive and asserting themselves. She wanted a forever after marriage like her parents' and Myra's. She recognized Judd's attraction to her, and the possibilities frightened her. He didn't look at her with marriage on his mind. Katie knew this, and the fact she didn't care was unnerving. *Am I getting desperate?*

Judd's dark, handsome looks and the heated intensity of his eyes appealed to Katie's feminine side. He overpowered Gunnar's cold, Nordic persona. Judd was sophisticated, but not in a suave, narcissistic way. His confidence came from authority, the mantle of responsibility as heir apparent of Stetson Enterprises. It amused him that she didn't know about wine and also the fact she was running from the inevitable. This knowledge embarrassed and excited her. She felt young, a new violin awaiting the hand of the master to give it identity. And Judd had a vulnerable side that attracted her. Katie's eyes settled on the sensuous lips that changed his demeanor when he laughed. What would it be like to be kissed by this man, loved by this man? *He's a Stetson, a fairy tale. No point going there.*

"I told you I wasn't married, but I have been."

Katie didn't even blink. If he wanted to tell her about his marriage, she was a good listener. Had he divined the pattern of her thoughts?

"I met Rita in Paris the summer after graduating from Princeton."

She was a goddess. Her golden hair, alabaster skin, and taunting green eyes dared me to take her. Theirs had been a tempestuous affair that ended in marriage one month later. "We were married eight years." Eight years of hell had hardened his resolve not to repeat the experience. He had managed Stetson Enterprises an equal number of years. The enormity of the task kept him busy. The women who allied themselves to him knew the relationships were not permanent from the beginning.

"I have a daughter, Dori. She's seven and lives with her Aunt Helene in Connecticut. I've been happily unattached six years."

Well, that was a neat package, hand-delivered. His proclamation left no room for doubt about his intentions. "Thank you for the warning. It will save me from making a fool of myself," she said with a hint of sarcasm twisting her lips. He was clearly warning her. She would be a fool not to heed his words, "happily unattached." She dropped her eyes and waited to see if he would try to rectify his remark. He hadn't planned on a reply, and she bet this wasn't the reaction he wanted.

Judd hadn't expected a response, especially the one he received. Katie didn't accept his words as a challenge She wouldn't be trying to change his mind. *Face it Bucko, she's different from your other women.* Why did her response matter? Once he delivered her to Aaron, he'd be shed of her.

CHAPTER SIX

Katie thought about Judd's revealing speech. His hard expression softened when he spoke of his grandmother and his daughter. Dori held a special place in his heart, and the situation begged the question of why she was living with her aunt. "How awful," she began, "about your daughter. Do you get to see her often?"

Wariness formed in his eyes. Dori was off limits. She didn't expect an answer, but he surprised her.

"I see her as often as possible," he said, and added, "not often enough." *Helene sees to that.* She seemed to know when he was coming and had Dori away on some pretext or other that left more time squiring her. She wasn't subtle about her ambitions. Her efforts to make herself invaluable to him were beginning to wear thin. Rita immunized him from Helene's wiles, even though she was not like her sister. He thought again of Dori. *I wish … no, my wishes aren't practical.*

"I live on an isolated ranch. My home doesn't provide the social graces a young girl needs, and my time is limited by my work." He said no more on the subject.

They declined dessert but stayed for a second cup of coffee. Judd paid the check, and they walked out onto the deserted patio. He took her hand, and his warm touch felt natural.

Colorful lanterns swayed in the breeze casting soft light into dark corners. The ambience of music piped to the dock made the parking lot seem a romantic spot. Limbs of water oaks reached across the still, dark water, the silvery moss barely skimming the surface. Crickets sang in unison, and frogs croaked. The starry sky had never been clearer.

When Judd stopped and gently pulled on her arm, she turned into his embrace as if she had never left. *What are you doing? He gave you fair warning. You'd be wise to heed it.* She shut down the warning as his eyes focused on her lips. Her heart raced, and she didn't pull away. She wanted him to kiss her.

Julie London sang, "Sentimental Journey," the words indelible in Katie's mind. Judd wrapped his arms around her, and guided her head to his chest. His warmth, his scent, and the sound of his heart soothed. She sighed as he began to move with the music. They danced until the song ended.

Judd's hand smoothed her hair behind her ears and tangled in its strands, drawing her head back.

He was beautiful. His black hair blending with the sky, and his silvery blue eyes promising wondrous things as that sensuous mouth lowered to her own. Judd's lips and breath were warm. They lightly touched her own and moved on to her eyelids, temple, and down to the hollow of her throat. The kisses, tender awakenings of her senses, caressed her lips again, gently nudging them.

"Open for me, Katie," he breathed against her closed lips. And with the touch of his tongue, she abandoned the post, and welcomed his possession. She responded with the ardor he demanded, her own mouth searching satisfaction. Her arms went around his neck wanting him closer.

The kiss ended as other couples invaded their space. She tried to control her emotions, aware by his breathing, he was as affected as she had been. She savored the thought as they walked to the car. He kissed her lightly before helping her inside the car and after buckling her seat belt. As he closed the door, she looked back at the dock where several couples danced. The Blue Adagio would always be a special spot to her because here she had been awakened from the dead. She lived a dream if only for a few minutes.

They drove in silence a couple of miles. Judd asked her about her family, and she enjoyed sharing them with him. "Mom was on track to be a concert pianist. Instead she went back to school and got a degree in music education. She teaches music in a private school and gives piano lessons afterwards. She also writes and illustrates children's books." Her mother allowed her to stretch creatively. Katie loved music and playing the piano.

"My dad loves history. He's a college professor with his doctorate in Ancient Civilizations, but he also teaches a New World History course. Horticulture is a second passion. He propagates hybrid orchids and plants a large vegetable garden each year. Dad always has plenty for neighbors and friends." Her father instilled in Katie an interest in the past and a love of books. He was as sensitive as he was inquisitive. His gentle nature had taught her patience. He had never raised his voice that she could remember.

Katie and Myra were four years apart, but they had always been close. She told him about Myra's family, her husband, Paul, their children, Hank and Karen, and about their Golden Retriever, Freebie. This reminded her of the pictures Hershal Cleeland had told her about, and her thoughts went in another direction.

Katie chattered on and on about her family. *He hasn't interrupted once.* She thought about the Will and wondered if he thought about it too. Friday was two days away. Judd would be there.

Judd slid the BMW into a spot near the front of her apartment building. He turned off the ignition and reached out lightly rubbing his knuckles across her cheekbone, his fingers pushing back tendrils of hair framing her face. He opened his hand behind her neck and pulled her toward him for a kiss. "It's been too long," he whispered before parting her lips for a searing kiss.

Too long, too long, echoed in her mind as she touched his face and buried her hand in his hair. *Too long!* her conscience screamed. *Glory!* She'd only known him one evening, and he already had one foot in her bed. She drew back and didn't meet any resistance. She must be losing her mind, too. When had she ever kissed anyone on a first date? When had she started thinking of this meeting as a date? *Lord, I'm in trouble.*

"I think it's time to go in," she said when she caught a breath.

"Umm, my sentiment exactly," he agreed.

She watched him, her eyes wide as he strode around the car, confident of tonight's outcome? *Lord, how did I get in this predicament?* She could hear her mother saying, "Well, Katie, you'll just have to get yourself out. You make your bed, and you have to lie in it." In another few minutes, he'd be sharing her bed if she didn't think of something fast. He obviously expected every woman to succumb to his advances. His conceit and her weakness sobered her. She pulled back on his hand as they entered the foyer, stalling for time. If he noticed, the ploy didn't deter him.

He pressed the elevator button and the doors opened.

"I've had a lovely evening," she said as she watched him punch number five. His hand was tanned like his face with a sprinkling of black hair in sharp contrast to the white cuff of his shirt. A gold cuff-link winked in the light. She swallowed and looked up. His face was closed to her.

"The dinner was excellent."

The doors slid open, and he gently nudged her toward her apartment.

Katie began to panic. She fumbled in her purse for the keys. When she found them, Judd covered her hand and loosened them from her nervous fingers.

"Allow me," Judd said, his voice low and intimate. He opened the door and waited.

Katie didn't move. If she went past him, she knew he would follow, and all would be lost. She worried her lip, and he raised an eyebrow.

"It's been a long day, Judd. I'll . . . I'll see you around two on Thursday." She put her hand out for the keys and found herself pulled into a crushing embrace.

He grinned down at her, his unmasked desire evident, his will thwarted. "Well, well, Little Red Riding Hood in Shreveport."

Left unsaid, his role as the wolf. His lips, hard and unforgiving plundered her own. She let herself go limp, and Judd's kiss became less punishing, his arms easing their hold on her. His hands traveled up and buried in her hair, massaging her scalp, and making her tingle all the way down to her toes.

"I want you, Katie." His eyes consumed her, his voice husky and filled with need.

All the tender points on her body were swelling, aching to fill that need. She backed hard into the door jamb, her flight response activated.

Judd recognized fear, reluctance, and something he couldn't quite identify in her golden eyes. He touched her lips with his finger and frowned. His eyes softened and withdrew their hold. "I'm sorry, Katie, if I expected too much."

The keys were placed in her hand, and she escaped into her apartment.

Judd heard the door lock, the dead bolt slam shut, and the rattling chain hastily put in place. Was that also a sob he heard? He wanted to pound on the door and demand to be let inside. His mangled pride was one thing, but something went deeper. He had listened as she spoke lovingly of her family, and as she talked, they became real to him. She was secure in the knowledge she was loved in return. He yearned to feel that kind of security, but he knew it wasn't possible in this lifetime. His parents were somewhere in Europe. He hadn't heard from them in months, not until they heard J.D. was dead. Their call had left him cold.

Judd could picture Hank, Karen, and Freebie all too clearly. He had seen a picture of them in J.D.'s office. His grandfather had a place in Katie's life, he didn't share. That nagged him. He stabbed the elevator button and stepped in as the doors opened.

Tonight, Katie had kissed him passionately. She wanted him. He wasn't mistaken about that. The wide-eyed innocent he pulled from the car left him frustrated and disbelieving. He was too old to start over and with a woman not of his world. He'd take the proverbial cold shower and not get involved. *Involved!* She scared the hell out of him.

CHAPTER SEVEN

Katie shook her alarm clock and checked the trigger. The toggle hadn't flipped off, so she must have slept through the alarm. She groaned and pulled the sheet over her head. The nights had been long with little sleep. She must get up. Judd would be coming at two. She groaned again. *I'm not going to start thinking about him.*

After she turned on the coffeemaker, she rummaged around in the fridge for a raspberry yogurt. A note on the counter reminded her to call her mom and Myra to let them know she'd be gone a few days. She didn't want them to worry if they called.

Her mother wanted to know where she would be staying. "Are you staying with him?" The question had been tentative. She didn't want to believe Katie was going off to New Orleans with a man.

Katie reassured her. "No, Mom, he's just taking me. We aren't going to be together. It has something to do with J.D. Stetson's Will. I don't even want to go, but I guess my declining any part of the estate has to be done in person. Why is he so persistent, even in death? I didn't know him. It's been five years." She didn't tell her mother about his investigation of her life. *The reality is too creepy.*

"You know, Katie, it might not be so bad to take what is offered. He's gone now, so ..."

"Don't go there, Mom. You know the ethical reason I tore up the check. It wasn't easy, and Gunnar went with it. I'm glad about that now. We weren't suited. Better to find out before doing something I'd regret later."

Her mother's silence spoke volumes.

"You never understood me not going to the dedication. I didn't go because I didn't want to give him a reason to believe I was like all the others sponging off him. You have no idea how bitter and twisted he was."

~

Katie's sister, Myra, had been more direct. "This trip to New Orleans is about the Will, isn't it?"

"Judd hinted it was the reason."

"Tell me about Judd Stetson. What's he like?"

Katie looked around the kitchen and tried to think of a way to describe Judd that wouldn't give her sister a hint of her emotions concerning the aborted evening. "Well, he's all business. He said I had to go to New Orleans for the reading of the Will, and he told me he'd pick me up on Thursday."

"That's it? And you said ... you'd be happy to go?"

"Not exactly. I said there was no point in going. I didn't want anything of J.D.'s. He sort of challenged me to go and tell the attorney in person."

"Okay, Sis, what are you *not* telling me? I've seen his pictures in the Society Pages and celebrity magazines. I know what the wealthy, mysterious scion of the Stetson family looks like. He's a hunk." Myra lowered her voice as she confided, "He's gone missing from magazine coverage the last couple of years, and I've read he shuns publicity. Why did *he* come to persuade you to go to New Orleans?"

Why indeed? "I don't know, Myra. He was actually angry. He's a younger version of J.D." Katie swallowed and prayed her sister would leave it at that. She did. And Katie was thankful her sister couldn't feel the heat shrouding her body and burning her face. She said, "You know, I have a lot to do. I'll call you when I get back."

Once the calls were accomplished, Katie poured a second cup of coffee and headed for the shower. Her parents thought of more questions, and she didn't have the answers. Judd said Hershal had given her time off. Surely, she could sign whatever paperwork needed signing and be home this weekend. *Well, dwelling on it isn't going to get you answers, kid.*

The jets of hot water pelted her with relaxing heat. Steam covered the glass door and mirrors. She wrapped her hair in a towel and pulled on her terrycloth robe. Fifteen minutes later, her suitcase was packed. She looked at the contents, mostly casual clothes, and tried to feel good about her choices.

When she realized she was pacing the floor, she raided the fridge again. This time she ate a peanut butter and banana sandwich followed by a diet drink.

J.D.'s family was probably the Social Register type, very formal. Somehow, her act of rebellion seemed petty, so she repacked and felt a little better. This time she packed along with her PJs, a suit, two casual dresses, a short evening dress, slacks outfit, and accessories. Satisfied she had everything, she dressed in a taupe pants suit with an amber blouse and topaz earrings and necklace. Two *faux* tortoise combs pulled her hair away from her face. *Why worry? Treat today like any other day.*

Katie needn't have worried about Mr. Judd Stetson. His motto for the day echoed hers. She was now Miss Mulholland. No deference, hint of friendship, or memories of unleashed passion acknowledged. The atmosphere crackled, but she played her part with aplomb. Hadn't she spent two days chastising herself for her behavior and feeling foolish? Katie knew Judd Stetson wanted what every healthy male wanted. He and Gunnar were cast in the same mold. His intentions were clear enough. She didn't need to learn the same lesson twice, so she relegated Judd's nearness to be as necessary to her as a hair shirt.

Judd's aloofness eased her mind, but nothing had been able to douse the excitement of the flight to New Orleans. She had been to the Big Easy many times, but she had never flown anywhere. She was awed by the sleek lines of the five passenger Maverick Solo Jet and impressed that Judd was its pilot.

A second pilot, Clem Masterson, climbed on board after doing a last minute check-up on the plane while Judd stowed the luggage and finished the paperwork. Clem looked to be in his forties or early fifties. "You're Katie, I'm Clem," he announced.

"You'd be right about me. I'm pleased to meet you."

"That's a ditto." He laughed and talked about his love affair with flight. He kept up a lively conversation while they were in the air and pointed out plantations bordering the Mississippi River. He was proud of his family and took out a picture of his wife and two children. Judd maintained his silence except when talking to the tower.

As they taxied down the runway at Louis Armstrong International Airport, Judd said, "Clem, see to her luggage and get her a taxi. She's staying at The Royal Orleans."

Clem looked at Katie. "I'm happy to help. Let me know if you need anything special."

"And Clem, I need you to pick up Mr. Aguilar Mojica at the Hotel St. Pierre at ten on Saturday. I'll meet you here. We'll be flying to Corazon."

"Yes sir, happy to oblige."

Judd parked the plane and turned to her. "I'm sure Aaron will be contacting you about the time and place of the meeting. He'll send a car around to pick you up. Until then, Ms. Mulholland." He nodded his dismissal.

"Ta Ta," she responded airily to his little speech and deplaned in Clem's company.

Friday arrived overcast and rainy. Katie dressed carefully for the meeting. She wore a smart outfit with white pants, pleated tuxedo shirt, and a jade, raw silk jacket. The buckle on her green suede belt closed to become a gold-toned dragon. She wore her hair up in a chignon that gave her an older, more professional appearance. Her eyes looked larger and her cheekbones more prominent. She lightly dabbed on White Shoulders, her favorite day scent since high school and wore her pearls, a gift from her parents at graduation. Wearing them gave her confidence.

She was surprised to see Judd when she entered the lobby. He stood when she entered and indicated the door with an outstretched arm. Outside, he put up his umbrella and ushered her to another black BMW. *Is this a different car, or did someone drive his down for him?*

"Thank you for picking me up," she said after several minutes of silence.

"You're welcome," he said, not taking his gaze off the road. Katie looked out the window as they drove down Canal Street. He was giving her the silent treatment again.

"You know, this is silly. I don't know why we can't be civil to one another. You picked me up. I told you I wanted no part of the inheritance. I meant it."

"That remains to be seen. Aaron told me to pick you up. It wasn't a request. After today, I doubt we'll be seeing one another again." The finality in his voice contained an angry edge.

He reminded her of his grandfather. "Oh, is that your excuse for being rude?"

His eyes cut a path to her and narrowed. "Forgive me, then. I didn't mean for you to take my silence as rudeness."

Katie nodded but decided not to say more. *Lord, why have you brought this man into my life? It's going to take a lifetime to get him out of my mind. It's unfair. Every man I go out with is going to fall short by comparison.* Katie folded physically, her arms across her abdomen as thoughts of his kisses ignited passionate thoughts. *Enough! This is unproductive, unrealistic.*

A few minutes later, Judd pulled into a parking garage. They got out, and Judd took her elbow, steering her into the building and to Mr. Pickering's office.

Mr. Pickering stood as the door opened. He walked around the desk, his warm hand clasp and cheerful greeting friendly. He hadn't changed much. He still exuded courtly gentleman. His trim physique wore a charcoal suit, crisp white shirt, and a maroon tie that matched the leather upholstery of the two wingback chairs.

"Here she is, Aaron, safe and sound. As you can see, it wasn't necessary to give her the letter," Judd drawled with all the quiet confidence of a man who had accomplished his mission.

His mission, in all ways but one, she reminded herself smugly.

Judd pulled a sealed white envelope from his jacket and handed it to him.

Mr. Pickering tapped the envelope against his finger tips and smiled. He held out his hand, thanking Judd for being prompt, and advising him they were meeting in the conference room at 10:30.

Katie was surprised when Judd walked out leaving her alone with Mr. Pickering. He pulled back a maroon leather chair for her and sat beside her in its twin. This was not going to be a lawyer, client talk across a desk.

CHAPTER EIGHT

"I want to thank you for coming in view of all that's happened," he began. "I hope you will forgive me for the trials ahead and understand J.D. was a law unto himself."

Katie cocked her head listening to his tone of voice and its cryptic message. "Mr. Pickering, I appreciate your position, but please believe me when I say, I want nothing from J.D. Stetson, alive or dead." *There. I said it and meant it. So, I told him, Mr. Judd Stetson, and you can put your accusations in your pipe and smoke it.* "Can't I just say I want to be left out of his Will or sign myself out of it?"

The envelope began to tap again as Mr. Pickering searched for the right words. "In a perfect world, we might have what we wish, but ..." His voice dropped. He opened his arms, reaching out as if pleading forgiveness. Apology and distress were evident in his face and demeanor. *Maybe I assumed too much. How humiliating!* Her face flushed, and she began to rise.

Hastily, he stood and touched her shoulder arresting her motion. "No, please don't leave. There's too much at stake and too many lives depending on your decision. I've begun badly, and I should have foreseen this. I hoped, no, I prayed you might have softened your stand just a little."

He was so sincere and agitated, Katie felt sympathy for him.

"I'm sorry; I just don't understand what you're trying to say."

"Yes, I can see that." He held out the envelope. "I asked Judd to give you this, in the event he couldn't persuade you to come. I have an idea or two about it, but only J.D. knew its content. I hope this will explain all or part of his plan." He turned and walked around to sit behind his desk, the lawyer once again. "J.D. entrusted it to me, and he told me to give it to you before the reading of his Will. He empowered me to answer some of your questions. Please open and read it now."

Katie turned the thick envelope over in her hands several times before opening it and taking out several thick sheets of embossed stationary. J.D.'s handwriting was small and scratchy. The black ink was most pronounced where the fountain pen lingered over certain words like, "dearest," "forgive," "joy," "please," "must," and lastly, "heartfelt." She held a love letter. Her eyes brimmed, and as she looked up at Mr. Pickering, a tear spilled over followed by another and another.

He handed her his maroon silk handkerchief, nodding his understanding.

Between "My dearest Katie," and "My heartfelt thanks," was the testimony of a changed man's life. It was the most touching and most beautifully written letter she had ever received. The date read almost one year ago to the day.

She tried to speak, but the words choked back on a sob, and she had to blow nosily into the now crumpled hanky.

Mr. Pickering leaned across the desk patting her hand in comfort. His own voice wavered. "J.D. lost almost everything he held dear beginning with his parents in a freak avalanche."

Katie sat back in the chair and listened.

"He grew up in the strict, unforgiving environment of an uncle. He met, married, and lost the only woman he ever loved to the man he thought his best friend. The son of their union, Maxwell Lincoln Stetson, fell short of J.D.'s expectations. Max left home at the first opportunity.

"The family barely survived the crash of '29. When J.D. took over the reins of the business after his uncle's death, he was determined to build an empire for his son. He's built more than one, and family, organizations, and the needy hounded J.D. for money. The line never ended. He hired people to take care of requests and to keep the press and the public at bay. He squirreled himself away from contact with anyone other than his managers and closest associates.

"Then you saved his life in more ways than one and didn't ask for anything in return. No one was in place to protect him from the media blitz that followed his rescue. I had the pleasure of putting your torn check in his hands." Aaron Pickering's voice cracked. "It broke him. He sat at his desk with his head in his hands and cried. We both did. It was the first time he realized some things, some people can't be bought. I gave him the Lee Strobel book you sent me to give to him."

Katie had forgotten about sending the book, *A Case for Christ*. The book had answered many of her own questions and increased her faith. She wanted J.D. to know why she believed.

"J.D. read it, and he met with the author and consulted with ministers. He gave his life to the Lord and became one of the happiest and most generous of men. I've known J.D. since we were boys, and I can tell you, he was a changed man."

Katie nodded her understanding and asked the question bothering her. "Judd told me I'd been investigated. Did you know about the pictures?"

Aaron Pickering sighed. "I tried to dissuade him from an investigation. But he told me, 'Ari, I have to know how this girl ticks. Is she the real thing, or is this whole thing a charade?' I think he believed at some point, you'd change your mind, and it tickled him you didn't. He thought of you as family, the one he never had." He sighed. "I know, it doesn't sound rational."

Katie sat stunned by these revelations. For the first time, she saw the rescue in a favorable light and forgave J.D. the intrusion of her privacy. The man had changed because of her actions, her belief. *No, it wasn't me.* God wanted him to be saved, and He used her. It was humbling.

"You said J. D. has a son."

"Max is weak." Aaron Pickering looked like he didn't want to say what had to be said. "Max shrank in the shadow of his father, shunned responsibility, and chased every glittering rainbow and *light skirt* he could get his hands on. Money flowed through his hands like water, his friends siphoning their share and then some. He was expelled from two universities, got involved in several scandals, and was finally caught by a gold digger, five years his senior and ten times more experienced." Mr. Pickering's mouth and demeanor turned grim as he recounted the distasteful story. "Adrienne is selfish, aggressive, and manipulative. She has, however, managed to keep Max out of the greedy clutches of mistresses.

Her finest hour was producing Judd, and she's never let anyone forget it."

Katie listened to the account, fascinated.

"Max and Adrienne shuffled Judd through a series of nannies, governesses, and boarding schools in Europe. The miracle is he weathered his unfortunate youth and turned out to be a decent, conscientious young man."

"It sounds like he had a horrible upbringing. Surely, something good happened."

"Judd was one of the world's most eligible bachelors when he graduated from Princeton. He met his wife, Rita, on a business trip to Paris that summer. They married a month later. It was a rocky marriage from the start. Their fights made headlines in the tabloids, especially after Rita left him and moved to Los Angeles." Mr. Pickering's voice dropped . "She had a love affair with the film industry, leaving Judd at home with their three-year-old daughter. Rita was killed in an automobile accident along with her latest boy toy two years later."

"His wife is dead?" Katie couldn't believe it. She thought they were divorced.

"Judd didn't tell you?" He paused, "It's a sore spot; I guess he wouldn't. He's on the same solitary track J.D. drove himself. Judd has removed himself from most society functions, going only to those related to the family industry's promotional advancement. He has become a recluse at Corazon, the Stetson Ranch in Florida, and only makes time for business."

"But he has a daughter?"

"Yes, Dori is the best thing to happen in Judd's life. He loves her. J.D. doted on her."

"But he told me she lives with an aunt in Connecticut."

"Yes, Rita's sister, Helene. No, I know what you're thinking. She's a lovely young woman but not cut from the same pattern as Rita. She runs a successful real estate business, and she has convinced Judd, Dori is better off living where there are advantages for a young girl."

Appalled, Katie asked, "Did Judd and J.D. get along?"

"When Judd graduated from Cambridge and then Princeton, he had begun his own import, export business. J.D. was impressed and proud of Judd's business acumen. He was able to hold his own with his grandfather, and J.D. eventually turned over the reins of Stetson Enterprises to Judd, not Max."

He looked at her with serious intent. "I'm truly sorry about this."

Katie sank into the upholstery. *This is going to be worse than I expected.*

"I can't tell you what is in the Will before I read it, but you have an important part, and you need to know, it's a vital role." He leaned forward seeking eye contact. "I asked you to come early because it is imperative you say nothing during or after the reading of the Will. This may be difficult. You must only think about the people who will be hurt if you do speak your mind. I can only appeal to your inherent spirit of humanity."

Mr. Pickering leaned back in his chair and sighed, his hands again expansively wide and apologetic. "As to the year, you must look at it as a fully paid vacation, or even a learning experience. A year will go fast and needn't be a millstone," he quickly explained before Katie could ask anything. "You'll lose nothing. Your job at Centaur will still be yours if you want it, and after one year," he continued, "you'll be free to do whatever you want with the inheritance. And the best part, you'll make a lot of people happy," he added.

"Mr. Pickering, you've lost me. What year?"

Once more he sat forward, only this time, a finger pointed toward her. Katie twisted her own in her lap. *What will I be doing?*

"No one in the conference room will be aware of your part in all of this, but everything," he paused to emphasize the point, "and I mean everything, hinges on your cooperation. Say nothing. We'll discuss your part later. I hope you will look upon me in the future as a friend. I would have liked to have done things differently, my dear, but there you are, J.D. prevailed."

"But where will I be?" Katie asked. The setup sounded mysterious. "What people will be happy?"

"You'll have these answers soon. I can't give you any more information than this," he said as he stood, indicating their meeting was over.

Katie stood on shaky legs and followed him more perplexed than ever. His hand rested on the handle of the double doors, and he half turned to remind her. "Remember to say and do nothing, no matter what transpires." He faced her, a question in his eyes. "May I depend on you, until I can fully apprise you of the whole situation?"

Katie met his eyes and made a decision. He depended on her. "I'll try." She knew her answer fell short of his expectations, but he nodded gravely and opened the door.

CHAPTER NINE

Katie was escorted into a large room where Judd and a number of others sat around a conference table. Everyone stopped talking and turned to look at Katie and Mr. Pickering as they entered. Their expressions were unguarded for a moment, and she was assailed by everything from overt curiosity to unbridled hostility. Katie balked and stepped back. Mr. Pickering's hand at the base of her spine brought her up short. He gently pushed her into the room and closed the door.

The introductions began. The dark-suited elderly gentleman leaning to the side, one hand folded over the ornate head of a cane was Randall Stetson, J.D.'s brother. His rheumy eyes were pale blue and assessing. He nodded, his mouth pursed in speculation. To his right, were his two daughters, J.D.'s nieces, Merit and Madeline. The former was a slender, fortyish edition of her father. She smiled and nodded, her curiosity evident. Madeline, a plumper, plainer edition of her sister was clothed in black and rigid with distain. Her dyed, black coif stood stiffly away from her face and disapproving eyes.

Facing her across the table were Judd's parents. Max was of medium build and nondescript in coloring. His jaded expression and puffy eyes appreciatively sized her up as a woman, and Katie shifted uneasily from one foot to the other embarrassed.

Judd's mother, Adrienne, was a stunning Amazon with broad shoulders, and a carefully made-up face. Her green eyes narrowed in cold appraisal, the hostility earlier transmitted, now hidden. Her provocative, bright coral dress didn't clash with her hennaed hair as one might expect. This woman was the enemy, and she wanted Katie to know it.

Katie was introduced to Judd as if this were the first time. He sat at the end of the table by himself, a couple of seats from his parents.

His grooved face and arrogant expression bore no trace of recognition or welcome.

Mr. Pickering pulled out a chair for Katie on his right. Her unease was acute as she sat down. *Are these the people I'll make happy?*

The door opened and a stunning, strawberry blond woman entered. "I'm sorry I'm late," she said, "The traffic you know," her voice a breathless drawl to garner attention. She smiled widely at all present, enjoying the surprised expressions.

"This is Helene Forrester," Mr. Pickering said as he stood. "I'm glad you were able to join us, Ms. Forrester." Katie was introduced, and Helene moved down the table to take a seat next to Judd, who looked poleaxed.

Katie guessed by the startled expressions, this woman wasn't expected. Judd's mother turned her hostile stare down the table, and Katie breathed a sigh of relief.

Mr. Pickering frowned as he unlatched a large briefcase, extracted a stack of papers, and sorted them into three piles.

Katie wanted to jump up and leave before he started.

As though divining her thoughts, he looked up and pinned her with his eyes. Their expression reminded her of the promise.

"Everyone is present now, except Dori," Mr. Pickering's formal voice returned. "I know you will all understand why I didn't want to put her through this legality." He turned to Katie. "J.D. and Dori were close. She's seven, and she loved her gramps unconditionally. He returned that love."

Dori. Judd's daughter. Katie looked down the table at Judd and saw Helene put her hand over his. He slipped it out and put it in his lap. At least, her hand didn't follow.

Mr. Pickering opened by informing them that J.D. had been examined by three well-known physicians. His physical and mental states were judged sound, and their reports had been notarized.

The first pile he put his hand upon, he explained were charities. Among them, J.D. left approximately twenty million dollars.

Katie was stunned by such a large amount, but she saw relieved faces.

The second pile represented bequests to people who had served him faithfully over the years. They were in the main, monetary amounts, but he also included some tangible assets and deeds to properties. This pile came to approximately twelve million dollars.

No comments were forthcoming when he asked if there were questions about either pile.

The atmosphere became charged when his hand went to the third pile. He began to read the portion of the Will that dealt with the rest of the estate.

Katie tried to dismiss the legal jargon and understand the meat of J.D.'s bequest.

J.D. left to each, Max and Judd, twenty percent of his stock and another twenty per cent was to be divided among Dori and any future offspring Judd might father. It would be held in trust until she, or they, as the case may be, reached the age of thirty. He left thirty per cent to be divided by his brother and his two nieces, Merit and Madeline, and ten per cent to Katie.

A few gasps were heard, including her own, and everyone looked at Katie with varying degrees of interest. She twisted her fingers painfully in her lap and bit her lip to keep from rejecting the bequest outright.

Mossy Cove would go to Max, and he looked relieved.

Judd's face was carved in stone.

Mr. Pickering cleared his throat. He handed each person present a check for $100,000., including Helene, who had not been mentioned in the Will. The checks were dated the Christmas of the previous year. It was now May. Mr. Pickering informed them that after the Will was probated, they would each receive a balance of $400,000 for the remainder of the fiscal year.

"Helene, you have received your part. J.D. appreciated your care of Dori."

Katie looked at Helene as did they all. She smiled appreciatively. *So this is Rita's sister, the aunt who takes care of Dori.* Judd looked grim.

The rest of his assets, tangible and intangible, he left to his grandson, Judd Stetson, with the exception of Corazon. This property would be divided equally between Judd and Katie with the stipulation they would live on the ranch for a period of one year, and Dori would also live there for the same period.

Feeling Judd's anger, Katie closed her eyes not wanting to see his own accusing ones.

Judd would remain CEO of Stetson Enterprises. Family members would have an equal say and vote at Quarterly Board Meetings. Several stipulations were listed for the meetings.

With the exception of the $500,000, no one present would receive any property, stocks, or other assets for the period of one year from the date of J.D.'s death. Those in the other two piles would receive one-quarter of their monetary bequests the first year. Should the Will be contested, or if the contents of the Will not carried out to the letter, the whole estate would be divided among the charities previously named.

The words seemed to echo from a great distance. Katie's mouth was so dry, she couldn't swallow.

At the end of one year, the estate would be turned over to the beneficiaries. The stocks could be sold, but family had to be given the first option to buy.

In an instant, Katie knew what J.D. had in mind. Her eyes flew to Judd's and confirmed it. His eyes glittered with the knowledge. His mouth tightened into a thin line, his face a mask of fury.

Katie scrunched down in her seat as the swell of indignation became a chaotic verbal barrage aimed at her. She burned as a tide of red washed over her, and her heart thudded erratically.

Adrienne was the first to leap to her feet. "He can't do that!" she screeched. "Say something Max," she angrily commanded the dazed man at her side. When he didn't respond, she slapped him hard, the sound reverberating around the room.

Everyone collectively held their breath.

"Are you contesting the Will, Ms. Stetson?" Aaron Pickering asked with dead calm. The chilled edge of his question tightened a band around Katie's heart and added a hint of fear to appalled faces around the table.

Adrienne changed tact. "It's your doing, you hussy!" she accused, pointing a finger at Katie. "You've wormed yourself into his life, into his bed," she spat venomously.

"That's enough, Adrienne!" The voice of authority rang from an unexpected source. Max leapt to his feet and restrained her from behind before she could launch a physical attack. "For once in your life, think about what you're doing," he grated in her ear. "Think about what you'll lose," he continued. "Think about all those lovely stocks going to the homeless."

Adrienne stilled in his arms, her dilated eyes focusing somewhere in the future. She shook him off, and dropped heavily onto her chair in a magnificent sulk.

Stupefied, Katie looked at Judd. The disgust plainly written on his face alternately hurt and repelled her. Did he believe his mother's accusations?

His clenched fist was the answer. Without speaking, Judd stalked from the room, and a dazed Helene followed him out, still clutching the check in her hand.

Katie tasted bile and knew she would be sick. She rushed to the Ladies Room and relieved herself in misery. She leaned against the cold marble wall. The cream and brown pattern blurred as the tears became sobs and the sobs great shudders until she was heaving once more, swamped in a mire of denial and self-pity.

A long time passed before she regained control. Katie rinsed her mouth and washed her face. She wasn't one of the lucky ones who cried beautifully. Her eyes were puffy, her pale skin making the red blotches around her eyes, nose, and throat more prominent. She dropped down in one of the upholstered, wicker chairs decorating the lounge. Katie didn't want anyone seeing her like this. She snuffled several times as she wound down to an uneasy calm.

Closing her eyes, she drifted into a drained semi-sleep. Her mind formed a picture of Freebie, the golden retriever, running playfully away from Karen, who waved a daisy chain in her chubby little hand. He ran by her several times until Karen tackled him and rolled with him in the grass. She placed the chain around his neck. The feat completed, she rose and pumped her arms over her head, victorious. The pride in her wide smile and sparkling eyes was not diminished by Freebie when the chain broke, and he raced back to the house. Karen had won.

Katie felt hope burgeoning in her breast. She would win, too. J.D. had given her a formidable task and one year. He entrusted his two greatest treasures into her keeping, his grandson and his great-granddaughter, hoping their lives would be changed.

"Thank you, Lord," she whispered, acknowledging His will for her. "I can do all things through Christ who strengthens me. Nothing is impossible with You." These two verses sustained her and had seen her through hard times.

Mr. Pickering was alone when Katie returned for her purse. Only one look at her pale face had him by her side in an instant.

"Do you think he'll ever forgive me?"

He knew she was referring to Judd. "Yes, my dear, he'll forgive you," he said with an encouraging hug. "He'll forgive you." *And love you,* he added silently. *J.D., you may have done something right.*

CHAPTER TEN

Chester "Slim" Wiggins felt like a hammer in the produce department. His sun-leathered face, dirty work clothes, and scarred boots were not the fashion here among the well-heeled and famous. Several raised eyebrows and open stares had him shifting uneasily from one foot to the other. He scratched a bristled jaw and wondered for the umpteenth time what had goosed the boss man. He'd been mighty moody of late, and this mornin', he'd been downright irrational.

The last place Slim Wiggins needed to be was at this airport pickin' up this female. He needed to be puttin' in a fence on the back section. A rough man of few words and fewer social graces, he worked long hours and was satisfied only when the job was done. Already hot and sweaty from loading creosote posts and barbed wire onto the back of his truck, he'd headed to the barn to clean up when the boss stopped him and gave him new orders. He would have got out the company Expedition but was told to get a move on and use his own truck. Slim hawked and spit, stopping long enough to clean his hands and wipe some of the grime from his face.

When he and Sam had exchanged glances, the younger man had just shrugged his shoulders and grinned.

Yep, I'm goin' to be the laughin'stock for a week 'cause I'd been sent after a durned female. He could only guess she was goin' to be trouble with a capital T. *Me bein' at the airport is goin' to make a scene, or whatever, worse.*

Bein' raised by a passel of females had soured Slim on the species. "This's not my job, anyways," he griped under his breath as he crossed the floor to Baggage Claim. His pocket watch told him he was twenty minutes late.

The conveyor belt was spittin' out the luggage in one area, so he checked the flight number. "Yep, right one, wrong person," he told himself as he slewed his eyes around looking for a black-haired woman with golden eyes. He saw her immediately because she stood out from the crowd. "Yessir, attractive, an I'm not jest whistlin' Dixie," Slim mumbled to himself as he got closer. He had expected some society dame the boss wanted to humiliate, but she seemed casual and young. The girl struggled with a large box, pulling it off the belt and draggin' it over to a woman with two small children.

"I can't thank you enough for your help," the young mother said. "Benji and Sara will miss your attention."

The freckled boy pulled on the woman's pants. "Sing *The Wheels on The Bus* again," he pleaded.

"Yeah," the pig-tailed girl chimed in, "I want to be the baby on the bus. Wah, wah, wah," she pretended to bawl as she rubbed her fists in her eyes to wipe imaginary tears.

"You two will have to teach the song to your mom. I've got to find my ride."

A tall, balding young man with a harried expression arrived amid a cacophony of, "Dad," and "Daddy," as the boy and girl glued themselves to his legs.

"I'm sorry I'm late, Hon," he murmured, planting a quick kiss on the young mother's lips. "The traffic was horrendous, and there's one lane closed because of an accident." He picked up the two live wires, who proceeded to smother him with hugs and kisses.

Katie envied the family their closeness and love.

"You're just in time for the heavy work. This is Katie Mulholland from Shreveport. She was a big help on the plane."

Slim straightened, dumbstruck. *Katie Mulholland from Shreveport?* He hadn't put it together afore. There weren't enough girl here to pull a man like J.D. out of a canal.

The young man put the children down and pumped Katie's hand. "These two can be a handful even when they're good. Do you need any help?"

"No, thanks, I'm supposed to be met." Katie's eyes searched the crowd for Judd.

Slim mangled the hat in his hands and waited until the family took their leave before approachin' her.

"Miss Mulholland," he rasped and cleared his throat. "Chester Wiggins here. Mr. Stetson tole me to pick you up."

She didn't hesitate to hold out her hand, and Slim self-consciously wiped his hand on his pants before it was clasp in a firm, warm grip.

"Uh, if'n you'll show me what's yorn, I'll haul it out to the truck."

Katie watched him mash the sweat stained felt hat down on his head, stretch his neck, and tug at his collar. He shifted uncomfortably, and Katie felt sorry for him. She pointed to two blue suitcases and picked up the matching overnight piece.

Even carrying two heavy suitcases, Mr. Wiggins left so fast, Katie almost had to run to keep pace.

When he stopped at the battered, red pick-up loaded with black poles and barbed wire, she was speechless.

Chester scratched the back of his neck as he tried to decide how to get her luggage back to the ranch undamaged. He grumbled as he rummaged around behind the seat and brought out a faded, long-sleeved, blue shirt and a length of rope. He stretched the shirt across the ends of the poles and wedged her suitcases between the shirt and the cab of the truck.

"Reckon they won't be movin' none, so I won't need the rope," he grumbled as he threw the cord back behind the seat. He walked to the passenger side and opened the door. More grumbles assailed Katie as he moved things on the floor and off the seat to make room. He took her overnight bag from her and set it on top of some unopened oil cans. He walked around the truck and got in, leaving Katie to fend for herself.

With no running board to help her, she struggled to get inside. Katie had to stifle her own grumble about Judd's welcome.

Chester waited patiently, not saying a word.

Katie tried to squelch her ire and the questions besieging her. The dusty interior of the truck contained used oil cans, rags, discarded soda cans, and an assortment of tools. "Where's Mr. Stetson?" she finally inquired as he shifted gears and moved out into traffic.

"Don't rightly know, ma'am," he drawled. "Guess somethin' come up, or he'd a come for you hisself."

Katie was not convinced he believed his explanation. The silence stretched over the next few miles.

"Have you worked at Corazon long, Mr. Wiggins?"

"Call me Slim, ma'am. Everbody does."

"Then you may call me Katie, Slim. Ma'am makes me feel a lot older."

"Yes ma'am, Miss Katie," he amended her request to suit himself. "Guess I've worked for the Stetsons purt near seventy year. Goin' to be eighty soon, and I was took in when I was 'bout ten years by Mr. J.D. hisself. I was just a young pup then."

"What happened to your family?"

"Oh, I had family after my grandpa and grandma was drownded in the big lake. Hurricane of 1928. My pa run off and got hisself kilt poachin' after my ma passed on with consumption. Ma had two sisters what took me in. They and four daughters brung me up, but it weren't easy for 'um, me bein' a boy an all. We was livin' in a one room shack on the next property, but we wasn't makin' it. My pa was the one what hunted and fished for food 'fore he got hisself kilt." He wiped his nose on his sleeve. "I weren't too good at it, but I was the man now, and I got lucky sometimes. We was tole we was squattin' and to move on.

"Mr. J.D. musta heard 'bout it and rode over on his horse an tole us to pack up an move on his ranch. Said he needed help and had work for all ah us. I still live in the place what he give us. The rest is married, passed, or moved on." Slim hawked and spit out the window. He couldn't remember talkin' so much in a long while. She hadn't interrupted once. *This un was a rare female.*

They drove for miles wrapped in their own thoughts.

Katie leaned her head back and let the balmy Florida breeze whip her hair. The warm sun heated her arm resting outside the window. She was in Florida, and she had pinched herself to be sure she wasn't dreaming. Katie had no idea what to expect. Slim and his work truck would probably be the first of many surprises.

She dozed off and awoke when the truck bumped over what Slim called a cattle guard. He explained the metal poles laid over a hole took the place of a gate. Cows wouldn't walk across the poles. They bumped over five or six more. Straightening in her seat, Katie looked around. They were on an elevated marl and grass road that passed through palmettos, oaks, and pines. A prairie of brown grass waved beyond the trees. Clusters of palm tree islands dotted vast expanses. She saw cattle in most of the pastures. They were mainly black but some bore different colors. The terrain looked a lot like places in Louisiana, but she never had occasion to ask about them. Large white birds with long legs, curved beaks, and black wing tips waded in the marsh.

"What kind of birds are those?"

"Wood storks."

"And the palms?"

"They's cabbage palms. The pines, palms, oak, palmetto, and hickories is on higher ground. They's called hammocks. Indians at times has camped or lived there. We got some mounds here."

"Seminoles?"

"Mebbe. But there was Indians a fore the Seminoles. They was here thousands ah year ago and was wiped out by those Spanish and Indian enemies. The boss man's interested in them sites. He can tell you plenty if'n you want to know."

After this welcome, Katie didn't think she'd ask.

The road was bumpy in places, the scenery changing as they wound through several hammocks.

Katie marveled as Slim pointed out the bromeliads, wild orchids, and resurrection fern. He explained the fern which grew up the trunks and on the limbs of trees turned brown and looked dead in dry weather, but turned green and healthy looking when it rained. The fern was in the green stage now.

Slim stopped talking abruptly when he realized how dry his mouth had become from talking. When had anyone ever listened so long to what he had to say? Her golden eyes rested on him as he reached for the round tin in his back pocket. They was almost there. *I can wait. No sense dippin' and offendin' her when we is this* close. He didn't know what the boss man was thinkin', but he'd better not have brung this girl out to Corazon to hurt her. She looked like a fawn what lost its mama. *Mebbe she's here 'cause she pulled Mr. J. D. outtah that canal.* His hands gripped the steering wheel, and he sniffed as an unfamiliar emotion clenched his insides. *The boss better not be messin' with this girl.*

CHAPTER ELEVEN

A large, rambling wooden-framed house came into view.

Moisture welled in Katie's eyes unbidden. This house represented one year of her life. *One year, a lifetime.* She closed her eyes. *I'm not wanted here.* Mr. Pickering had told her to look on the year as a vacation. At the time, his words held possibilities. After Judd's welcome, second thoughts muddled her thinking. Prickles of dread assailed her senses. *Will the sacrifice be worth the loss of one year of my life? Judd ... his daughter. I have to try.* She opened her eyes to look at the surroundings.

The white, painted main house had a second story. The annexes might have been added later. The white columns and spacious porch reminded Katie of the plantations back home. Three dormer windows sprouted from the tin roof that had a brick chimney at each end of the main house. Surreptitiously, she swiped the tears, not wanting Slim to see her as weak. *Look at the house. Think about something else.*

Katie assumed the wide green shutters served an aesthetic, as well as, a practical purpose. They could be locked closed in a storm. Seasonal storms were common in Florida like in Louisiana. She had seen first-hand the damage wind and water could cause.

The gravel on the circle drive crunched noisily as they pulled to a stop near the front steps. Large trimmed boxwoods skirted the porch and were interspersed with hibiscus bushes loaded with brilliantly hued pink and red flowers. The beautiful array welcomed her. *Think about that.*

Slim hopped out of the truck and began to retrieve her luggage. The front door opened and a screen door strummed shut. A petite, stout Hispanic woman in an oversized apron walked out, a puzzled look furrowing her brows. "Ay dios mio!" she exclaimed as her eyes took in the scene. She digressed into rapid Spanish, her tone of voice conveying her displeasure as she negotiated the steps.

Katie tried to hide her amusement as the little dynamo planted herself in Slim's path, her flashing, black eyes and poking fingers punctuating her speech.

Slim halted and straightened to his full height, not the least intimidated by her assault.

"Enough, Zita! Save it for Mr. Judd. This here's Miss Katie," he drawled.

Katie slid down from the cab of the truck and smiled.

Dark, expressive eyes scrutinized her.

I guess my visit is a surprise.

"She's a guest," Slim said, indicating her luggage.

Katie put out her hand as a peace offering, and Zita grabbed it with both hands.

"Ay dios mio! Mr. Judd, he have much to answer. Dios, what's in his head?" She dropped Katie's hand and placed her hands on her ample bosom. "My name Rosita. I happy you here. Yes, yes, happy to see you. Come. Come." She clambered up the steps, motioning Katie to follow, lapsing once more in Spanish, shaking her head and clucking incoherently. Opening the door, she ushered her in, but rounded on Slim. "The boots," she pointed at Slim's feet, "no come in."

Slim set the suitcases down, sat in one of the rockers, and proceeded to pull off his boots, grumbling under his breath all the while. "Females," he muttered, climbing the stairs in his stockinged feet. The luggage alternately banged the wall and the stair railing, before he put one in front and one behind.

"Men!" Rosita countered loudly as she followed in his wake. "You trying to break something? Here. Here," she said pointing to the first room on the right. "This room."

Slim dropped his load inside the door and beat a hasty retreat down the steps, passing Katie without a word. He was out of the door and grabbing his boots without stopping.

Katie didn't have time to thank him.

The truck door slammed, and the wheels spun, spitting out gravel as it took off down the drive.

"Now," Rosita called from the top of the stairs, "you come up and rest. Zita call you to dinner in a hour."

A savory smell permeated the house, and Katie's stomach rumbled. She looked around as she ascended the stairs. She liked the homey atmosphere, the muted greens and golds, and the fragrance of waxed wood.

Katie's bedroom was large and airy. A four poster bed, without a canopy, sat between two windows. The bed was covered by a beautiful quilt with the rings of a lover's knot in pinks, greens, and blues. At its foot sat an antique chest. The wide plank floors were a little uneven, but they gleamed and complemented the blue and green oriental rugs. A chest of drawers, tapestry wingback chair, ottoman, bedside table, and reading lamp completed the furnishings.

Rosita emerged from the bathroom after putting out fresh towels. "You rest now. We unpack after dinner. Yes, I help you," she said as she began to leave.

"Is Mr. Stetson here?" Katie asked tentatively, her curiosity growing.

"Yes, he somewhere. You no worry. He no miss dinner when Zita cook," she said proudly. She closed the door, and Katie sank down on the side of the bed. Obviously, Judd Stetson was chafing and determined to show her that he didn't want her in his life. She bet he wouldn't be at dinner either. Slipping off her shoes, she lay back against the quilted pillow sham fully intending to unpack in a few minutes. The day had been long, and she needed to rest a moment.

Insistent knocking on the door woke her. "Miss Katie, dinner ready." Rosita's voice seemed a long way off.

Katie opened her eyes and tried to orient herself to the surroundings. She remembered where she was and swung her legs over the side of the bed and sat up.

"Miss Katie, you awake," Rosita questioned, and another spate of knocking sounded.

"Yes, Rosita, I'll be down in a few minutes." The unopened suitcases mocked her across the room. She had planned to unpack, take a shower, and change before going down. Now there wouldn't be time.

Katie walked to the sink, splashed cold water on her face, and patted it dry. Rummaging through her overnight case, she found her brush and ran the bristles through the windblown strands, pulling her hair back with a barrette. Smoothing down her rumpled clothing, she set out to find the dining room. Her hand slid down the polished oak railing of the staircase, and she took time to appreciate the quality of the workmanship. They didn't make houses like this one anymore. The beveled wood wainscoting and carved ogee moldings graced the ceiling and windows. They showcased a master's craftsmanship.

The formal dining room was empty, so following the sound of voices, she pushed through the door of the butler's pantry. Katie found herself in a room separated from the kitchen by paneled, double doors. Six curious pairs of eyes watched her enter. Rosita wiped her hands on her apron and picked up a serving spoon.

"Slim, you tell Miss Katie everybody, and you," she waved the spoon at the men, "you close the mouths, or you catch flies. This lady, a guest."

"Yes ma'am," a young man in his twenties jumped up and wiped his hand on his pants before holding it out.

Katie moved forward and clasped it warmly without hesitation.

"Hi, I'm Sam."

Slim harrumphed. "Sit down, Sam. You'll make the rest ah us look bad. Don't know what causes him to be so jumpy. Too much sugar, I reckon."

The others nodded their agreement.

"Now this here's Mike." He pointed to a husky man who looked to be in his fifties.

Mike nodded, and a gap-toothed grin followed. Slim looked at the young man next to Mike. "That's Melvin. He don't talk much." Melvin blinked at her behind a pair of thick-lensed glasses. His prominent Adam's apple bobbed up and down as he swallowed.

"Hello, Melvin," Katie said.

He nodded and looked owlishly at her.

"That's Pliny accrost from you. He's been here about forty year." Pliny was a black man of indeterminate age. His weathered face could have seen fifty or as easily seventy years.

Pliny flashed his big, white teeth at her. "Ma'am," he said and nodded.

Judd was conspicuously absent.

Rosita bustled around, setting bowls of steaming black beans and rice on the table to complement a platter of broiled chicken.

"You go in dining room now, I fix you plate quick, yes?" Rosita stammered nervously and nodded encouragingly toward the door.

"You mean eat in the other room?" Katie said, thinking of the big empty table.

"Yes, you a guest at Corazon, and …"

Katie didn't let her finish. "If you don't mind, I'd rather eat here." She looked around at the mixed reactions of the men. The older ones looked uncomfortable, but the others smiled, pleased.

Sam jumped up and pulled out a chair next to him. "You can set here, little lady."

Rosita shook her head. "Mr. Judd, he no going to like this."

"Well," Katie interjected, "Mr. Stetson isn't here to mind, now is he?"

She slid into the seat and pretended not to see the glances the men shot at each other. Surely, they didn't think she was a snob.

Hands reached for the food as it was set on the table, and they guffawed at a story Sam was relating about an armadillo. A couple started eating before everything was passed.

Katie smiled indulgently. "We forgot to say grace," she commented quietly.

They looked at each other, and Rosita stepped into the breach.

"Take hats off," she ordered, and the hats disappeared under the table.

"These men good, but no so close to the Lord, you know. Maybe they learn."

Katie smiled and bowed her head. "Thank you, Lord, for a safe trip. Keep our loved ones safe, and bless this food to the nourishment of our bodies. Bless the hands that prepared our meal. In Jesus name, Amen."

A few seconds passed before the men dug into the food, and Katie joined in the camaraderie. She told the men about an armadillo ad she drew for a soda company, and they laughed heartily as she told them the ways she tried to give the animal expression. "I called him Pierre, and he had a nose for the ladies."

Judd walked in after she raised her hands to her face to form Pierre's nose.

The men stopped laughing, and Katie lowered her hands.

"What's up, Boss?" Pliny asked Judd. Sam and Mike elbowed each other at the remark.

Katie imagined Judd with a thundercloud over his head and almost laughed again.

Judd left the question unanswered. "Zita," Judd hollered toward the kitchen.

Zita appeared, a big smile on her face.

"I need a place setting."

"Yes, Boss." She disappeared, and a drawer opened and closed. Rosita appeared with another place setting and drinking glass.

The men scooted their chairs down and left room for Judd to pull up another chair.

Food passed to Judd's end of the table. His clothes were dirty, but his hands and face were clean. His wet, slicked back hair looked like he washed it under a hose. His collar and shirt were wet.

Judd nodded at Katie and spooned food on the plate Rosita set before him. The men continued to eat quietly and Katie spoke.

"Slim was kind enough to pick me up at the airport. I'm surprised you were able to spare him. I think he planned to build a fence today."

Pliny guffawed and nudged Melvin with his elbow.

Judd looked at her. "I'm glad you enjoyed the ride."

"Indeed I did." she responded with a smile at Slim. "You left before I could thank you, so I'll do it now."

Slim grunted in embarrassment at being singled out.

All the heads turned from Katie to Slim, to Judd, waiting.

Judd sighed and put down his fork. "You probably have already met, but Katie Mulholland will be living here on the ranch for a year."

"Mulholland?" Mike said and came around the table and pumped her hand. "This here's the girl that pulled Mr. J.D. out of that canal."

"Well, I'll be," Sam chorused his thanks with the others.

"You done good, Miss," Pliny spoke again. "Mr. J.D. come back here changed and happy as I ever seen him."

"Yessir, that canal water washed all his bad times away." Melvin spoke for the first time.

Katie swallowed. She looked at Judd and bit her lip. She wanted to say canal water might do Judd some good, too. She hid her smile behind her napkin, but she could tell Judd got the message.

"All right, the introductions are over. Let's eat." Judd said, picking up his fork again.

"It's okay, Boss, we done said a prayer," Sam said, grinning.

Judd looked around the table at the men watching him. He looked at Katie before continuing to eat without a word.

Rosita brought in a massive chocolate cake and dessert plates. She began removing the dirty dishes, and Katie got up and helped.

Judd still said nothing, and the men looked at each other.

Rosita had plenty to say in the kitchen. She closed the doors. "You no help with dishes. Zita's job." She thumped her chest with her fingers. "Mr. Judd, he not pleased." She put dishes in the sink and then turned and hugged her hard.

"You make Mr. J.D. new man." Tears glistened in her eyes. "I know him long time and first time he happy in years. You so special. Many candles lit for you."

Katie wiped tears from her eyes, too. She nodded, unable to speak. She remembered J.D.'s letter and his words had been humbling. These were the people she would make happy, the ones J.D. would help at the end of her year.

Katie looked around the kitchen. "You clean off the table, and I'll rinse these dishes."

"No, no, you guest here. No dishes." She pushed her toward the door. "Call me Zita."

When Katie returned, Mike jumped up and pulled out her chair. "You're gonna love Zita's chocolate cake." He kissed the ends of his fingers in appreciation.

"I love chocolate," Katie said, and a large piece came her way.

Judd watched but said nothing. His eyes narrowed as he watched the men accept her. Even the trip from the airport with Slim didn't faze her. Why did he feel bad about it now? Because it was petty. Because she accepted his rude welcome graciously, without striking out at Slim. Katie had made herself at home.

Katie used her finger to scrape icing off of her plate and put the dab in her mouth.

Sam slapped Mike on the back. "You see that? Welcome to Corazon, Miss Katie."

She looked at the men grinning at her and figured she was now one of the boys.

Later, after Zita helped her unpack, Katie summed up Judd's reactions. His rudeness made it plain she wasn't welcome, but he seemed unsure or wary when the men accepted her so openly in spite of his obvious disapproval.

Katie determined this year of her life would be an adventure. She planned to enjoy her stay, despite Judd. With that in mind, she prepared for an early night. Later, when sleep eluded her, she lay propped up in bed reading Randy Wayne White's, *Sanibel Flats,* another Doc Ford novel.

CHAPTER TWELVE

The time was after seven when Katie walked into the kitchen the next morning. Rosita was finished with the dishes and wiping the stove top.

"Buenos Dias, Miss Katie."

"Buenos Dias Zita. I'm going to have to learn some Spanish from you. I learned French in Louisiana."

"I help you if you want. Now, what you want to eat?"

"Do you have cereal or a couple of pieces of toast? I'm not a big breakfast eater, but I have to have a couple of cups of coffee to get started." The coffee smelled strong. "Umm, it smells so good." She walked to the half-full coffee pot and took a clean mug from the drain. She tried to stifle the yawn, but it slipped out.

"I make you fresh pot. That one stay too long."

Katie felt the pot, and it was still warm. "It's okay. I'll nuke it," she said, adding some milk from the fridge and carrying the cup to the microwave. "You don't have to wait on me. I'll find my way around in no time."

The bread box held a half loaf of whole grain bread and a half dozen bagels. She took a couple of the whole grain slices and put them in the toaster.

Katie sat down with her hot cup of coffee and asked, "Tell me, what does Corazon mean? The word is Spanish, isn't it?"

"Si, yes, it mean heart. Many years, place called *Mi Corazon,* My Heart. Mr. J.D. bought place for *su esposa,* his wife. She no like here. She city girl. Go back to city with man, not J.D. Break Mr. J.D.'s heart. Now it just Corazon."

The toast popped up, and Zita rushed to get it.

Katie watched and saw which cabinet held the dishes.

"You want butter? jelly? Mr. Judd got Orange Blossom Honey. You like honey? They bring bees to pollinate groves."

"No thanks, I eat mine plain." Katie dipped the toast in the coffee and ate a bite.

"I get you something more. That's no enough," Zita insisted.

Katie smiled. "You're spoiling me. I'll eat a banana."

Zita set the basket of fruit on the table. It held bananas, apples, and pears. Katie peeled a banana and began eating it. She was anxious to look around.

~

Katie wandered through the rooms, finding where everything was located. Her big find was in the parlor. A Steinway baby grand piano was revealed when she lifted the white cover. Katie overcame her resistance and decided to play. She pulled out the bench, sat with her feet on the pedals, and opened the lid revealing the keyboard. Her fingers moved down the keys in a series of riffs and began to play Chopin's most beautiful Etude OP 10 No 3 from memory. She closed her eyes and let the haunting melody lift her soul to new heights.

When she finished, Zita stood in the doorway, tears streaming down her cheeks. Katie got up and went to her. "Who played the piano?"

"Miss Adele. She play, and she like your song. I no think I hear it again."

"Miss Adele?"

"She Mr. Judd's *abuelita*, grandmother. She love to play, only sometime make her sad."

"Was Adele, J.D.'s wife?"

"Si, she leave him, and he no heart to give away. No one play but her. I so happy to hear again," she said, her hand pressed over her heart.

"It's a beautiful piano, but it needs tuning. Do you know who fixed the piano?"

"No good. Man die. Mr. Judd, he may know person." Zita shrugged her shoulders.

"Let's keep the piano uncovered. I'd like to practice," Katie said. She would look in the Yellow Pages later and call music stores to see if anyone near the ranch tuned pianos.

Zita gathered the cloth and left the room.

Katie ignored the temptation to sit and lose herself in the music because she wanted to explore outside.

She opened the front door, and a large brown dog bounded up the steps and put his paws on her chest, his weight pushing her backwards. She was used to Freebie's antics, so she wasn't afraid. The dog appeared to be friendly. His tail wagged and his slobber flew as he tried to lick her face.

"Okay, dog. Get down." She grasped his front paws and pushed them away from her.

"Here Jammer," Judd's authoritative voice called from the corner of the house. He watched Katie's head swing in his direction. "He's usually not so friendly with strangers."

Left unsaid was he couldn't imagine why the dog liked me, Katie thought. "I like dogs. He surprised me."

"Did I hear you playing the piano?"

"Yes, I hope you don't mind. It's a beautiful instrument, but it needs tuning."

"I guess it does. It hasn't been played in years." For a moment his face had a wistful expression that turned hard. "You may play it, but locating a tuner might not be easy."

"Leave it to me. I'll find someone. Is it all right if I walk around and explore?"

"It's half yours. You don't have to ask." His voice conveyed his disapproval.

"I told Mr. Pickering I didn't want the inheritance."

"Sure you did. That's why you're here," his sarcasm, an emotional blow.

"It's why you're here, too," she said softly. "Did you really want me to contest the Will?"

Judd looked at her and grimaced. "I guess not, but I don't have to like it." He turned to leave.

"When will Dori be coming to Corazon?" Katie's curiosity got the better of her.

"She'll be coming after school is out for the summer. I don't want her torn from her school or friends when she only has a couple of weeks left."

"You're wise to be thinking about her future. I'm looking forward to meeting her."

Judd half turned and said, "Dori is not your responsibility. I'd like for you to stay out of our business."

"Is that how you see your daughter, as business?"

"Look," he said turning back fully to confront her, "you know what I meant. She's my daughter, and I don't need your help or interference. Do we understand one another?"

Katie understood all too well. "I hope we'll be able to get along while Dori is here. Children pick up vibes, especially the discordant ones. I'll try to keep out of your way, for her sake."

Judd accepted her answer and nodded. He walked away without a word. *What's wrong with me? I'm never going to have a relationship with Katie if I snap every time I speak with her. Relationship?* He thought about the kiss on the dock. She had surrendered to his kisses, and her passionate response enflamed him. He had felt confident of the night's satisfying end when Katie denied him and left him frustrated. Sleep deprived nights cost him when he tried to concentrate on business. He couldn't get her softness or smell out of his mind. Knowing she had a year to satisfy his grandfather's diabolical plan, he dug in his heels. What galled him was her ability to ignore him.

The dog remained at Katie's feet. "Okay Jammer, it's just you and me. Let's go see what's happening around back." She walked toward the garage, Jammer at her heels. A dark green King Ranch Ford truck was in one bay and a shiny silver Expedition in another. Judd meant for Slim's truck to set the tone of welcome she might expect. The third bay held a golf cart and a John Deere work cart with tools on the back. Both held keys.

Across the way, she saw a shed and heard grinding, so she walked in that direction.

Pliny was sharpening a shovel on a round electric whetstone. He took off his safety goggles and spoke to her. "Good morning, Miss Katie. Can I help you?"

"I'm just looking around. Where is everybody?"

"The boss is probably in his office." He pointed to a modern building set apart on the other side of the shed. It had a big satellite dish, several smaller ones, and wiring that terminated at the site. "Mike's the Harvest Manager. He's probably overseeing the picking." He indicated another direction, down the wider road.

"What's he picking?"

"Valencias. The crews is finishing up picking this month. Them's the late oranges what mostly goes to juice. Slim, Sam and the boys, they's probably building or repairing fence. Leastways, that's what they was going to do yesterday, but Slim was gone with the poles. The other men what works the ranch don't come here. They meets at the 'quipment barns down the road. They's another road they use."

"Would it be okay to use one of the carts to drive around?"

"Sure thing, Miss Katie. Let me check and see if the cart's got gas."

They headed back to the garage. "This here's a puny thing," he said pointing to the golf cart, "what doesn't have the power of the other. It's electric an probably not charged up." He walked to the John Deere. "Thisn's a workhorse." He took some of the longer tools and buckets off the back, pulled up the seat, and used a stick to check the gas. "Yep, somebody's done topped it off." He looked at Katie. "You ever drove one of these?"

"No, I'm afraid not. Is it hard?"

"No ma'am, easy as driving a car." He pointed to the key in the ignition. "You turn it on and put it in gear. It's marked. Drive's up. Reverse's down, and Neutral's in the middle. That's all you got to know. Oh, keep your hands on the outside of the wheel. If it jerks, it could break your arm if'n it's inside the wheel. And stick to level ground 'til you get the feel of it."

"What's this? Katie asked, pointing to the toggle switch under the seat behind the leg area.

"Oh, that's if'n you want to dump something." He pulled the switch up, and the back started to rise, and when he pushed it down, the back returned to its original position. "You got a phone on you?"

"No, I left it in the room. It said, 'no service' this morning."

"Figured as much." He took a phone out of a belt holster and gave it to her. "If'n you need anything, push that first contact button. That's the boss. We'll have to see 'bout getting you communication. You shouldn't oughta be driving around here without it." Pliny got in the driver's seat and drove the cart out for her. He got off, so she could get on.

"Thank you, Pliny. I appreciate your help and the use of your phone." *I'll make sure I don't have to call Judd.*

Jammer jumped on the seat beside her. Pliny waved at them, a big smile on his face.

Katie put the cart in gear and mashed the gas. The only other pedal was the brake. Feeling comfortable, she drove down the road. Jammer sat up straight beside her, his tongue out, enjoying the wind.

CHAPTER THIRTEEN

A hive of activity greeted Katie when she reached the barns. Long lines of equipment were parked under sheds. She recognized the huge John Deere tractors and counted nine of various ages and types. Some of the larger ones had closed cabs. A*ir conditioned, no doubt.* Other equipment, like disks, also shared the spaces.

Across the way, empty fruit trailers were parked on a large, shell bed lot next to the road, and a semi-rig was being attached to one of them. A man came out of a building rolling an oversized tire, and sounds of hammering and clanking could be heard from open bays down the line.

Mike came out of the office when he heard the cart pull up. He greeted her cheerfully. "Good morning, Miss Katie. You're out and about early this morning. You want a tour of the place?" Mike's gap-toothed smile conveyed his pleasure at seeing her again.

"I'd love a tour. It looks like you have a lot going on right now. I don't want to take you away from your work if you need to be here."

"I've got my phone if anybody needs me. Cheryl's in the office, and she can handle just about anything that comes up. Let's go inside, and I'll introduce you."

Cheryl Hubbard was a plump, middle-aged woman with brown curls. A wide mouth held a chewed up pencil clasped between her teeth, and her hands raced over a computer keyboard. She took the pencil out of her mouth and straightened when Katie and Mike came into the office.

"This here's Katie Mulholland, Cheryl. She's going to be here a while, so you'll probably be seeing her around." Cheryl's eyes widened when she heard the name, but she didn't comment. She held out her hand, and Katie took it in friendly acknowledgment.

"Let me know if you need anything while you're here, Katie," Cheryl said.

"It's a pleasure to meet you, and thank you for the offer," Katie turned and looked around the room with interest. Binders of paperwork lined the shelves, and a cork wall behind Cheryl held a myriad of papers, cards, and tickets tacked to it in bunches. A copier, FAX machine, and weather computer also took up space. Family pictures were scattered about.

Mike led her through the rest of the building. His office held a large desk and a book-lined wall. Folders, Rolodex, and a phone covered the surface along with a large desk calendar filled in and with phone numbers scratched in the margins. A family portrait sat on the desk. "So, you're married," Katie said. "When I saw you at dinner, I assumed all the men were single."

They moved down the hall. "Sam and Slim are the only ones not married. This is their office." The room had wood paneling and photographs of hunts, cattle, dogs, horses, and cowboys. Two desks had piles of paperwork, but only one computer occupied the room.

Mike chuckled. "Slim calls the computer, 'The Beast', and he won't touch it. Sam's a wiz with gadgets. Each cow has an electronic ID tag placed in her ear with Corozon's ranch number. The microchip is a quality control record that gives its age, history, and medical record. And knowing a cow's origin prevents the spread of disease. We know a lot more about cows today because of technology. The tag follows the calf or cow to slaughter. Sam uses an iPad to store the information. When a cow goes through the chute, the ID tag is read by a device. We've had to modernize some things to keep up, but there's still lots of old ways used on this ranch."

Katie was amazed. She had no idea cattle were worked using today's technology.

"Slim has seniority and cattle smarts. He's always figuring ways to make the product better, like AI, artificial insemination, to make a better bull, or good conformation before they ship heifers and steers to western feedlots. He rotates the cattle to different pastures, so grass can regrow, and since our cattle are grass fed, he makes sure we have good grass. Slim also sees to working the cows, getting cowboys to help round up, castrate, and brand. He sets up times for the Vet to vaccinate, worm, and see to the cow's health. Slim has a full-time job.

"We each head up different jobs on the ranch and meet on Thursday evenings for supper to go over the week and plan what to do the next."

"I'm sorry if I interfered or kept you from leaving on time. I hope your wife didn't mind," Katie said.

"Oh, I've got the best wife a man can have. Julie's got the patience of Job, and that's a real good quality in our line of work. She was tickled pink you were going to be here a while. You'll meet her at some point."

"I'll look forward to it. What does Melvin do?"

"He's water management. It's important work in these parts. We work with Southwest Water Management to make sure excessive nutrients from fertilizer, pesticides, and the by-products of cattle manure get filtered out before going into Lake Okeechobee or flowing into the Everglades. You'll see ditches and a dike around the place. Water quality is paramount in Florida, and the boss takes it serious. Melvin can tell you more."

Mike led her into a room where she was introduced to another man, Ralph Medders. He was in the fruit lab, containing an oversized juicer and shelves of fruit bags, glass containers, and beakers.

"We depend on Ralph here to tell us when and where we can pick. He goes into a block and picks a selection of fruit from different areas of the grove. There are standard requirements for how much sugar is in citrus. Sugar is measured in Brix. If you pick too early, and you don't meet the standards, a load can be turned down at the plant, and that's an expense you don't want, so we check the fruit before we harvest it."

Ralph was an older man in his seventies or eighties. His courtly demeanor reminded her of Aaron Pickering "Good morning, Miss Mulholland. I've finished testing the fruit until August. I'm just cleaning up before vacation."

Katie asked, "Do you pick fruit in August?"

"Not usually. We'll most likely start picking the early fruit in October, but a few times we've started in early November. I check to see which blocks are ready to be picked first."

They said goodbye to Ralph, and Mike said, "If you're interested in the operation, you'll learn more by keeping your eyes and ears open over time. It's a lot to take in all at once.

"In here, we have a conference room and a kitchenette." Mike pointed into a large room with several tables and chairs. A counter at one end of the room held a microwave. The refrigerator sat back in its own nook. Two large coffee pots sat next to the sink, one half-full.

"The restrooms are there," Mike said, pointing down the hall. "Now, if you're ready, we'll drive down to where the men are harvesting."

They walked outside and passed a soda vending machine. Jammer jumped up in the cart.

"Sorry, Jammer, I'm taking Miss Katie in my truck." Mike led her to a white Ford 150 and opened the door for her. The running board helped her ease into the cab.

Jammer whined around the truck, and Mike relented. He opened the tailgate, and the dog jumped onto the bed without any help.

"I see you already have a devoted friend," Mike commented.

"We met this morning, and he hasn't left my side."

"Jammer is Judd's dog, but I guess the boss doesn't have much time for him. Dogs make good companions. We have two of our own," he said, making conversation.

"I passed a couple of dirt roads on the way here. Where do they go?"

"Let's see, the one on the left goes to a cabin behind the boss's office. It's an interesting old place that hasn't been used for years. The original homesteader, Cletus Baker, built it, so it's a true Cracker house."

"What's a Cracker house?"

"Cracker's the name they gave to the first cowboys in Florida. The name comes from the sound of the cracking of their whips to move a herd of cattle. A Cracker house is a cabin built by the settlers."

"I don't usually think of cowboys in Florida."

"Florida has a colorful history when it comes to cattle and cowboys. The Spanish brought in the cattle, and they ran loose until somebody rounded them up and branded them. Range wars began over fencing, and men were shot for cutting a fence or stealing cattle.

"You'd be surprised, Miss Katie. Florida is either the third or fourth largest producer of cattle east of the Mississippi. The cowboys here still work the cows in some ways they used to a hundred years ago with the exception of a few modern changes. Slim can tell you stories, and Sam can fill you in on the technology if you want to know."

"Where does the second road lead?"

"That one leads to Slim's cabin. I'd leave him be, if I were you. He doesn't like people around his place, and he has no use for women in his life. He grew up in a houseful of women, and they just about ruined him. He has a kennel of cur dogs there which work the cattle."

Mike changed the subject before she could ask more about Slim. They pulled up to a grove with several trailers filled with oranges. Corazon Harvesting was displayed on the back of the trailers, and they were numbered. A semi-truck backed up to hook onto one of them.

"The Valencia orange is a late orange and makes the best juice." They got out of the truck, walked over to a bin full of fruit, and he selected an orange. With his pocket knife, Mike began to pare away the outer rind about half way down the orange, leaving the white inner pulp. He opened a hole in the top, reamed it a little, and handed the orange to Katie.

"You just squeeze and drink. Juice doesn't get any fresher than this."

Katie squeezed the orange and sweet juice filled her mouth and dribbled down her chin. "The juice is really sweet." She had to lean over to keep juice from running down her shirt. Mike selected one for himself and repeated the process.

"Where do you take the fruit?"

"The juice fruit goes to Southern Gardens in Clewiston, but some of our loads go to other plants. I call each plant, and they tell me how many loads a day we can bring in. If we have more than the quota for that plant, we take them to another plant where we have contracts. We have to keep our harvesting crews going, or they leave to pick blueberries, go north to pick apples in the Carolinas, or work for someone else. Some of the early, fresh fruit is packed and sent to different markets."

When they finished the oranges, they threw the remains on the ground under a tree. Mike handed her a wet wipe from the back of the truck seat to clean off her sticky fingers and mouth.

Katie noticed the majority of the pickers were Latin American. "How do you find your workers?"

"We're part of an H-2A program that provides legal, temporary workers from Mexico. That's another expensive program. We have to house workers, guarantee fair wages, and meet other requirements. You'll see some of the housing in a bit."

They drove down the road, and the grove seemed to go on forever. In a couple of areas, tall ladders were set against the trees and men and women on them picked and put oranges in the bags around their necks and across their shoulders. They emptied the bags into large, round bins, that Mike said held ten boxes each.

They drove past hundreds of acres of groves. Every once in a while, sign placards on stakes carried identification, Block Numbers, and at times, varieties. They came to a place with houses lined along each side of a couple of roads. Chickens ran around the area. Goats and pigs were penned. A few trucks were parked in yards, and wash hung on lines. A couple of old school busses painted white were behind one building with Corazon Harvesting emblazoned on the sides. A few young children played outside.

"These houses are where the pickers live while they're harvesting. The older children go to schools in Okeechobee."

Returning, they stopped to watch a strange vehicle pick up a bin and empty it. An orange crane-like device was moved by a driver, working different levers to pick up the bin and empty it into its back holding area.

"That's what we call a *goat*. When the driver picks up enough fruit, he'll take it to one of the trailers. The back lifts up and he'll pour the fruit out into the trailer. Each trailer holds about five hundred boxes of fruit. You'll probably see that process at another time."

They arrived back at the office around noon. Katie thanked Mike for the tour, and she headed back to the house. Jammer sat beside her, enjoying the wind in his face.

Judd stood outside as she drove the cart into the garage. He walked over, and Jammer jumped out to greet him.

"You've been gone all morning," Judd said, and he didn't sound happy.

"I went exploring. Mike was kind enough to show me your fruit operation, and I met some of the people who work here. You have a nice staff." She turned off the ignition and stepped out of the cart.

"You should have let me know you were going farther than the yard. Pliny had to tell me where you were."

"I didn't think you cared. And I didn't want to bother you."

Judd seemed somewhat mollified and followed her out of the garage. Kati pulled the phone out of her pocket. "I have to give this back to Pliny. He let me borrow his because mine doesn't have service."

"He told me. I'll take care of it," he said, reaching for the phone.

He left her standing there, and as she watched his back, she knew this man was going to be a tough nut to crack. Her next thought got her attention. *Are you sure you want this nut?* Katie laughed and tried not to remember how it felt to be held in Judd's arms, to know his passion, his kisses.

CHAPTER FOURTEEN

Rosita greeted Katie when she opened the kitchen door. "Miss Katie, you come in. Zita fix lunch for you."

"You don't have to fix my lunch. I can make a sandwich."

"No, no, all ready for you. I fix chicken salad. Mr. Judd, he eat early. You no have to do it." She opened the refrigerator and took out a bowl of chicken salad. "See, all ready." She set the bowl on the counter. "Now what you want to drink?"

Katie sat at the table. She couldn't argue with the woman. "Just water and lemon. Thank you."

Zita beamed. "Now, you want sandwich or salad?"

"Just the salad would be fine. Zita. Do you make all the meals and take care of the housework, too?"

"Oh no, Zita have help. Isabel come three times a week to clean. I help with wash and meals. This my job. You a guest, Miss Katie. I no want to get in trouble with boss."

"I don't want you to get into trouble. I've never had anyone cook or do my work for me. I'm not comfortable having you do it."

"*Si*, I know this, but Mr. Judd, he pay me good. So you not get in way of job, okay?"

"Okay, Zita, I understand."

Rosita put the chicken salad on a bed of lettuce and set it on the table. She returned with utensils, ice water, and a slice of lemon. "I still have chocolate cake," she said, nodding encouragingly.

"No thanks. Your cake is really good, but this will be enough for now." Katie said a silent grace and ate the chicken salad with Rosita hovering over her. She would have to watch her weight. Too many tempting food items were available.

"Zita, do you live here?"

"Oh no, Miss Katie. I live near Buckhead. Not far."

"Do you have a family?"

"*Si, si,* Zita have big family. Juan, *mi esposo,* husband, five children, eight grandchildren. Mama and Papa still alive. We all close."

"That's a big family." Katie missed her parents and sister's family. A wave of homesickness washed over her.

"Is it okay to use the house phone until I get one that works?"

"*Si,* yes, of course." Rosita left the room and came back with a phone. "You plug in room. I take one from hall. House number on phone."

Katie thanked her, took the phone to her room, and looked for the jack. She found it by the bed, and called Myra first because she knew her parents wouldn't get home from work until later in the afternoon.

Myra sounded like she was in the same room. *Telephones, what a marvelous invention!*

"Well Sis, how is it down in Florida?"

"It's warm and sunny, but I miss you. I'm homesick. How are Paul, Karen and Hank?"

"They're fine. Paul loves his job, and you know how it is when school is almost out. The kids can't wait for summer. Will you be able to come back for a visit?"

"I'm sure I'll get some time off for good behavior," Katie said and laughed. "I'm going to call Mr. Pickering later. I want to come home and get my car and a few things I need to feel independent. It's a bit suffocating here."

"It can't be that bad. Why did you say it like that? What's it really like there?"

"It's a beautiful place, but Judd Stetson didn't put out the welcome mat."

"Well, you know my feelings about this whole situation. J.D. Stetson must have been crazy to think you and his grandson would ever get together. Mr. Stetson doesn't sound like a very nice man, and he's certainly not your type."

Katie mulled her sister's words. "Judd Stetson may have been born with a silver spoon in his mouth, but the tarnish has left him with a bad taste. He's not a happy man, and who can blame him? The problem is he's becoming a recluse like his grandfather, and I think this was what J.D. was afraid would happen?"

"Tell me you aren't feeling sorry for him. You're not going to try and reform him."

"That's a negative on both counts. You know me. I'll find something to keep me busy, so the time will go faster."

"Is his daughter there yet?"

"No, Dori is supposed to arrive after her school lets out in a couple of weeks. She and Karen are the same age. Maybe you can come here for a week or two this summer."

"I like the way you think. My curiosity is killing me. I'll see if Paul can get away."

Katie and Myra talked for quite a while before saying goodbye. Katie lay on the bed and revisited The Blue Adagio and Judd's kisses. She tried to tell herself he had been using her, but she knew deep down, he was as affected as she had been. *And maybe you're dreaming. Admit it. You're way out of his league.*

Yet, despite his tough façade, she saw his vulnerability, and she hurt for him. *No, feeling sorry for someone is not a good way to begin a relationship.* Besides, they were from two different worlds, and she'd never fit into a jet set mold.

Mr. Pickering answered his phone on the second ring. "How are you doing, Katie?"

"Well, I don't think things are going to turn out like J.D. hoped. Judd has dug in his heels and is spoiling for a fight every time I see him. He doesn't want me here, Mr. Pickering."

"Please call me Aaron. We're friends now." His voice conveyed sincerity, and Katie appreciated this friendly gesture. He continued, "You knew before you left, it wouldn't be easy. Don't give up. You just be you. He has to learn to trust you, the person you really are, if that makes any sense."

"It doesn't. I wouldn't try to be someone else, and I'm not exactly in his type of woman category." She remembered his stinging words, "Little Red Riding Hood in Shreveport" comment. "He treats me like an unwelcome child who gets in his way, which is the reason for my call. Is it all right to fly home, get my car, and visit my family a few days?"

"I don't see why not. J.D. would understand. He wouldn't want you to feel cooped up at Corazon." Katie thought of Adele, J.D.'s wife, and wondered if she had felt isolated.

"Okay, I'll probably go home sometime this week."

"You have full use of the money you were given," he reminded her.

"No, Mr. Pickering, Aaron. I'm going to use money I earned if there's a need. I have some set aside, and it's not like I'll have any big expenses this year. You paid my rent a year in advance, so I feel like I've already been compensated."

"Yes, I paid the rent. J.D. made all the plans. He foresaw what could happen, and he didn't want you to lose anything. Just so you know, I spoke with Mr. Cleeland, and he said he'd take you back at the agency, even a year later. You are that valuable to him."

Relief eased some of the tension she felt about leaving the agency so abruptly. Her job was safe. "Thank you, Aaron. I really appreciate your help and understanding."

"I'm here if you need me, Katie, and J.D. would tell you the same thing I'm telling you now. Please, don't give up on Judd. He's bull-headed, but he does have a heart. Your presence will provide the beat."

Katie told Aaron about some of the things she was learning on the ranch. "I've met some nice people and now I know who I'll be helping this year. They're the incentive I need to stay."

She tried not to think about Judd in a romantic context. It would be best not to think of him at all, but his daily presence reminded her of the brief passion they shared, and the memory clung like a remora on a shark.

When she finished speaking with Aaron, she began making plans to go home. She wouldn't ask Judd to take her to the airport. First, she needed to make a reservation, and then she'd think about how to get there. She found a phone book downstairs and called the airline.

She also found a music store listed in Palm Beach. The man who answered the phone knew a piano tuner and gave her his number.

Judd had set a mobile phone on the kitchen table and left Zita to tell her how to use it. He avoided contact with her whenever possible.

The following day, Katie met Slim outside the kitchen. Zita had a bag of vegetables from the garden for him. When she asked him if he'd take her to the airport on Sunday, Slim's face reddened, and he hesitated.

"Does the boss want me to take ya?"

His immediate deference to Judd irked Katie. "The boss isn't asking you. I am." She reined in her impatience. Judd was his employer, and Slim probably had no idea she was now a partner. Judd's overt actions were not encouraging.

"It's okay, Slim. I'll make sure it's all right if you don't have anything else planned on Sunday. I'll pay you for your time."

"No, no, ya don't have to pay me. If the boss don't need me, I'll take ya. Might even take in a show" He grinned at Zita. "Didn't know I like the movies, did ya?"

His comment surprised Katie. She thought of Slim as a homebody, not wanting to get out and do something frivolous.

She had to find Judd, and she wasn't looking forward to another confrontation. She walked to his office building. The satellite dishes and power boxes were overwhelming. Judd ran an international business, so if he lived at Corazon, communication with the outside world was imperative. Katie knocked.

The door opened and an irritated Judd Stetson put his face into her space. "This building is off limits. You are not welcome here unless there's an emergency, or you are invited. Understood?"

"Yes, Sir! Understood, Sir!"

Judd's eyes narrowed to slits, and he appeared to bite his lip to hold back a retort.

"Permission to speak, Sir." Katie clicked her heels and gave him a smart salute.

Judd's mouth quirked on one side and with a huff of exasperation, backed off without moving inside the doorway.

"What do you want?" His voice conveyed his exasperation at being interrupted and at her childish response.

Katie told Judd she wanted Slim to take her to the airport if he wasn't needed on Sunday.

If her request or her choice of the driver bothered him, he didn't let it show. She also told him she had spoken with Aaron and received approval for the trip. "I'll drive my car back to Florida."

"You can use the Expedition," Judd said, his first acknowledgment of her decision.

"Thank you, but I want to be free to move about without your permission."

"I told you ..." he began.

"Yes, you did," she interrupted. "Corazon is half mine, but I'm not comfortable with this arrangement. How would you feel?"

Judd nodded as if understanding, and Katie left before he could close the door in her face or before anything further could be said.

Talking didn't solve their problems. The less she had to do with the man, the easier it would be to stay at Corazon the remainder of the year.

Katie spent a couple of days with Myra's family and saw her parents. They plied her with questions and wanted to know more about her life in Florida. She tried to have a positive attitude about her situation, and extended an invitation for them to come to Florida and see everything for themselves. Remembering the number of bedrooms upstairs, she told them there was plenty of room.

Five days later, Katie returned to Corazon in the green Pathfinder she had bought last year when she traded in her Taurus. The vehicle had more room for her folios of designs and work items. She put down the seats and packed the back with clothing, personal items, and the Bentley rocker.

When she pulled around to the back of the house, she noticed the third garage bay had been emptied for her vehicle. The carts sat under a nearby shed.

Zita met her at the back door with a big smile and willing hands to help her unload. The gesture made her feel like she was returning home. That in itself was a bit disconcerting.

CHAPTER FIFTEEN

The time flew by, and Katie's days began to take on a pattern. She woke early but waited until Judd had eaten and left for the office before coming downstairs and eating in the kitchen. She arranged to have Zita fix lunches to take with her on the cart while she explored the ranch and hammocks. Jammer looked forward to the rides and met her at the vehicle each morning.

The piano tuner came one afternoon. He was an emaciated man with a bad cough, and he reeked of tobacco.

Katie suspected smoking was consuming his health. She wanted him to leave as soon as possible after tuning the instrument, but he sat at the piano and played several sentimental pieces by memory. "You got a good piano here," he said when he finished playing. "Let me know if you need any more work on it."

Katie opened the windows after the man left and sprayed the room several times to get rid of the tobacco smell.

She had found sheet music in the piano bench and in the cabinet behind the baby grand. Katie practiced on the piano a couple of hours each afternoon. Adele had eclectic tastes ranging from Gospel to Classical. The music relaxed her and filled her with harmony and peace. Sometimes Zita and Isabel stopped by to listen and comment on her playing.

Isabel came to the house on Monday, Wednesday, and Friday to clean. She was younger than Katie imagined and probably in her early twenties. A purple birthmark covered the left side of her neck and face, but it didn't mar the beauty of her features. Isabel was slender and had the most beautiful and expressive eyes of anyone Katie had ever met. Zita spoke to her in Spanish and acted as an interpreter with Katie, who was patient and tried to teach her some English. Isabel was the wife of one of the crew leaders, and this was her second year to work at Corazon.

Every week, a couple of workers arrived to mow and do the lawn work. They kept the yard manicured.

At dinner, Judd sat alone in the dining room. Katie preferred the kitchen, and he didn't object to the arrangement. The obstinate man was unwilling to bend, so Katie ignored his rudeness and kept to herself. On Thursday, when the men met for dinner in the kitchen, Katie took her supper to her room, so she wouldn't interfere with their business discussions.

Katie's evenings were spent checking the news on her computer, responding to emails, and reading on her Kindle. Unlike home, she retired early and woke refreshed. She had no deadlines to meet or a stack of work to sort through. The lack of work made her restless, and she widened her exploration outside of Corazon.

On Sunday, Katie got up early and drove to a small church she had found while driving around the area. It was situated on the bank of Taylor Creek. The church had been established in 1917. An old cemetery rested under the shade of heritage live oaks just down the road from the parking lot. She walked among the tombstones looking at the names, dates, and epitaphs. It looked as if families were buried here. These were the early pioneers of Florida. "What stories you could tell," she said aloud as she walked. Tombstones of parents and children dying on dates close together were the saddest. Entire families had died in 1918, the influenza epidemic, she guessed. The next most common date of death was 1928. Maybe that was the date of the big hurricane Slim had mentioned. 1926 was also recorded a lot. *Another hurricane?*

Katie noticed a nice-looking young man walking toward her from the church parking lot. He had auburn hair, wire-rimmed glasses, and wore a blue-striped seersucker suit.

"Hello, are you looking for someone in particular?" he asked, a friendly smile on his face.

"Oh, no. I was early and thought I'd soak up some of the local history. These tombstones represent the lives of some Florida pioneers."

"You'd be right about that," he said, holding out his hand. "I'm Luke Albritton, and a number of my ancestors are resting here."

Katie clasped his warm hand. "Albritton, a big family going way back according to these inscriptions. I'm Katie." She didn't want to give out her personal information, but she didn't want to be rude either.

"That's right, Katie. I'm a sixth generation Floridian, a rare breed these days."

Katie was impressed. A lot of Florida's residents were Snowbirds, people who came to Florida for six months from other states during the winter.

"Are you planning to be in the area a while?"

"I might be. Florida's an interesting state."

"Are you coming to the church service?"

"Yes. Do you work and live in the area, or are you visiting?"

Luke laughed. "I live in West Palm Beach, but I work in Okeechobee a couple of days a week. I grew up here and have family in the area. Come on, I'll walk back with you."

On the way, Katie asked about the two most prominent dates, 1918 and 1928. She had been correct on both, the dates of the influenza pandemic which killed millions, and the Hurricane of 1928. The storm caused the most devastating loss of life in the history of the country. Another damaging hurricane had happened in 1926.

When they reached the church, a couple met them at the door, and Luke introduced them. "Susan and John, this is Katie ...

"Mulholland," Katie supplied. "I'm visiting the area."

"Welcome to God's country," John said. "We hope you enjoy your stay."

Katie thanked them and walked inside.

Luke introduced her to several more people. The congregation was friendly, and if they recognized her name, they didn't mention it. *Stop being paranoid about people's reactions. Five years have passed.*

One older man, Bill Smith, said, "Well, you're in good company, young lady. Luke is a bright young attorney, and an up-and-coming political star."

"Are you running for an office?" Katie asked.

"Not right now, but I may run for the Florida House in a couple of years."

"You'd better," Bill said, "We need good men like you."

After the service, Katie met Luke's parents, uncle, and sister's family. She thanked Luke for his hospitality and told them she needed to go.

Luke asked if she'd join them for lunch, but she declined, saying she had plans.

Katie drove west along the shore of Lake Okeechobee to a seafood restaurant recommended to her. On the way, she detoured up a levee ramp and saw the big lake for the first time. She remembered Slims's story about the hurricane that had killed so many people. Because the lake was shallow, the wind picked up the water and slammed into communities drowning a large portion of the population. A levee had been built to contain the water. The lake looked peaceful enough at the moment.

The restaurant was packed, and it took a half hour before she was seated. The wait was worth it. The seafood was delicious.

Nearby Okeechobee began as a series of fish camps by the big lake, then became a cattle town which displayed an old-time charm. Katie spent a couple of days driving around some of the historical sections, looking at the earlier homes.

She returned to Corazon later one afternoon, and Zita met her at the kitchen door.

"Mr. Judd, he fly to Connecticut early to pick up Miss Dori. She be here today." Zita put a hand over her ample bosom. "You gonna love Miss Dori. Mr. J.D. and her, they close." She clasped her hands together for emphasis.

Katie knew Judd would be going to pick up his daughter soon, but she didn't realize it would be today. She was looking forward to meeting Dori, but remembered Judd telling her, "Dori is not your responsibility," and then he told her more or less to mind her own business.

CHAPTER SIXTEEN

Katie heard the gravel in the drive crunch and Jammer barking. She put the piano lid down over the keys and walked to the front door. The seven-year-old had left the car and had her arms around Jammer's neck. The dog licked her face, overjoyed to see her.

"Dori," a feminine voice called from the car. "Please don't let that filthy animal get your good clothes dirty." Red patent stilettos and long legs preceded the person of Helene from the car, with Judd giving her a helping hand.

"Hell!" she exclaimed as her heels sank into the gravel. "My shoes are going to be ruined. Why don't you pave your drive like other civilized people?" She directed this salvo at Judd, who left her to take the luggage from the trunk. He set the bags on the porch. The number of suitcases made Katie think Helene might also be staying a while.

Judd ignored Helene's complaints and declined to put his thoughts into audible words. *Great legs, but you shouldn't have worn the heels. You know from previous visits, they're not practical.* Helene was a beautiful woman. If she had not been related to Rita, he might have had fun with her.

Dori was tall for seven, like Katie's niece, Karen. Her long blond curls were held away from her gamine face by beribboned barrettes, and her outfit, knee socks, and Oxfords made her look like an escapee from an Ivy League prep school.

Katie walked outside and greeted them. "Hello, you must be Dori," she said, holding her hand out to the little girl.

Jammer jumped between them, and Judd commanded, "Go!"

The dog raced up the steps and waited, his tail wagging like a flag, periodically thumping it on the porch in excitement.

Katie stooped and held out her hand again. "Hi, I'm Katie. It's so good to finally meet you. I hope we'll be friends."

Dori's response was immediate acceptance, but when Katie faced Helene, her expression was frozen with disapproval. Her face immediately arranged itself into the more superior acknowledgment of a peon.

Katie looked at Judd, who turned and said, "You remember Helene. She'll be staying with us a while. It will take time for Dori to acclimate to her new surroundings."

"Spoken like the chief environmentalist," Katie responded and turned to Helene. "I hope you enjoy your stay."

Judd looked from Helene to her. "Dinner will be served at six. Please be on time," he said, looking pointedly at Katie. At first, Judd was surprised that Katie did not attempt to seek him out. She had been here two weeks. Now, her avoidance annoyed him. *Maybe a little competition will bring you around.* He decided having Helene at Corazon might get Katie's attention.

The dinner directive had Katie's heart racing. Judd expected her to eat dinner with them, and she wondered about his wording. Other than the first Thursday dinner in the kitchen, she and Judd had not had a meal together and therefore, she had never been late. She held her tongue, called Jammer, and walked around the house and down the road to collect her thoughts.

So Helene is staying at Corazon with Dori. She made it crystal clear she isn't in favor of my presence here. Maybe she has designs on Judd. They deserve each other. No, Dori deserves better than to be parceled out. She needs her father.

Katie picked up a stick and threw it down the road. Jammer retrieved it and brought the branch back to her. He was in a playful mood. A few minutes later, Jammer raced past her, and Katie turned to see Dori walking in their direction.

The dog jumped around her, his tongue hanging out, and Dori stopped to hug him once more. "I've missed you sooo much," she told the dog, and Katie's heart went out to her. She didn't seem to be the girly-girl her aunt wanted her to be.

"Hello, Dori. How did you escape?"

Dori looked up at Katie with a mischievous grin and then down at her feet. "My aunt didn't want me to hear her talk to my daddy." She kicked larger pieces of gravel and shell down the road.

Katie started to mention she might scuff her Oxfords but then thought better of the idea. Shoes can be replaced. She'd need a good pair of everyday shoes on the ranch.

"Oh. Grown-up talk, I guess."

"Yes ma'am."

They walked in silence for a while. Katie asked Dori if she liked flying.

"Yes, sometimes. I don't like it when it bumps."

"Same here." Katie changed the subject again. "Is Dori your real name or a nickname?"

"Dorita's my name, but daddy calls me Dori. He hates my mother. She's dead. Her name was Rita. Is yours real?"

Katie put her hand on Dori's shoulder to let her know she wasn't alone. *What a burden for a child to bear.* "Yes, but it's short for Kathryn. I've always just been Katie."

"My daddy says I'm going to live here this year." Dori looked up at Katie with a tight expression, like she might cry. Her bottom lip trembled, and she looked down again.

"How do you feel about living here?"

"I'd love it, but my Aunt Helene doesn't like it. She wants me to stay with her in a cibilized place. She'll take me away again."

"I think you mean civilized." Katie corrected and added her reassurance, "I'm *sure* your aunt will let you stay for a year."

Her face lit up at Katie's positive statement. "Yes ma'am, civilized. What does civilized mean?"

Dori was inquisitive, a sure sign she was eager to learn. Katie determined to not use the child to get information on Helene and Judd or to become a hindrance to their relationship.

"It means your aunt believes you should live in a place where there are advantages, like good schools, libraries, churches, and entertainment. A place you can grow up having friends nearby. She and your daddy only want good things for you."

"I want to stay with my daddy. I have friends. Jammer's my best friend." She picked up a clam shell and threw it. Jammer ran after it but didn't pick it up.

"I'll be your friend, too. Please call me Katie. We can go exploring together on the cart if your daddy says it's okay. Jammer and I have found some interesting places to visit."

Dori turned left on the dirt road that wound around the back of Judd's office. The Cracker cabin came into view. The outside and roof looked like they had been kept up.

Dori ran ahead and jumped from a large rectangular rock onto the porch. The door was locked, so she looked in the window, her hands shading her eyes. "This is my best place. Gramps read to me here. He was old, but he was my friend, and he told me lots of stories." She looked at Katie. "He's dead, you know. I wish he was still here."

The sadness in her voice made Katie think about the old man again in a new light. Zita said Dori loved J.D. Children saw more than adults. He read to her and told her stories. Katie remenbered Mr. Pickering saying, "J.D. loved Dori."

Katie joined Dori on the porch and looked inside. This was the first time since coming to Corazon, she had the courage to come here. The building was too close to the forbidden office building. Through the windows, she saw primitive furniture, books, and stacks of boxes.

Katie looked at her watch. "We need to walk back and get ready for dinner."

CHAPTER SEVENTEEN

Katie made sure she was in the dining room by six. She was actually a few minutes early, and Judd stood as she walked to the table. He smiled and Katie's heart began to race. She looked back to see if someone else had walked in behind her. She heard Dori running down the stairs and Helene telling her to slow down and behave like a lady.

Dori burst into the room and ran to her father, giving him a big hug. "Guess what Katie and me did today?"

"It's Katie and I, darling," Helene said, "and you should call her Ms. Mulholland, not Katie." Helene had changed into a blue-green paisley dress that hugged her figure. A matching scarf pulled her golden hair back, revealing her long neck and exquisite features. She had the look of a model.

"Yes ma'am," Dori said as she pulled out a chair next to Judd and plopped down. Her smug smile as she looked at her aunt revealed friction between the two.

Helene frowned as she walked around Judd, and he seated her to his right.

Katie sat next to Dori, who wore a blue dress and a white bow in her arranged curls. She too, had showered and changed into a clean slacks outfit, but in the present company, it seemed too casual. Judd didn't have on a coat or tie, so she relaxed. "I believe Dori was about to tell you about our walk."

"Daddy, Ms. Mul… Mul…"

"Mulholland" Katie supplied. "I told Dori to please call me Katie." She looked at Judd and Helene to gauge their reactions. "The name is easier to pronounce, and I won't feel so old."

Dori looked up at her. "You're not old. You're pretty."

"Thank you, sweetheart. Kindness is honey to me. It gets my attention every time."

"I love honey," Dori said. "The bees make honey here. Daddy, Katie and I walked on the road and played with Jammer. We went to Gramp's place, but we couldn't get in. Can we go inside? Please."

Katie smiled at the way Dori wheedled out the "please."

Judd looked at Dori's excited face. *She likes Katie and seems to like it here.* Dori had visited the ranch several times last year, over Spring Break, Christmas, and a month during the summer. He had flown to Connecticut to visit when he had time. *I need to spend more time with my daughter. She's growing up too fast.*

"May we?" Helene corrected.

Katie heard the coolness in Helene's response.

Helene turned to Judd. "You can see why the dear needs guidance."

"She's just seven. Give her some room. She'll learn by example," he told her.

Katie silently cheered Judd's response and smiled at him.

"Whose example?" Helene's voice rose as she drove her point. "The cook's, the men you have working around here? Who will be an example?"

"I'll be here and Judd, too," Katie volunteered. "Her father will know how to handle the example part."

Helene bristled at the reminder that Katie would be staying at Corazon a year.

Rosita entered with a tray of food and set it on the sideboard. "I get the tea. You want sweet, unsweet?" Zita asked Helene.

"You see what I mean," Helene rounded on Judd. "Her speech is incorrect."

Zita stopped, rooted to the spot.

Judd's eyes narrowed as he looked at Helene. His face registered surprise followed by disapproval. *Helene, can't you just keep your mouth shut for once.* Her outburst reminded him of Rita's complaints. *Don't think about Rita.*" He turned to Zita to say something.

She had stepped back, ready to retreat, the smile wiped from her face.

Katie spoke up, changing the conversation. "Dori, Zita is going to teach me Spanish. We can learn together. Zita, you can speak to us in Spanish, and we'll begin to learn the names of things in the house. Helene, if you know Spanish, you can help or you can learn with us."

"I don't want to learn Spanish. If I did, it wouldn't be Mexican Spanish." She didn't look at Zita again. "Maybe *she* can learn proper English," she mumbled.

Zita looked stunned.

Judd gaze swung toward Helene. "Are these the manners you spoke with me about this afternoon?" His voice had a stern edge, and Katie was glad she wasn't on the receiving end.

Helene placed her napkin on the table and stood. "If you'll excuse me, I'll have a tray in my room later."

If Helene's comments or leaving the table bothered her, Dori didn't show it. She looked at Zita. "I can count to ten in Spanish." Dori proceeded to count. "And I know *agua* means water."

Judd nodded and smiled at Dori. "Where did you learn your Spanish?"

"On Sesame Street. I watched it every morning, until I went to school."

"Well, I think it would be a good idea for you to learn Spanish. It may one day become Florida's second language."

The rest of the meal went smoothly. Judd softened his tone and gave Dori his attention.

His daughter dominated the conversation, and she chattered about her teachers, the friends she had made, and about her dance lessons. She was taking ballet. "I missed the recital, but that's okay because I'm here." She beamed at Judd. "Aunt Helene was mad she had to come here and miss my recital. My pretty dresses were 'spensive. You won't let her take me back? I don't want to go back." Her eyes pled with him to let her stay.

"I'm very glad you're here. I appreciate your aunt's help, but she won't be taking you back for a long time."

Dori laughed, her relief plain. "That's what Katie said. I like Katie."

"I like you, too, Dori. Maybe you can show us your dance steps or give us a show one evening after dinner," Katie said. She remembered Hank and Karen's performances for family.

Dori jumped up, her hand pumping down, "Yesss! I can give you a show."

Katie suspected Dori had a flair for the dramatic. She wondered if this was a natural gift or a learned behavior.

Later, when Dori ran upstairs to get ready for bed, Judd spoke to Katie. "I don't know why Helene made such a scene. It's not like her to be unpleasant. She must be tired from the flight. Thank you for coming to Zita's rescue." Agitated, Judd ran his hand through his hair. "I was trying to think of something to say that wouldn't make the situation worse."

He smiled at Katie with warmth and appreciation. "Learning a second language is important. Spanish will be easier while Dori's young."

"I agree," Katie said. "And thank you for inviting me to eat with you." She looked at Judd, trying to assess his actions. *The invitation is a concession on your part. Why did you do it?*

"I think having our meals together would be a good idea. What do you think?"

Katie thought about her answer. "If you want me to share meals with you, I'm fine with it." *This is unexpected. What else are you going to spring?*

The next morning, Judd was in the kitchen when Katie came downstairs. Dori sat at the table in her pajamas, eating cereal.

"Good morning." he said with cheer in his voice. *Was Judd's welcome a precursor of an attitude change?*

Katie returned the greeting, and Zita poured her a mug of coffee and returned to get the milk. "*Buenos Dias,* Miss Katie, you want toast this morning?"

"*Buenas Dias,*" Katie said, choosing an orange from the fruit bowl and taking out a paring knife. "Toast will be fine."

"No, no, I tell you, I get your food. How you want orange?" She took the paring knife.

"Sectioned would be fine. How do you say orange in Spanish?"

"*Naranja* mean orange. *El fruta es una naranja,* The fruit is the orange, or *El color es el naranja,* the color orange," Zita said as she peeled the fruit.

Katie and Dori both said the words in Spanish. They practiced both ways to say orange as a fruit and a color. Zita had to coach them with the proper accent several times.

Judd patted Dori on the head, a pleased expression on his face. "What are your plans for today?" He looked at Katie for the answer, his eyes softening as did his words.

The question seemed a natural one, but Katie knew this was a new direction for Judd. "I was going to ask you if I could take Dori down to the pasture to see the cows and calves."

Dori jumped up. "Please, Daddy. Please."

"I don't see a problem. Just stay on the road and be sure you carry your phone."

He took a key off the hook by the back door and placed it in front of Dori. "This is the key to Gramp's hideaway. Put it on the hook when you come back."

"We'll be careful," Katie said as she dipped toast in her coffee.

Dori stood and hugged her father around the waist. "Thank you, Daddy. Me and Katie won't lose it."

Judd put a finger under Dori's chin and lifted it, so her eyes met his. "Katie and I, Dori."

She repeated the sentence correctly.

"That's right." Judd looked over her head at Katie. "I'll see you both for lunch around noon," he said as he opened the back door. They heard him whistling as he walked to the office.

CHAPTER EIGHTEEN

Helene didn't put in an appearance before Katie, Dori, and Jammer walked to the shed to get the cart. Katie lifted the seat of the cart and checked the gas. She patted her pocket to double-check she had her phone before they left the house.

Katie circled around the groves on the way to the pastures. She stopped the cart to watch a "goat" raise its orange-filled bed and dump the oranges into an almost full trailer. Dori said she had never seen a "goat" work, and Katie explained the process as told to her by Mike.

Leaving the grove behind, Katie drove along the elevated marl and grass road between the fence and a ditch that paralleled the pasture fence. They stopped several times to see alligators sunning on a bank or turtles basking on a log. The gators were all less than four feet in length. They appeared to have evolved from early prehistoric lizard-like dinosaurs which fascinated and repelled Katie.

Dori pointed out birds along the way, and Katie told her some of the names she had learned. "During the winter months, migratory birds will be here. They've probably flown home by now."

"Where do they live?"

"Some live up north or in Canada, the country above the United States on the map. Maybe some come from the mid-west. I'm not an expert on the subject. We have birds that fly south for the winter in Louisiana because it's too hard for birds to find food up north during the winter months. Some birds come back to the same place year after year."

"How do they know where to come?"

"I guess it's instinct, something they're born with that tells them when to leave and when to return. They see the earth from the sky and maybe they remember landmarks. What we need are some books with pictures of birds, trees, and the flowers of Florida. Maybe your daddy has some at the house. If not, we'll find a bookstore."

Katie finally spotted some cows, but they were too far from the fence to see. She stopped at a gate and found it unlocked. She opened it and drove through, making sure she closed the gate before driving into the pasture. The ground here was uneven with cow plops, and they had to watch out for wallow holes hidden in the grass.

Dori loved seeing the calves. She made cow sounds when they came close, and laughed at their antics. The cows and calves were a mixture of colors, but the bulls were Angus and Charolais. One white calf looked brand new. He was still wet and had an umbilical cord visible. The cow had separated herself from the herd. She looked at them and stepped closer to her calf when they stopped to watch.

"I don't want to upset his mama, so we need to keep some distance between us," Katie told Dori.

"Ahhh, he's sooo cute. He has the sweetest face. I'm going to call him Snowball," Dori said. "Do you think Daddy will let me have him?"

"I don't know, Dori. Snowball needs to stay out here with his mama. He needs her to feed him. There are other white calves out here. How will you know which one is yours?"

"His mama has brown spots on her white tummy and that white mark on her head and around her eye. He'll be with her."

"Good thinking, but Snowball looks like a she. I guess we'll find out later." They drove around the pastures about an hour. Katie glanced at her watch. "We need to get back for lunch before your dad sends out the troops to look for us."

Dori laughed. "He doesn't have any troops, silly." She tucked a stray lock behind her ear and waved goodbye to Snowball as they turned to go home.

Katie thought about how children took words literally. Once Paul had mentioned a close associate of his was fired, and Karen started crying. She knew the man and thought he had burned up.

They met Judd on the road when they were almost home. He was in his truck, and he pulled off the shoulder alongside of her. "I was beginning to think you two were lost," he said through the open window of the cab.

Katie took out her phone. "You could have called."

Judd smiled a crooked smile at her, and her heart began to race. *Why did he have to be so good-looking, so masculine in his jeans and boots?"*

Dori jumped off the cart and ran to Judd's door. He opened it, and she crawled up onto his lap. "Daddy, we saw the cutest white calf. I named him Snowball. Can he be mine? I love him. Please Daddy. Can I, can I, please?"

Judd looked into his daughter's excited face, and at that moment, he would have promised her the world. He touched her pink nose. "It's *may* I, and Snowball is yours if you want him. Do you think you can find him again?"

"Oh yes, me and Katie," she began and corrected herself; "Katie and I know his mama, so we can find him again. But can I still have him if he's a girl?"

Judd laughed, hugged Dori, and looked at Katie. "If it's a heifer, she's yours, too.

"Thank you, Daddy, thank you."

"We'll meet you back at the house," Judd said, and he let Katie drive in front of his truck, so the dust didn't cover her.

Katie thought about Judd's laugh and realized she was half way in love with him. Even crumbs he threw her way gave her hope. *Don't be stupid. Helene is more his type.*

Helene came out the back door when Judd parked his truck in the garage. She looked cool and relaxed in her white linen skirt and aqua-striped blouse. Helene had traded her heels for white, open-toed sandals that showed her long legs and feet with mauve-painted nails to full advantage. Her smile was for Judd. "I see you found them. I told you they'd be back for lunch."

"So you did, but I wanted to see if Dori was enjoying herself." He put his hand on Dori's shoulder as they approached the door. Dori looked up at him, adoration shining on her face.

Helene turned her attention to Dori. "Did you have fun, Dori?" Her question sounded stilted, more like an afterthought than an interested inquiry.

"Yes ma'am," was Dori's short response as she pushed by her to go inside.

"You'll have to tell me all about it," she called back to her as she looked in Katie's direction.

Katie felt like a limp noodle next to a cool cucumber. "We need to wash up. Excuse me," she said as she eased by Helene.

Ten minutes later they met in the dining room. Zita placed the food on the side board without speaking.

Katie said a silent grace. She took her plate and filled it with the spring mix and fruit salad. Strips of ham and turkey were on a separate plate and the condiments to make a sandwich were by a basket filled with bread. She noticed Helene left off the meat and only ate the fruit and lettace.

Dori picked the fruit out of the salad and made a ham sandwich. She told Helene about her daddy giving her Snowball and talked about the gators and turtles they saw. "Can we go back this afternoon?" Dori asked Katie.

"We can do a lot of things, Dori, but you say, May we, when asking permission."

Helene looked surprised that Katie corrected Dori, and explained the difference between the two words.

Dori accepted the correction and said, "May we go back this afternoon?"

Helene looked at Judd. "I think she's had enough excitement today. I'd like to have her read to me this afternoon. We want her to stay on top of her reading this summer."

Dori didn't complain. She turned to her father. "Do you have any bird books and books about Florida things? Katie and me want to learn the names. That's reading."

"Katie and I, sweetheart." Judd looked pleased. "We'll have to look after lunch, but I'm sure there are books on those subjects around here."

Dori looked up at Helene. "We can take you with us tomorrow and show you Snowball and the gators."

"That's sweet of you, honey, but I planned to go to Palm Beach tomorrow and look around. Maybe another time."

Katie would be surprised if "another time" ever came.

"Daddy, you can come with us, can't you?"

Judd looked at his watch. "I need to get back to work." He looked at Dori's fallen face. "I'll tell you what. If I can finish a few things this afternoon, maybe I can get away a while in the morning. Of course, I have to see Snowball."

Dori ran after her father when he left the room. "Daddy, where are the books?"

Katie saw Judd take his daughter's hand and head outside, probably to his office.

Helene wiped her mouth with the cloth napkin. "Dori is full of energy. If we aren't careful, she'll become a wild child."

"We need to remember she is a child, and her needs are different from ours," Katie said. "She's enjoying being with her father and wants to stay."

"I know. This arrangement is upsetting. J.D. should have learned something from his marriage to Adele. Corazon is not the place for a woman who wants a social life. Dori thinks she wants to stay here because everything is new. A month from now, she'll want to get back to Connecticut and a more interesting life."

"I believe Dori wants to stay here because she wants to be with her father. She's missed him."

"That may be, but when she finds out Judd doesn't have much time for her, she'll get bored."

"Life at Corazon has a lot to offer," Katie said. "She shouldn't get bored."

"We'll see." Helene said, eying her speculatively. "What do you expect out of this year at Corazon? Do you have hopes that Judd will keep you on permanently?"

Katie decided Helene's direct speech wasn't much different than looking down the barrel of a shotgun. "Judd may not have a choice as my home is now here."

Helene bristled at the reminder.

"I try not to anticipate" Katie said. "J.D. may have had different thoughts on the matter, but proximity doesn't guarantee what he hoped would happen. May I ask what you hope by staying? Are you interested in a permanent relationship with Judd?"

Helene pursed her lips as the question returned and made a decision. "Judd needs a woman who will be an asset to his business and social life. I've loved him for years, even before he married my sister." Her eyebrows raised, her head tilted, and she smiled with confidence. "Yes, I'm hoping he'll want to share his life with me. I love Dori, and she needs me. As for you staying on, Judd can do business anywhere. He needs to get out more."

Katie nodded her agreement. She knew it was true. Judd needed to socialize more, and she didn't feel adequate for the part. Corazon was his shelter and becoming his prison. "I won't interfere with your plans," she said, and hoped Helene would be more amiable for Dori's sake.

"Thank you for that. It eases my mind." Helene's smile appeared genuine.

Katie found solace in her music. She took out an old Cokesbury Hymnal and played several selections.

Dori returned with some books. "Daddy had books. Look at these."

She held up one on Florida trees, another on insects, and a plastic foldout on Florida butterflies. "He didn't have anything on birds or flowers. I like the piano." She touched the keys and played several notes. "I want to play the piano."

"Maybe I can give you some lessons. You have to practice if you want to play."

"Can we do it now?"

Katie closed the lid on temptation. "I believe your Aunt Helene is waiting to read with you. Run along and we'll work on the piano afterwards."

Dori left and Katie sat for several minutes, her heart heavy.

CHAPTER NINETEEN

Katie took the cart and drove to the field office. Jammer was nowhere in sight. She stopped and spoke to Cheryl Hubbard and asked if she would be working through the summer.

"I'll be here until the end of June. Bill and I take off two weeks and go visit my family in North Carolina. They live near Boone, and I can't wait to see the mountains and maybe enjoy some cool evenings outside on the porch."

"I hope you enjoy your vacation," Katie said as she walked into the hall.

"Thanks. I'll see you when we get back. The operations start up again the first of August."

Mike came down the hallway. "Hello, Miss Katie. Are you looking for anyone in particular?"

"No, I just thought I'd stop and say hello. Will you be working through the summer?"

"Everyone usually takes off the first two weeks of July for vacation. Slim and a few of the temporary laborers don't leave. They stick around to take care of any problems. Slim's not a big one for vacations, and the boss is usually here part of that time."

Katie looked at some of the posters hanging on the walls.

Mike noted Katie's interest and told her about some of the problems citrus people were facing.

"Canker is a big concern. Everybody sprayed equipment at first, going in and out of the groves, hoping they wouldn't get it, but the hurricanes spread canker to all the groves. The oranges aren't as pretty, but they're still good to juice, and canker doesn't kill the tree," Mike explained.

"Greening, on the other hand, does kill the tree, and the citrus industry is trying to find a solution to the problem. We've ordered a bunch of resets to replace dying or distressed trees, so you'll see them being planted after the old ones are pulled and burned."

Mike pointed to the poster with pictures of rust mite, scab, aphids, and other diseases and pests found on leaves. "We have a spray program to keep these problems in check, and someone is in the grove daily looking to make sure our trees stay watered and healthy."

"I can see you have your hands full," Katie said.

"Oh, that's not the half of it. We have to irrigate and make sure none of the irrigation heads are stopped up or blown out. Most growers now use drip irrigation instead of the tall rain birds. This process conserves water because it doesn't evaporate before reaching the ground. Contrary to the notions of the environmentalists and general public, farmers are good stewards of the land. Take care of the land, and it'll take care of you."

Mike spoke about the operation with pride, and Katie was enthralled.

"You know, Miss Katie, what would happen if the agricultural community got fed up with all the regulations put on them and decided to sell out? The land would be grabbed up and developed. You better believe it would."

"We fertilize and spray groves, as well as, pick and harvest the fruit. Then we have to keep the equipment in good, running condition. It's a full time, year round job that requires a large work force."

They walked down a hallway lined with grove pictures, showing the trees being planted and then trees in different stages of growth. Several of the pictures had trees with icicles hanging from them and snow on the ground.

Surprised, Katie asked, "You had snow in Florida?"

"Only once I can remember. It was January of '77, and it snowed clear down to Miami. We did a lot of replanting that year."

"Is there anything I can do to help while I'm staying here?"

Mike scratched his head while he thought. "I can't think of anything right off hand, but if something comes up, I'll get ahold of you."

As Katie walked back to the cart, Mike called after her. "Around the first of September, the boss has a barbeque or fish fry for the employees. Maybe you can help Zita plan it."

"Thanks, Mike." Katie wondered if she made him uncomfortable.

The men probably didn't know why she was here. She doubted Judd would discuss her presence or J.D.'s Will with them. Speculation probably birthed more than a few rumors.

Outside, a couple of men were painting fruit trailers.

Jammer greeted her when she returned to the house, and Katie heard someone picking on the piano. She found Dori.

"Reading didn't take long," Katie said. "Did you look in the Florida books?"

"No. Aunt Helene wanted me to read a story, but she got sleepy and told me to go to my room and read. The books are in her room."

"I heard you picking out a tune on the piano. Have you taken lessons?"

"No, but I like it. You can teach me, can't you? I want to play like you."

"It took years of practice to play like I do today. We won't have enough time for formal lessons. I can show you some chords and see if you like the sounds they make."

Dori nodded, and Katie placed her hands on the keys and named them. "You'll have to learn the names to read sheet music." She showed her a page in the hymnal as an example. The way she heard the little girl picking out the sounds, she thought Dori might be able to play by ear. "What if I show you the chords and you see if you can make them sound like a tune."

Dori practiced some of the chords over and over again, getting used to their sounds. If she continued to show interest, Katie would teach her the basics.

After fifteen minutes, Dori's interest flagged, and Katie taught her Chopsticks. Dori loved playing the tune. "Tomorrow, we'll play it together," Katie promised.

"I'm going to see Daddy and tell him I can play the piano." Dori ran out of the room and Katie heard the back door close. *I wonder how Judd will react to his daughter's invasion of his private space. Shelve it; he's a good father. Judd saves his roars for me.*

Dori returned, her face furrowed in a frown. "Daddy's talking to some people on TV. He said he'd see me later."

Judd must be in a conference call. Katie tried to explain about conference calls and why he couldn't talk to her right then.

Dori's face cleared, and she took something out of her pocket and handed it to Katie.

It was the key to the Cracker cabin Judd had given Dori this morning. He had called the place, Gramp's hideaway.

"Do you feel like exploring?" Katie asked, and Dori nodded.

The door to the cabin opened easily. Katie tried the switch by the door, but the lights didn't work. *Electricity's probably off.* Enough afternoon sunlight filtered through the window to see the contents of the room. A musty smell greeted them, and as they moved, motes of dust rose and floated in the sunlight, held in suspension. An old refrigerator had its doors open and a gas stove sat beside a galvanized sink. A window mounted air conditioner looked like the newest addition, but it was unplugged. The cabin hadn't been used for a long time.

"I think we're going to have to clean the place up before we do much exploring." Katie turned away from the stacks of boxes they had seen through the windows earlier. A leather recliner sat in a corner, an ottoman nearby. The surface of a side table held a stack of books. One she easily identified as a Bible, and it looked like it had a few miles on it. Under it was the book, The Case for Christ, by Lee Strobel, a journalist, who set out to disprove the Biblical account. His investigation led him to become a believer. She had sent the book to Mr. Pickering to give to J.D. Stetson. Katie wanted him to know why she had faith and believed. Chill bumps skated up her arms. "Come on, Dori, we need to get out of here until the place is cleaned." She locked the door and put the key in her pocket.

Dori squealed as she jumped off the porch.

Katie looked toward the office. The window slats were partly open, but she couldn't tell if Judd watched.

"When will it be cleaned?" Dori asked.

"Soon," Katie said. She'd talk to Judd about it later.

Katie hung the key on the hook by the kitchen door when they returned to the house.

"What can we do?" Dori asked. "It's too hot to play outside."

Katie agreed. "Why don't we practice a program for tomorrow night after dinner? You can show us your dance steps, and we can play Chopsticks on the piano together."

Dori clapped her hands. "I can say the Pledge of Allegiance, too."

"Excellent."

Helene claimed the seat on the sofa beside Judd for Dori's program. She took charge of the conversation, and Katie noticed she casually touched Judd whenever they were together. The touches underscored her claim that she had every intention of winning.

Dori began with the Pledge of Allegiance. She stood an open book on the piano and said it was the flag. They followed Dori's lead by standing and putting their hands over their hearts before reciting the pledge.

Dori didn't have the music for her dances, but she put on a show. If her moves were wrong, no one knew. Everyone clapped and she took several bows, enjoying the attention. Katie and Dori played Chopsticks together.

Judd asked to have his memory refreshed. He had played Chopsticks with his grandmother as a child. Dori showed him the keys, and they played it together a dozen times, laughing as they played it faster and faster.

Helene smiled and tried to look interested, but she stifled several yawns and said she had a headache.

Katie lay in bed later and went over the day. Judd drove the cart, and they finally found Snowball. She was definitely a heifer. The morning had been fun and relaxing. Dori hugged her father and told him she loved living on the ranch with him. He made an effort to be nice and include Katie in his conversations with his daughter about birds, bugs, and gators. He told them about the time a bull had chased him as a boy and about times they had to pull cattle from ditches when they got mired down. Cowboys on horseback rode over the ranch daily to check fences, water control, and the ditches for cattle.

They had returned before lunch, and Katie excused herself and headed to her room. Helene greeted her with snide remarks when they were alone in the hallway, "You know, you're going way beyond the call of duty with the little princess." As Katie walked away, Helene sniped, "Did you enjoy your outing with Judd?"

At this, Katie turned and replied as pleasantly as she could muster, "We had a good time. I'm sorry you didn't want to join us." Helene had a way of making her feel uncomfortable.

Katie went to her room with the newspaper, which was delivered to the house by a worker each day. She enjoyed the crossword section, but hadn't figured out how Sudoku worked. A stack of books from the local library and her Kindle lay on the side table to read at night.

Dinner had been quiet. *Did Helene also say something to Judd?* Only Dori chattered about her day and her program after dinner. She told her father about the dirty cabin and said, "I'm going to help Katie clean it. What's in the boxes?"

"I didn't think about cleaning," Judd said. "The cabin hasn't been used except for storage since your Gramps passed on. I'll get some of the men over there to clean it up. Who knows what's in the boxes. It's probably some of J.D.'s old things."

"Can we look? Is it a secret?"

"You *may* look. There are no secrets," Judd said, his voice low and mesmerizing. His eyes fell on Katie, and she imagined them probing her innermost thoughts. She knew color flagged her cheeks. Even his voice affected her.

Katie rose from the table, excusing herself, and walked to the door, trying to make her exit appear casual. She was drawn to Judd like a magnet. His face haunted her dreams, and she wanted to feel again the warmth of his embrace and the passion of his kisses.

Judd entered her mind whenever she lay in bed. Katie tossed and turned as she tried not to think about him. *Maybe I should call Hershal Cleeland and see if he has something for me to work on at Corazon.* No, she didn't want to start thinking about deadlines now.

CHAPTER TWENTY

A crew of men helped clean the cabin the next morning. The boxes were stacked on the porch while the rooms were aired, dusted, mopped, and polished. The air conditioner hummed along with the activity. Katie opened the refrigerator door and found a stock of bottled water, cooling. Contents of the filled ice trays were partially frozen. She handed water to the appreciative men and took a bottle for herself. The day was hot and muggy. The workers placed the boxes in a corner of the second room and left.

Katie sat in the worn recliner, sipped water, and looked around. She thought about the pioneers who had lived, loved, and maybe died here. Did they have children? Where did they sleep? She thought about Slim's family, six women and him in a one room shack.

This cabin had two rooms, or three if you counted the tiny space blocked out for a shower, toilet, and sink. After spotting a dilapidated outhouse in the back, this newer improvement was a welcome sight. The toilet bowl and ceramic sink exhibited rusty stains. Probably iron in the water. *From a well?* Neither room contained a bed, unless you counted the canvas cot, which looked like Army surplus. *Did J.D. sleep on this? I'm sure Adele didn't.*

She set the water bottle on the table by the chair and picked up the Strobel book. Inside she saw the words she had written five years before, "*Why I believe. Katie.*" inscribed on the flyleaf. She thought about J.D.'s letter to her and Aaron's explanation of a changed life. She had learned God didn't deal in half measures.

Katie sat down, closed her eyes, and prayed. It was a prayer of thankfulness and a plea for God to continue to use her. She flipped through the book and noted uneven highlighting and some notes in J.D.'s scratchy hand. A paragraph at the end told about meeting the author four years ago.

She placed the book on the table and picked up the Bible. On the cover, *J.D. Stetson* in gold gilt proclaimed his ownership. The leaves rustled as she turned them. Verses were underlined in ink or pencil. Some were highlighted in yellow. The margins contained notes and references. J. D. had studied the written Word, the markings more prevalent in the New Testament. He had made time to study. The Bible contained handwritten notes, pictures of family, pressed leaves, and prayers. One note was particularly poignant. Katie read,

"Del, my love, I'm so sorry for the years we wasted. No, I wasted. I'd give everything I own to go back and start over. You were right. I was a greedy SOB and too full of myself to accept your love and forgiveness. I can't tell you this now because you're gone. They say to a better place. You might be surprised to see me there one day. Sandy was a good man. Today, I mourn the loss of my friend. So, my dearest Del, I have been set free, and have been trying to make right, everything I can.

If you have any influence up there, I could use some help. Your repentant husband, Judson."

So, the J. stood for Judson. Katie folded the note and put it back in the Bible. She reflected on its contents. The words must have been written in the last five years. *Who is Sandy?* Was he Adele's rescuer and second husband? He must be dead, too. Del had to be the name J.D. called Adele.

She heard voices and footsteps crossing the porch. She put the Bible back on the table and stood as Judd, Dori, and Helene walked inside. The room shrank with four people taking up space.

Dori ran and hugged Katie. Then she turned round and round, her arms out. "I love it! It smells so good. Do you like it?" she asked Katie.

"I do." She looked at Judd, who had been studying her. Today he wore khaki jeans and shirt with the sleeves rolled to his elbows. His cowboy boots were scuffed, his appearance overall, one of a rugged, outdoor working man. Katie had difficulty fighting his magnetic aura. "The men worked hard this morning. Thank you." She turned to the others, away from the intensity of his eyes. "Would anyone like a water?"

Dori ran to the refrigerator. "I'm getting some. Do you want one, Aunt Helene?" She held a bottle out to her aunt, who hadn't said a word.

Helene shook her head as she looked into the next room. "No, thank you," her tone dismissive. She wrinkled her nose as if assailed by an unpleasant odor. "Rustic. Small. Hard to believe someone actually lived here."

"A family of five lived here," Judd said, looking around. "The original homesteaders were a hardy group. They had to be, to survive." He walked the perimeter of both rooms checking windows, walls, and ceiling. "My grandmother stayed out here sometimes when I was young. She loved this cabin and its history. In fact, she was responsible for most of the improvements. She baked me cookies in that old stove."

Helene grimaced. "It must have been a real mess if these are improvements."

Katie looked at Judd with renewed interest. His voice as he recalled an earlier time, made her think he had been happy here as a child. He loved his grandmother, which must have put him at odds with J.D. when she left. He had mentioned The Blue Adagio was his grandmother's favorite restaurant, and she had brought him there.

Helene shook her head. "I can't imagine more than one person in this place, and Adele? She must have been very angry. Why else would a woman of refinement want to stay out here?"

"I'd stay here," Dori piped with enthusiasm.

"Well, that I understand," Helene said, speaking to Dori in a childish, sing-song voice. "You don't know any better."

"She wasn't angry," Dori said, defiance in her stance. "She loved Gramps. He told me so, and he loved her." Dori's brow creased and her forehead furrowed with the telling.

"Then why did she...?" Helene began.

"Of course, they loved each other," Katie interjected, bending down to Dori's level. "You only have to look around to see all the details that make this a special place." She remembered Dori saying her daddy hated her mother, and Katie wanted to reassure her, love once filled this cabin.

Judd walked to one of the corner posts. He pointed out something to Dori in the shadow.

Dori squinted as she looked at the inscription and read aloud, "J. loves A." She looked up, grinning, "and a heart's around it." She read the words carved under the heart. "Del loves you more."

"I remember finding this, and Gramps telling me about carving the initials and the heart soon after they married. I didn't know the other inscription was here."

Dori cocked her head as she asked her father. "Who's Del?"

"Gramps called your great-grandmother, Del, short for Adele. She never liked her name. Your gramps spent many nights here after she left. He spent his days here, too, the last few years."

"Why did she leave?" Dori's earnest expression begged an answer.

"Gramps said she was lonely," Judd explained. "Corazon is too far away from people and the places they go for entertainment. She wasn't happy."

"But she loved Gramps. He was here. Why was she lonely?" She looked at each of them in turn and exclaimed. "I'm not lonely! I have you and Katie and Jammer and Zita, and you too, Aunt Helene," she added. "I could stay here forever and ever." Dori stopped talking and checked both rooms. "Where are my books?"

Judd shook his head. "I don't know, sweetheart. What books do you want to find?"

"Gramps bought me some books. They had stories about Sampson and Noah. David was my favorite, and Gramps said he was his, too."

Judd raked a hand through his hair. "Maybe Zita put them in the boxes. You can look for them later. Come on, Helene wants to see the cows."

"Maybe we'll see Snowball. You'll like her, Aunt Helene."

"I'm sure," her aunt responded with a forced smile. "I can't wait," she said, her voice less than enthusiastic.

Katie watched them leave. She had to give Helene points for trying. Katie sat in the recliner and picked up the Bible to read in Psalms. A while later, she leaned back to meditate on what she read. In minutes she was asleep.

Thunder clapped and woke her. Rain drummed on the metal roof and sluiced off the eaves in a waterfall. The room had darkened, but Katie didn't turn on the light. She thought about how peaceful and cleansing a summer rain could be. *How long did I sleep?* She didn't wear a watch.

Lightning lit the room followed in seconds by another drum roll of thunder. She had read Florida was in a lightning belt. Bright bursts continued to punctuate the sky, lighting the room. Several strikes sounded close by. Time passed, and it looked like the rain wouldn't let up. She wondered if the trio had gotten caught in the downpour.

A few minutes later, footsteps stomped on the porch. Judd entered, caked mud on his boots leaving a trail. The large, folded black umbrella dripped water in a puddle where he dropped it. "I think the storm has socked in for the duration, so I came to get you. Dinner will be ready soon."

Katie stood up and looked at Judd, her heart in her throat. His wet pants and shirt clung to him, his masculinity a feast for her eyes. Another streak of lightning outlined his powerful physique. Judd moved toward her and she backed to the wall, heart hammering, away from the danger emanating from him. "Uh," was the only thing she could manage, and then he was there, close, so close she felt the heat of his body, his breath on her face.

Judd instantly saw Katie's attraction flare and then her retreat. His hands gently traced her face, her ears, released the pony tail, and buried in her hair. Her vulnerability piqued his desire, her golden eyes widening on the verge of panic, inciting his predatory instincts. He dropped his brow onto her head, trying to control the tremors of passion slamming through him, losing ground.

His lips moved over Katie's face, warm as they caressed the outline of her mouth and moved to her eyelids, the tenderness melting Katie inside. She leaned into him, submitting to the sensual awakening of her senses.

He smiled his intent, and moved in to take her mouth, remembering her passion, wanting her. Judd molded the softness of her to his aroused body, and deepened the kiss.

She tried to put distance between them, but the wall didn't give.

Lord help me, I want this man. I need him. She twisted her head, and his mouth found the pulse at her neck, nipping and moving along its length to her shoulder. "Katie," he rasped, "Katie."

His voice awakened powerful urges unfamiliar and frightening. Katie thought about drowning, loss of air scalding her lungs. Her body trembled, and frightened of the powerful emotions, she retreated. "No, *not like this ...* Please," she murmured, more a feeble mewl than a denial.

Every fiber of Judd's body responded. He had never mistaken a woman's need, and the naked desire on Katie's face registered in his aroused state, as continue. *She's mine.*

When he swooped in to plunder her mouth in another searing kiss, Katie panicked and bit his lip, tasting blood.

He pulled away from her, stunned, his fingers at his lip. "You bit me!" Judd's eyes bore into her. "You bit me ..." Disbelief cooled his passion faster than a pail of ice water. He had blood on his fingers. He backed up. *God, what am I doing?* "Katie."

Horrified, Katie pushed him away and ran to the door, not bothering to retrieve the umbrella. She heard him call her name, but didn't turn back. She scrambled to the house, mud sucking at her feet, rain pelting her. The screen door slammed the wall with a crash.

Zita looked up from the counter, both hands going to her mouth as she took in Katie's soaked, disheveled appearance. "What happen?" She rushed toward her, pulling a dishtowel off a rack. "You okay?" Concern covered her face.

Katie sidestepped her and ran to her room. She had the misfortune of meeting Helene on the stairs, but she pushed past her and managed to reach safe haven. She leaned against her closed door, trying to control the heaving gasps and convulsions that shook her body.

Several minutes passed before she crossed to the bathroom, lightning the least of her worries. She stripped off her wet clothing and turned on the hot water. *I bit him. Oh God, I bit him.* She tried to settle down by scrubbing her skin, washing her hair, thinking about nothing and everything. The shaking subsided, and she climbed into bed, her hair wet, nothing but a towel wrapped around her. Dinner was now out of the question. In fact, she might never come out of her room again. *What am I going to do?*

A knock sounded on the door, and Katie held her breath.

"Miss Katie, I have you dinner. You awake, Miss Katie." Zita knocked again.

Food hadn't entered her mind. "I'm sorry, Zita. I'm not hungry," she called out. "I've gone to bed."

"Okay, Miss Katie, I save for you, for later." Zita's voice sounded muffled, but Katie understood her words.

"Thank you, Zita. You're a good woman." Katie reached and turned off the lamp. She lay in the dark, the storm still raging and wondered what Judd was doing. How bad was his lip? How would he explain it? *I can't believe I bit him.* Katie pulled the pillow over her face. She tossed and turned. Sleep eluded her, and her body burned for his kisses, his touch. She loved him. *I don't want to be one more of his conquests.* She'd call Myra in the morning. Katie hoped her sister would be coming soon.

CHAPTER TWENTY-ONE

Katie woke Sunday, just before noon. She had missed breakfast and church. Zita had Sundays off, and Katie found food left for her in the refrigerator. The floors and stairs had been cleaned. Helene and Dori were gone, the Expedition not in the garage. Neither was Judd's truck. A note from Judd leaned against the coffee maker. *Flying to Miami. Back Thursday afternoon.* It wasn't signed. *Coward.* Who was she to throw stones? *I'm the coward. He's just saving me from embarrassment.*

Famished, Katie ate almost half of the roasted chicken. She set the note aside and brewed coffee. Would his lip be healed by Thursday? *Doubtful.* Did she leave teeth marks? *Stop thinking about it. You have five days to get over this fixation.*

She had dressed in a jeans outfit and wore her loafers. The muddy tennis shoes mocked her from the bathroom floor. She scraped as much mud off of them as she could and added them to the pile of laundry she took downstairs. She filled and ran the washer, taking the sneakers outside to hose off the mud before adding them into the mix.

Katie found a mop and went back to her room to remove all traces from the night before.

Satisfied the floor looked clean, she carried the mop to the cabin.

Skirting the puddles she hadn't missed yesterday, she reached the porch when Jammer made an appearance and leapt toward her, his muddy paws in the air. She fended him off with the mop. "Down," she commanded, her irritation growing. *This isn't his fault.* She patted his head when he sat. "Good Jammer. I'll be out in a few minutes."

The door was unlocked. She had left the key on the stove. It lay half hidden under a dish towel. Several towels from the bathroom were piled by the door, wet and muddy. One of them had blood on it. Judd had used them on his face and to mop up the mess. The umbrella was gone. She finished the task and carried the towels back to the house, Jammer running in circles around her. She found his food and filled his dish outside. His water bowl didn't need filling.

The trees and moss still dripped a surplus of water. The resurrection fern on the trees had changed from dead brown to emerald green, and the sun broiled everything the rays touched. Today was a good day to stay indoors and let the air conditioner do its work.

Katie sat at the piano and played over an hour, but the music didn't give her solace or soothe her spirit. She was restless and dropped into an overstuffed chair when she realized she was pacing the floor, her thinking in turmoil. Thoughts of Judd, his intent, and her temporary escape didn't subside. Something had to give, and she feared it would be her.

She walked back to her room and called Myra.

"Well hello, stranger," her sister said. "Haven't heard from you in a while. How is everything?"

"Fine," she answered. A silence followed. Katie didn't trust her voice past the one word.

"Are you sure? You sound a little subdued."

Katie swallowed and tried to keep her voice even. "Everyone's gone and I'm all alone, counting the knots in the wood paneling."

"Poor thing. So, you thought about calling me. Should I be happy to know I'm a last resort?"

"Don't be silly," Katie said. "I just needed to hear your voice, and … I admit to feeling a little homesick. Do you think you'll be able to visit this summer?"

"We've been talking about the third week of June. That's just around the corner. Will that work for you, or should we plan for a later time?"

Relieved they would be coming soon, Katie sighed her relief. "Anytime will work for me. It's not like I'll be going anywhere. Tell me what's happening."

Myra filled her in on Hank's basketball camp and Karen's cheerleading class. "They want to know if they'll see alligators. We have them here, but it's not like we live in the wilderness."

"I know what you mean. Yes, they'll see alligators, and cows, and cowboys."

"They'll love that. So, anything *interesting* happening with you?"

Katie knew Myra wanted to know about her relationship with Judd. She didn't go there.

"I'm fixing up an old homesteader's cabin. They call it a Cracker house. Dori's a tomboy and a delight to have around. She's short on outdoor clothing because her aunt is insisting on her dressing and acting like a lady. I'm thinking about taking her shopping. She's interested in learning to play the piano. Judd's grandmother played and left a baby grand here. Helene is on the fast track with Judd. She has marriage on her mind. How are Mom and Dad?"

"Humm. Something's happening," Myra drawled. "You've gone from subdued to chatterbox." She didn't say more on the subject.

"Mom and Dad are busy planning a trip to Alaska. You know they've always wanted to go, and they're renting a travel trailer."

"I'm glad. They'll have a lot to tell us when they get back." They talked about ten minutes more, and when they hung up, Katie felt better.

∽

Katie made a chicken and pasta salad for later and put it in the fridge. She sat at the table working on the Sunday Crossword Puzzle.

Dori bounded through the door and hugged Katie. "Are you okay? Zita said you didn't feel good and went to bed. I was going to get you up, but Aunt Helene said to leave you alone."

"I'm fine. Just tired. I got in some good sleep." At *least a half a day.*

"Guess what?"

Before Katie answered, Helene's exasperated voice preceded her up the steps. "Open the door, Dori. You might have waited and helped me. Some of this is yours, you know." Helene dropped two armloads of bags and packages on the floor when she came inside.

"You've been shopping," Katie said to Dori.

"Yes, I got a new bathing suit. My other one's at home."

Helene sat down at the kitchen table. She kicked off her high heels and sat back. "I'm exhausted. We went to the Palm Gardens Mall."

Dori searched through the bags and brought out several outfits and a pair of tan leather, closed-toed shoes that looked practical. She held up her bathing suit. "See, it has green and pink polka-dotted ruffles on it. I'm going to try it on." She took it and ran from the room.

"Would you like some iced tea?" Katie asked Helene.

"Thank you. I need a refresher. Dori has energy to spare. I didn't get half of what I needed."

Katie prepared a sweet iced tea and set it on the table with a napkin. "It looks like you made inroads. I have a chicken pasta salad for dinner."

"That sounds good." Helene looked at Katie, her speculation obvious. Curiosity won.

"What happened last night? You came running in, looking a mess, and leaving one. Judd didn't make it to dinner either, I might add."

"I guess he was getting ready for a business trip. He left a note."

"Yes, I saw it, but that doesn't answer my question. You don't show up for dinner and neither does Judd. Dori said he didn't come for breakfast or see her before he left."

Katie told Helene what she wanted to hear, without telling an outright lie. "Judd and I didn't see eye to eye on something, and we had a bit of a fight. This whole thing about me staying here a year is uncomfortable for both of us. I'd like nothing better than going home, but I promised I'd stick it out."

Helene nodded, mollified. She had been present at the reading of the Will and knew the conditions specified. "I guess you must feel like a prisoner. Maybe Adele thought of her stay here the same way, only you're not married, and after the year is up, you'll be free to leave, a wealthy woman. Judd said your boss is holding your job for you."

"Humm," Katie murmured. *What else does Judd tell her about me?* "You're right. The year can't pass fast enough."

"Next time, go with me. Shopping's a panacea for the doldrums." She finished her tea and retrieved the packages.

According to named bags, Bloomingdales, Saks Fifth Avenue, Victoria's Secret, and Jimmy Choo were favored stores. *Victoria's Secret. A negligee, a revealing teddy, or sexy underwear? Stop it. Stop thinking about Helene and Judd together.*

Dori ran in wearing her new bathing suit as Helene left.

"I like it," Katie said as Dori turned to show the ruffles across her bottom. The suit looked good on her.

"Daddy's taking me swimming in the ocean."

"That's nice." *I hope he follows through.*

"You're coming, too. Do you have a bathing suit?"

"I didn't think I'd need one."

"I'll help you pick one out. Can we play the piano?"

"Why don't you go upstairs, help your aunt unpack, and change. If she doesn't need you, then we'll practice." *I'll dream about swimming with Judd. Get real. Why punish myself?*

CHAPTER TWENTY-TWO

The next few days, Katie spent time riding the work cart and looking at Corazon's ranch operation. The staff's efficiency and organization impressed her. She took side trips getting to know locations in and around Okeechobee.

One day she drove up the east coast to Titusville and back. Dori traveled with her some of the time. They enjoyed stopping at bookstores, looking through the books, and adding to their Florida collection. The evenings were spent reading or watching a few programs on television. Katie hadn't been back to the cabin since she cleaned the floor.

Zita didn't mention Saturday night, but she was more reserved than usual. When Katie caught Zita looking at her, she read concern on her face and wondered if she had guessed what happened. *Maybe it's a common occurrence. Had she seen Judd? Did Judd bring his women here? Myra had hinted that Judd had an active social life.*

Katie was playing Checkers with Dori when Judd returned Thursday afternoon. Zita had cooked more for the evening meal because tonight was the men's weekly meeting.

Dori ran and jumped into Judd's arms, glad he was home. She touched his lip, "You got a boo-boo. Does it hurt?"

Judd looked at Katie over Dori's shoulder.

Katie looked down, not wanting to read whatever his eyes conveyed. A cut remained. The swelling was down, but a light bluish, bruised area under it had not disappeared. The lip took longer to heal.

"No. Not anymore," he said, his voice subdued.

Judd remembered his loss of control in the cabin and berated himself. His actions embarrassed him, not because she rejected him but because it was wrong ... wrong for Katie. He knew better, but he couldn't help himself. She had just awakened, and her somnolent look was incredibly sexy. When he approached, she backed away, attraction widening her eyes, and her vulnerability, a siren's call. *I need to apologize.*

Helene walked in all smiles and welcome. She noticed his lip, and her smile widened, but she didn't mention it.

Katie thought about her talk with Helene. No doubt, she thought Katie had hit him in the altercation.

Judd turned to Rosita. "Zita, Saturday, two members of the Stetson Paris office will be here. We'll have an early dinner. They have a flight out of Ft. Lauderdale at eight Sunday morning.

"Is this private, or may we join you?" Helene asked, her smile enough to win any match.

"Sure, you may. I expect you to eat with us anytime we have company. We're one big, happy family."

Katie detected sarcasm in his remark, but she kept her head down, looking at the checkerboard.

Dori sat down and resumed playing by making a move.

Judd carried his flight bag to his room down the hall, and Helene sat down trying to look interested in the game. She had spent most of the last three days in her room and had encouraged Katie to take Dori with her.

That night Katie, Helene, and Dori ate in the dining room. The men had their work dinner in the kitchen addition. The meal was quiet. Helene remarked she had to decide what to wear Saturday night, "something chic, but not too dressy."

Katie hadn't given it a thought until then. *What should I wear?*

Later, that night, Katie came down to the kitchen to get some cold apple juice as she did many nights. Sleep eluded her, and the time was well past midnight. Judd must have heard her moving around. He stood in the doorway after she closed the refrigerator. He had on shorts, his torso bare. *God, he's beautiful.* She clutched the cold bottle to her chest and backed into the counter.

Judd held up his hands in surrender as he drew near. "I just want to apologize. I'm sorry about the other night." He kept his voice low and sounded sincere. "I don't know what came over me. The whole thing is making me crazy."

What whole thing? "I'm the one who should apologize" Katie said. "I've never in my life bitten anyone." Her gaze focused on his damaged lip, and she shuddered.

"Maybe not, but it was effective. Can we forgive each other? I promise not to attack you again."

His words and tone sounded sincere. Katie nodded and left the room in a hurry. She still had the bottle of apple juice in her hands. *I'll never get to sleep now.*

Judd picked up the Parisians at the Fort Lauderdale-Hollywood International Airport. They retired to Judd's office for an afternoon meeting before dinner.

Zita prepared the meal for four-thirty. Accustomed to serving business dinners, she planned every detail to perfection. Isabel helped her in the kitchen and then helped her serve and clean up. The table looked beautiful, set with fine china, silver, and red hibiscus. Wines and wine glasses sat on the bar.

Dori and Katie arrived in the parlor on time. The men stood when they came in and remained standing while they were introduced. They both shook hands with the visitors.

Katie wore a green summer dress with a white, short-sleeved cotton jacket she brought for church. Dori had on a ruffled, white Swiss polka-dotted dress with blue trim and a big blue bow in her hair.

Judd smiled approvingly at them both, the cut on his lip visible, a constant reminder. The blue tint was faint, still discernible. He had on a coat and tie as did the men.

Helene made her timed entrance as they walked to the dining room. She floated down the stairs in ruby stilettos and a striking scarlet dress that hugged her figure. Her golden hair was, arranged in loose curls, held back with rhinestone bows. She looked regal and welcomed the men with an alluring smile and sparkling come hither eyes.

The men watched her approach and when she gave them her hand, they each kissed it in turn and said, "*Enchante.*"

Her red lips smiled in appreciation, and she led the way to the dining room, choosing the hostess chair opposite Judd. One of the men pulled out her chair and the other did the honors for Katie. Judd pulled back Dori's chair, and she grinned up at him, pleased by his attention.

Dori sat next to Katie and followed her example. As she did at every meal, Katie lowered her head and said a silent grace. Dori had told her that Gramps did that, too. She also bowed her head, but Katie didn't know whether she said a blessing or just copied her action. She put the napkin in her lap and picked up the salad fork on the outside like Katie. When Dori stared at the men who ate and held their knives and forks in European fashion, Katie leaned over and asked when she was going swimming to distract her.

"Daddy, Katie wants to know when we're going swimming."

A red tide crept up Katie's neck. Leave it to a child.

"Maybe one day this week or next weekend, sweetheart," Judd said.

"Katie's going, too," Dori said, her fork capturing a piece of tomato.

Judd looked at Katie. "If Katie wants to go, she's welcome." His tone of voice seemed normal, a little stilted maybe, but she knew he seethed beneath the surface.

Katie let him off the hook. "No, I'm sorry, I'm not prepared. I'm going to church next Sunday."

"I told you I'd help you find a bathing suit," Dori said.

"I know, and I appreciate the thought. I missed church last Sunday, and I don't want to miss it again this week." She imagined Judd's eyes on her, making her nervous.

Dori looked downcast, but she didn't pursue the subject.

Helene, who had appeared rapt in her conversation with the men said, "I'll go to the beach with you, Dori."

"Great." Judd said, his enthusiasm a bit stale.

Mr. Gerard, who sat to Helene's right, asked Katie if she was a visitor on the ranch or a family member.

Katie told him she was visiting and talked about her job in

Shreveport. When she mentioned creating the French armadillo ad featuring Pierre, she had both men's attention.

"Very clever, *Mademoiselle*. It's easily our favorite ad in Paris. It will probably get a Clio." They asked about how she came up with the idea and more about the ad business.

Helene did not like being ignored, even for a few minutes. She quickly brought their attention back, her animation and laughter a sight to behold.

Katie didn't dare look at Judd. *Did he really apologize, or did I dream it?*

CHAPTER TWENTY-THREE

Katie took a seat in one of the back pews of the little country church. She admired the diminutive, stained glass windows framed in simple molded arches above the plain opaque glass windows on either side of the sanctuary. Each little gem portrayed a named apostle and she wondered if they had been donated by a patron member. Such exquisite art usually decorated large cathedrals. The sun cast multi-colored designs on the opposite wall. A larger stained glass portrayal of Jesus as a shepherd looked down at the congregation from behind the choir loft.

The choir sat behind the altar rail with nine chorus members present. They did not wear robes. People here dressed casually for church. She saw denims and boots. Luke Albritton and his family sat on the left side near the center. He seemed like a nice young man.

Announcements began with the pastor reminding people about the pot luck dinner on the grounds the following Sunday and to bring a dish. Katie mentally marked the occasion. She would bring a fruit cobbler.

After church, Luke saw her and headed her way. "I missed you last Sunday. I was afraid you might have left the area. I'm glad you haven't." He had on the same blue seersucker suit he wore the last time she saw him, but with a different shirt and tie.

"Thank you. It's good to be back." She didn't elaborate. They talked about some of the church events coming up and moved toward the parking lot.

"How about lunch? I know a good seafood restaurant on the lake," he said.

"If it's the same one I found a few weeks ago, I know it's good."

Luke named Sal's Seafood Place, and it was the same.

"I'd like to go. Thank you for asking me," Katie said.

"I can follow you home, and we can go from there, or I can bring you back here to your car. Your choice."

I'm not ready to take him to Corazon. "Or I can follow you to the restaurant, and you won't have to drive out of your way."

Luke laughed. "I like the way you think. Let me tell my folks not to expect me for lunch today. I'll be right back."

Katie watched him walk toward his parents' car and speak with them. They looked her way and nodded. She liked the fact he had a good relationship with his family. He was an attractive man in looks and personality, the kind of man who might take her mind off of Judd.

She followed Luke in her car to Sal's. The restaurant exhibited local color. Fishing tackle, paintings, and photographs of fishermen and their catches lined the walls. The aroma of fried fish and fresh bread permeated the atmosphere, and the salad bar's contents abundant and inviting. They had to wait but not as long as she had before. A lot of people knew Luke and approached the table to speak with him.

"You're a popular man in these parts."

Luke had a nice laugh. "When you live in a rural area all your life, you went to school with them, used their services, or were friends of the family. In my case, I'm related to a number of them. Okeechobee's growing. I have to admit, people have moved here from the coast, and I'm seeing more unfamiliar faces. Tell me about where you grew up. You sound like a Southerner."

Katie talked about Shreveport and her family while they ate their meal. When he asked her about where she worked, telling Luke about the ad agency was easy. When he asked where she lived while visiting the area, she reluctantly told him she lived at Corazon.

He sat back in his chair and regarded her with a curious expression. "Corazon? The Stetson property?" He didn't say ranch. He was silent, like he was mulling over her answer.

"Yes." Katie swallowed. *Is there a way to mention my stay at Corazon nonchalantly?* She asked if she might order a coffee. He looked around for their waitress and caught her eye.

"Are you a Stetson?"

"No. I'm a friend of the family."

"Judd Stetson's friend?" The way he asked specifically, sounded like he suspected a personal liaison. He tensed ever so slightly, but she saw it.

"If you're insinuating I'm one of Judd Stetson's women, you're wrong."

He relaxed but persisted. "I didn't know anyone but Judd and his workers lived on the property."

"Well, his daughter, Dori, and her aunt are living there now, and next week, my sister and her family will be coming for a visit."

"So, how did you become a friend of the Stetsons? J.D. was practically a hermit, and Judd has become as mysterious and elusive as his grandfather. They shunned publicity and weren't known for cultivating friends, just businesses."

Katie rubbed her forehead, trying to decide how much to tell him. If she wanted to continue seeing Luke, she had to be forthright. The truth was a good place to begin. "Look, this isn't for public disclosure. May I depend on you being discreet? It would be embarrassing if my presence at Corazon became a public issue."

"I have to say, I'm intrigued. As an attorney, privacy is implicit. Anything you tell me will be confidential. I'm telling you this not because you're a client. You're a friend, a person I want to get to know better. Understood?"

Katie nodded. The waitress brought two coffees. Luke drank his black, but Katie added cream. She told him about pulling J.D. from the canal, about his conversion, his changed life, and said only a little about the settlement of the Stetson estate. She told him she didn't want anything of J.D.'s. Katie said nothing about what she inherited, but told him she was committed to stay on the ranch for a year so others would benefit.

"Humm. Sounds like J. D. was hoping for a match. Is that how you see it?"

"It's how everyone sees it. Believe me, J.D.'s Will is a bone of contention. Judd is angry. He has to accept my presence or lose everything. I'm not thrilled to be away from my work and my family. If J. D. knew me, he would have known we aren't suited."

"The way I see it, J.D. knew you well enough to know you would acquiesce to his bidding. How are things working out at Corazon?"

"Dori, his daughter, makes the stay bearable. She's in the same boat, but she wants to stay on the ranch and not go back to Connecticut to live with her aunt. I agree with her. She needs her father, and he needs her even more. I'm hoping by the year's end, he'll realize that."

They sat a while in silence, drinking their coffee. Katie hoped she could trust him. Maybe, Luke wouldn't want to see her again or get involved. She wouldn't blame him.

Luke's forehead furrowed in thought and then cleared. "May I continue to see you, or will that be awkward?"

"It will only be awkward if we make it so. I'd like to continue seeing you." She meant it. The more she learned about this man, the more she admired him.

Luke smiled, his spirits restored. "Great! Are you coming to dinner on the grounds next week?"

A little after midnight, Katie was awaked by a distraught Helene. "Dori's sick. I can't help her. She's upchucked, and I'm going to be sick, too." Her hand clutched her throat as she swallowed hard. Katie had a brief glimpse of Helene in a black teddy, so sheer it left nothing to the imagination.

Katie found Dori sitting on the bathroom floor, hugging the toilet.

"I'm sorry. I tried to make it," Dori wailed, rising on her knees and heaving again. Helene made gagging sounds and began backing out of the bathroom.

Katie held Dori's head while she was sick and pulled her hair back to keep it out of her face. "Don't worry about that, sweetheart. It's not your fault; you're sick." To Helene, she said, "She's burning up. Do you know where to find a thermometer?"

Helene hurried away.

Katie gave Dori a cup of water. "Here, rinse your mouth and spit." She took a washcloth, filled it with cool water, wrung it out, and wiped Dori's face. "You're going to be fine. Let me help you out of your nightie and get you cleaned up."

Dori stood in the bathtub while Katie gave her a quick bath. She wrapped her in a towel, and took her back to bed. She sat the little girl down after ascertaining the bedding was clean and moved the wastebasket closer in case she was sick again.

Katie was going through the dresser drawers looking for a clean nightgown when Judd entered the room, followed closely by a concerned Helene, still wearing the flimsy teddy. She hadn't stopped to put on a robe.

Judd came into the room and went right to the bed and knelt before Dori. "How are you feeling, sweetheart?" He had on pajama bottoms, riding low on his hips, and no top. A brief glimpse revealed black hair, on his exposed chest, channeled down to a vee below his belly button. His hair was mussed from sleep, and he had the shadow of a beard.

Katie turned away, feeling guilty for staring at his toned physique.

Dori began to heave again, and Judd held up the wastebasket. This time the heaves were dry.

Katie found a gown and held it out for Judd to dress her. "She has a fever. Do you have a thermometer?"

"I don't know," he replied, pulling the gown over Dori's head. "There may be a thermometer in my bathroom medicine cabinet, but I don't remember seeing one."

Dori folded in her dad's arms, crying and shaking uncontrollably. Judd held her close to his body.

Teeth chattering, Dori said, "I'm ... so ... cold."

"She's having chills. Put her under the covers to warm her. I'll look for a thermometer. She probably has the flu." Katie had to get by Helene who still stood in the doorway, her teddy hiding little, and her hair arranged provocatively over one shoulder. She hadn't tried to cover-up.

Katie went down to Judd's bedroom and to the medicine cabinet in his bathroom. She found an array of bandages, muscle wraps, liniments, condoms, and adult over-the- counter pain medications, but no thermometer. The room held a faint smell of musky cologne with a touch of lime, and she noticed the rich brown towels hanging by the shower. *Condoms*.

As Katie walked back, she surveyed the masculine bedroom lit only by a hall light. The king-sized bed with its massive, carved wooden headboard ate up most of the space, and bedding thrown back, trailed toward the floor. Katie hurried from the room.

Halfway up the stairs, she turned around and went back to the kitchen and picked up a roll of paper towels, the mop, and a bucket.

Helene had left, probably because gagging was unattractive and because Dori held Judd's attention. He was stroking Dori's hair back from her forehead.

The little girl looked pale beneath the covers in the dim beam of the bedside lamp.

"No luck," Katie said, "I didn't find anything useful. I'll go to the drugstore tomorrow and stock a cabinet with a children's pain reliever, antihistamine, and a thermometer." *Condoms. Stop thinking about them.*

Dori kicked off the covers when the fever began again, and Katie brought a folded, wet washcloth for Judd to put on her forehead. She went into the bathroom to clean up the mess.

Judd came to her side and took the paper towels from her hand. "Why don't you keep the washcloth cool, and I'll clean up in here." He looked at her and with a grateful smile, thanked her for helping, and added, "Fatherhood has its challenges."

Katie heard the water running in the bucket followed by the sounds of cleaning in the next room. *Judd is a natural at fatherhood.*

When Judd was finished, he left the bucket and mop by the door and pulled up a chair near Dori. "I'll stay with her. You go on to bed."

Katie gathered the dirty towels, washcloth, and nightgown to take downstairs and start the washing machine. She also carried the bucket and mop, before washing up and returning to her bed.

As she lay awake, Katie relived the night's events, her thoughts lingering on Judd's physique and his masculine bedroom. She had never been in his room before, and now she felt like she had an intimate acquaintance with the area. *Condoms? For here?*

Remembering Helene's appearance took her mind off of Judd. Her revealing teddy made Katie's cotton pajamas look old-fashioned and uninteresting. *Enough of that, Katie. Think about tomorrow.*

Judd stayed busy in the office most of the week.

One night at dinner, Katie mentioned church and dinner on the grounds. She asked if anyone wanted to go with her.

"I do, I do," Dori said, holding up her hand and waving it. She still looked a little pale from her ordeal, but it didn't dampen her enthusiasm.

Katie looked at Judd. "Is that all right with you?"

He stared at her a few seconds too long, and Dori turned to plead with him. "Please Daddy. I *want* to go."

Judd nodded, but didn't look happy about it.

Helene's lips twisted into a knowing, satisfied smile that read, "too bad, so sad."

Later, Judd approached her as she was checking to see if the cart had enough gas.

"Look, I don't want Dori learning a lot of nonsense. She's a child and susceptible to being led astray."

"Astray?" Katie looked straight into his eyes, direct, and unwavering. "What do *you* want her to learn? Greed? The almighty dollar is more important than loving, compassion, family? You want her to hide herself away from life in an office, not trusting, becoming a cynic like you and J. D.? Tell me what do *you* deem important?"

Judd backed up a step as if he had been hit in the chest.

Katie dropped the seat and hung up the measuring rod and rag. Her eyes misted, and she kept them down. She refused to say more. *I've said too much.*

"Okay," he said in a grudging tone of voice. "She can go."

Katie nodded, took her seat, and started the cart. Jammer ran after her down the road, so she stopped and let him get on.

Judd watched her until she was out of sight. *Is that how she sees it? She thinks I'm an unfit father? I don't care about anything but money? I did a credible job with Dori's sickness. Surely, she couldn't fault that.*

He thought about his grandfather, who had spent more time with him in the last few years than in his entire life. Yes, his grandfather had mentored him in business, but it was too late to make up for all of the lost years. J.D. tried to get him to go deep sea fishing or go out West and learn to snow ski. He had learned at eighty-five, and became one of the happiest of men. *But everything was about Jesus, forgiving, and salvation.*

He remembered the time J.D. clapped him on the shoulder and said,

"Son, you're not alive until you have a personal relationship with Jesus Christ." Judd dismissed his grandfather's change, thinking he had become a Jesus freak, unhinged.

J. D. didn't go to church. He said church was anywhere he chose to commune with the Father. He spent a lot of days in the cabin communing while Judd kept the businesses going.

Judd walked to the cabin. The door was locked, and he returned to the kitchen for the key. The dirty towels were gone and the floor cleaned. Katie had come back. He walked around again remembering his grandmother and how special she had been to him. He had seen her at least once a year, sometimes twice. Sandy had been good to her, but Judd couldn't bring himself to like J.D.'s former best friend. He blamed Sandy for the break-up, as did his grandfather.

Judd sat in the chair remembering his childhood. His parents traveled and shuffled him around to private schools where he boarded. They didn't see him often. He loved Corazon, his grandmother, and then along came Rita, who had taught him love was just a word, a fleeting one at that. Dori was the only person in the world he truly cared about. *How can Katie think Dori's well-being isn't important to me?* Everything he was doing was for Dori. He gave her everything and made sure she had the best. The air-conditioner hummed along with his thoughts.

Judd had promised Dori a trip to the beach, and he would make that happen. He knew Katie would be watching. He was less enthused about taking Helene. She was becoming a thorn in his side.

CHAPTER TWENTY-FOUR

Sunday morning, Dori helped Katie make a blueberry cobbler. Katie washed and dried the two containers of blueberries while Dori used a whisk to stir the self-rising flour and milk. Katie turned on the oven and melted the butter in the microwave. She poured the batter into the glass baking dish over the melted butter and let Dori put in the blueberries and distribute them with a spatula. Katie put their cobbler in the oven.

They cleaned up their mess and satisfied, went upstairs to dress. The dessert would be ready in an hour, so they had plenty of time.

The cobbler, packed in a warming carrier, sat on the back seat. Dori talked about the beach trip they took Saturday, all the way to church. She said she liked trying to outrun the waves. "My daddy helped me build a sand castle, and we dug a moat. Do you know what a moat is?"

"A ditch of water that circles the castle for protection."

"That's right. You're smart like my daddy."

I need wisdom not smarts. Katie enjoyed Dori's chatter about the beach. Her account sounded as if she had a good time.

"Aunt Helene kept saying she was going to burn. She had daddy put some white stuff on her, like he did on me. He had to put a lot on her because her swimming suit was too small and she made these funny noises like it hurt. But I know it didn't." Dori recounted every detail.

Katie set her teeth and tried not to visualize Judd and Helene together at the beach. She recognized jealousy and looked in the mirror to see if she had turned green. Of course, it was a silly reaction, but the insidious feeling was becoming an issue she didn't want or need.

"Everybody looked at Aunt Helene when she walked down the beach. I asked Daddy if she was a star. He said she was a beautiful woman. People just liked to look at her. You know what he told me?"

"No, what did he tell you?" *Do I really want to hear this?*

"He said some people are beautiful on the outside but not on the inside. How do you know what people look like on the inside? I wanted to ask daddy, but I didn't want him to think I'm stupid. Amy Stimpson says her daddy thinks she's stupid, and he doesn't like her."

"Amy's a friend of yours in Connecticut?"

Dori nodded.

"Do you miss your friends back home?"

"I don't have that many. I guess they're okay. Aunt Helene doesn't like them to come to our house. She says we're too loud, even when we're not."

Yes, Helene, for all of her good points, falls short in the patience department. The more Katie learned about Dori's life in Connecticut, the more she hurt for the little girl.

"You're very lucky to have a daddy who loves you. He doesn't think you're stupid. If you want to know something, asking is the *smart* thing to do. That's how everyone learns. I'm still learning new things every day."

"You are? Really?"

"Yes, really. Not being beautiful on the inside means when a person opens his mouth, and ugly words which are not nice come out, it's not from a pretty place. So we need to be kind to people and only let good things come out of our mouths, so people know we're beautiful on the inside."

"Gramps said God made people that looked like Him, so God looks like everybody in the whole world. God made everything."

"Your Gramps was a smart man." *J. D., you old goat. You were giving Dori a foundation. Heavens! I'm beginning to like you.* "God doesn't make ugly, Dori. Only people do."

Katie parked the car in the church lot, and Dori wanted to carry the cobbler. The container was heavy, and she struggled, using both hands.

Luke must have been looking for her. He came out to meet them and told Dori he was there to help. She handed him the cobbler and took Katie's hand.

"Dori, this is Luke Albritton. He's a member of this church, and he has lived near here all of his life. And this is Dori. She helped me make the cobbler this morning."

Dori moved closer to Katie, acting shy, which surprised her.

Luke bowed at the waist and held out his hand. "I'm very pleased to meet you, Dori. Katie has told me so many nice things about you."

Dori looked at his hand a few seconds and then gave him hers.

Luke smiled. "You'll have to tell me how you make a cobbler. I've never made one, but I like to eat it." He started walking to the church kitchen. "What do you do first?"

Dori soon filled him in on every step of making a cobbler.

Luke introduced them to the ladies in the kitchen as Katie and Dori, no last names. A girl about Dori's age came in to ask her mother something, and Luke introduced Dori to Bobbie Jean, who was eight and had auburn hair and freckles.

Bobbie Jean's mother said, "Maybe Dori would like to go and help my daughter with the toddlers. An adult will also be present."

Katie sensed Dori wanted to go with the girl, but she didn't want to hurt Katie's feelings and hung back. "You may go with Bobbie Jean if you'd like. I'll see you for lunch after church."

Dori smiled and followed the girl to the door. Katie heard her say, "You have two names. Why?"

The girl shrugged, and Dori said, "Maybe your mother liked both names but couldn't make up her mind. You're my first friend with two first names."

Bobbie Jean grinned and led Dori down the hallway.

Luke and Katie went into the church and sat together. His parents sat beside him and his sister, Janet, and her family sat behind. The small choir had good harmony, and four men sang *Swing Low Sweet Chariot* acappella, giving Katie goose bumps.

The sermon focused on the Apostle Luke's road to Emmaus account where Jesus appeared and walked with two of his followers after his crucifixion. They told him the account of what had happened in Jerusalem and that the body of Jesus had disappeared. They didn't recognize him until later when he was urged to stay and eat with them. As Jesus spoke and broke the bread, their eyes were opened, and they recognized their risen Lord. They hurried back to Jerusalem to tell the disciples Jesus lived.

Katie remembered this account as one of the turning points in her belief. This news and other appearances of Jesus gave the disciples courage to come out of hiding and preach the gospel. Human nature caused the disciples to hide. They feared crucifixion, a horrible death. What happened to bring them out of hiding to preach the gospel and die gruesome deaths as martyrs? Jesus appeared alive to many, and they believed. They experienced the reality of life after death. A hoax would not have had the same power.

After the service, everyone proceeded to the fellowship hall for dinner. Dori and her new friend, Bobbie Jean, joined them. Round tables of eight filled quickly. The minister, Rev. Tom Dickon, said the blessing, and two tables at a time formed a line to the buffet. Luke's family joined them, but his sister's family sat at another table. Bobbie Jean brought her plate to their table to sit with Dori.

Mr. Albritton asked Katie about her family and growing up in Shreveport. Luke's family conversations, in the main, dealt with history and agriculture. Luke's father had a sod farm and grew cabbage and potatoes. Corazon was not mentioned.

Bobbie Jean talked about her dog having puppies. Katie was silently thankful to hear they were all promised. Her parents, Jan and Joel Madsen, brought their dinner plates over and joined them. Joel leased agricultural equipment, and Jan was a fourth grade school teacher at River Bend Academy.

Katie thought about Dori needing to be registered in a school and asked questions. River Bend was a non-denominational Christian school that served kindergarten through eighth grade.

Jan believed the school had an advantage because of lower student ratio classes and discipline. Although a Christian school, they had students who were not churched or were of other faiths. Jan asked Dori what grade she would be going into, and Dori told her second grade.

Jan looked at Katie and said, "If you're thinking about enrolling Dori, you need to do it right away. Some of our classes have waiting lists, and a couple of days ago, second grade had only two openings. They may be filled by now."

"Thank you for the information." Katie wondered if Judd had given any thought to the school year. She asked about the location of the school.

Jan said, "Another thing to consider if you enroll her is shopping for uniforms. I get Bobbie Jean's on line."

Dori went to the dessert table and brought back plates of blueberry cobbler. She put a large serving in front of Luke. "I wanted to be sure you got some to see if you like it, so you can make it."

Katie smiled. Dori thought he'd remember how to make it from her description. She tasted hers. It was good and still a little warm.

Luke ate his and told his parents, "Dori helped Katie make the cobbler." He said to Dori, "This is the best cobbler I think I've ever eaten."

Dori's grin couldn't have been bigger. She hurried back to the dessert table to bring the others a serving.

A couple Katie noticed watching her on several occasions stopped by their table to talk. Luke stood and hugged the woman. He appeared to be fond of her. "Katie, this is John and Sandra Raulerson."

Katie nodded in acknowledgment and wondered if they were relatives. The Albrittons greeted them like old friends.

"How is Pam?" Luke asked. "I haven't seen her since we opened the office in Palm Beach."

"She's doing all right. You know Pam. Her heart is in her work. She loves helping the children, but she calls me when she has a tough situation to handle. The outcomes are sometimes heart breaking and even tragic."

Luke nodded, and Mr. Raulerson squeezed his wife's shoulder in support. He said, "Someone told me you might run for a political office in a couple of years."

"Yes sir, I've been giving it some thought, but I haven't made a final decision yet."

"Well, it goes without saying, you'll have our support." He clapped Luke on the shoulder, his action friendly. "Come on Sandra, we should see the Smithsons before they leave. It was nice meeting you, Katie."

The Raulersons said their farewells and left.

Everyone at the table remained silent, until Katie felt like she had missed something.

"Who are the Raulersons?" she asked.

Everyone spoke at once and then realized the jumble of words were unintelligible. They lapsed into silence again.

Katie was intrigued.

Mr. Albritton said, "The Raulersons are an old cattle ranching family in our area. Their daughter, Pam, and Luke were in the same class together. We've been friends for years." He looked around the table, his voice lifting. "Would anyone like a refill on their drinks?"

Katie glanced at Luke. His mouth folded inward as he pushed away from the table. "I'll give you a hand, Dad."

Jan Madsen leaned toward Katie. "I'm so glad Bobbie Jean has a new friend. She's usually shy around other children, but she and Dori hit it off right away."

"Yes," Katie responded, her mind lost in thought as she watched Luke walk away. He appeared unhappy. *Did the look have anything to do with Pam?* She pulled herself back into the conversation. "Dori doesn't have many friends her age. She's grown up around adults. I'll tell her father what you've told me. Maybe we can arrange for them to get together before school begins."

~

Katie and Luke walked outside where children played in an enclosed recreational area. Dori, Bobbie Jean, and another girl were on the swings.

"I'll be in Tallahassee most of the week on a court case, but I'll be back by next Sunday. Will I see you then?"

Katie looked at Luke. "Tallahassee is the capitol of Florida isn't it? That's a good distance. I passed by there on the way here."

"Yes, but this is a Florida Supreme Court case. It probably won't take longer than a few days. I'll be back for the weekend. Our family is planning a barbeque."

"Unless something unforeseen comes up, I'll be here. Dori might be with me."

"Good. I like her. Do you think she'd like to ride a pony? We have one my mom uses for therapy rides. Lady Bug's patient with children."

"Dori might like that. I'll ask her father."

"Bring her a change of clothes. I wouldn't want her to mess up her Sunday best."

"May I bring something?

"Not unless it's one of Dori's famous blueberry cobblers," he said.

"You've got a deal."

Katie called Dori to say they were leaving as Luke put the carrier in the back seat.

Dori was full of questions on the way home. "Are we coming next week? Do you think Daddy will let me go to Bobbie Jean's school? Can we make a cobbler for Daddy?"

⁂

That night, Katie took out the deli meats and condiments. They made sandwiches for dinner. Dori was still excited about her morning, her chatter incessant.

She told Judd and her aunt about Bobbie Jean, her new friend, and about Mr. Luke, Katie's new friend.

The last part garnered some attention. Helene raised a questioning eyebrow, and Judd didn't take his eyes off of Katie, making her nervous.

"Mr. Luke loved my cobbler." Dori looked at Katie. "Our cobbler. Katie taught me to make it. He asked me how to make cobbler, and he's going to make one. And the dish was empty, so everybody loved it. Katie said I could make one for you. Do you want me to?"

"Yes, I'd like that, sweetheart," he said, and then addressed Katie, "Mr. Luke?"

"Luke Albritton. He's a sixth generation Floridian and has a lot of history and relatives in the area. I've met his family, and they're very nice."

"Luke Albritton, the attorney?" Judd asked.

"Yes. Do you know him?"

"Only by reputation." Judd's voice deepened. "J.D. had some dealings with him when Aaron wasn't available. Is he a member of the church?"

Before Katie could answer, Dori asked her father if she could go to Bobbie Jean's school. "Her mom's a teacher there."

Katie told Judd what Jan Madsen had told her at lunch. "I don't know how schools are in this area, but a smaller private school might be a better fit for Dori. Jan says it's academically sound, and they have discipline. If you think River Bend's a possibility, you need to register her right away." She told him about the need to do so quickly and about the waiting list.

"I'll look into it." Judd hadn't given school a thought. *What kind of a father doesn't think about school when he knows he'll have his daughter for a year?*

"Tell me about this Luke Albritton?" Helene asked. "What kind of attorney is he?"

"I don't know, but he has a Florida Supreme Court case this week in Tallahassee."

"Ooh, an important one. What else?

"I know he's well-liked, and people want him to run for the state legislature next term."

"I like him already," Helene cooed.

Judd frowned as his thoughts churned. *I'll have to look up this Luke Albritton and find out more about him.*

CHAPTER TWENTY-FIVE

True to his word, Judd registered Dori in River Bend Academy. He brought home a rule book and several pages of items she would need. "It's a good thing I went in today. Dori got the last opening. Helene, I need an update on her vaccinations, and make an appointment with a pediatrician. I'll take her, but her doctor will have to sign her medical records before she can attend." He handed the sheaf of papers to Helene. "I'll let you do the shopping. You're better at this. I'll be in the office if you need me."

Helene perfunctorily scanned the pages and handed them to Katie. "You're definitely going on the next shopping trip. I've done my part. So tell me, what does Luke look like?"

~

Dori showed up in the parlor each morning to play the piano. Katie was right about her playing by ear. With the chords she had learned, she could pick out tunes when she heard them. One day she played Amazing Grace. Judd was impressed with her ability.

"I think it's important for Dori to get some formal training, so she can read music," Katie told him afterwards. "I'll help her as much as I can while I'm here."

Even Helene told Dori how proud she was of her new talent, and the accolades gave Dori the incentive to practice.

After reading in the afternoon with Aunt Helene, Dori and Katie walked to the cabin to go through the boxes. The first day, the key was not on the hook, so they stopped by the office to see if Judd had it.

Judd opened the door and didn't bark at her when he saw Dori.

"Do you have the key to the cabin?" Dori asked him.

"As a matter of fact, I do," he said, walking to his desk.

Dori pulled on Katie's arm. "Come here. I want to show you Daddy's gym."

Katie resisted. "I don't think that's a good idea. This is your father's private space, where he does his business. Other people have to have permission to enter, from him."

Dori looked at Judd. "Daddy, can Katie see your gym?"

Judd stood behind the desk, holding the key. He didn't answer right away, so Dori asked him politely, "May I show Katie your gym?"

"Go ahead," Judd said reluctantly. His eyes bored into Katie's. She remembered their previous encounter. *What is he thinking? I've invaded his space or contaminated it?*

Judd's office was spacious, bigger than it looked outside. One wall held a series of clocks recording international times. Books lined one wall and wooden file cabinets another. A map of the world took up most of the third wall and had different colored pins stuck all over it. Despite the numerous electronic gadgets and computers, the room was comfortable. A large oriental rug covered the wood floor and three comfortable leather chairs sat before the desk. One end of the room had a conference table and ten arm chairs.

Dori pulled her into the next room, separated from the first by a bathroom on the left and a kitchenette on the right. The gym contained state-of-the-art equipment along one wall. One corner had a punching bag, and another a futon, where he could rest or nap. Floor mats were stacked against the wall. Katie saw how Judd kept in shape.

"Thank you for the tour, Dori." To Judd she said, "You have quite a set-up here. Your own private man cave. I'm impressed."

Katie held her hand out for the key, and Judd dropped the key on her palm, folding her fingers over it, an intimate gesture Katie didn't expect. She flushed and hurried to the door.

~

Several days were spent going through the boxes. The older books had a musty smell, but Katie looked through them and set some aside to read later. They were mainly books about early Florida history written at the time the events happened.

A smaller box held a number of newer books by well-known evangelists, preachers, and motivational speakers. She found books by Billy Graham, Norman Vincent Peale, Zig Ziglar, C.S. Lewis, Charles

Swindoll, and Max Lucado. Many were signed by the authors. *Did J.D. visit with these men?*

Dori found the set of books J.D. had bought for her. "You'll have to read to me," she told Katie. "I read pretty good, but not so good with these. The words are too big, and I like to hear the story."

"You pick one out, and I'll read it to you later."

One box held some women's clothing and accessories. Katie assumed they belonged to Adele. She found hats, gloves, purses, a feather fan, and some vintage dresses from an earlier era.

Dori picked up a sequined royal blue shawl and draped it over her head. She took it off and twirled around the room with it. "Is this Del's?"

"I think so. I don't know who else would own it."

Katie found framed and loose pictures in the bottom of the box. Some of the names inscribed on the backs identified family. Pictures of a younger J.D. and Adele during happier times and of Max growing up were mixed with pictures of unidentified people. The one of J. D. in cowboy attire on a horse made her think of Slim's story where J. D. rode to their shack and ordered the family to move to Corazon. A studio portrait of Judd when he was at Princeton revealed a handsome man with the fire of ambition in his eyes. She found a ripped picture of Judd in a tux and later the other half of the photo, a bride. Rita, she assumed, a stunning woman. Something about her reminded her of Dori. She put it in one of the books she had left out. Katie would trim it and save it for Dori when she was older. Every girl should have a picture of her mother even if she wasn't popular. Several snapshots showed Judd in various stages of growth. One framed photo showed Judd as a young man, standing by his grandmother. She took it into the other room and put it on the side table with the books. Katie repacked the box, leaving out half a dozen framed photos to take back to the house. She told Dori she could help with another box tomorrow.

"Okay, let's see which story we're going to read today."

Dori handed her the book of Joseph and The Coat of Many Colors. She pulled the ottoman to the side of the recliner, and Katie read the story. They talked about it afterwards.

"How could Joseph be nice to his brothers after they were so mean to him?" Dori asked. "They sold him and wanted to kill him."

"Forgiveness is when you're nice to someone who hasn't been nice to you. When that happens, the other person usually feels bad for hurting you, and sometimes you can be friends."

"What if you can't be nice to them because they hurt you real bad?" Dori asked.

"If you can't forgive someone, it makes you feel like something is eating you on the inside, and you get sick. The best thing to do is to pray for that person. God is in the heart-changing business. He can change that person's heart and change yours, too."

"My mother's dead, so God can't change her heart. I get sick when I think about her. How do I keep from being sick inside?"

"Do you remember your mother?"

"A little bit."

"What do you remember? Was there anything good you remember about her?"

"She sang to me, and she got me a white, fuzzy coat."

"Those are the things you should try to remember about her. Ask God to help you remember the good things and not the bad. He likes those kinds of prayers."

Katie put off telling Judd that Luke had invited Dori and her to his family's home for a barbeque after church. She hadn't mentioned it to Dori, in case Judd didn't let her go. But it was Saturday, and she needed to ask if it was okay to take her. She waited until he left his office and came to the house for dinner. No one was around. Zita left food in the fridge, and Helene and Dori were still upstairs.

"How well do you know Luke Albritton?" Judd asked when she mentioned tomorrow.

"I've met him at church a few times and he took me to lunch once afterwards. Everyone I've met likes him. He has a close family relationship and a good reputation."

"Does he know why you're here at Corazon?"

"Yes. I had to tell him something. I told him the truth, or part of it.

His first reaction was to think I was one of your women. So, I set him straight on that point."

Judd wanted to retaliate, but he held his tongue. Inside, anger began to build. *That's all I need. Having everyone and their mother know the arrangement J.D. planned for me. The media will have a field day.*

"I asked Luke to keep anything I told him in confidence. He agreed, and I believe him. I did not mention being an heir, only my presence at Corazon for a year, so beneficiaries could receive their portion of the inheritance." She stared at the floor unable to look him in the eyes. *This is so embarrassing.* "Luke took this information the same way everyone did at the reading of the Will. J. D. hoped for a match. I assured him we were not suited, and J.D. had made a mistake. He was fine with that."

Judd gritted his teeth. *What do you mean, not suited?* He couldn't believe he was hearing this. He had sleepless nights thinking about her, and his concentration on business suffered. He saw her as a desirable woman, no longer the naïve child. Judd's lip seemed to throb, but he knew it was a figment of his imagination. He had no idea what to say.

He turned and walked to his room before he said what he really thought about her interest in Luke Albritton. Katie made him sound like a saint.

"What about tomorrow? Is it okay for Dori to go?" Katie asked his departing back.

Judd stopped but didn't turn around. "She can go if she wants to."

~

Dori and Katie made another blueberry cobbler the next morning. They left a third of it for Judd and Helene before putting the dish in the warming carrier.

Dori carried a bag with a change of clothing when she gave her father a kiss goodbye. "You can come with us if you want," she said.

Judd's lip curled in a parody of a smile as he looked over her head at Katie. "Not this time, pumpkin. Thank you for the cobbler. Have a good time."

On the way to church, Katie told Dori about the pony and maybe getting a ride. Dori pumped her arm in the air and shouted, "Yesssss!"

CHAPTER TWENTY-SIX

The days had passed quickly. Katie made sleeping arrangements for her sister and her family. Paul and Myra would have her room and the kids would stay in Dori's room. She had twin beds, so Katie bought an inflatable mattress for Hank.

Katie also bought a full-sized bed for the cabin and had it delivered and set up by the store's delivery men. Pillows and linens to fit the bed were also purchased. She acquired some needed furniture from a local thrift shop. A small oak dining table and four chairs added character, their scarred surfaces proclaiming use and that beauty is not always perfect.

Katie knew Judd was keeping an eye on her. He opened the slatted window panels in the office, so he could see what happened at the cabin.

Judd made an appearance when the men left. "Are you planning on moving out here?"

Katie thought about his observation. "What an appealing idea! The house is a little crowded." *With Helene in residence, Biltmore would be crowded.* "Myra and her family will be here in a few days. I plan to stay out here and let them have my room. Hank might decide to stay with me when he finds himself in a room with two female jabber mouths." She added, "Look on my improvements as my contribution to Corazon."

"I'm looking forward to meeting your family." Judd meant it. He felt like he knew them from Katie's descriptions over the last couple of months.

"They're anxious to see the ranch and meet you also. Maybe the trip will save a hundred questions they have."

~

The Paul Hennessey family arrived late one afternoon after a two day drive from Louisiana. Myra hugged Katie and told her how much she had been missed. Hank and Karen raced around the yard with Jammer.

Paul opened the trunk to take out their luggage and Judd came out to greet them. Dori followed, her eyes fixed on Hank and Karen. Katie called them over and made the introductions. Judd helped Paul with the luggage and told them dinner would be served at six-thirty.

Myra yawned, and put her hand over her mouth. "I'm having trouble staying awake. I may have to take a nap before dinner."

Katie hugged her sister again. "I'm so glad Paul was able to get away. I've missed you so much. Come on, I'll show you to your room." She called to Dori and asked her to show Hank and Karen where they were staying. She heard Karen telling Dori about looking for alligators on the trip down and not seeing a single one from the road.

"Mom said you have alligators. Where are they?" Hank asked.

"We have lots of gators," Dori replied. "Maybe we'll see some tomorrow. Let's go upstairs. You're going to be in my room." The three of them raced up the stairs.

Katie marveled how children bonded in minutes while adults tiptoed around each other looking for words to start a conversation.

Judd and Paul followed with the luggage.

Dinner was a lively affair. Helene put in an appearance, ever the gracious hostess. Myra raised an eyebrow at Katie when everyone's attention gravitated south to Helene's end of the table. She had a knack of drawing attention and making someone feel special. Tonight, Helene worked her wiles on Paul, an engineer and consultant for a large oil company. She made his work on drill rigs in the Gulf of Mexico and remote areas of the world sound romantic. Paul was too savvy to fall for her obvious ploy and nipped it in the bud early on. "I'm on vacation. I make it a policy not to bring my work home, and vacations are definitely work free zones. Right, honey?"

"Darling, if only you didn't bring your dirty clothes home, our marriage would be perfect." Myra smiled at Helene. "Tell me about your line of business. Are you taking a leave of absence or are you also on holiday?"

Helene looked momentarily uncomfortable, but she managed to talk about her real estate business and her hiatus. She explained her presence at Corazon was to ease Dori into ranch life, a radical move from her life in the city.

"Is Dori having a problem adjusting?" Myra asked Helene.

Dori looked at Katie. "What's adjusting? Does that mean I don't like it here?" She looked from one adult to the next. "I love it here. There's so much to see and do," she told Karen and Hank.

Judd said, "We know you love it here, sweetheart. Aunt Helene thought you might be bored, and she wanted to help you. She also knows how important it is to keep up with your studies during the summer months."

When Hank asked Dori about Jammer and told her all about Freebie, their Golden Retriever, the "adjusting" subject was dropped.

Helene took the hint, became quiet, and let the family catch up.

Myra said, "Mom and Dad are planning their trip to Alaska, but await our return because they're keeping Freebie."

Listening to the family's escapades made Judd feel he was missing out on something special. He saw Dori shine as she planned adventures for Hank and Karen at Corazon. For the first time, he thought about having more children. He thought about the Will and J. D.'s provision for any future children and grimaced. *Forget that. Marriage is out of the question. Hell will freeze over first.*

Katie and Myra rocked on the front porch after dinner, leaving the men to bond. Cricket and frog song surrounded them, lending their orchestration to the balmy evening. Clouds pregnant with rain hung low overhead, threatening to burst at any time. A distant rumble of thunder, a prelude to an impending storm, drummed its message. Katie' thoughts turned to another stormy night.

Myra opened the conversation. "Do you want my take on the situation?" Her eyebrows rose with anticipation. A smile deepened her dimples.

"I'm sure you'd give it to me anyway." Katie said.

Myra rested her chin on intertwined hands, one knuckle touching her lips. "You and Judd are cautiously circling each other, doing an egg shell dance. Helene has the *hots* for Judd, but he's either not paying attention, making him a dull boy, or his heart is otherwise engaged. Any other females on the horizon?"

Katie blushed. "Not that I know about. Judd has business trips away at times. There's no telling who he sees."

"You get newspapers with a Society page, don't you? If the paparazzi get wind of him socializing, it would be news."

Katie nodded and fiddled with a lock of hair. She turned to the Society pages first whenever he was away. "You're right." *Maybe he has a secret mistress … or two. Makes sense.*

"So, has the hunk made moves on you?"

Katie's color deepened and Myra pounced. "He did! Tell me." She sat forward eager for details.

Katie folded inside not wanting to share the intimacy, the embarrassment.

Myra softened her tone. "Tell me about him. He owns the room when he walks in, not as cold-blooded as Gunnar, your last heart throb. Did he kiss you?"

Katie stood. "I don't want to talk about it."

Myra rose and put her hand on Katie's shoulder. "That bad?"

Katie turned, her eyes misted, and hugged Myra. "I guess I'm just destined to love the wrong men. He's not for me."

"Why ever not?"

"I'm not in his league." *Why torture myself? It's true. Now get over it.*

"Honey, don't sell yourself short. You're beautiful, educated, talented, and a genuinely nice person. What's not to love?"

Katie shrugged. Judd dressed casual around the ranch and looked most days like one of the workmen. Except for the business dinners, the jet set seemed a long way off. "I haven't acquired the society gloss, the small talk. Knowledge about wines, cocktails, and travel are deficiencies."

Myra laughed. "Then I hope you never acquire the gloss. As for travel, you have plenty of time to catch up." She arranged a lock of hair behind Katie's ear. "People like Judd are either too jaded to appreciate the difference or they're socially inept. Judd doesn't strike me as either. Did you hit him?"

"What?"

"I noticed Judd had a cut on his lip when we arrived. You don't get lip cuts from shaving." Myra cocked her head waiting, a knowing smile teasing her lips.

"Worse. I bit him."

Myra's peal of laughter was so loud, Katie put a hand over her mouth.

"It's hardly noticeable."

"Oh, you marked him all right. Only someone blind wouldn't see it."

Helene came to Katie's mind. She hadn't mentioned the cut, and Katie remembered Helene probably thinking their fight led to her hitting him. Any other scenario and Helene's hackles would be up.

"So, what happened?"

Katie refused the details. "He flew to Miami and spent five days. When he returned, he apologized."

"That's a good sign."

"Maybe. Now, he pretty much ignores me. On the positive side, I've met another man at church. He's very nice, and I like him a lot."

"Tell me about him."

Katie told Myra about Luke, his background, and being with his family.

"Luke sounds special, more like you. Can you love him?"

"Not like I love Judd. The spark isn't there. I didn't know the spark was missing with Gunnar until Judd kissed me." Details of the kiss assailed her senses. *Will I ever stop wanting him?*

Myra brought her back to earth. "Passion is highly over-rated. We're talking about a possible lifetime commitment."

"I know."

CHAPTER TWENTY-SEVEN

The household rocked with three children playing, laughing, and screaming. The energy level increased exponentially. Dori planned something for each day. At breakfast, she taught Hank and Karen the Spanish words she had learned from Zita. She would touch an object and say it in Spanish. She soon had them counting to one hundred and learning phrases in a new language. They learned more Spanish when they helped Isabel with her English. Myra and Paul saw the ease the children learned and the benefit. They decided to continue the lessons at home. A local, private school taught French and Spanish as a second language during the summer months.

Helene reserved several days at the Breakers in Palm Beach. She packed her bags and said she was in the mood to explore the coast.

Judd took Katie, Dori, and Paul's family out on the swamp buggy. The open vehicle with huge tires traversed swamps, prairies, and palmettos with ease. They saw wild hogs, deer, turkeys, cows, and numerous alligators and turtles. Dori pointed out and named pond birds she had learned. Katie recounted the history she'd read about the area.

Judd came across several wild piglets in a pasture surrounded by three ditches. Mama didn't make an appearance, so the kids jumped from the lowest step and chased them. Katie and Paul took pictures. The squeals of the baby pigs and the children filled the air. Karen caught one and dropped it. Hank jumped on it. He picked up the squirming piglet, grinning from ear to ear.

Judd kept a look out for the mama. The sow didn't appear, and he figured she must have been killed. Just about everyone trapped or killed the hogs. They were a nuisance and dug up the land with their powerful snouts. The hogs quickly multiplied, having several litters a year. Most of the workers killed them for food. Local men were hired to hunt them.

"Can I keep him?" Hank shouted up to Judd, trying to get his attention over the motor's noise.

"That's not a good idea, son. He's cute now, but he grows fast. These hogs are not pets."

After Dori and Karen petted him, Hank let him go, and Paul and Myra sighed their relief.

Judd climbed down from the buggy and encouraged the children to clean their hands and arms after holding the pig. Water and a cleaning goop were attached to the back of the buggy.

On the way back to the house, the kids saw several cowboys on horseback moving cattle into a dryer pasture. Katie recognized Slim. He had a coil of rope in his hand and brought it up and down, slapping his leather chaps. The sound and his voice kept the herd moving. The cur dogs brought up the rear and ran along the sides to keep the herd together. Strays were coaxed back into the herd. The trained cow dog's presence alone kept the cattle going in the right direction.

The day ended on an exciting note. Everyone had fun and talked of little else the next few days. Paul and Judd spent time together and seemed to enjoy one another's company.

Every day it rained, usually in the afternoon, and during those times, stories were read or games played. During the mornings, they took field trips.

Katie had scheduled a fishing guide to take them fishing on the big lake. The loquacious guide, Johnny Dee, told them the history surrounding the shallow lake, enriching the trip.

"Lake Okeechobee is the second largest lake totally inside the United States, with an average depth of nine feet." He taught them to bait their hooks with wild shiners, the natural food of the bass. Johnny Dee talked about the fossil history, prehistoric Indians, and the Seminole Wars. He told them about Hamilton Disston, the developer, who in 1847 opened an outlet for the lake to the Gulf of Mexico. Until that time, the lake drained to the Atlantic and Everglades. Johnny talked about the destructive hurricanes and their aftermath with thousands of lives lost and was recounting the story of building the levee when Myra hooked a nine pounder.

The excitement of the moment delayed his spiel. Myra was generous and let the fish go when Johnny Dee determined its life wasn't compromised. All of them caught fish. The ones deemed too small were thrown back, and they ended up with a credible mess of fish for dinner.

Johnny Dee filleted their catch, which Zita fried. The children were so proud of their catches. Hank and Karen said it was the best vacation ever.

Helene returned, and the children regaled her with their stories. She listened politely for five minutes then escaped to her room, unable to take the clamor.

Myra raised an eyebrow. "She's not very patient with children. I guess Dori, as an only child, is quieter and better behaved than most. I wonder what Dori's life was like with her?"

Katie had wondered about Dori's life in Connecticut, but she kept silent. She believed Helene cared for Dori, but Katie saw by her inhibited behavior how restricted her life had been with her aunt. Dori blossomed at Corazon with her father's support. Helene chafed at the loss of control. Katie believed the year Dori had with her father was going to change them both.

~

Katie , Dori, and Paul's family went to church on Sunday. They had to put up the extra seats in the Hennessey's Suburban. Dori tried to get her father and Aunt Helene to come, but they declined. Judd said he had to catch up on his work, and Helene mumbled an excuse about having other plans for the day.

The family met and liked Luke. They went to Sal's Seafood Place for lunch. Katie invited Luke to Corazon for dinner on Friday before her family left.

Judd wasn't consulted. Katie had grown comfortable enough to make her own plans. She told Zita the dinner would be casual, not the business, formal fare.

Myra mentioned at dinner one night that they were leaving on Saturday, a few days early, to take in Disney World. She asked if Katie and Dori wanted to drive up and meet them.

Dori begged, "Please, can I go, please?"

Judd acquiesced, and Katie made their reservations in the same hotel.

Judd said he had a business to run, and Helene informed them, the attractions were not her thing.

Katie knew this side trip would leave Helene a clear field with Judd. *Get over him. If Judd falls for her conniving, he isn't worth the trouble.*

~

Thursday turned out to be a beautiful day. Katie planned to take everyone to the Big Cypress Swamp and the Ah-Tah-Thi-Ki Museum. The Seminole people fascinated her, and Luke told her she would enjoy the trip and what to do while there. She took out her road map and the brochure she picked up in town.

Judd said he needed to catch up on some business, and Helene declined the invitation. Katie briefly thought about the two of them left behind, and a worm of jealousy began to burrow in to dampen her spirits. She quickly perished the thought and applied her mind to the fun day.

The car was full enough with excited kids in the back. They were having fun, and if Myra and Paul weren't put off by the noise, she'd hold her tongue and concentrate on driving. Paul did the navigating and before long, they reached the museum.

The Seminole Museum was state-of-the-art. They watched a short film about the Seminole history and toured the museum.

Life-sized mannequins, attired in authentic clothing were found throughout the building. Daily activities, Indian technology, relics, and a ceremonial scene made up of many Indians dancing the Green Corn Dance amazed them.

"I'm impressed by the displays of traditional practices and culture," Myra said. She pointed out various patterns in the patchwork, and the girls tried to guess the pattern.

"This is lightning," Dori said about a zigzag line, "and these straight up and down lines are rain."

"I like the Seminole dolls," Karen said. "How do they get their hair to poof up like this doll?"

"I think they put their hair over a form of some kind to make the hair stand up," Katie answered. "I'd love to get a doll in the gift shop before we leave. They're so colorful."

Hank and his father checked out the weaponry and the canoe.

Outside, they took the boardwalk tour which circled about a mile through the middle of the Everglades. The walkway was sturdy and handicap accessible. They stopped to read information about plants and trees identified along the way. Some were used as medicines.

Paul noted the wooden corridor even sported a sprinkler system. "I guess they planned to keep the walkway safe in case of a fire. This must have cost a lot of money."

The walk took them to a small, replicated Seminole village from the past with chickee huts made of poles, with a raised floor, and palmetto thatched roofs.

Hank walked around one of the chickees, looking at the construction. "Daddy, we need to build one of these in our backyard to give us shade when we have a party. I'll help."

"This structure is harder to build than it looks," he replied. "I think the screened area we planned is a better solution."

Myra snapped more photographs for their family album. "I have already taken ninety-two pictures!"

Indian artisans in traditional clothing made and sold items such as beadwork, carvings, and patchwork clothing. Paul bought each of the girls a beaded bracelet and Hank a carved canoe as souvenirs of their visit. Back at the museum store, Myra bought a sweetgrass basket and Katie a small Seminole doll she would use as a Christmas ornament, another treasured memory.

They ate lunch down the road at Billie's Swampwater Café where they tried and liked the Indian fry bread. While they ate, they discussed Seminole history. Myra commented on the survival of a people hiding and fighting the U.S. Military in such an inhospitable environment.

Paul said, "The Seminoles had an advantage because they knew the swamps and how to evade the soldiers. You have to admire a people who survived three wars and remained an unconquered nation."

Hank and Karen talked about playing cowboys and Indians. "Hank always wants to be the cowboy, and I'm the Indian." Karen looked at Hank. "The Seminoles won, so now I can win, too."

"Mr. Luke said the Indians weren't treated right," Dori told them, and they all nodded in agreement.

"Life is rarely fair," Myra said. "We used to talk about the survival of the fittest. If the members of a species didn't adapt, they became extinct." Her voice became cynical. "Now, we want to save everything, except the human species."

"Hon, this isn't the time for a discussion on political correctness," Paul said.

Myra nodded. "You're right. Sometimes, I think about having a tee-shirt made which says, "Save the Mosquito."

"Why would you save the mosquito? We know they can make you sick," Hank said.

"And they make us itch when they bite," Karen added.

"Your mom is trying to be funny. She doesn't really want to save the mosquito," Paul told the children.

The day ended at dinner when the kids told Judd and Helene what they had learned on their outing. Karen and Hank were excited and couldn't wait to tell their classmates about their adventures in Florida.

~

Friday evening, Luke arrived at Corazon on time, and Judd greeted him graciously. "I've been looking forward to meeting you. I know you and my grandfather, J.D., had some business dealings. He mentioned you had a good head on your shoulders."

Luke laughed and said, "I believe he said the same words to me when we parted. We met several years ago, and I was impressed by his shrewd mind. He wasn't at all like the hermit I expected."

Katie spoke for the first time. "I had no idea you and J.D. had met. You never mentioned it. Please come in. The family is looking forward to seeing you again, and Dori wants to fill you in on their big adventures. We enjoyed the Seminole Museum, by the way. Thank you for giving us the information."

Zita was ready to serve dinner, so they walked to the dining room. The children sat at one end of the table, each trying to outdo the next, telling of their exploits during the week.

Paul refereed and finally told them to settle down and speak one at a time.

Helene joined them at the table and thanked Paul for his intervention with the children.

While they gave their accounts, it was obvious to Katie and Myra that Luke and Judd were sizing each other up.

Katie resumed her old habit of picking at her cuticles when she was nervous, and Myra slapped her hand under the table.

Helene took charge of the conversation early. She flirted with Luke, and he looked at Katie, an amused expression on his face. Katie smiled at him, knowing he showed his immunity to her charms. If Helene was trying to make Judd jealous, she missed the mark.

Dori told everyone about the pony ride at Luke's parent's house. She also told them about helping make a blueberry cobbler, and she would show them how to do it.

Hank and Karen updated Luke on their trip to the Seminole Museum and told him about their souvenirs. Dori and Karen had on their bracelets which they proudly held out for Luke to see.

After dinner, Dori took Luke's hand and led him to the parlor where she played Chopsticks. She and Karen played a duet. Then Dori played Amazing Grace, and Luke sang along the second time around. He was joined by everyone but Judd and Helene, who sat on the sofa and listened.

Myra encouraged Katie to play some oldies, and they had a song fest. Helene and Judd joined in when family members prodded them and they knew the words.

Judd watched the evening progress. Luke made himself at home, and the children brought him into their conversations. Judd liked the man despite his growing jealousy. Luke resisted Helene's wiles and his interest in Katie presented a problem. They had met at church and spent Sunday afternoons in each other's company. *What if their relationship becomes serious?*

CHAPTER TWENTY-EIGHT

Judd looked around the empty house, the silence deafening. Everyone had left for Disney World. Helene slept late, and he wanted to be ensconced in his office before she got up. He knew he would have to fend off her advances now they were alone. It was easier when Katie and Dori were at home.

A desirable woman in another situation would not have been a problem, but he wanted Katie, not Helene. The more Katie denied him, the more he wanted her, an age-old psychological ploy Judd understood. But Katie bit him, and horrified ran, not a game to her. *She's not in play.* The last time Judd had lost control involved Rita. *I don't need this.*

Zita rattled some pans in the kitchen, a welcome sound taking his mind off the personal and onto work. He asked Zita to bring his lunch to the office.

Predictably, Helene showed up with lunch for both of them. He opened the door with a smile, took his portion from the tray saying, "I have a lot of catching up to do. I know you understand why I'm behind." He thanked her and closed the door. Judd knew Helene steamed, but his hints fell on deaf ears. He thought about sending her back to Connecticut, but he needed Helene as a buffer against J.D's plans for his future. *Man, you cannot seriously be thinking about Katie and permanence. She's a child! No. Erase that. Katie's more woman than Helene will ever be. Katie has substance, a woman comfortable in her own skin, not trying to be someone else. Not trying to catch me. Okay, that stings. Don't lose your head over it.*

Judd remembered the time Katie and Dori visited his office. Katie called the place his "man cave," an apt description. Judd surveyed the area and imagined making love to Katie on his desk, on the exercise mat, and as he looked around, everywhere. The thought of Luke squelched his lustful thoughts.

Luke Albritton, more than a formidable opponent. He's got Katie in his sight all right, and he's not going away. Helene couldn't turn his head, and he let Katie know it. Hell, he let me know it. He's enjoying his coup in my house, at my table, in my face. Irritated, Judd understood Luke's attraction to Katie, and the green-eyed monster had him pacing, lunch forgotten.

Okay, he's *better than average looking man and successful. So am I.* Judd turned and headed into the gym. *Admit it; the cherry on top is he's a church-going family man, Katie's ideal. Not your bailiwick. Worse, I like the man. And St. Luke is at least five years younger than me. Ouch.*

Judd stripped and pulled on gym shorts. He took his frustration out on the machines and punching bag, sweat stinging his eyes.

The phones rang numerous times, but Judd let the message machines do their work. He'd get back to the callers when he was exhausted. He satisfied himself by believing he was in better shape than the younger man.

~

Katie remembered returning from Disney World and Epcot. The family had fun, more fun than Judd. He was a bear when they returned and Helene aloof to the point of giving everyone the silent treatment.

Dori asked Katie what was wrong, and she told her sometimes people became unhappy when they were under a lot of stress. This explanation led to a discussion on the meaning of stress.

Katie came to her own conclusion. *I don't think anything romantic happened while we were gone. Be careful. You know what they say about a woman scorned.*

The uncomfortable situation led Katie to call the attorney, Aaron Pickering, to see if it was okay to move into the cabin. Her time in the Cracker house proved restful while Myra's family visited her. It would be her cozy nest and maybe ease some of the tension.

Aaron told Katie the cabin was on the ranch and satisfied the content of the Will. They talked quite a while, Aaron wanting to know about life at Corazon.

"I love Dori. She's really a special child. We spend time together exploring and learning about Florida and the ranch operations. We're learning Spanish, and I'm helping her with piano." She paused remembering how much fun they had last week with Myra's family.

"Judd enrolled Dori in a private Christian school. She's been going to church with me, and she's already made some friends."

Aaron said, "Dori couldn't have a better example. What else?"

"Judd has his hands full with business and Helene," Katie continued. "My sister says she's a piece of work. As far as I can see, Helene hasn't made much progress with Judd. She's in love with him and believes she's what he needs. I'm not so sure. But his life and how he spends it is up to him."

"Umm. How are you handling everything? How does Judd treat you now?"

"We circle each other. He accepts my presence, and he seems to be happy I spend time with Dori." Katie wasn't disclosing the kiss and bite incident. *He apologized. Now forget it.* When she hung up the phone, Katie went to her room and packed.

The hardest part was telling Dori of her decision. She cried and made Katie feel like she was abandoning the child. "Dori, I'm only going to be in the cabin at night. I'll still be here for you during the day. I miss having my own place, and I'd like to cook some of my own meals. You can come over and help me cook. I didn't learn to cook until after I left home."

Katie's parents both worked. They spent their evenings together rehashing the day's events with little thought to planned, homemade repasts. Frozen meals and take-outs were the fares of choice. Cereal, soup, and sandwiches were staples. On Saturdays, her dad fired the grill and barbecued enough meat for two days. Baked potatoes and salads rounded out the menus. Special occasions meant referring to her grandmother's cookbook for some seriously delicious repasts they all enjoyed.

When Katie moved to an apartment, she used some of her grandmother's recipes as a guide. She couldn't afford to eat out every meal. A co-worker gifted her with a recipe book to plan meals for two people.

Gunnar had enjoyed her dinners and complimented their presentation. Katie thought her cooking sparked her boyfriend's interest as much as anything.

Judd revealed at dinner, the cattle would be moved to the pens in a couple of days. "We'll be selling the calves. You might find the process interesting."

Dori began to cry. "You can't sell Snowball. You promised."

Judd said, "Dori, we won't sell Snowball. She has to stay with her mother until she's older."

"How do the men know she's mine?" Dori wailed.

"The men are trained to know which calves weigh enough. Don't worry about it."

"No, you can't sell her!" She slid back her chair and ran from the room.

Judd began to stand and follow, but Helene said, "Ignore her childish theatrics. She'll cry it out and accept the situation. You can't give in to her, or it will continue to happen."

Judd hesitated, conflicted.

Katie said, "She's a child and doesn't have an adult's understanding. She needs comfort. I'll check on her."

"How do you know what she needs? You don't have any children," Helene sniped.

Katie put her napkin on the table and stood. "No, I don't. I rely on common sense." *Children aren't produced by one person. Stop thinking about having children.*

"Thank you, Katie," Judd said as she left the room.

Dori lay across her bed, crying into her Teddy bear.

Katie knocked on the open door. "May I come in?"

Dori nodded and snuffled.

Katie plucked a tissue from the box on the dresser and sat on the bed. "Here, blow your nose." She waited for Dori to speak.

Dori blew and said, "Aunt Helene thinks I'm stupid. Now, Daddy will think I'm a stupid cry baby."

The revelation surprised Katie. "No, Dori, your father is hurt you don't trust him to keep Snowball safe for you."

"But he said she wasn't big enough yet, so he'll sell her when she's bigger."

Katie saw the problem from Dori's perspective. "I'm sure he didn't mean what it sounded like. Your father made you a promise. He wouldn't break it, knowing how strongly you feel."

"You think he'll keep her even when she's big?"

"Yes, I believe he will." She pushed Dori's hair out of her eyes and snugged the strands behind her ears. "Why don't you come downstairs like a big girl and show your aunt she's wrong about you."

Dori stood and hugged her.

Katie savored the feeling. "You might give your daddy a hug and tell him you believe he'll save Snowball. He needs to know you trust him to keep his promise."

CHAPTER TWENTY-NINE

The day they worked the cows on Corazon arrived. Katie and Dori rode the work cart to the pens. The cattle bawled for their calves, eyes rolling their distress. The pungent odor of manure filled the air. Dori climbed the outside rail for a better view. Katie joined her and thought the operation sad, but this was business. They watched as hundreds of cows and calves came through the pens. Cowboys herded them down a corridor and into chutes. They separated larger calves in holding pens until they were loaded into waiting trailers. Cows and calves passed quickly through the pens.

Cowboys were everywhere. Katie recognized some, but a larger contingent must have been hired to do the work. In the distance, they heard several cracks.

When Slim pulled up beside the fence, Katie asked, "What's that noise? Is someone shooting?"

"No, Miss Katie, that's a whip cracking. The sound keeps the cows moving," he shouted over the noise. Several more cracks were heard, and a dog barked.

Dori spied her father. "There's Daddy," she yelled above the din.

Judd rode a large bay horse into the pen. He was dressed like the wranglers in jeans, khaki shirt, sweat-stained cowboy hat, and boots. He cut a romantic figure, and Katie thought him the most handsome man she had ever seen.

He moved a new group of cows into the pen, and rode over to the fence. "Hey, what do you think about this?"

Dori said, "It's exciting." She spotted Snowball's mother but not the calf.

"Snowball's in here," Judd said. "I've been looking for her. I saw her mother first and followed them in." He rode through the crowded pen, pointed down and nodded, indicating he found the calf. He herded Snowball in Dori's direction and reached into a saddlebag, bringing out a can of spray paint.

She watched her dad lean over and spray a red spot on Snowball's rump. "The men will know this calf is yours. She's safe."

"Thank you, Daddy," Dori hollered. "Can I ride on the horse with you?"

Judd brought the horse near the fence. "Not today, too much activity" he told Dori. "We'll do it another day. Count on it."

Judd glanced at Katie as he steadied his powerful mount. "Thank you for bringing Dori." When the horse calmed, he examined Katie's slim figure in jeans, blue plaid cowgirl shirt, and red bandana. A straw cowboy hat gave her a rakish look. The toes of her plain cowboy boots peeked through the rails, and he thought how good she looked. Katie had taken Dori shopping, and the cowgirl outfit she bought his daughter was perfect. The two of them made quite a picture.

"Will you be finished sorting today?" Katie asked.

"No, if the weather's good, it'll take several more days. You don't have to stay out here in the heat, you know. The scenery's not going to change anytime soon."

"I want to stay, please," Dori said, looking at Katie, "at least a little longer."

Judd's laugh and deep voice affected Katie, weakening her legs and her will to deny his advances. *Stay the course.* Her mantra needed backup.

"You'll make a cowgirl yet," he told his daughter.

Judd noted his attention to Katie's physical attributes caused her eyes to light with excitement and the color in her cheeks heightened her natural beauty. The possessiveness Judd had felt in Shreveport slammed him to the core. *I can't let this happen. J.D wins. I lose. Not going to happen. God, what a mess! I need to visit some of the stores and check on management, anything to remove the temptation.*

He turned his horse to bring the next group through.

Summer ended mid-August when school began. River Bend Academy had an evening orientation to visit the school before it opened for the year. Judd took Dori to meet her teacher and to see her classroom. Helene wanted to go, but Judd said he'd handle it, and the two of them left.

Helene stormed up to her room, and Katie retired to the cabin for a light dinner and an early night. Her evenings were spent reading about the early history of Florida. She found in *Morse's Geography of 1812*, that Florida belonged to Spain, and its inhabitants traded in furs and sterling. Florida was listed as "proper missionary ground". She marked the place for Luke.

She also leafed through J. D.'s Bible, reading margin notes and familiar verses that spoke to her spirit. J.D. had studied some of the written Hebrew words in Greek and Latin. *You are just full of surprises.* She thought about J. D. when she first met him and about how far he had progressed in five years. *Thank you, Lord, for using me to make a difference in one man's life. Thank you for showing me why judgment is reserved for You alone. Lord, help me not to judge others.*

The next afternoon, Judd walked into the kitchen to meet Katie and Dori as they were reading the directions to make chocolate chip cookies. He announced that he had to fly to Belgium and would miss taking Dori to her first day of school. "I'm sorry, sweetheart," Judd said as he squatted before her to give her the news. "I really want to take you on Monday, but some business has to be conducted in person, not on a conference call. This is really important, or I'd take you. Do you understand?"

Dori tried to put on a brave face, but her disappointment showed. She hugged her daddy and said, "It's okay. Katie can come see my room." She ran out, but not before they saw tears welling in her eyes.

"God, why does something have to come up now?" Judd turned, his arms out in supplication. "This is why it's hard to live on Corazon, run a business, and try to care for my daughter. She needs continuity."

"I don't know anything about Stetson's business, but surely you have a second in command that can step in and take some of the burden," Katie responded.

Judd appeared to be conflicted by his obligation as the head of Stetson Enterprises and his role of being a parent.

Katie did not see his dilemma as a bad thing. He wanted Dori to be at Corazon with him, and he took on the mantle of responsibility whenever possible. It was a step in the right direction. "Don't worry, this is just a bump in the road. Dori will be over it before dinner."

"Thank you for taking her. I feel better knowing you're here."

Katie's mouth dropped open, and she turned to close it with her hand. For the first time, she didn't feel like a wart on Judd's life. She watched him leave, deep in thought. Katie decided she would come to dinner and smooth things over if needed.

By dinnertime, Dori was her usual, exuberant self.

Helene remained quiet and sullen throughout the meal.

Judd seemed to be miles away, so Dori and Katie talked about school, and after dinner, they went upstairs to prepare for Monday.

Dori put out her khaki skirt and blue polo shirt, the school uniform, and everything else she would wear. The school also allowed red shirts, red and blue plaid skirts, and khaki pants. Belt loops required a belt. Dori took school items out of her backpack to show Katie before putting them back. She was proud of her princess lunchbox. Her organization impressed Katie. Helene knew how to organize, and she had taught Dori well.

~

Mrs. Markham, the second grade teacher, welcomed Dori to school and met Katie. She reminded Dori where to put her lunchbox and backpack.

Dori pulled Katie around her classroom to see the different stations for reading, games, and geography. Colorful posters filled two walls and encouraged good behavior. Everything about the room was conducive to learning. Dori took Katie to her seat. Her desk had a bright cardboard ruler across the top with Dori's name in red foil letters. Placed between two boys, Trevor and Jim, the three took up the short front row.

Katie kissed Dori goodbye and told her she would pick her up after school. She took the envelope with the necessary medical forms to the office before leaving.

~

Judd called Zita and told her he had some meetings in Austria before returning. He said the following week would be the soonest he could make it home. *Condoms. She couldn't get the sight of them out of her mind. What do you expect? Abstinence?* Katie tried without success to dismiss the jealous twinges when she thought Judd might have female companionship abroad. *He's a man with a strong libido. Of course, he's out with women. He isn't committed to anyone. He believes in safe sex.* The thought didn't make her jealous leanings any easier. *Get over it.* Katie lost the battle and bought several entertainment magazines looking for photos and print about him. She saw Helene bring in similar magazines and knew she also kept tabs. *We're hopeless.* And Katie didn't like her thoughts.

Dori wrote Karen and Hank, and they exchanged drawings. Katie had showed Dori how to draw animals using circles and ovals to give shape and size. Shading added values to the drawing and depth gave perspective. As a graphic artist, she taught Dori the lessons she learned from her mother as a child. Dori's drawings of people showed maturity. People had bodies and the arms didn't extend out of the head.

Katie let Dori call Karen on her phone, and they traded school stories. Myra and Katie enjoyed the children's desire to stay in touch. At times, Hank added his sports stories to the conversation, not to be outdone by his sister.

Dori practiced chords on the piano, and if she hummed a tune, she soon played it. Katie began teaching her the keys and to read notes in a beginner's book. Dori tried and practiced the scales, but soon became frustrated with the slow pace. She accomplished playing *Brother John* and *Twinkle Twinkle Little Star* reading the notes, and Katie gave effusive reviews.

Katie invited Bobbie Jean to the house for a sleepover on the weekend. Katie and Jan had become friends and her daughter visited several times. The girls played well together. Bobbie Jean brought her doll, Ruby, and they had a tea party with Dori and her dolls. Katie was invited, but opted out, on the pretext of practicing piano.

Bobbie Jean brought some dolls with magnetic clothing. They reminded Katie of the old paper dolls she and Myra made and enjoyed, growing up. The girls proved to have creative imaginations, and their laughter alleviated some of the pervasive tension.

When Judd returned, he would see some of Dori's schoolwork and drawings displayed on the refrigerator. Katie added photos of Dori on the first day of school, of Snowball, and one of Dori, Karen, and Hank, all hugging Jammer.

Katie hid the gossip magazines she picked up at the store in the bottom of the bag. She thumbed through them looking for pictures of Judd when he traveled. She found one of him with Lily Taranova, the Russian opera singer. The dark-haired beauty held Judd's arm possessively and smiled into the camera, a look of satisfaction in her eyes. The caption read, "Prima donna, Lily Taranova, is seen being squired by the eligible Judd Stetson in Vienna. Has the young scion of the Stetson Dynasty finally met his match?"

Katie closed the magazine and stuffed it in the trash among the day's newspapers. *What did you expect? You're only on the radar as the plaything next door.*

~

Judd's return to Corazon was met with overwhelming joy by Dori, who jumped into his arms, driving him back to the kitchen counter.

Helene gave him an unexpected hug and said, "We've missed you. I hope you won't have to leave again anytime soon." Her smile of welcome would have done in a lesser man.

Katie watched the scenario unfold, amused by Helene's demonstration of affection and Judd's retreat. When he looked her way, she turned and busied herself with cups and utensils in the sink. "Did you have a successful trip?" she asked as she opened the dishwasher.

Judd walked to her side. "I think my trip was necessary," he said to her. "How successful remains to be seen," he said, his voice barely audible, a cryptic message for her alone.

Katie reddened as she realized the trip had more to do with her than with business.

Wiping her hands on a towel, she glanced at Helene, who stared at her, recrimination in her eyes.

"*What now?*" Katie decided to stay in the cabin a few days and let emotions cool. Dori had her dad and Aunt Helene to keep her company.

CHAPTER THIRTY

The last week of August heralded the arrival of another member of the Stetson family. The doorbell rang as Katie came downstairs. She opened the front door and came face to face with Merit Stetson, J.D.'s niece and Judd's cousin. Katie remembered Merit as being the only family member who appeared halfway friendly at the reading of the Will.

Merit smiled and said, "I guess Judd hasn't informed you about my visit."

"No, I don't think he has told anyone. Do come in." Katie stepped back and allowed her to pass. She looked outside and saw a silver Lexus.

Merit stood in the entryway looking around. "The place hasn't changed much. Believe it or not, I enjoyed coming here as a child. My Aunt Del made this house into a home. She loved family visits."

"Do you have luggage, anything I can help you move?"

"I have a bag in the trunk, but Judd can handle it. I'll only be here a couple of days. Judd summoned me last week."

Katie thought the statement odd. "Have you travelled far? Please, come into the parlor."

She thought her actions and questions awkward. *Don't be a ninny. I don't have any reason to be embarrassed.*

"No, I live in Palm Beach most of the year."

"Can I get you something to drink? An iced tea or lemonade?"

"A sweet tea would be divine," Merit said as she sat on the edge of one of the upholstered high back chairs. "You might let Judd know I'm here."

"Yes, of course," Katie said and escaped the probing dark eyes of this fashionable woman. Merit was no longer dressed in black. She wore an apple green sheath and matching heels. Her slender, toned physique and facial expressions exuded confidence. Katie in denim jeans felt dowdy in comparison. *Stop it. You're dressed for ranch life, not high tea.*

When she reached the kitchen, she told Zita that Judd's cousin, Merit Stetson, was in the parlor and asked her to prepare a sweet tea. Katie walked out to the office and knocked on the door.

Judd answered with raised eyebrows and, "To what do I owe this momentous occasion?"

"Merit Stetson is in the parlor. She asked me to let you know."

Judd's face registered surprise. "I didn't expect her quite so soon. I'll be there in a few minutes. Thank you."

Katie was already returning to the kitchen as the last words were spoken. She picked up a napkin and the tea, telling Zita she'd deliver it. "You need to set an extra place at the table. She'll be here a couple of days."

Zita nodded and smiled as if she welcomed the visit.

On entering the parlor, she found Merit standing and looking at framed photographs of family members Katie had placed on the piano. They had been packed in the boxes.

"I see the piano is uncovered. Do you play?"

"Yes, it's a lovely instrument. I've enjoyed using it."

Katie handed Merit the tea, and she returned to her seat. Katie sat across from her. "Judd said he would be here in a few minutes."

"I remember when a few of those photos were taken. You must have put them out. J.D. didn't believe in being sentimental."

Then why did he have pictures of me in his office? No wonder everyone thought there was something going on between us. "I found the pictures packed in some old boxes and thought it time for them to be seen again."

"How is everything working out for you at Corazon?" Merit asked, her demeanor friendly and curious.

Judd walked in before Katie answered. "Merit, you look wonderful." He took both of her hands in greeting and kissed her on both cheeks. "Thank you for coming so promptly."

"My dear boy, when Stetson's CEO speaks, I listen; when he summons, I drop everything and come." She smiled up at him, a saucy lift of her lip, revealing a dimple.

"You're incorrigible." He grinned. "Seeing you here is like old times."

"Yes, and the times we see each other shouldn't get so old. It's been too long. We have some catching up to do."

Katie stood, transfixed by this friendly exchange. They appeared to be friends, as well as, family. She noticed similar genes in the cousins. "I think I'll leave you two to reminisce. Would you like for me to pick up Dori this afternoon?"

Judd looked at his watch. "Right. School will be out in an hour. Thank you. I'd appreciate your help."

"No problem." She looked at Merit. "I'll see you later at dinner."

~

Merit and Judd spent the afternoon in his office and arrived at the dinner table on time. Katie and Dori met them in the doorway. Dori grabbed Katie's hand and stepped behind her.

Judd noticed and called Dori to come and greet her "Aunt" Merit, even though she was a cousin. Katie knew she wasn't a real aunt, because Max didn't have a sibling, but it helped Dori with her name.

Dori squeezed Katie's hand and walked over to her daddy, not letting go of her hand.

"Hello, Merit," Katie said, "Dori seems to be a bit shy lately. Maybe it's an age thing. Dori, this is your Aunt Merit."

Judd smiled at Dori. "Your great-aunt and I are good friends. You met her several years ago, but you might have been too young to remember."

"I remember," Dori said, her voice low. "Hi." She pressed closer to Katie.

Helene arrived a little late as usual. Her mega-watt smile faded when she saw the company. "I didn't know you were here, Merit."

Merit lifted an eyebrow, her lips pulled back in a feigned smile. "Well, well, the surprise is mutual. I wasn't expecting you either."

Judd pulled out the chair to his right for Merit. "We're all glad you're here now. Right?" Judd said, looking at each in turn, and they nodded.

Katie wondered what had happened several years ago. *Dori acted strange. Merit and Helene appeared to be at odds.* She looked at Judd for his reaction.

He ignored the tension and began handing around the bowls of food. Silence reigned.

Merit spoke first. "How long are you staying, Helene?"

"As long as Dori needs me." Helene shifted uneasily in her chair.

"Her father's here. Does he need your help with Dori?"

Judd answered. "I asked Helene to come to Corazon to help with Dori's transition. Uprooting and moving to a new environment isn't easy."

"I see," Merit said and dropped the subject.

Dori found her voice and began to talk about the fishing trip with Hank and Karen. "Do you think we can go fishing again?" she asked Katie.

"Maybe your daddy will want to take you next time." Katie and Dori looked at Judd.

Her father gazed on Dori's eager face. "I think it can be arranged."

"Yes!" Dori pumped a fist.

Merit looked on amused.

~

Merit found Katie on the front porch the following morning. She set her coffee on a side table and sat in one of the rockers. "I've always enjoyed the sunrise. So, you're also an early riser?"

"I enjoy the coolness of the morning. I'm afraid the heat and humidity enervate me. The climate in Louisiana is a bit different." Jammer raised his head when she spoke. He lay by her chair as he did most mornings.

"How are things going here at Corazon? The family has been curious about arrangements and are reluctant to interfere. They're awaiting my report with bated breath."

Katie cocked her head and tried to read Merit's expression. The woman didn't mince words. *At least she's not unfriendly … to me.*

"Things are going about as well as you'd expect. Everyone but Dori is counting the days."

"That bad, huh. I see you moved into the cabin. Is Helene giving you a fit?"

"We get along most of the time."

"Judd's *not* getting serious about that woman."

A statement, not quite a question. Interesting. "I wouldn't know. She's still here, and I don't interfere." Katie lifted her mug of coffee for a sip and counted the hibiscus blossoms on the nearest shrub. *Ask her what happened three years ago.*

Katie looked at Merit and said, "I couldn't help but notice the swords out at dinner last night. Have you and Helene crossed paths before?"

"You noticed," she said, her smile enigmatic. "I came to Corazon after Rita's death. Judd went through hell while his wife was alive and after the tragedy, he locked himself away. He was angry, not only at Rita but with himself for being taken in by her." She leaned forward, taking and holding the mug between her hands.

"Dori was four. Helene didn't waste a moment, trying to ingratiate herself with the family. J.D. was sick about Judd's decision to send Dori back to Connecticut with her."

Katie prodded. "You and Helene didn't get along?"

"I was wearing black at the time, and Helene called me a witch after I confronted her about her intentions. Dori overheard, and after that, she ran in fear whenever I appeared." Merit sighed. "I can't really blame her. She's had Helene saying who knows what about the family for three years." She glanced at Katie for a response.

Katie thought about Dori saying her father hated her mother.

"We're really not as awful as we appeared at the reading of the Will." She set the mug on the table. "Well, maybe Adrienne is.... no, I shouldn't have said that. She *is* Judd's mother. I have to admit though, her reaction shocked all of us. I know, I know.... *our* actions were inexcusable, and I apologize. Tensions were off the chart, and I'm afraid we all jumped to the wrong conclusion. Judd has personally set every member of the family straight on your non-relationship with J. D. It is curious though."

Katie was stunned at this news. Loss of words left her mute.

Merit continued. "I think J.D. decided to make sure Dori returned to her father, the only way he knew how. He's still in control and probably having a good laugh at our expense about now." She grinned at Katie. "Yes, I believe he made it to the Hereafter. You saved his life twice. He was vocal about that. So, are you going to forgive us our bad behavior?"

"How could I not after such a speech." Katie smiled and held out her hand. "I'm so glad we had this talk. Thank you."

Merit took her hand. "No, I'm sure we'll all be thanking you at the end of the year."

CHAPTER THIRTY-ONE

Luke called Katie frequently and took her out to dinner several times in Palm Beach. They enjoyed each other's company, but the relationship didn't progress to something more serious. It was a surprise when their picture appeared on the Society page of the Sunday edition of a Palm Beach newspaper. The caption under the picture read, "Luke Albritton, Palm Beach attorney and aspiring political hopeful, is seen squiring a lovely young woman at Jacque's Chez Jardin Restaurant."

Helene tore the page out and handed it to Katie at dinner. "I see you and Luke are on society's radar. Will we be hearing about an engagement anytime soon?"

Katie's face burned when she saw the picture. *No way am I checking Judd's reaction.*

"Well?" Helene drawled, enjoying the moment.

"Well, what?" Katie said, her question tart. "We're friends. That's all."

"Right. You look like friends in the picture."

The photographer had caught Luke leaning toward her ear. It looked like he was about to kiss her, but Katie knew it was so she could hear him. The dining room was packed and a loud birthday celebration was going on at the table next to theirs.

Dori leaned over to look at the picture. "Katie has a boyfriend," she sang, increasing Katie's embarrassment and discomfort.

Judd's eyes narrowed at the disclosure. He felt the weight of a stone in his stomach. *You can't be getting serious about him. I know you have feelings for me. No, this can't be right.*

~

Luke's sister, Janet, had made a point of befriending Katie over the past several weeks. Janet and Luke shared genes of generosity and hospitality.

After the photograph in the newspaper, Katie wasn't surprised when Janet called to ask her out to lunch.

They met at Chef's Delight, a small deli tucked back in a wooded area next to a strip mall. Everything offered was organic and home baked. They ordered two of the specialty salads.

Janet's strawberry blond hair was pulled back and held with butterfly clips. Her blue eyes, the set of her mouth, and mannerisms reminded Katie of Luke.

Janet talked about growing up in the area and about her children, Alan and Debbie. She asked about Katie's family. The subject of Corazon was not mentioned. *Luke must have told his family the Stetson ranch and her stay there were off limits. He's keeping his word.*

Over Key Lime Pie, Janet asked her how she liked Luke. "You appear to be an item," is how she put it.

Katie believed this was the reason for lunch. "I like Luke. He's special. I admire his love of family and his involvement in community service. What's not to like?"

"Humm, Luke likes you, too. Our family is happy he's found someone else."

She wants me to know about a former girlfriend? "Someone else?"

"Well, that didn't come out right." Janet tortured her napkin while she made up her mind if she should continue. "Luke's been in love with Pam Raulerson since his sophomore year of high school and through four years of college. When he left for law school, they broke up, and he hasn't been serious about anyone since. Everyone assumed they would marry. He's been somewhat depressed."

Ah, the Raulersons. I remember them. They came by our table when the church had the pot luck supper. Luke seemed unhappy and distant. "We're just friends," Katie told Janet.

"Yes, I know, but he talks about you a lot. He's been different, happier than we've seen him in a long while."

Katie thought about the times they had gone out. Luke seemed more like a big brother than a lover. They laughed and shared jokes, talked about current events and family stories, nothing serious. *Maybe Luke still loves the girl.* "Pam lived around here?"

"They grew up together. She's from an old Florida family, too."

Unlike me. "Where is Pam now? Did she marry?"

"She works with a children's social services organization in Palm Beach, and last I heard, not married. I'm sure her family would get the word out if there was anyone else on the horizon. Her family goes to our church, and Luke's interest in you has been noted."

Janet put the distorted napkin on the table and took a deep breath. "I was wondering if Mr. Stetson was okay with you dating Luke." She kept her eyes on the napkin and didn't raise them to see Katie's reaction.

"You were wondering?" Katie left the question hanging.

Janet had the grace to color and stammered, "I'm sorry. I shouldn't be so nosey." She leaned forward, a plea in her voice. "Really, my interest is about Luke not getting hurt again. We're very close, and I wouldn't want him to be led on ... romantically ... and dropped. I know this sounds juvenile and awkward. Luke would die of embarrassment if he knew I talked to you about him."

"Yes, it is awkward, and I do understand your concern for Luke. But he's a grown man, who will make his own decisions about his future. I'm not romantically involved with anyone. That's not saying something won't change in the future. Right now, you have nothing to worry about." *And there is no way I'm going to discuss Judd with you.*

"Thank you for your honesty. I knew you were the genuine article the first time we met."

~

Katie decided she needed curtains in the cabin for privacy and a screen door to catch the breeze on nice days. Luke stopped by to measure the windows and doorway and drove her to town to shop.

A young man helped them choose a screen door and said someone would bring it to the ranch and install it for them. This suited Katie. She hadn't asked Judd's permission, and she wanted the job to be done right.

For the windows, she chose sets having wooden dowels and ecru, cotton curtains with cloth loops to go over the dowels.

Luke nodded his approval and said, "Rustic. A good choice."

As they carried their load across the hot tarmac, he said, "How about an ice cream cone?"

"I think your finger is on my pulse."

Luke laughed and minutes later, he pulled into the parking area of an ice cream parlor.

While waiting in line, they watched a group of children trying to decide what to get with their money. They waffled on the flavors several times and carefully counted out the coins after ordering. Luke impressed Katie with his patience. *He'll make a wonderful father. And husband.*

Back at Corazon, Luke helped Katie mount the dowels and hang the curtain panels. They made a good team.

Katie noted Judd's interest. The closed wooden slats in his office were now partially ajar. She started to wave but thought better of it. *Don't antagonize him.*

Dori had heard the car return, and she joined them in the cabin.

Katie shared some of the history she had found in J.D.'s books. Luke was fascinated, especially with the books that contained old maps.

Dori looked through her books for one he could read to her.

Luke sat in the recliner with Charles Hallock's book, Camp Life in Florida, published in 1875. One chapter described the first expedition down the Kissimmee River and into and around Lake Okeechobee after the Indian wars in 1843.

They laughed about the advertisements in the back of the book. One advertised steamship passage between New York and Key West, Florida, at $50.00.

"My, how times have changed! These books need to be protected," Luke said. "I have an attorney's cabinet I'm not using. I'd be honored if you'd accept the donation to your nest."

"I like that description." Katie thought about how she was feathering her nest. "Thank you, Luke. Your addition will ease my mind. I've been worried about the condition of the books deteriorating after being stored in corrugated boxes. I'll have to fix dinner for you one night, to show my appreciation for your help."

"No need to go to any trouble." He grinned at her. "How soon can you do it?" His voice lifted in anticipation.

"Can I come? I helped." Dori asked.

"Sure you can, peanut. Anytime. In fact, you can help cook."

"Yipee!" Dori danced in a circle, her arms raised.

Dori handed him the book about Sampson and Delilah. "Did you know that if you cut your hair, you aren't strong anymore?"

Luke took the book. "I think we need to read the story. Not everyone with long hair has the strength of Sampson."

When they walked to the house, Katie noticed Judd's window panels were closed.

CHAPTER THIRTY-TWO

September arrived and the ranch bustled again with activity. Judd had planned a barbeque for his workers under one of the sheds with a concrete floor. Workers came early that morning to clean the area and to set up tables and chairs. Some of the men sang songs in Spanish as they knocked down spider webs and swept the area.

The men's work ethic impressed Katie. They worked cheerfully as they joked with each other and spoke of families back home.

Dori came out looking for Katie and wanted to help. Katie rolled out red and white checked rolls of plastic and cut them. Dori held them in place while she taped the edges under the table. Judd came out to check on the men and their progress. When he gave the nod of approval, the workmen left.

Dori had put two rolls of paper towels on each table and opened and added the inexpensive salt and pepper shaker sets Katie had found in the spice section of the grocery. Katie wrapped individual sets of plastic utensils in large napkins and put them in a box for convenience.

"Very nice," Judd said. "Everything looks good, better than ever. This is the first time we've used tablecloths, but I like them."

Katie was surprised at his unexpected compliment. "Thank you. I wanted to contribute something to the day since others are doing the cooking."

Cheryl Hubbard arrived with sturdy paper plates, cups, and condiments. "Hey, this looks really good. Mike said you had gotten the utensils. Now I know why."

Judd helped Cheryl unload her car. He put the large igloos for drinks on a separate table, and igloos of ice out of the sun. He walked back to the area where the men were barbecuing and Dori tagged along.

Savory aromas permeated the area. Katie's stomach rumbled. The piece of toast she had for breakfast didn't last long.

Earlier in the day, Katie had watched Sam and Slim strip outer layers from hearts of palm stacked on the back of a pickup truck.

Sam told Katie, Zita would cut them up for a big pot of swamp cabbage. "She knows how to season it just right,"

Slim gave Katie a raw piece to chew. "People eat 'em in salads, too."

Katie tasted the piece Slim gave her. It was crunchy but not real hard. She had never heard of the dish made from the hearts of palm trees. "Does it kill the tree?"

"Yep, 'fraid so," Slim answered. "They's hard to get which makes 'em taste better. But not to worry, they's lots of cabbage palms, and we don't fix'em often."

A large, black kettle sat on a grill over hot coals. Ears of corn steamed in their husks.

A Parker Catering truck with a large, commercial grill attached cooked chicken halves, and another large enclosed oven by the side of the truck contained briskets.

Big Jim, the caterer, a husky man of color with grizzled black hair and large ham-like hands, wore an apron printed with flames leaping up and the words "Trial by Fire." His crew, attired in the same aprons, worked at each station readying the meal for consumption. He brought out bags filled with chunks of meat that caught her attention. Baskets containing paper towels were placed on the table nearby. He hummed as he worked.

A smaller kettle over a gas grill contained hot oil. On a nearby table, Big Jim mixed seasonings on a stainless steel pan and rolled the pieces of meat in the mix.

"What are you fixing?" Katie asked.

"Gator tail," he said, grinning at her expression. "It tastes real good. You'll like it."

Katie wasn't so sure. "Did *you* kill the gator?"

"Nope. I had to purchase it from a gator farm that has the permits and gets the meat inspected." He dropped a seasoned batch in the oil and the pieces sizzled. "Stick around. It'll be ready in a few minutes, and I'll give you some. You can be the first to get a taste of this delicacy."

Workers along with their wives and children began to show up and walked over to watch Big Jim work. He used a large slotted spoon to drain and scoop out the offerings and put them in the baskets of paper towels. Taking a napkin, he placed three of the pieces on it and handed it to Katie. "Let it cool a minute. It's still hot."

Everyone standing by, pressed in to get a morsel, and their enthusiasm gave Katie the courage to try hers. Gator tail was delicious. She laughed. "This tastes like chicken," she said, "and the seasoning is really good."

Big Jim grinned. His black, mutton-chops twitched as he put in another batch. "I hear that a lot from people who haven't ever tasted frog legs. Better get you some more before it's all gone. This is one appetizer that doesn't last long."

Judd showed up to get his share. Helene, who arrived with him, wore blue pedal pushers and white sandals. Her shirt tied under her breasts, showed her bare midriff, and Katie thought it strange attire to wear to a barbecue for the workers.

Helene was having none of it. "How can you eat that reptile?" Her mouth and face screwed in distaste.

"Ma'am," Big Jim said, "you're missing out on one of the great pleasures in life. You've got to learn to live a little." His plump cheeks split in a big grin, showing white Chiclet-sized teeth. "You must be a Yankee."

Helene was not pleased by his comment, and she left in a huff to check out the food table.

Sam and Mike unloaded a large pot from the back of the cart, and Zita trailed behind with large spoons. Several men unloaded pans from the back of the truck to add to the food on the table.

"How do you like gator?' Judd asked Katie, bringing her attention back to the treat.

"It's really good. You sure know how to put on a spread." She looked around for Dori and found her playing tag with some of the children. "I think I'll go see if Zita needs any help." She needed to get away from Judd's disturbing presence.

Judd watched Katie walk away. She had a nice swing to her hips. Dressed in jeans and a blue, gingham cowgirl shirt, her attire was appropriate for the setting. He held his tongue when he wanted to send Helene back to change. He knew how that would have ended.

Katie had been a help today, and her extra touches were appreciated. Judd always enjoyed this occasion, but this year's barbeque seemed special. He attributed that to having Dori here, but he couldn't deny Katie's presence added to the pleasure. *What am I thinking?*

Katie filled her plate, and when she didn't think she could add another thing, one of the men brought an ear of corn out of the big kettle with tongs. He shucked the ear down to the end, using gloves, and holding the husk, dipped it in butter, and laid it across the top of her plate.

Katie enjoyed the day. She had tried gator tail, swamp cabbage, brisket, and found a new way to eat corn on the cob. The food was excellent, and Katie knew why everyone looked forward to this day. She went back for another helping of swamp cabbage and didn't eat dessert, only because she was stuffed.

Two of the men brought guitars to play, and almost everyone joined in singing some of the songs. A few couples danced, and some of the children joined them, including Dori. All that was missing from the festive occasion were the lanterns and piñatas.

Katie sat at the table with Mike, his wife, Julie, and with Cheryl and her husband, Bill. She met Julie and Bill for the first time. The women talked about education, shopping, and local politics. No one talked about work.

Bill, a surveyor, enjoyed fishing. He and Mike talked about fishing tournaments and shared saltwater fish tales.

Judd, Dori, and Helene sat at another table, and Katie tried to quell feelings of unwanted jealousy because the three of them together looked like a family. *Grow up, Katie. You have to give them room to decide what they want.* She turned away several times, trying to put these thoughts out of her head and keep her mind focused on the conversations around her. *But I don't want to, Lord.*

Big Jim provided coconut cake, carrot cake, and apple pie. Katie took a small slice of each and carried the plate back to the house. She planned to eat dessert later with a cup of coffee.

Mid-September, Katie attended her first virtual Stetson Board Meeting. She had missed the one in June. Judd sat at the conference table in his office with the wall map behind him, a laptop in front, and a camera facing him. Large white boards stood at the other end of the table.

He punched in a site and password. The first order of business was to get his Executive Secretary, Martha Geary, online. A middle-aged woman behind a desk with her own computer looked into the camera. Ms. Geary had short white hair, a lantern jaw, deep-set inquisitive eyes, and a no-nonsense look about her. Katie imagined she was probably efficient and discreet. *So this is how he gets all of his work finished without an Executive Secretary underfoot.*

Judd asked Katie to come forward and introduced her to Ms. Geary, so she could be added to the list of those attending the meeting. Judd spelled out her last name and asked her to spell out Kathryn for his secretary.

"Hello, Ms. Mulholland. I'm pleased to meet you." She looked down at some papers on her desk. "I have the documents sent to me by Mr. Pickering, and everything appears to be in order. You have the right to vote on any matter that comes before the board and requires a vote."

Judd nodded, but his mouth was set in a grim line as he went over additions to the agenda.

Five minutes later, the other Board members checked in. The roll was called even though all of them were shown on one screen. Ms. Geary, the compiler, added their names and put the minutes of the previous meeting up for them to see.

Judd called the meeting to order, and asked if there were any additions or corrections to the minutes they had received several days earlier. The minutes were unanimously approved, and Judd went on to the first order of business on the agenda.

Katie sat in the background and listened as the meeting progressed. Astronomical figures were brought up, stores which needed upgrading, reports from various entities with maintenance or management problems.

Katie's head swam with all the figures. Spread sheets filled screens and few questions were asked. She stayed quiet and tried to send her mind to another realm away from business, but Judd's authoritative voice kept bringing her back to the present. Katie worked to keep her expression bland as her face appeared on the screen with the others. She studied Judd's movements, nuances of meaning in his voice, and his control over the meeting.

The faces of other Board members registered everything from avid attention to detail at one end of the spectrum to ennui at the other end. Katie turned her head and squelched a smile when Adrienne yawned.

Attempts to go off on a tangent were not tolerated, and two hours later, the next meeting was scheduled and this meeting adjourned.

Judd asked Ms. Geary to archive the business meeting after transcribing the minutes. He stayed on with Ms. Geary to add notes about correspondence needed to be sent or changes needed to be made in management.

Katie had said one word, "Here," when the roll was called.

Judd turned to Katie after he disconnected the equipment. "Do you have any questions?" His granite face did not invite comment.

Katie shook her head, and said, "No." She got up to leave, and Judd stopped her.

"I hope if you have questions, you will come to me with them. We do not want our business bandied about outside of the family. Understood?"

He meant Luke, of course. "I have no reason to speak with anyone about Stetson's business. I have no wish to even be involved."

He nodded, and she left, closing the door quietly.

Judd looked at the closed door. In his mind, the door represented the barrier which stood between them. J.D. Stetson. The old man had unleashed a Pandora's Box of feelings he didn't want or need in his life. Whenever he felt himself weakening where Katie was concerned, he visualized J.D. saying, "This is the woman I picked for you." The vision dispelled any welcome thoughts her presence brought to Corazon. The pleasant ones he squirreled away were of Katie under him, surrendering to his passion. *I have another use for her, old man. You lose.*

CHAPTER THIRTY-THREE

In October, Dori's school had a Fall Festival instead of a Halloween party. Her second grade class had the fishing booth. Judd surprised everyone by not only going, but taking part in the festivities. He volunteered to sit in the class booth for an hour and put prizes on the end of a fishing line. Katie told him if the child was a boy or a girl and the approximate ages. Dori helped her dad choose the prize.

Dori had a fist full of tickets for the cake walk. She wanted a cake, so she and her father walked in the circle until Judd ended up on the right spot and won. All of the grades took part in the cake walk, and numerous cakes, pies, and cupcakes were donated. Katie baked and decorated Zita's chocolate cake, but it had already been chosen. Dori picked a chocolate cake with orange icing and candy corn decorations.

Judd looked like he enjoyed the evening, and Dori was proud he came with her. She held onto his hand while they walked around the various booths and played some of the games.

Katie laughed at Judd when he sported blue cotton candy on his nose and chin. He stuck out a blue tongue at her, and Dori loved it. "Look at my tongue. Is it red?"

Judd and Katie both smiled and nodded. She skipped a circle in delight.

Luke spotted the trio and stopped to talk with them. Dori showed him her red tongue. "My daddy has a blue tongue. He looks like a lizard when he sticks it out. I'm going to have my face painted like a clown so my nose will match my tongue." She waggled her tongue at him.

They walked and played a few games together. Luke performed well in the bean toss and gave Dori and Katie matching glow in the dark necklaces and bracelets he won. "I pitched on the high school baseball team, which gives me an edge when aim counts," he told them when they remarked on his success.

Katie gave Judd high marks for being pleasant when Luke joined them. She guessed he wanted nothing to get in the way of Dori having a good time.

Before Luke left them, he tried to give Katie a dozen cupcakes decorated with orange icing and Jack-O-Lantern faces. He won them in the cake walk, but Katie declined the offer.

When Luke walked away, Dori looked at Judd with adoring eyes and said, "I'm glad you won the chocolate cake, Daddy." Her simple statement melted him, and he stooped to give her a big hug. "Thanks baby, you made my night."

Dori beamed.

In that moment, Katie believed Dori would not be leaving Judd at the end of the year to go back to Connecticut. She realized the year would pass quickly, and the thought left an ache in the region of her heart. Tonight she saw Judd, the ideal father, the caring parent, giving his daughter the gift of his time.

Uncle Luke also spent time with his niece and nephew, making sure Debbie and Alan had plenty of tickets. Their paths crossed several times. Later, Katie saw his sister, Janet, and her family carrying Luke's cupcakes to their car. They exchanged waves.

Judd watched Katie's facial expression change from smiling to thoughtful. He saw her put a hand to her chest and sigh. *Is she thinking about Luke?* He had not minded the young man joining them because Katie was with him.

His thoughts turned to Katie and Dori. *Tonight we made a great team, and we had fun, especially Dori.* He pictured them as a family. *Whoa. We're not a family. Banish that thought.* He visualized J.D. smiling and said, "I think it's time to call it a night. Let's go home." *God what am I thinking? Family. Home. Are you nuts?*

One of the local churches had a pumpkin patch fund drive for charity. Katie asked Judd if they could have a Jack-O-Lantern painting party with Dori's friends.

He said, "Do it," and Dori made invitations on the computer using graphics with Katie's help. Dori handed them out to everyone in her class and to Bobbie Jean.

Katie and Dori chose twenty pumpkins in different sizes and shapes. The feat was getting all of them loaded into her car. They picked up acrylic paints and brushes from a craft store along with bags to decorate for candy and favors. Painting the pumpkin faces would be easier than cutting the features. They also made a grocery list and shopped for food items.

Saturday arrived, overcast but not raining. Tables were set up outside between the back porch and Judd's office with plastic cloths covering them. Most of the class showed up for the party, and some of the parents stayed to help.

The day was cool, and smocks made from garbage bags kept most of the paint off of the children's clothes. Parents cut holes in the white bags, fitting them to each child.

"Acrylics use water and the paints dry quickly," Katie told Judd when he asked her about her choice of paints. She picked up her camera and began to take pictures of the activities.

Helene came outside and picked one of the remaining pumpkins to paint. She painted a silly face on her pumpkin, and was delighted to see some of the children tried to copy hers.

Katie was happy she chose to participate. Helene's attitude had deteriorated over the past week, and it was good to see her come out of the prison she had built for herself. She made an effort to be friendly to the guests, probably more for Judd's sake.

The night of the Fall Festival, Helene had accused Katie of monopolizing Judd's time. "You think you're so smart to be part of all the cutsy activities for Dori." She harrumphed indelicately. "You're trying to turn Judd's head through his daughter." She preened and gave Katie a knowing smile. "Dori's important, but it's a woman Judd needs to satisfy his desires. I'm still here and available, so he won't be wanting in that department." She turned and sashayed to her room, leaving the impression something of a sexual nature existed between Judd and her.

I don't believe you. I won't believe you.

Her thoughts returned to the project at hand, but she couldn't put the scene out of her head. She watched Judd and Helene as they interacted throughout the day, but she didn't see any sizzle, and she berated herself for giving Helene's taunts an iota of credibility.

Judd laughed a lot and helped some of the children perfect their faces. He fired up the grill to broil hamburgers and hot dogs.

Zita brought out buns, chips, condiments, and punch when it was time to eat. After eating and cleaning up, she and Katie strung a line with donuts hanging from it. Three children at a time tried to see who could eat a donut the fastest without using their hands. Prizes were handed out.

Everyone had fun, and Dori passed out the decorated bags full of candy, fruit, and knickknacks when they were leaving.

Judd put his hand on Katie's shoulder as he waved goodbye. "That went well, I think," Judd said. "I know Dori had fun. Thank you for making today possible." He looked down at her, a smile on his face.

Katie's heart turned over. She didn't want him to drop his hand, but of course, he did. She glanced around to see if Helene watched, but she had disappeared when the cleanup started.

CHAPTER THIRTY-FOUR

The silver salver on the hall table held the day's mail. An important-looking, embossed ecru envelope addressed in gold metallic ink rested on top. Curiosity lured Katie to the pile. She guessed the contents might contain an invitation to the *Fete de Noel*. Luke had asked her to go with him last week. He told her the annual gala was a fundraiser for local children's charities. She told Luke she'd think about going and hadn't given him an answer.

Katie looked through the mail for a note from Myra or her parents. Mostly junk, nothing for her today.

Later, before Zita brought in the appetizer, Helene waved the ecru envelope in front of Judd. "Open this one. Let's see where we're going."

Judd glanced at the writing. "It's an invitation to an annual ball. You can put it back on the table. I'll take it to the office."

"Ooh, what kind of ball? May I peek?" Helene wheedled.

"Sure you may, but I'm not going. I'll send a check."

Helene used her knife to carefully open the flap and brought out the fancy invitation. She read the contents. "This is an event to help children."

Dori spoke, her eyes sparkling with excitement. "Do they have games?"

"No, sweetheart, this event is not for children, only adults, Judd told his daughter."

"Aw, nutters!"

"I beg your pardon," Helene admonished. "Where did you hear that?"

Dori looked abashed. "Is it bad?" She looked at her father.

"No, it's an unusual expression, that's all," Judd answered, cutting off further comment. He knew she had heard Slim say it.

Helene brought the conversation back to the invitation. "Judd, you should go. Katie will be here with Dori. It'll be fun, and this is to help children, after all," she cajoled using her eyes and sultry, come hither smile on him.

"That's right," he said, his voice lowering to indicate the end of the discussion. "I'll mail them a big check."

"I'm going," Katie announced, surprising herself. She kept her eyes on the salad plate, wishing she hadn't spoken. She didn't want to think she said it to irritate Helene, but she knew it was the very reason.

Katie welcomed Zita's entrance carrying the night's fare.

"You're going to this?" Helene's voice rose as she waved the card.

"Yes," Katie said not looking in Judd's direction. "Luke asked me last week. He must have known about it ahead of time. Believe me, I'm not looking forward to shopping for a formal dress to wear."

Helene pouted the rest of the meal and except for Dori who talked non-stop about Thanksgiving vacation, the dinner ended in silence.

Katie excused herself and retired to read the latest Greg Iles novel.

~

Two days passed and Luke arrived at the cabin with the barrister's bookcase standing up and anchored in the back of a pickup truck. "I borrowed the ride from my dad. It wouldn't fit in the back of my car." He let down the tailgate. "It's two pieces. I think we can handle it together, or we can see if Judd will help."

"No," Katie said. "Let's see if we can do it ourselves." The cabinet looked like it was made of walnut and had the fine patina of age. The panes of glass looked original. *Maybe we should call Judd. This is a valuable piece. No. We can do it.*

Luke maneuvered the bottom piece toward the back end and jumped off the truck, pulling the blanket it sat on toward him. "Grab the other end as I bring it back, and we'll set it on the ground."

Judd walked around the side of the office. "Do you need some help?"

Katie figured Judd heard the truck arrive and peeked to see who visited. *Naturally, he wants to investigate.*

"Great timing," Luke said, like he wasn't thinking the same thing. "I'd hate for Katie to hurt her back."

Judd took the rear end, and they eased it off of the truck and up the stone step.

Katie held the door open and smiled at Judd. "Thank you for your help."

"I wouldn't want you to hurt your back," he said, his voice low and laced with an undertone of sarcasm.

Luke tried to lighten the moment. "Your grandfather has a treasure trove of rare Florida books. I'm not using this cabinet, so I brought it along as a donation to the cause."

"And what cause would that be?" Judd asked his voice cold.

Luke did a double take at his tone. "Why, the books need to be preserved. The acid in the boxes will fox them, hasten their deterioration."

"Right," Judd said. Then walking outside to help bring in the top half, he murmured, "I know what foxing means." As soon as the case was situated, he returned to his office, grinding his teeth in frustration.

"Is everything okay?" Luke asked. "Judd seemed out of sorts."

"He's fine. The business is stressful at the moment. He's had to travel a lot." She changed the subject. "Thank you for the cabinet. It's beautiful." The bottom had three shelves and the top had two. All five had glass fronts that pulled up and slid inward to open.

Luke wiped down the shelves and helped Katie load the books into their new home. "I'm glad you decided to go to the gala with me. You'll enjoy the festivities. The foundation puts on a good show, and they raise a lot of money."

They went outside and before Katie stepped off of the porch, Luke took her arm and turned her around. He wrapped his arms around her, drawing her close. "You know Katie, I think I'm falling in love," Luke said. "I'm glad we found each other." His kiss lingered and deepened, unlike the other kisses he gave her on occasion. Katie put her arms around his neck and responded, but her heart wasn't in it. The desperate need only Judd could give her was missing. The spark didn't ignite.

Luke must have known because he set her back and lifted her chin so he could look into her eyes. "You don't have deep feelings for me," a statement not a question.

Katie swallowed. "You're the nicest man I know. I love being with you, but…"

"It's him, Judd Stetson, isn't it?" He sighed. "Why am I not surprised." He pulled Katie back into his embrace.

"I'm sorry," Katie said and laid her forehead on his chest. "It's not what you think. He sees me as an intruder, not someone to share his future after the year is up. I'm not his type of woman. You know it's true."

"That's his loss," Luke murmured in her ear and hugged her closer. "You deserve to have someone who will cherish you."

From his office, Judd watched the couple with clenched fists. What had they been doing in the cabin? She certainly didn't fend Luke off. When she put her arms around his neck, he felt a knife twist in his gut. When Luke looked directly at the window and smiled over Katie's head, Judd went ballistic. *The bastard.*

He strode to the gym, not bothering to change, and charged the punching bag, pounding it until he was exhausted. He stood, leaning into the bag, sweat rolling down his body, knowing if he let go, he would fall. A loss he couldn't explain sucked at his soul, leaving grief in its wake.

~

The following afternoon, Helene came to lunch jubilant. "Judd relented. He taking me to the gala and …," a significant pause followed to underline her announcement, "he's giving me his personal card to buy a dress from Stetson's of Palm Beach." She twirled around, hugging her chest in delight.

Dori looked at them. "Who's staying with me?"

"I'll be here," Zita said. "Mr. Judd asked me this morning."

Katie noted Helene's buoyant expression. She believed Judd changed his mind for her, but Katie knew Helene read too much into his mind change. She believed Judd kept tabs on her and looked out for his interest. If she and Luke became serious, half of Corazon and a percentage of Stetson Enterprises would be shared with yet another interloper. She didn't blame him. His grandfather had put him in an untenable position.

Luke's kiss came to mind. Did Judd see them? *Yeah, he probably did. It makes sense now. Why else would he change his mind? He's taking Helene to keep an eye on me. Better be on guard and stay around people.*

More than once it had crossed Katie's mind that Judd's pursuit of her was connected to the Will. She remembered his pronouncement at the Blue Adagio about being "happily unattached," a warning not to expect more than a temporary arrangement. No, Judd and permanence were like oil and water. He wanted a convenient lover, and if he could seduce her, keep her here without commitment, so much the better. Helene reminded Judd of Rita, and he wasn't chancing that pain again.

Katie relaxed. No sparks detected from that quarter. *How long will Judd keep Helene at Corazon? Not long. He'll be going to Plan B. soon.*

CHAPTER THIRTY-FIVE

November arrived with gusty winds and chilly weather. Harvesting citrus was in full swing, and sounds of music playing and tortillas cooking over small fires permeated the air. Florida had passed through the hurricane season unscathed. Fall brought in drier conditions, and oaks, hickories, and cypress trees dropped their leaves. Maple trees, a few shrubs, and sumac showed color, but not the spectacular event found in northern climes.

Katie and Dori saw deer, turkeys, and hogs almost every trip despite hunting season. Early mornings were the best times for them to see wildlife because they avoided being too far from home at dusk. Dori held Jammer's collar to keep him from running after the animals.

Gators and snakes were digging into their holes as the cold arrived. They had also seen a couple of black bears, which ran away when they were spotted. They, too, were preparing to hibernate, even in Florida.

Katie never failed to express her thanks for God's blessings. One day, Dori lifted her face and her voice skyward and shouted, "Thank you, God, for Daddy, and Katie, and Bobbie Jean, and Jammer, and all the blessings you give me. Please let me stay here forever and ever."

Katie reached across the cart and hugged her.

"Do you think God heard me?" Dori asked.

"I'm sure He did. They probably heard you back at the house."

Dori giggled. "No, they didn't, silly." She raised her voice again and shouted. "If you hear me at the house, tell me when we come home." She looked at Katie with a grin on her face.

Katie and Dori explored some of the hammocks on weekends. The foliage was sparse and the ground exposed. Rains had eroded one side of a mounded area near the eastern edge of the property. The spot was probably two miles from the house and the farthest they had ventured.

Jammer jumped off the cart to explore the wooded area.

Dori picked up a black object. "What's this?" She handed the piece to Katie.

Katie turned it over in her hand. The item had a flattened rim. "I think it's old pottery."

Dori picked up a roundish, flat white rock. The chipped edge looked man made.

"This looks like a tool. Maybe we found an Indian site." Katie said, looking around and seeing more pottery pieces.

"Seminole Indians live near here," Dori said. "Do you think they lost these?"

"I don't know much about the Indians that lived in Florida before the Seminoles. These look old. You'll have to ask your daddy."

They returned to the house, and Dori ran to the office and opened the door without knocking. Excited, she handed Judd their artifacts. "Look what Katie and me found in a hammock."

Judd swallowed his annoyance at being disturbed and checked their finds under a light.

"Katie thinks they're Indian. Is it Seminole Indian?"

Judd laid the pieces on a sheet of typing paper. "No, these are older. They belonged to Indians who lived here before the Seminoles came into Florida. They might be Calusa, who came here from the west coast, or the Tequesta or Ais from the east coast. Only an expert can tell us." He picked up the rock tool and held it up to the light. "This is a fine scraper made out of coral." He pointed to some roundish markings that looked like tiny sunbursts at one end. "These are polyps, the coral animals. They grow together in colonies off of the coast. When they die, they harden over the years. Reefs are made of coral."

"How did the Indians get it?"

"That's a good question. Reefs must be close enough to shore for them to dive down and chip pieces off."

Katie leaned against the door jamb. "We didn't pick up everything. I thought the pieces were Indian, and I didn't want to disturb the site."

Judd looked up and smiled his appreciation. "You did the right thing. Where did you find these?"

Katie described the hammock and area.

Judd nodded. "I think I know the place. We've found other sites on the ranch, but this must be a new one. Maybe we can take a look tomorrow ... after church," he added.

Dori jumped up and down. "I can't wait to tell Bobbie Jean. Can I call her?"

"Sure you may." Judd looked up the number and punched it in for Dori.

Judd and Katie listened to Dori tell Bobbie Jean about the site. They both smiled at her enthusiasm.

"Will you go with us tomorrow?" Judd asked, leaning back on his desk and folding his arms across his chest.

"If you want me to," Katie said hesitant to commit. He looked so good in his jeans and red plaid flannel shirt. Her heartbeat increased, and she knew her face and neck reddened.

"You know I want you to come," Judd said, his tone intimate, his eyes intent.

Her insides melted in the heat of his gaze. She realized he had started his campaign to win her over. Katie turned from temptation and hastened her steps to the house, unsure of her strength or will to thwart his plans for her.

Judd watched Katie flee the inevitable outcome. He'd bet the ranch she loved him. He saw it in her eyes, her physical response to his voice, and yes, in her need to escape. He had warned her, and unlike most women secure in their confidence to beat the odds, she heeded the warning. Her head wasn't turned by money or power, which made her the most challenging and interesting woman he had pursued. Luke might be in the wings, but he would never generate the passionate response he elicited from Katie. He smiled.

Dori hung up the phone and hugged Judd's legs. "I love you, daddy."

Judd bent and gathered his daughter in an embrace. "I love you too, sweet thing." As he said it, he had a sobering thought. *Luke can give Katie marriage and a family.*

Katie and Dori arrived at church to find Luke and Bobbie Jean waiting for them. Katie was surprised when Luke continued to seek her company. He told her again how happy she made him by still wanting to go with him to the gala. They enjoyed the same interests.

Dori showed them the artifacts they had found. A plastic bag protected her treasures and kept them together. "Daddy named the site after me. It's called Dori's Mound. When he sees where we found these, he'll put the name on a map in his office."

"Wow!" Bonnie Jean exclaimed. "Your name will be on a map. You are so lucky. Can I see the place?"

"Sure," Dori said as they walked toward the Sunday School classes.

Luke smiled at Katie as they left. "Dori is certainly feeling important this morning."

"Well, it's not every day you have a site named for you. I didn't know Judd did that."

"I'm not surprised. Does Judd know anything about your finds?"

Katie told him Judd's guesses.

"We should see if we can find books about Florida Indians, preferably with pictures. I didn't see any in your library. We could go to West Palm this afternoon and check out the bookstores."

Katie shook her head. "That's really nice of you. I'm supposed to take Judd and Dori to the site this afternoon. Maybe we can do it another time."

"Humm," Luke offered as a response. It wasn't mentioned again.

The second Stetson Estate check arrived the week before Thanksgiving. Katie paced her room agitated, discontent, and what? Sadness that half of a year had slipped away far too quickly or the responsibility the draft pressed upon her? The check arrived as promised after probate and six months after the reading of the will.

Katie recognized the envelope from the attorney, Aaron Pickering. Judd's check also arrived. The payment would remind him of J.D.'s ironclad commitment to arrange Judd's future. Would the money change Judd's attitude? He had mellowed toward her. Katie was torn between her love for Dori and the reality of the situation with Judd. The idea of leaving Dori squeezed her heart. J.D's plan half-succeeded. Judd saw Dori thrive at Corazon. She would not be going back to Connecticut with Helene.

Judd was attracted to her, but why? Was she a means to an end to reclaim her half of Corazon and the ten percent of Stetson Enterprises, or did he really care for her? At times, she saw him looking at her as if he did. The answer to that question should be answered in May. She remembered again what he said at the Blue Adagio about being happily unattached. *Oh Judd, how can I leave you? How can I stay without commitment?*

Katie thought the last check a temptation, and she had put it in a money market account. Taxes after the first check put her in a higher bracket. This check added four times that amount. Her mother had commented after she tore up the first one five years before that the next one could be used to support any number of worthy causes. The thought nagged her.

Taking out her checkbook, Katie reviewed her balance and chewed the inside of her lips. Having her apartment and room and board paid by J.D.' s estate, left her with substantial savings. She had never held so much money in her hands. She stuffed the checkbook in her underwear drawer until she could think clearly.

~

Meredith Stetson Wilcox and her husband, Bob, were coming to Thanksgiving dinner, and Judd asked them to stay a few days to go over business. They lived in New Orleans but were staying with Meredith's sister, Merit, in Palm Beach for a couple of weeks. Merit had other plans for Thanksgiving Day.

Judd watched the work pile up on his desk. He had never let his duties suffer because of his lack of focus. His dark mood fed his frustration. Katie showed no interest in her Stetson investments. He knew she received the check, but she asked no questions about acreage, numbers, or stock information. She sat silently through the quarterly meeting, watching family members question his decisions and trying to finagle more personal funds into their accounts. How could she be so nonchalant about her future ownership? Maybe he needed to ask her to the office where he could apprise her of her holdings. Had it been six months already? Where did the time go? *Katie will be leaving Corazon in May.* To top everything off, Katie announced she would be sharing Thanksgiving with Luke's family. They also invited Katie, Dori, Helene and himself to dinner. He was not happy that Katie accepted the Albritton's invitation.

Judd had been short-tempered all week, and Katie looked forward to getting away from a house of doom and gloom. She wished she could save Dori, but knew that possibility was out of the question. Katie spent her time in the cabin reading history or practicing with Dori on the piano.

Dori came to the cabin after school to do her homework, and Katie bought some watercolor paint and paper to give her a creative outlet. Her artwork decorated the old refrigerator, lending bright colors to an otherwise rustic décor. Dori exhibited some real talent. She was creative and innovative. One of her pictures was a mosaic scene created by tearing up smaller pieces of construction paper and pasting them on another sheet. "This is the funnest art."

"Funnest isn't a word," Katie said.

"Why not? Funnest says what I mean." Dori had made a house, a cabin, a man, a woman, a little girl, and a dog. "This is my family," she said. That's you, and daddy, and me, and Jammer."

Katie loved the picture and tacked it to the corner post where the initials were carved.

Sometimes, Dori stayed to have dinner, just the two of them. These occasions were when Judd had a business trip or when Katie declined the invitation to eat with the others. She stayed true to her bid for independence and was grateful to have a choice.

Judd had not complained about the arrangement, so Katie was happy for the company.

Luke came to the cabin for dinner on a couple of occasions, and Dori was present for those meals. They enjoyed a unique camaraderie.

The three of them pored over the books on Florida Indians Luke had purchased for the library. Robin Brown's book, *Florida's First People,* was a favorite. The book included a lot of pictures and told about Indian technology, giving instructions for replicating cordage, baskets, weaving, and other job skills, using natural materials.

Luke collected palm fiber and they sat on the porch making cordage by following the directions in the book. They wove the strands into strings and doubled them to make a stronger rope. Indians used cordage to carry or hold items and to make fishing nets. Dori couldn't wait to show her daddy and take her work to school to show her teacher and her classmates.

Meredith and Bob Wilcox arrived at Corazon an hour before Katie left to drive to the Albritton's for Thanksgiving dinner. She had cooked in the cabin, making a pan of yams with pecans and topped the dish with melted marshmallows. This was her grandmother's recipe, and she knew everyone would like her contribution.

Zita had her hands full in the kitchen, and Katie put on an apron and helped her by chopping ingredients for the extra stuffing. Zita no longer looked at her as an intruder in the kitchen or as a threat to her job. She welcomed Katie's company and help.

Judd brought his cousins into the kitchen after they arrived. Katie hurriedly washed and dried her hands before greeting them. "Hi. You caught me at a disadvantage."

Embarrassed by the amused look on Judd's face, she took off the apron and faced the woman who had peered scornfully at her during the reading of the Will. Meredith was not as pleasant as her sister, Merit, nor as elegant. The tight, plum dress she wore did not enhance her full figure or coloring. Her dyed, black hair was severely coifed and her unfriendly, dark eyes assessed Katie from under drooping lids. Meredith acknowledged her presence with a nod. Meredith's mouth was set in disapproval, her expression dismissive.

Bob expressed his acceptance in a jovial voice. "A woman in the kitchen has my heartfelt appreciation, and my appetite isn't far behind. I'm starving. Will we be eating anytime soon? The smell is killing me." He closed his eyes and took an exaggerated breath to savor the aroma and smacked his lips, leaving Meredith to roll her eyes in disgust. The pair certainly bore out the saying, "Opposites attract."

"Maybe a couple hours," Zita said, "if Mr. Judd, he carves the turkey on time." Zita looked at Bob as if she liked him, and Katie was inclined to do the same.

Unlike his wife, Bob's ruddy face displayed dimples on his cheeks that winked and eyes that sparkled when he spoke. His thinning hair, shiny bald pate, and rotund body added to his mischievous persona. With a cap and white beard, he'd make the perfect Santa Claus.

"I'll make sure he does," Bob said. "It's a pleasure to finally meet you, Katie. I didn't expect to see you working in the kitchen. I've heard all sorts of tales about you, and I confess, I couldn't wait to get here and see you for myself."

"I'm sure everything you've been told is true," Katie responded with a tight smile. "Family members tend to support one another. If you'll excuse me, I'll be leaving soon. I need to get dressed for dinner." She hung the apron on a peg by the door. "I hope to see more of you during your stay. We can trade war stories, if you like."

Judd no longer looked amused. She brushed by him as she went out of the back door.

"I say, old man, where's she going?" Katie heard Bob ask before the door closed.

Meredith and Bob stayed several days. Meredith spent time in the office with Judd, and Bob read or watched television in the parlor. Dori played the piano for him and taught him Chopsticks. He was patient with her, and Katie asked him if they had children.

"Yes, we have two, a son and a daughter. They live in Louisiana. Junior is a CPA in Baton Rouge, and Audrey lives in Slidell. She teaches second grade.

"Now, tell me about your family. I believe Judd said they live in Shreveport."

Katie sat down, and they exchanged family stories. Bob was easy to like. He didn't ask awkward questions about her stay at Corazon, and she was grateful. He talked about history, art, and their travels.

By the third day, Meredith loosened up and joined their conversations. Judd sat back and listened. He wasn't as close to Meredith as he was to Merit and their conversations were stilted, more formal. He and Bob seemed to get along just fine.

Meredith and Bob left Corazon in a better mood than when they arrived, and Katie relaxed and breathed a sigh of relief.

CHAPTER THIRTY-SIX

Katie procrastinated until the *Fete de Noel* was days away. She had to consciously stop chewing her cuticles, a nervous habit she thought cured. Katie dreaded the thought of shopping for a suitable ensemble to wear at the formal event. She needed to find someone in town to do her hair and a manicure, luxuries she had done without over the years. She opened the phone book, ran her finger down the list of salons, and made an appointment.

Formal affairs left Katie feeling inadequate. Her mother had helped her select a prom dress her senior year. She remembered thinking she looked good in the rose satin gown. Her mother supplied the finishing touches and called her Rose Red after a fairy tale princess.

Swallowing her pride, Katie called Merit Stetson and asked her for help. The call took a while to get through.

Merit encouraged her to come by Stetson's in Palm Beach. "I'm so glad you phoned, Katie. I was hoping to see you again. We would be honored to help you find a gown for the *Fete de Noel*."

"Will you be going to the gala?"

"I wouldn't miss it," Merit said, setting a date and time that included lunch. She also gave Katie her personal cell phone number for future calls.

Stetson's Department Store, an imposing structure, straddled an entire block of Worth Avenue. Mannequins in the artistically appointed windows wore fashionable outfits for the season.

Katie's heart hammered as she walked inside and gaped at the gorgeous Christmas decorations. Huge golden deer seemed to leap across the space above the brass railed balcony. Wreaths of frosted red and white poinsettias enhanced with greenery surrounded their necks, and gold streamers curled behind. Every department shone with unique and festive seasonal displays. Christmas music played softly in the background.

Katie took the escalator to the third floor and approached the executive offices. She gave her name to the tastefully dressed receptionist, who stood with deferential demeanor and a gracious smile. The nameplate on her desk read Callista Gordon.

"Ms. Stetson is expecting you. Please come this way." She led Katie through a private waiting room, which gave an impression of understated opulence with its leather seating, oriental carpet, and a gas fireplace.

Merit stood behind a massive, polished mahogany desk with a patina only acquired by age. She came around and extended her hand. "You're a welcome sight this morning. I'm so glad you called. Have a seat." Merit settled into a chair next to her. "Would you like some refreshment? Callie has an assortment of beverages from hot tea to diet drinks."

The receptionist listed the offerings, and Katie chose water with lemon.

"Now, tell me how everything is going at Corazon, and please don't stint on details." Merit looked elegant in a burgundy gabardine suit with black grosgrain piping. Her hair swept back and held with a black velvet bow gave her a chic business look. She crossed her legs and leaned forward as if to catch every word.

Katie blushed. Even dressed in her best Sunday outfit, she looked like the Country Mouse visiting the city. She recounted the Fall Festival and the pumpkin painting party. She explained Judd's involvement in both events.

"I'm impressed. You're drawing my favorite cousin out of his self-imposed seclusion. Splendid! Judd used to enjoy travel, adventure, and the outdoors. Rita managed to suck all she could from their marriage, and she took his fun-loving, good-natured optimism with her."

"I believe Dori is the catalyst. She hungers for Judd's attention, and he basks in her adoration. She'll stay on at Corazon."

"What about you? Will you also be staying?" Merit's sincere question contained no rancor.

Her concerned interest hit a tender spot and Katie's eyes misted. Embarrassed by an emotional revelation, she looked down. "No, I don't think that's going to happen. Judd is too stubborn, maybe too proud to admit J.D. was right. His grandfather tried to make amends in his last five years. I'll really miss Dori though. I love the child."

"And the man," Merit interjected. She placed a hand on Katie's folded one and squeezed her support.

Katie looked up at Merit not quite believing this accomplished business woman cared.

Merit retrieved a tissue from a desk drawer and handed it to her. "I want Judd to have a complete life, free from J.D.'s cynicism and the massive burden of responsibility he placed on Judd's shoulders. The family has discussed ways to move forward and give him some time to enjoy life again. Even his father has offered to help." She ran her hands briskly down her skirt. "It's a hard sell. Judd feels responsible for everyone."

Callie returned with a tray and the beverages. She handed Katie a napkin and a crystal goblet of water, poured Merit's tea into a china cup, and left the room.

Merit stirred in a teaspoon of sugar with a silver spoon. "Judd and I had some interesting discussions while I was at Corazon." She folded her napkin and continued. "He has feelings for you. I heard it in his voice whenever your name was mentioned, which was often. I don't believe he'll let you go."

Katie's heart swelled with hope, but she knew wanting something and committing to it were two different things. "I'm afraid the checks we received this week have set Judd back on square one. He's been in a dark mood the past few days."

"Possibly," Merit said. "Judd, like J.D, has to feel in control. Stay the course, Katie. He's beginning to melt, and that's saying a lot. Is Judd bringing you to the gala?"

"No, I'm going with Luke Albritton, a man I met at church."

"Humm, the young man pictured with you in the Society section of the newspaper?"

"Yes, he's a good friend."

"I wondered. When I heard Judd sent a reservation for two, I knew something was happening. He hasn't attended a gala since Rita left him. Is he taking Hellacious Helene?"

Katie swallowed the smile forming at Merit's appellation. "Yes. He committed after he found out Luke was taking me. Helene is feeling her power."

"Helene came last week to be fitted for a gown. She put everyone off with her demands and waved Judd's credit card in several departments to let everyone know of her important connection. He's too smart now to fall for her machinations ... I hope," she added softly.

"How did you hear Judd was attending?"

"I'm actually on the Board. You'll sit at our table, of course, unless Mr. Albritton has asked for a special seating arrangement. Now, let's go up to Fantasia and see what wonders Nadine can do for you."

Upstairs in *Fantasia,* The Formal Department, Merit introduced Katie to Ms. Nadine Decatur, a dignified, white-haired lady dressed in a conservative, gray suit with pearl buttons and accessories. "Nadine, we want Ms. Mulholland outfitted for the *Fete de Noel.* I believe she's lovely enough to wear a simple, sleek look in a color to bring out the gold in her eyes."

Merit turned to Katie. "Nadine is our treasure. She has the eye of an artist and the instinct of a couturier. I leave you in capable hands. When you are finished here, we'll go to lunch if you have time. She looked back before leaving. "Thank you, Nadine. I know I can count on your expertise."

After Merit left, Nadine commented on her mentor. "Ms. Stetson rarely gives her personal attention to clientele. You are special indeed. Turn around and let me see where to begin."

Several hours sped by while Nadine worked miracles. She not only recommended her choice of color and the gown but had all of the accessories from shoes to jewelry delivered to the private dressing room. Triple mirrors reflected a woman Katie had no idea existed.

"Magnificent" Nadine said as she turned Katie around. "You have the looks and figure designers can only dream about. The dress is made for you. Heads will be turning, I guarantee. Now, let us talk about cosmetics and how to wear your hair."

Nadine introduced Katie to Lola, who chose her cosmetics and gave her tips on their proper use. They included creams and moisturizers for her skin.

Katie left for lunch with Merit a couple of thousand dollars lighter, but definitely worth every penny. "I feel like Cinderella," she shared and thanked her mentor effusively for her help.

"I'm looking forward to seeing the results," Merit said.

CHAPTER THIRTY-SEVEN

The Saturday of the Fete de Noel, Katie had a manicure and her hair styled by Abby in a local salon. She could hardly contain her excitement.

Katie dressed at the house because she wanted to luxuriate in a magnolia-scented bubble bath. Dori lay on her stomach across the bed, watching Katie's metamorphic change as she put the finishing touches on her face and donned the gown. "I wish I could go. Why do I have to grow up before I can do fun things?"

"Dori, you'll be grown before you know it. Enjoy youth while you can. Besides, you have to save something to look forward to when you reach adulthood."

"Yeah, but it's so slow." With a sigh she said, "I wish I had my crown here, so you could wear it."

Katie gathered her clutch and wrap before the two walked down the stairs. "Thank you for the thought. You have a good heart, Dori."

Judd met them as they reached the bottom step. His eyes widened and his mouth pursed, expelling a held breath like a "whooo".

Katie stunned in a sleek, amber taffeta sheath gown. A burnt sienna accent border crossed the top of her bust line gathering at one shoulder and leaving the other bare. She pivoted around. The gown exposed her long neck, one creamy shoulder and her back. The dress hugged her figure, and his immediate thought was inappropriate for the occasion. *I'd love to taste every inch of you.* Her hair styled back in a chignon at her nape registered understated chic. Judd remembered burying his hands in that glorious hair and the urge to take out the pins stimulated thoughts best shelved. Her only jewelry was a simple gold and topaz necklace with matching earrings.

"Isn't she beautiful!" Dori exclaimed. "Like a princess."

Judd was speechless as he tried to curb his thoughts, unlike the suave playboy the publicity rags portrayed him.

"Well, do I pass muster?" Katie asked, turning around again and bringing him back to the present.

The carefully applied cosmetics brought out her features and her golden eyes mesmerized him. *Is this the same girl who runs around the ranch in jeans and a ponytail?* "You look ... fantastic!" He struggled to bring the right word out. *Luscious, Desirable. Whoa! Not advisable.*

Judd was saved by crunching gravel, heralding the arrival of Luke, who bounded up the steps and arrived with a grin on his face. He had no trouble relaying his thoughts.

"You look incredible! I'm completely captivated." He took her hand and kissed it.

Dori giggled in delight, and they laughed when she pulled Katie down and kissed her cheek saying, "You know what happens at midnight?"

Luke escorted her outside and helped her get into his black Lexus.

The gala was held in the Guinevere Ballroom at the Age of Camelot Hotel. The decorations sparkled their gold and silver magic. Adorned Christmas trees donated by various organizations to be auctioned ringed three sides of the room.

Luke and Katie were escorted to the Stetson table where Merit, who was dressed in winter white, greeted her. "You look fabulous, like you stepped out of Vogue." And then she whispered mysteriously, "I can't wait until the family sees you."

Family?

Introductions were made. The distinguished gentleman with Merit, Michael Corinth, was also a member of the Gala Board and an executive at Stetson's.

Merit took Katie's arm and moved her away from Luke. "Handsome devil," she said, eying Luke. She then said, "I'm so sorry, but I didn't really have a choice, unless I wanted a scene. Adrienne and Max called last minute, and I had to make other arrangements for a couple of guests to accommodate family at our table. Just wait until Adrienne sees Helene with Judd. I'm expecting fireworks."

Katie turned to Luke to bring him into the conversation. "We can sit at another table. Believe me, we don't mind."

"Oh no, you will lend our table some stability," Merit said, "and you can't deny me the pleasure of seeing their faces when they realize your identity." She spoke to Luke. "I'm impressed with your involvement in the community. Maybe we'll have time to talk about several projects later."

Katie and Luke walked to the display of upscale offerings for the silent auction. They both wrote bids on several and returned to their table as the program started.

Judd and Helene arrived after the welcoming speech, and his parents arrived a few minutes later. Helene wore an eye-popping scarlet dress with a plunging neckline. Adrienne wore a dress of a similar hue with a plunging back. Katie couldn't help but hide her smile at the similarity between the two women.

Adrienne sailed forward and addressed Merit. "Words cannot express how appreciative we are that you found a place for us at the Stetson table. Aren't we Max?"

Max nodded and embraced Merit.

Merit smiled crookedly, reminding Katie of Judd. "We couldn't ignore your generous check. Thank you, Max. You've always come through for us."

Max, who had hung back, his eyes down, looked up sheepishly. "Good of you to mention it, Merit. It's for a good cause."

Merit made the introductions and said, "You remember Katie Mulholland, I expect?"

Adrienne, whose sharp eyes were visually cutting Helene to pieces, moved her attention to Katie.

Max smiled at Katie appreciatively and said to Adrienne, "Close your mouth before you say something you'll regret."

Adrienne had no intention of being silent. "My god, you're *that* girl? Well, you've certainly made good use of Stetson money."

Luke found and clasped Katie's hand under the table. She didn't flinch or wait to be defended. "I have no need of Stetson money. Some wise person once said, 'True happiness is wanting what you already have.' I'm happy. Are you happy, Adrienne?"

Adrienne clamped her mouth closed, and Judd looked at Katie with new respect. When had anyone bested his mother? *Katie has backbone. Her fire tempered by restraint. Unusual for a person her age.* The thought occurred to him that Katie, unlike Helene, had not turned in a single receipt for any shopping for herself, Dori, or the cabin. Mike had told him Katie didn't use the company gas for her vehicle, and he realized she must be using her own funds.

Katie faced Luke, apologetic and appalled by her audacity. He squeezed her hand and leaned over to kiss her cheek. "Well done," he murmured in her ear. "Is the dragon lady Judd's mother?"

Katie nodded. "Very perceptive of you," She refused to look in Judd's direction.

"For the first time, I feel sorry for Judd. What a cross to bear!" Luke said.

Merit ate her salad, keeping her head down, so no one could divine her thoughts, and Adrienne looked astonished and peeved. The lines between her eyes furrowed and her mouth pursed as if she tasted acid. The dinner progressed mostly in silence.

Michael spoke with Merit throughout the meal, their words indiscernible. Katie wondered if their relationship went beyond the business.

The emcee announced the Christmas tree auction would follow dessert and to take time for a closer inspection of the trees. "Be sure to update your bids on the silent auction. We'll be closing the bidding in ten minutes.

Katie spoke to Luke. "I'd like to check out the trees."

Luke rose, pulled out her chair, and said, "I'd like to get a look at them myself."

They inspected each tree. One of the smaller, live trees had traditional, old-fashioned, handmade ornaments that stole Katie's heart. "I want this one. A lot of love has gone into these." She fingered a hand sewn angel. "I'm going to bid on this one for the cabin, even though I'm spending Christmas with my family in Louisiana." She read the card, "Made by the girls at Sutter's Home."

"Sutter's Home is for girls who have emotional problems following a traumatic experience or an unplanned pregnancy," Luke told her.

Dessert had been served while they were gone. Unlike the other women at the table, Katie enjoyed eating her rich, chocolate cheesecake topped with cherries.

Helene leaned forward and spoke to Katie across Luke's plate. "You look good. May I ask where you found the gown?"

"At Stetson's of Palm Beach," Katie said proudly. "Nadine is incredible. I'm sure you must have met her."

"Yes, I remember her." Helene murmured without elaborating.

The emcee returned, and bidding on the trees began. The bids started at five-hundred dollars, and the first four artificial trees brought seven-hundred to eleven-hundred dollars each. A couple of them were laden with ornaments Katie suspected cost much more. Her tree came up, and Katie opened the bidding.

"I have a bid of five-hundred from the vision in gold. Do I hear six?"

When the price reached one-thousand, Katie sighed and said, "That's a little over my budget." A bid of eleven-hundred followed.

Luke raised his hand and shouted out, "Twenty-five-hundred."

The emcee beamed and became enthused. "Thank you, Mr. Albritton. You understand what this night is all about. I have twenty-five-hundred, do I hear twenty-six?"

Luke said, "Looks like it's yours, Katie."

Impulsively, she threw her arms around Luke's neck and hugged him.

"Going twice," was being called by the auctioneer.

Katie gasped when Judd raised his hand and shouted, "Five-thousand."

The emcee and those sitting at the table were stunned.

Heads turned, looking for the bidder.

"Thank you, Mr. Stetson!"

No bids followed, and the emcee beamed and said, "Well now, I think we started the bidding too low. We'll now start the bidding at one-thousand."

Helene was clapping and jumping in her chair. "Thank you," she said, turning Judd's face with her hands and kissing him on the mouth.

Judd said quietly, "I'm sorry if you were misled, Helene, but the tree is my Christmas gift to Katie."

Humiliated, Helene excused herself and left the table with as much dignity as she could salvage.

Luke leaned across the seat she vacated, his hand extended to Judd. "Good job! I knew you had a heart," his tone good-natured and sincere.

Judd took his hand. "I'll try to take that as a compliment." He gazed at a stunned Katie, her blush unmistakable. Sure she wouldn't run around and hug his neck, Judd said, "I'll claim a dance with you later."

"Well, that should set tongues wagging," Merit interjected. "I knew there was a reason why you were my favorite cousin."

Adrienne gaped and Max again admonished her. "Close your mouth and look pleased." He smiled at Judd, "I'm proud of you, Son."

Judd looked at his father as if he hadn't seen him before this moment.

Katie knew the comment was precious to Judd. She hurt for the years they had lost.

When the last tree sold, envelopes were handed to the winners of the silent auction. Everyone at the table received one, except Helene, Judd, and Katie.

A lovely young woman, smartly dressed in a cerulean blue velvet gown with satin insets, stopped by the table, and the men stood.

"Pam," Luke said, his voice rasped when she hugged him.

"I just wanted to thank you for getting the ball rolling tonight, and I want to thank you, too, Mr. Stetson. Your bid was most generous, and we appreciate your support."

Judd nodded his acknowledgment.

Luke introduced Pamela Raulerson to guests at the table.

Pamela smiled at Katie. "I've heard a lot of nice things about you from my family. They attend the same church."

"Yes, I remember meeting them, and they're proud of the work you're doing. Thank you for volunteering to help with the gala. It's a huge success." Katie held out her hand. "I'm glad we had the opportunity to meet."

"Likewise and thank you," Pam responded taking her hand.

To Luke, Pam said, "I hope we won't continue to be strangers."

Her eyes held a wealth of sentiment translated into words, before walking away.

Katie was sure Luke noticed. *So this is the woman Luke has been in love with since his high school sophomore year. Looks can be deceiving, but I think she still has feelings for him.* "Pam seems to be a nice young woman. I believe someone told me you were in school together," Katie said.

Luke nodded as his eyes followed Pam through the crowd.

The host announced the five live auction trips were about to be bid. "After the live auction, you are free to dance and enjoy your evening. Thank you for coming tonight. If you were outbid and still want to contribute, we will be pleased to accept. See the registrar in the lobby. The Board extends its thanks for your generosity and hopes you've enjoyed the meal and festivity." Extended clapping followed.

Judd bid on and won a ski trip to Colorado.

Max said, "When did you take up skiing?"

"I decided tonight. I'm planning on taking Dori skiing over Spring Break. The trip is her birthday present. We'll learn together."

Helene had returned to the table, and her lips compressed at the announcement. She was not included.

Merit said, "I'm so glad you're taking time to have some fun, Judd."

Michael added, "You'll enjoy Breckenridge. The community has a lot of activities for children. If you have time, you and your daughter should try the dog sledding, my family's favorite activity."

"I'll remember that," Judd said and stood. He looked at Katie. "The music has begun. May I claim my dance?"

They joined others, and Judd took Katie in his arms and led her around the floor. She thought he looked handsome in his tux, and being held like this reminded her of their dance in the parking lot of the Blue Adagio, a lifetime ago. She closed her eyes and savored the memory.

"Ummm, you smell good," he said, his warm breath caressing her neck.

A *frisson* of delight rocketed through her pliant body. *Oh, Judd, why did I have to fall in love with you?* Not for the first time, she thought, *It's not fair.*

Feeling the tremor, Judd pulled Katie closer. "You're more than eye candy to me, Katie." Judd looked up to the ceiling, exasperated. *Why did you say it that way, you fool?*

His voice, deep and sexy, ignited a flight response, but she tamped it down. Katie nodded. "I know," she said, laying her head on his shoulder, believing he did care for her a little even if it was because Dori loved her … even if it was just to get her in his bed.

"Will you go skiing in Colorado with us?" The invitation came as a surprise.

Katie closed her eyes. *Temptation, your sting is killing me.* "I can't, Judd. My mom's fiftieth birthday will be celebrated during that time. Birthdays are big in the Mulholland family. I planned to go home during the break."

"Well, nutters!" Judd responded, eliciting a smile from her. "Maybe it's time to introduce me to the "golden" Christmas tree," he said when the dance ended. "I'll have to arrange for it to be delivered."

"Thank you for the tree," Katie said sincerely. "I'm sorry I haven't told you before now." She looked him in the eyes. "You have a heart, Judd, but you expend a lot of effort trying to hide it." She walked toward the trees, leaving him to follow.

What are she and Luke trying to tell me? Of course, I have a heart. Why do I feel like I'm missing something? He frowned.

His eyes focused on Katie's back and the feminine sway of her hips as she walked away. *And how long can you hang from the tree of temptation without falling?* The answer came unbidden. *With God all things are possible.* Judd stopped in his tracks. Where did that come from? *J.D.? Divine intervention? J.D., you old coot. You said that more than once.* He was beginning to like the old man. *Did I decide to go skiing because you did it?* The direction of this line of thinking needed to be addressed.

Luke was not at the table when they returned. Katie saw him dancing with Pam, and she had her arms wrapped around his neck, her long blond hair draped over his arm. Maybe, just maybe, they would become an item again. If they did, it would relieve some of the guilt Katie felt about not loving Luke to the extent he needed to be loved. She crossed her fingers in her lap, feeling foolish for the childish gesture.

Helene found her voice and said, "I'd like to dance." She looked around the table and Max, bless his heart, stood and said, "I'm up to it. Lead the way."

Adrienne's face reddened, and Katie thought she might smack him down, like she did at the reading of the Will. He had asked Adrienne to dance a couple of times, but she rebuffed the offer. Katie felt sorry for Max.

Judd rose and spoke to his mother. He extended his hand, "Would you care to dance with your son?"

Adrienne's face registered astonishment, and she slowly rose to her feet, her expression not quite believing, to precede him onto the dance floor.

Katie didn't know what Judd and his mother discussed, but Adrienne returned to the table with moist eyes and a mellowed attitude.

Luke danced several more times with Katie, and she said, "I like Pam. Do you think you might get back together?"

He stopped and looked down at her. "Someone has been telling you tales."

"Are they tales, Luke? I'm not an expert on love, but if there's something special between you two, it's worth pursuing. I'm thinking Pam dropped a hint."

Luke continued movement around the floor. "I'd given up hope, but Pam made the first move tonight, and you're right, I'm going to pursue her." He held her closer. "You're a wise and generous woman. I cherish our friendship and want it to continue. What say you, friend?"

"I wouldn't have it any other way," Katie said.

CHAPTER THIRTY-EIGHT

Christmas was only two weeks away. Katie planned to drive home next week to celebrate Christ's birth with her family in Louisiana.

Dori wanted to buy Karen and Hank Christmas presents for Katie to take with her, and Judd took her shopping at Palm Gardens. They spent the entire Saturday together. When they returned, their arms were loaded with bags and wrapped gifts. Dori giggled and ran upstairs with several of the bags saying, "You can't look, yet."

That night at dinner, Helene picked at her food and made several disparaging remarks about the workers. She brought up seeing Slim chew tobacco, a disgusting habit, Mike's problem with stuttering around her, and Zita's slowness in bringing their dinner. "That woman is lazy. Have you ever thought about hiring someone else?"

"No. Zita is competent, a good cook, and I can rely on her discretion," Judd said, his jaw hardening with Helene's rebuke.

"You know what Katie said?" Dori asked Helene.

Her eyes swung in Dori's direction. "No, what did Saint Katie say this time?"

"People who say things that aren't nice, aren't beautiful on the inside."

Katie cringed at Dori's pronouncement. She had no idea Dori would come out with something like this.

Helene erupted. She threw her napkin on the table. "I've had enough of your whining, little girl, and your hanging on Katie's every word. Tell Zita to *please* bring dinner to my room."

Dori stood. "I'm sorry, Aunt Helene. I shouldn't have said that." She looked at her dad and Katie, tears forming in her eyes. "I'm sorry."

If Helene heard Dori, she didn't acknowledge the apology.

Judd said, "Sit down, Dori. You've hurt your aunt's feelings. That wasn't a nice thing to say to her, even if it were true."

Dori hung her head. "She doesn't like me anymore."

"Of course, she likes you," Katie said. "Tonight, she was out of sorts and said things she didn't mean. We all do that sometimes."

"Look at me," Judd said, demanding Dori's attention. "Your Aunt Helene has been good to you over the years. She's always tried to do what is best for you, and I know she loves you."

Zita entered with the tray of food, and everyone was silent. She looked at the empty seat and the discarded napkin. "Miss Helene not having dinner?"

"Yes," Judd answered. "Helene wasn't feeling well and went to her room. She would appreciate it if you took hers up to her."

Zita nodded. "I hope she feel better soon."

"Thank you, Zita," Judd said. "We all hope that."

Dori hung her head, tears flowing down her cheeks. "I'm not hungry anymore." She covered her face with her hands crying. "Can I go?"

"You're excused," Judd said. "I hope you've learned a lesson. Words are important. Sometimes we need to think about things we say *before* we say them."

Judd watched his daughter as she ran from the room sobbing. Flashback conversations bombarded his memory. Words he had said to his mother and father, Rita, and J.D. cropped up unsolicited. Mired in his past, Judd said nothing as Katie left the table and followed Dori.

For the first time since he was a child, Judd felt helpless. His shoulders slumped as the memories hammered him. He had told his father and mother he hated them on more than one occasion. He blamed them when he didn't receive enough of their attention and love. Maybe they sent him away because he was hateful. The names he called his wife made him bow his head in shame. He had loved her once with an unquenchable passion, and he isolated her at Corazon, not listening to her pleas to move elsewhere. He drove her from Corazon as surely as his grandfather had driven his love out before him.

Oh Del, what have I done? His grandmother, Del, was the only person who had ever given him unconditional love. Judd's heart swelled with emotion as he thought of the good times she had planned for them. She always welcomed him with open arms and listened to him when he needed solace or advice. She tried to share her wisdom as he embarked on his course to build an empire of his own. His grandmother had told him, "Money will never bring you lasting happiness, Judd. Money won't hold you, comfort you, or warm you at night."

Judd thought of the words Katie said to his mother. "I have no need of Stetson money. True happiness is wanting what you already have. I'm happy." Katie had the wisdom he rejected for material things that didn't satisfy. *Dori makes me happy, and I criticized her.* They had had fun shopping today and looking at the Christmas decorations. Judd loved his daughter more than he ever imagined loving anyone.

Even J.D had not escaped Judd's scathing tongue, yet he seemed to let the vitriol go and tried to make amends in his last years. *I have to try and make amends.* Max popped into his mind. He had said, "I'm proud of you, Son," the last thing he expected his father to say.

He had asked his mother to dance, and she became emotional. Such little things swelled his heart, made him feel worthy. *Worthy?* That wasn't the word he sought. Scraping back his chair, he moved to check on Dori.

Katie stood halfway up the stairs and turned when she saw him. Putting a finger to her lips to silence him, she shook her head to slow him down.

Judd heard Dori's muffled voice between hiccoughing sobs saying, "I love you Aunt Helene. Please don't leave because I hurt you. I'm sorry. Please don't hate me."

Helene must have relented. "I don't hate you, Dori. I'll always love you and cherish the memories we made together. I said things I shouldn't have said because I'm not happy here, and you were right, they weren't pretty." A space of silence followed, and Katie imagined they hugged.

Zita entered the hallway with a tray of food. Judd motioned for her to return to the kitchen.

Helene spoke. "Dori, I'm not leaving because of what you said. My job here is finished. You don't need me now because you have your father to look after you, and I know he loves you. I need to go home and take care of business. I've been away too long. You can see me any time you want. You will come to visit, won't you?"

"Yes," Dori said, "Yes, yes, yes. I love you, Aunt Helene."

Katie backed down the stairs and Judd followed. They walked into the kitchen, and Judd told Zita she could take the tray to Helene.

"Dori puts me to shame," Judd told Katie. "I've said things to family members that were so much worse, and I'm castigating my daughter for her lapse."

"You have a daughter with a big heart. Dori loves you and Corazon. Helene was right. Her job here is finished. She'll be happier in Connecticut."

Judd nodded. "I've dreaded telling Helene she needed to go home. She's been with Dori a long time, and I didn't want to just tell her to leave after inviting her to stay."

Katie saw Judd's inner conflict registered on his face and in the hand he strafed through his hair and used to bracket his jaw as he thought of the ramifications.

His buffer was leaving, which left Katie exposed. She rubbed her arms to suppress a shiver as she realized when Helene left, Judd had a clear field to resume his seduction.

"I'm capable of caring for Dori," Judd said. "And right now, I need to talk with my daughter and tell her I've said things I regret. I'm going to try and follow her example."

"You're a good man, Judd Stetson. I believe you will. Go on. Dori needs reassurance from you."

When Judd left, Katie spooned food onto her plate and carried it to the microwave to heat. She was at once ravenous and relieved, but her legs wobbled. *Don't be a ninny. Dori's here.*

Katie puttered around the kitchen the following morning. She wanted to be here when Dori came downstairs. On Sundays, Zita always had the coffee pot ready to start, and Katie turned it on. As she reached for the cereal, she heard Helene enter the room, humming.

"You'll be pleased to know I'm going home as soon as I can get Judd to fly me back." Helene sat at the table, and Katie joined her.

"I can't say I'm surprised, but if you're implying I'm happy to be rid of you, you'd be wrong. We've had our moments, but I appreciate what you've done for Dori. She loves you, and I don't want you leaving and thinking she doesn't."

"I believe you. Dori and I had a talk last night, and she knows I'm not leaving because of her." She looked at Katie, a rueful smile on her face. "I'm leaving because Judd will never see me as anyone other than his wife's sister, and we know what he thinks of Rita. So, you win."

"The only winners are Judd and Dori. I'll be going home in May. Judd isn't looking for permanence, and I'm not the 'other woman' type." She rose as the coffee finished perking and poured two cups. Katie added milk to hers and a teaspoon of sugar to Helene's before setting the cups on the table.

Helene's eyes narrowed, her voice assuming a tart note. "I've seen how Judd looks at you. He'll marry you to keep Corazon intact. You're pretty enough, and you won't be an embarrassment to the Stetson family, certainly not a hardship for Judd."

Thinking about J.D., Helene's voice hardened. "Old J.D. had everything planned. What you can offer trumps any feelings I have for Judd. And Dori is the ace. She loves you and needs you. Judd sees that, too." Her eyes misted, and she ran her hand absently through her tousled strawberry blond hair.

Helene's words added salt to raw wounds, and Katie responded defensively. "I'll never settle for anything less than love, real love that comes with commitment. A merger is not in my future." She wanted to find strength in the words and believe them.

"If you say so, but you're deceiving yourself. If you can resist him, you're stronger than me. I'd settle for Judd in a heartbeat with or without love or commitment."

I have to resist him. If I give in, I'll never know how he really feels about me.

Helene stood and shook her head, her hair a swath of red gold swinging down her back. She had never looked more voluptuous and beautiful without makeup or pretense.

Hard to believe Judd foiled Helene's attempts at seduction.

"I'll be glad to get home and away from this infernal heat and the awful quiet. You have another five months. I'll be anxious to hear the end of the story." She added more coffee to her cup and left the room, her shoulders back and humming a tune.

CHAPTER THIRTY-NINE

Dori walked into the kitchen while Katie took the milk out of the refrigerator. She walked to Katie and wrapped her arms around her waist. "Aunt Helene is leaving," she said in a small voice.

"She told me, and you shouldn't feel responsible. Helene told me she was not happy here, and she wanted to go home." Katie smoothed Dori's hair. "Your aunt loves you and will miss you."

The little girl nodded her head against her, the scene Judd saw as he entered the kitchen. He stopped a moment and said good-naturedly, "Good morning, ladies. What's for breakfast?"

Dori hurried to hug her daddy. "Katie is having cereal."

"How about pancakes?" Judd asked. "I know how to read the instructions, but we have to check the pantry to see if we have the mix. Why don't you check, pumpkin?"

She left them to look for the mix.

"What are your plans for the day?" Judd was dressed in jeans and a khaki shirt, with the sleeves rolled to his elbows. His tanned arms with a sprinkling of black hair looked muscular, defined by work and exercise. A silver watch circled one wrist and his hands ...

Katie turned away while she still could. She had on pajamas and a robe, but she felt undressed. She certainly didn't need to dwell on Judd's physical attributes. "I'm going to Sunday School and Church."

"Are you still meeting Luke?"

"He'll probably attend. He usually does. Why?"

"Just curious. He hasn't been around all week and I thought..."

"I found the mix, Daddy," Dori interrupted, handing him the box, a grin of accomplishment on her face.

"Good job." He read the side of the box. "We're going to need an egg and some milk."

Dori ran to the refrigerator to get the ingredients and asked, "Can I mix it?"

"Yes, you *may*," he replied, emphasizing the correct use of the word. Judd opened a cabinet, took out a bowl, and cracked the egg into it. He handed the measuring cup for the milk to Dori and poured the correct amount.

Dori retrieved the whisk from the utensil drawer and pulled a chair over to stand on. "Do you remember us making the cobblers?" She answered herself before Katie spoke. "I do. We can do it again and give them to people. Remember when Slim said he had died and gone to heaven after eating the one we gave him?"

Katie smiled, amused at Dori's enthusiasm. She had blossomed with her dad's attention. "We'll have to wait a while until some fruit comes into season. Frozen fruit is okay, but fresh tastes better."

"I vote you make another cobbler as soon as possible." Judd turned on the stove, took out the skillet, and added olive oil.

Katie finished her cereal, rinsed her bowl, and put it in the dishwasher.

"Would you like a pancake?" Judd asked as she poured a fresh cup of coffee.

"Not this morning. Thanks. The cereal filled me up, and this is my second cup. I need to get ready for church. Are you going with me today?" she asked Dori.

Judd watched Dori deliberate her answer and knew she probably wanted to see what he was doing. "You haven't asked me if I want to go?" he said to Katie.

Judd's eyebrow raised as a mischievous smile pulled wickedly at his lips.

He watched Katie's face register surprise as she tried to gauge his ulterior motive. *Yes, I do have one, Little Red Riding Hood.*

"You want to go to church? Really?"

"I want to be with you and Dori." The minute Judd said the words, he knew they were true. If Katie said they were going to go to a poetry reading, he would have wanted to go with them.

Dori clapped her hands. "You're going to love it. Bobbie Jean and

I are in the same class. You'll have to go to a grown-up class, but I'll sit with you in church."

"They have a men's class you might like," Katie said. "You already know Luke and a couple of the fathers that came to the Pumpkin Party."

Whatever it takes. "Sounds like a plan. When do we leave?" Judd decided one morning couldn't be too bad.

Katie gave them the time and left to get ready, her head reeling with questions. *Why is Judd going to church? Has his strategy changed? Is Judd having second thoughts about J.D.?*

Luke waited for Katie and Dori in the church parking lot. When he saw Judd, he grinned and came over to shake hands and welcome him. "I'm glad to see you this morning. Will you be staying for church?"

"I'm sure we will. Katie usually stays, and I'm with her this morning."

Since Judd didn't include Dori, Katie thought he was making a point. "He's with us this morning," she said.

Luke's grin widened. "You couldn't be in better company. Pam is coming to church today. Maybe afterwards we can all go out for a bite to eat together."

"I'm happy for you, Luke." Katie had hoped Luke would see Pam again. She looked at Judd. "Do we have plans after church?"

Judd nodded. "We'll join you for lunch," he told Luke. "Thanks for the invitation."

"Great! You're welcome to visit the young adult men's class with me. Just so you know, some of the men are eighty years young. You won't feel out of place."

Ha. Ha. Luke knows how to get under my skin. "I certainly hope not. I'm not quite half that old," Judd returned with a smile. *So Luke is meeting Pam, and Katie doesn't seem to mind. Interesting. Things are looking up.*

Dori hugged her daddy. "See you later." She waved to Bobbie Jean and ran toward her.

They met again after Sunday School when the church bell dismissed the classes. As Katie walked to the front entrance of the church, she saw Judd standing on the front steps. He was talking to some of the other parents he had met. Luke was nowhere in sight. Dori hung from the monkey bars on the playground, but she ran to Katie when she saw her, and they walked up the steps together.

Judd said his farewells and followed Katie and Dori into the sanctuary. They sat toward the back, and Katie saw Luke sitting with Pam and her parents, the Raulersons.

Mrs. Albritton looked around, spotted Katie, and smiled when she saw Judd with her. *Yes, in a Utopian world, everything worked out ideally.* Katie had no illusions about a happy ending, but it was nice to sit here like a family and dream about it. She sighed and Judd looked at her. The attention brought her thoughts back to earth. His presence made it difficult to concentrate on the announcements, the music, and the sermon. Her mind kept wandering back to Judd's new strategy and how she needed to strengthen her resolve to counteract his next siege, which was inevitable when Helene left.

Judd looked around the sanctuary, noting the architecture, the exquisite stained glass windows, and the few members of the congregation he knew. He recognized faces of business people he had met, but the names escaped him. He had had a pleasant conversation with a couple of fathers he met at the Pumpkin Party, as Katie called it, and met a newly-minted young doctor setting up a pediatric practice in Okeechobee.

Dori's hand moved to cover Judd's, but her attention was elsewhere.

Judd looked down, noting the smooth perfection of skin covering the delicate network of veins, which carried the force of life. He pictured those long fingers, nails covered in light pink polish, playing the keys of the piano. Before long, Dori would be grown, and he visualized walking a radiant bride down the aisle. His heart swelled with the knowledge he had fathered this wonderful, talented being. Stetson blood coursed through her veins. Judd's eyes watered as he felt the inner stirrings of a love like no other. Dori's fingers splayed across his knuckles, curling inward as she leaned against him. Katie noticed, and Judd turned his head, not wanting her to see his vulnerability.

The minister was speaking about another child, one prophesized in the Old Testament, who would one day be the Messiah. He reiterated that to be a prophet, you had to hear God's voice and most importantly understand, to foretell events, and to be one hundred per cent correct while you lived. If you were ninety-nine percent correct, you were stoned as a false prophet. Isaiah was one-hundred percent correct during his lifetime, and he lived to be an old man. So what he foretold of future events carried weight. The minister read passages from Daniel, Isaiah, Micah, Zechariah, and also from Psalms, foretelling the birth of the Messiah, his life, and death. He would be a righteous man, rejected by men and suffering abuse, a man who would die for the iniquity of mankind.

Judd was not familiar with the Bible, but he knew something of the Christmas and Easter stories he had heard while growing up. These stories were celebrated yearly. The Old Testament prophesies were new territory, and like piecing together a puzzle, later New Testament events began to come together in his mind. He picked up the church bulletin. The minister's name was Tom Dickon. Judd was impressed by the man's eloquence in describing the unfolding history upon which Christianity was based. He read the passages verbatim and left the pulpit to speak directly to the congregation, his faith in the written Word unshaken, undiluted. You either believed the Word or you didn't. Judd imagined a giant, invisible finger pointed at him.

J.D. believed, and that belief changed his life. Seeing the new J.D. was a powerful testimony. Judd's resistance stemmed from the old man's gall and the implacable use of his Last Will and Testament to direct Judd's future. He glanced at Katie. J. D. planned for him to love this woman, marry her, and complete his family. *Not going to happen, Old Man. I'm older, and I've learned from my mistakes. My future is mine to determine, no matter how good the package looks.* Judd had no doubt Katie would be his in the end. She would stay for Dori and the inheritance she claimed she didn't want. *I'll never remarry, J. D. You lose.* Dori squeezed his hand and brought him back to the minister's Benediction.

~

Katie curled into the old recliner as she remembered the wonder of being held in Judd's arms at the gala. He had looked at her with admiration and a possessiveness that weakened her knees. He cared about her. "You're more than eye candy to me, Katie." She almost laughed out loud at the memory. His unplanned, verbal comment caught him by surprise and prodded her to take note of his train of thought. *Be careful girl, you're on thin ice.*

The gala would forever be Katie's Cinderella moment, a time when an ordinary girl morphed into a desirable woman, who attracted the Prince and danced in his arms. This fledgling confidence she attributed to God's favor, and she marveled at His blessings. Katie trembled at the thought of what the future might hold and quailed at what might not be.

Don't be a ninny, she chided herself. *You're a survivor. Just be you.* Katie strengthened her resolve to be true to herself.

Katie's mind turned to the dinner after church yesterday. They met Luke and Pam at Sal's Seafood Place and conversed as old friends do. Dori had looked confused at first, but she took the situation in stride. She livened the conversation with ranch stories and told Pam about Dori's Mound and how her father put her on his map. "He's getting a teacher to come out and tell us who lived there."

"An archaeologist, Dori. Archaeologists study what man has left behind over time," Judd told her. "I called Dr. Jan Mazore in Broward County to check our sites in January," he informed all at the table.

"Just think, Dori," Luke said, "hundreds of years from now, an archaeologist might dig up things from your bedroom. Those artifacts will tell him who probably used the space."

"I'll be famous again," Dori said, pumping her arm, and they all laughed.

Pam did not appear to be intimidated by Judd's presence or of Katie's. She must have heard that Luke was seeing someone and had to be curious. If so, her interest wasn't conspicuous. She spoke with confidence and lavished attention on Luke, who beamed, and at one point, held her hand.

Judd had let Luke know at the gala, he was not Katie's only contender. Katie wondered what Judd was thinking now, seeing Pam and Luke together. *Judd appeared to like Pam. He had met her at the gala, of course. What does he think about Luke's obvious interest in Pam now?* He seemed to relax, enjoy the meal, and didn't argue when Luke took the tab.

The little Christmas tree lights twinkled among the hand-sewn angels, their presence a sign she was not alone. Colorfully wrapped presents to Dori, Judd, Zita and Isabel rested below on the burlap tree skirt decorated with appliquéd angels. Even Jammer rated a gift. She had wrapped a red ribbon around a large dog bone and attached it to a box of treats.

Katie sat in the Bentley rocker as she often did remembering family. She was especially proud of Dori's gifts. She had met an old-timer named Emmitt Parker, who made rawhide whips for the cowboys. She commissioned three shorter, child-length whips for Dori, Karen, and Hank. They would have fun cracking them like cowmen, who used the sound the whip made to move the herd. She also ordered Dori a piano book of music for beginners and a CD player with a microphone to use in her impromptu programs.

She purchased Zita and Isabel colorful silk scarves and enclosed a gift card in each box. Judd's gift was harder. *What do you get a man who has everything he needs?* Katie settled on a midnight blue, down vest Judd could use on the ski trip or to cover his flannel shirts on cold days. She added a pair of thermal gloves in the same color.

Katie found Helene's favorite perfume in a local store and enclosed the offering in the gold-beaded clutch she had carried to the gala. Helene mentioned liking the purse several times, so she gave it as a gift to Helene before she left. Katie had been surprised when Helene said, "I hope Judd comes to his senses and realizes you are what he and Dori needs." She held out her hand and Katie took it. "I harbor no hard feelings," Helene said, "I've enjoyed meeting someone who doesn't compromise, a rare thing these days." She took her leave and returned a few minutes later with her gift for Katie, a book of Robert Frost poems. "He's one of my favorite poets," she told Katie.

Judd was flying Helene to Connecticut tomorrow. He told them he would stay in the northeast several days on business. He offered to fly Katie to Shreveport, but she said she wanted to drive. He was not happy about her decision, but what could he do? She would leave

Saturday, the day after Dori's last day of school before Christmas vacation and the day Judd returned.

That evening, Judd, Katie, Dori, and Helene met in the parlor for one last program. Dori played several songs on the piano. The rest of them sang along to Jesus Loves me, Twinkle, Twinkle Little Star, and Amazing Grace. Helene asked Dori to show her how to play Chopsticks, and Dori loved being the teacher. Helene did a credible rendition and the evening ended when she took her bow and received a standing ovation.

CHAPTER FORTY

Friday was a half day at school for Dori, so Katie picked her up and drove to Dori's favorite pizza parlor for lunch. They sat at a table by the window and watched the traffic move slowly down the highway. Dori seemed preoccupied and looked indifferently at the newly arrived extra-cheese pizza.

Katie placed a slice of pizza on Dori's plate and picked up a second piece by the crust. The rich taste of Italian tomato sauce and warm, melted cheese caused Katie to close her eyes and say, "Ummm. I feel the comfort all the way to my toes."

"When are you coming home?" Dori asked.

The question, direct and loaded with wistful thought, opened her eyes to another reality. Katie considered her words. 'Home' sounded permanent. She liked the sound, but she shouldn't take her stay for granted.

"I'll be back a few days into January. Probably before you're back in school."

Dori nodded and used her fingers to pick up her slice, holding it up by the crust to get the cheese that began to slide off the tip. "Are you staying forever?"

"Forever?" This child was precocious. Katie knew what she was asking, but she didn't have an answer. "We never know what the future holds. Forever is a long time." How much did Dori know about the Will and her required stay at Corazon for one year?

"You're growing up, and one day you'll leave home, go off to college, marry someone special, and have a family of your own."

"I'm coming back, so Daddy won't be by himself. Corazon is where I want to live forever."

"You have a good heart, Dori. Corazon is your home as long as you want."

Dori dropped the pizza slice on her plate and looked at her with welling eyes. "You're going to leave me, aren't you?" She worried her lip as she waited for an answer.

Dori's plaintive voice touched the hollow place where Katie's heart had been torn from her body. Katie looked down unable to keep eye contact. "I won't be going anytime soon," she said and tried to sound positive. Katie swallowed the lump growing in in her throat. Her answer sounded lame in her own ears.

Dori left her chair and ran around the table to hug her. "Please don't leave me, Katie. I love you."

Katie put her hand on Dori's head and smoothed down her hair. "I know, sweetheart. I love you, too." How could she leave Corazon in five months? She loved this child as if she were her own. "Whatever happens, we'll see each other. I promise. It won't be forever."

Setting Dori away from her, Katie looked into her eyes. "When we love someone, we hold the memory of them in our hearts and treasure it until we meet again."

"But I'll miss you." Tears ran down Dori's cheeks unchecked.

"And I'll miss you." What more could she say? "You know I love Hank and Karen, and I look forward to the times we get together. That's how it will be with us."

Dori nodded. "It won't be the same, but I'll see you. Daddy will take me, and maybe you can come back and stay with us sometime."

"Maybe." Katie swallowed hard, trying to keep emotion at bay. "But right now the pizza is getting cold, and pizza is one food that tastes better warm. Let's eat and think about how much fun you and your daddy are going to have this Christmas." Katie watched Dori return to her seat and pick up the discarded pizza slice. "He told me he has something very special picked out for you."

Dori's eyes lit up. "What, Katie. What is it?"

"If I told you, it wouldn't be a surprise. I guarantee you'll love it. How's that?" She watched as Dori finished the first slice and reached for another, the tears wiped, and the painful subject tabled for now. She marveled at children's resilience and forced herself to eat another slice of pizza. She buoyed her flagging spirit by thinking of joy coming with the puppy Judd had arranged for Dori's Christmas.

~

Katie packed the last of her presents and luggage in the trunk of her car. Tomorrow she would leave early in the morning to drive home for the holiday. She looked forward to a reunion with her parents and her sister Myra's family.

Inside the cabin, Katie took the ornaments off the Christmas tree and placed them in a special box she had purchased to store them. Tears formed as she remembered the gala, the auction, and being held in Judd's arms as they danced. She loved Judd, and her body ached with the knowledge she was leaving for two weeks without seeing him. How much worse would it be in May?

She sat back on her heels and spoke to the angel ornament in her palm. The little face looked down, eyes closed, wings folded at its side in an attitude of listening. "Why do I love Judd? Am I just attracted to a handsome face and his position of power?" She thought she had loved Gunnar for those very reasons. She concluded her feelings for Gunner weren't love, but pride because he had chosen her out of a lot of girls who would have fallen at his feet in adoration. She put off his amorous overtures because in her heart of hearts, she knew he wasn't the man she wanted as a life partner.

"We know how that relationship ended," she told the angel. "How could I have been so stupid?" Katie had only felt relief after she saw Gunnar for the last time. No, she felt more like she had escaped not only a bad choice but an unfulfilled marriage had it taken place.

Katie remembered her first meeting with Judd and smiled. She thought him a pompous ass, a Stetson with a privileged background and arrogant attitude, getting everything he wanted. Okay, so he was a handsome man, and she was attracted to his looks. At the Blue Adagio, Katie was drawn to the brief vulnerability he revealed. His kisses left her breathless, a heady emotion that left her wanting more.

Mr. Pickering had told her Judd's story and about the successful life he forged despite a dysfunctional family background and a tragic marriage. Judd's strength attracted her, as did his ability to overcome his past and continue to take on the yoke of Stetson Enterprises. She had felt the first stirrings of love before J.D.'s Will drove a nail into Judd's heart and left him saddled with a woman and a future his grandfather had chosen for him.

"Can love be born from such a mess, little angel? I wish you could tell me the end of the story."

She gently placed the angel with the others in the box and closed the lid. Standing, she folded the tree skirt, placed it in a pillowcase, and looked around for a place to store her treasures. They ended up under her bed.

CHAPTER FORTY-ONE

Katie had stopped by her apartment in Shreveport before going to her parent's home. She pulled back the curtains to filter in some light. The day was dreary, a study in black and white. Gray buildings sprouted in her district, uninteresting, without warmth or color. The temperature was cooler than the eighty degrees she had set on the thermostat before leaving. Cold weather outside helped, but the air inside smelled stale. Dust coated the furniture and the atmosphere oozed loneliness. How quickly unused space succumbed to neglect and disuse! Maybe her mother's efficient maid, Birgit, would have time to stop by and help her clean before she returned to the ranch.

Birgit came to her mother's house once a week, and she managed to sort the clutter, make the home presentable, and do the ironing. She had become an indispensable part of the family. Many times she came at night to babysit Myra and her. They enjoyed her tales of the Old Country, Denmark. The myths of Viking gods and the lore of Danes as they raided the northern coasts of Europe held them in thrall. Birgit said her Scandinavian name meant *strength*.

Katie sighed. *Lord, I need strength*. The pride of independence Katie once felt, no longer engaged her heart, leaving her feeling empty and depressed. She walked from room to room trying to recapture her former life before Corazon. The glass vase upside down in the drainer reminded her of Judd's peace offering, the red roses, and the magical evening at The Blue Adagio. His kisses. She closed her eyes, remembering, missing his touch, his voice, his presence. *Lord, I am so lost.*

Seven months had flown by since the night she fell under Judd's spell. So short a time in the scheme of things, yet it seemed much longer. Lifting the lid on the piano, Katie ran her fingers across the keys, uninspired. The walls seemed to close in on her until it became hard to breathe. She missed her daily forays into the outdoors and the vast expanse of prairie and hammocks. The birdsong, cricket orchestra chirping in unison was only broken by croaking frogs calling their mates, and the occasional grunt of an alligator.

She had no desire to stay here and closed the lid. Returning to this apartment after the freedom of exploring the ranch burdened her heart. Hurrying to the bedroom, she opened the closet and drawers, searching her wardrobe for a few winter garments to take back with her.

Locking the door of her apartment upon leaving became symbolic of the demarcation between her past and the unknown.

∽

Katie's parents welcomed her home. Their joy at seeing her again alleviated some of the pain she felt leaving Judd and Dori behind. Christmas in the Mulholland household celebrated the birth of Christ first and the joyful, holiday festivities followed.

A large, carved wooden crèche set, her parents bought during a trip to Israel, covered the table in the entrance hall, a reminder and focal point for family and visitors of the season's meaning. Katie rubbed each of the pieces, a yearly ritual, remembering its part in the Nativity story. She always marveled at the look and feel of the gold and sienna olive wood from the Holy Land. One day, she planned to make a trip to Old Jerusalem, the place her parents said was the most fascinating city on earth.

A ten foot blue spruce tree monopolized the den. The tree was surrounded by ornaments her parents collected on trips and those which were handmade by their children and grandchildren. Each had its own story. She picked up the replica of a birch bark canoe, loaded with camping items and two oars. The piece reminded Katie of the two weeks the family canoed in the Adirondacks, camping out when she was fourteen. The Laplander fur boots from Finland and the Dutch doll with wooden shoes from the Netherlands shared a box. Her parents told them about each ornament as it was placed on the tree, another tradition.

Several pieces had been handed down in the family, including the bisque angel which now topped the tree as the only adornment.

The tulle and satin skirts gracefully folded in the branches, her wings spread and her china hands lifting toward Heaven in praise. The wavy fall of golden hair and the beauty of her features never failed to fascinate. On closer inspection, Katie saw her father had also woven in the branches green cords of little white lights now circling the tree. When Myra and her family arrived tomorrow, they would decorate the tree together.

Katie loved this home built by her father's parents in the early 1920s. The wooden plank floors, open rooms, and the high beamed ceilings flooded Katie with memories of childhood. The house bordered the creeping urban landscape and was destined to be swallowed up in the future. The obvious path of destruction seemed unfair. She had played in the fields behind the house, picked fresh vegetables in the spring and fall, and helped her grandmother and mother fix dinner on special occasions. Her father's hothouse where he repotted and hybridized his orchids looked smaller than in year's past.

Katie's mother had taken out her grandmother's cookbook and planned a special meal for her return. The roast was tender and flavorful. Her father sautéed vegetables and creamed potatoes for the occasion. Katie made the salad. set the table, and served the iced tea.

The conversation at dinner was lively with her parents telling her about their adventures in Alaska. Katie could picture the vast landscapes devoid of human occupation, the majestic snow-covered mountain tops, and the rivers and streams which crisscrossed the state. They laughed and said the mosquito was the state bird, and they saw their share. They had close-up encounters with elk, moose, a black bear, and dozens of eagles going after the salmon fingerlings. Dungeness crabs, halibut, and salmon figured large in their menus, and Katie decided to save for a trip to Alaska one day. Her dad said if he were thirty years younger, he'd want to move to Alaska and pioneer. To that, her mother said, "I'm happy here, so I'm glad you are not thirty years younger."

The conversation turned to her circumstance in Florida, and they asked more questions than Katie was willing to answer. She mainly told them about the ranch, cattle, and groves. She told them about Dori, and skirted the issue of Judd altogether which increased their curiosity.

"Myra told us about some of what was going on, but she didn't say much about Judd Stetson except she liked him and Paul got along with him," her mother said.

"Hank and Karen certainly had a good time. They talked about the trip for weeks," her dad added. "Do you have plans for when the year is up?' he asked.

"I'll be returning to my old job, a whole lot wiser, and ready to get on with my life." She paused. "I've had an incredible time, and I've learned a lot about subjects I'd never considered. My main problem will be leaving Dori. I love that little girl, and I'm going to miss her." Katie's eyes misted as she spoke, and she saw her parent's anticipation as they waited for the rest of her future plans. When it wasn't forthcoming, her mother asked about Judd and the inheritance.

"I don't know the end of the story, Mom. I'm taking it one day at a time. Please let the issue rest for now."

They both nodded, but she could tell, this would come up again in another way, until they were satisfied with her answers.

~

The Hennessy family arrived a few days before Christmas, and the children's excitement added to the spirit of the occasion. They ate a light dinner, helped decorate the tree, and took turns adding the ornaments to the lower branches after their grandparents told them the story of each. The adults decorated the higher branches out of their reach.

Christmas music and songs piped throughout the house brought cheer and an occasional burst of spontaneous singing. Smells of baking bread, pumpkin pies, cookies, and dinner mingled with the fragrant aromas of fir and spruce coming from the Christmas tree and the garlands decorating the mantel and stair rail. The sights and smells brought back to Katie memories of Christmases past as new memories were made and stored.

On Christmas Eve the family would get together, share another delicious meal, and attend the church service together to hear again the story of the humble birth of the Christ Child. Afterwards, they would return to open Christmas gifts. The decorated Yule log, a tradition passed down through generations was lit as they sat around the den talking and watching the children enjoy their gifts. "The Cracker whips are not to be practiced inside," Katie told the children.

Myra tried unsuccessfully to get her alone and ply her with questions, but Katie successfully maneuvered to stay with the others, and the opportunity passed as it was time for them to leave.

Katie lay on the sofa in the dark, watching the leaping flames lick the logs, and hearing the crackle and pop they made in the hearth. One of her grandmother's quilts covered her legs as she contemplated her future.

What are Judd and Dori doing tonight? Do they miss me as much as I miss them? I've only been gone a week. Katie knew May would come in the blink of an eye. *What then?*

Why does love make me ache inside? The physical response of the body to an action, word, or thought mystified Katie. A Psalmist had written, "I am fearfully and wonderfully made," and to praise God. How could anyone believe the fragile intricacies of life were random?

The Yule Log still burned in the fireplace, a foundation for the fire they had enjoyed on Christmas Eve. Katie thought about passing traditions down in her own family as Myra was doing with hers. *What if I don't have a family?*

Katie would be twenty-six in July. Would it be enough to be an aunt and not a mother? Living alone stretched years ahead of her and did not give her peace. She knew there were good men like Luke, but would she settle for less than love to have a family? *There are worse things than being single.*

Luke. He had stopped by to see her at the cabin before she left. What a good friend he had been to her over the last five or six months! He shared the news he was going to propose to Pam on Christmas Eve, and he believed her answer would be positive. Katie had hugged him and wished Luke the best. She was genuinely happy for both of them.

Katie loved Luke like a brother, and even though she knew he would be a good husband and father, she wouldn't have married him. *Lord, I don't know what You have in store for me, but I have to believe it will be better than what I want for myself.* Her peace came in knowing He was in control.

CHAPTER FORTY-TWO

Katie returned to Corazon two days before school reopened after the Christmas and New Year holidays. She had enjoyed spending Christmas with her family, but she had longed to be back at the ranch with Judd and Dori. Homesick seemed a misnomer for what she felt now.

Katie pulled up next to the cabin to unload her luggage and gifts. Jammer greeted her with a wagging tail and welcoming yips. She patted his head and scratched behind his ears. He had been a faithful companion as she and Dori explored the ranch.

Dori came out of the house, holding her new puppy, all smiles and hugs. "I've missed you sooo much." She handed her the puppy, a brindle cur-mix, and hugged Katie's waist. "This is Scooby. Isn't he the cutest puppy you ever saw?"

Scooby wiggled upward in Katie's arms and tried to lick her face. Jammer danced around her, trying to reach the puppy. "No, Jammer. Down, dog," she said, turning away.

Judd left his office and walked to the car. "Welcome back," he said, smiling. "We've missed you." His smile looked genuine, and he sounded sincere. He was wearing the vest she had given him as a Christmas present, making his eyes look bluer.

Katie's hand went to her throat. She had on the gold necklace with gold cowboy boots. Katie knew Judd had helped Dori pick the gift. The boots were a reminder of her time spent on the ranch.

Katie remembered how she was met her first day at Corazon and compared it with this welcome seven months later. "Thank you," she said as she walked back to the trunk she had opened. *Don't just stand there and look all goo-goo-eyed at him.*

Judd reached for her luggage at the same time, and his hand folded over hers on the handle. "Allow me," he said, his voice low and his hand warm. Feelings of *déjà vu* swamped Katie as she remembered fumbling with the keys to her apartment in Shreveport, his hand over hers. Memories washed over her, leaving weak knees and a red face.

Judd gave her hand a little squeeze, and electricity arced up her arm. The puppy tucked under her other arm yipped, bringing her back to the present.

Katie made the mistake of looking into Judd's eyes. They crinkled with amusement, and his knowing smile had her mentally retreating post haste.

The screen door slammed as Rosita came outside to help. She greeted Katie as she walked between the house and the office. "So good you back home." She bustled around the car. "You come back safe. God watch out for you. We miss you, Miss Katie."

Katie glanced at Judd to see his reaction as Rosita pried her overnight bag from her hand. He looked on with a bemused expression, without a hint of cynicism.

Jammer circled them, vying for attention, the puppy now his main interest. Katie hugged the puppy to her chest. "No, Jammer. Be careful." She turned away to protect the little dog.

"Scooby is going to be an outdoor dog, Dori. He and Jammer need to become friends," Judd told his daughter.

"But Scooby is so little. Jammer might step on him."

"Where does Scooby sleep now?" Katie asked Dori.

"I fixed him a warm place in my bathroom. Daddy won't let him sleep in the bed with me."

"Yep, that's how it's going to be, Dori. Believe me, Katie, we haven't gotten much sleep with him crying most of the night. Jammer will take care of him."

"Your daddy's right. Scooby can snuggle up to Jammer to keep warm and get some sleep. He misses his mother."

Katie handed Scooby to Dori and retrieved two bags from the back seat. "Karen and Hank sent you a couple of gifts and a present for the puppy. My mom sent a couple of books she wrote. Let's go inside and check them out."

Katie and her entourage walked to the cabin. She couldn't help but smile at her welcome and felt a scintilla of hope where none existed before.

∽

School started and the days fell into a routine. Helene's absence lightened everyone's spirits. At least, Katie attributed the pleasant atmosphere to her leaving.

Judd filled the calendar with meetings, yet managed to spend more time with Dori. The plane arrived with business associates and left without Judd. He asked Katie to eat with them on Mondays, Wednesdays, and Fridays. The Thursday night dinner meeting with his ranch managers continued, and Dori ate with her in the cabin. Katie guessed Judd gave her Tuesday and Saturday nights off to satisfy her bid for independence.

Judd continued to attend church services with them if he wasn't traveling, and they ate dinner somewhere afterwards. On Saturday or Sunday afternoon they took road trips. Sometimes they took in a movie, walked on the beach, or around a mall or a park.

In West Palm Beach, they drove through Lion Country Safari, and Dori said she wanted to go to Africa on a safari. Judd laughed at her big plans. "You'll have to be older and take less equipment, or you'll have to charter a plane."

In Ft. Pierce, they spent an interesting afternoon at the Navy SEAL Museum, which Judd enjoyed. "I'd like to come back and read more of the material in depth. I didn't know the SEALS were formed by President Kennedy in 1962."

Dori enjoyed the museum's scavenger hunt, looking for clues in the different rooms, for a prize at the end. Katie and Judd helped her find them.

They walked outside, and Dori liked the boat with an open, shark's mouth painted on its bow and seeing the Apollo Space Capsule after her daddy told her about the NASA space mission. "I want to be an astronaut," she told them.

They walked on the beach at Vero Beach, and Dori looked for treasure from Spanish galleons which wrecked off her shores. Judd told her, "Be on the lookout for black, roundish metal which could be silver coins."

One Saturday, they drove around Lake Istokpoga, to see the vegetable farms and caladiums raised in the rich, black muck. They visited Sebring, famous for The Twelve Hours of Sebring, an auto endurance race, and spent time at an art complex on Lake Jackson. The Yellow House, one of several buildings on the site, displayed artwork by local artists. Katie made two purchases for the cabin, a mixed-media painting of nesting Great Blue Herons called "Changing of the Guard" by Rose Besch, and a smaller oil of sunflowers by Barbara Wade. Dori picked out a doll dressed in her Christmas outfit, which Judd presented to her, and he carried the paintings to the car saying to Katie, "Don't stay too long. We need to find a restaurant and get back. A storm is brewing."

"Can you believe all of the talent in this area?" Katie said, satisfied with her purchases and the reasonable prices.

"Yes. Florida is an artist mecca because of the climate. A number of cities and small towns have art festivals. I'm glad you're having a good time."

In February, they went to the Caladium Festival in Lake Placid, the Caladium Capital of the World. Some of the streets were blocked off, and they had to circle the area twice to find a parking spot near the festivities. After eating fried catfish and curly sweet potato fries, they topped off the meal with strawberry shortcake, and watched the clogging performance.

Judd wanted to get away from the crowds and see the murals. "We'll stop back by and pick up a box or two of the caladium bulbs to plant at Corazon." The large colorful leaves of the caladiums were impressive.

They walked through town and looked at the murals using the walking tour drawn in a mural booklet. They bought the color booklet in the Caladium Co-op, a large building displaying and selling artwork by Highlands County artists. Pictures of the murals and artists, along with information on each mural were included. Painted trash containers and bird plaques were featured in the back.

Dori's favorite mural was *Layers of Time,* the archaeology mural, because they had read about Florida Indians. She asked, "Why is the elephant painted in the picture?"

Judd told her that mammoths and mastodons once roamed Florida. "They're extinct, sweetheart. That means they died out and are no longer living today. They do look like they're related to elephants." He explained about how extinct animals left behind bones that became fossils over thousands of years. A conversation ensued about the difference between cow bones found in the field versus fossil bones. She asked, "Are we going to dig up my mound and find elephant bones?"

"I'm sure we won't be digging in the mounds. That's a job for archaeologists. We protect Indian sites, so archaeologists in the future can learn from them. I'll call Dr. Mazore and see when she can come for a visit," her dad promised.

Lake Placid was full of surprises. Dori laughed if the painted trash cans made noises or turned on their lights. The clown cut-outs and benches drew her attention. When Dori found out the town had a clown school, she claimed, "I'm going to this school and be a clown. What can my name be?"

They walked and talked clown names. Honki Dori became her favorite. "I'll have to get me one of those big red noses that honk when you squeeze it." She skipped down the sidewalk, pinching her nose and making honking sounds.

Judd took Katie's hand as they followed Dori down the street. His warm hand covered hers, and she struggled to keep the internal turmoil from showing on her face. *Don't make an issue out of it. No, accept and enjoy the moment.* They followed the walking tour in the mural book and looked for the items hidden in the murals by the artists.

In *Our Citrus Heritage* mural, Dori found three of the four oranges with sunglasses. Another spectator pointed out the fourth one.

Dori noticed the bird plaques first. She called out most of their names, but the Painted Buntings stumped her. "I've never seen those at Corazon."

They picked up the caladiums and started home by way of Highway 621 to see the Caladium fields, which were described as living, colorful patchwork quilts.

On the way, they stopped by a huge mural. *The Cracker Trail Cattle Drive* took the whole side of Winn Dixie and had a motion detector. They heard the cowboys, the sound of a whip cracking, a thunderstorm, and the cattle mooing.

"Wow! It took a long time to paint this one," Katie said.

"The project is certainly ambitious," Judd responded. He had to drop Katie's hand when she rummaged in her purse to retrieve the camera. She had let him hold her hand several times, and the connection felt good. *I'm wearing her down.* The thought gave him a smug feeling, but he realized this simple act was more of an intimate connection, a sharing unfamiliar to him. He wanted to hold more than her hand. He wanted to hold her heart, the essence of Katie, unlike anyone he had ever known. She dove into life, not content to sit on the sideline and watch. He looked forward to these side trips because of her enthusiasm, her eagerness to learn, and they knit Dori more firmly into the fabric of his life. *How did I get through the days without Dori in my life? She's phenomenal.*

Dori traced some of the brands with her finger. "Why do the cows have different brands?"

"The book says they're the brands of Highlands County cattlemen. Stand by the mural for a picture," she told Judd and Dori.

They walked and stood under the cowboy cracking the whip.

Judd reached for the camera. "Now, let me take one of you and Dori."

A man who had driven in with a group on motorcycles said, "Let me take a picture of your family."

Judd handed him the camera. Putting his arm around Katie, he pulled her to his side, and Dori jumped in front. Judd placed his other hand on her shoulder and smiled.

They thanked the man, and Judd said to Katie, "Be sure and give me a copy."

Sitting for meals together and traveling on weekend afternoons made Katie think of family. The man taking their picture thought they were a family. *Judd didn't contradict him.* She realized she was getting too comfortable with the idea, and tried to think of it as a job that would end in May.

Judd's attentive behavior and his unaccustomed, friendly banter rattled Katie. She related to the dragonfly she saw approaching a nearly invisible spider web, the spider hidden and lying in wait. *You're entirely too imaginative for your own good.* She brushed the insect and sent it flying in a different direction. *Sorry spider. Better luck next time.* If only the problem with Judd could be so easily solved.

That night at dinner while Dori prattled on about what the other children in her class were doing this weekend or what they did over the holidays, Katie became aware of Judd staring at her. No, not staring exactly, looking through her, his face a study in speculation. Then his eyes focused on her lips while the index finger of his right hand rubbed absently the spot on his own where she had bitten him.

Katie felt a red tide work its way up her neck to her face, and she looked down, panicked by the moment of passionate recognition she had tried to forget. The memory seared a path to her subconscious to return and haunt her in the night.

Flustered, she turned to Dori and asked her the first thing that came to mind. "Have you had much sickness at school? The flu was making its rounds in Shreveport. Paul had it before I left, and Myra was hoping Karen and Hank wouldn't catch it."

"I don't think so," Dori said, her eyes curiously searching Katie's face.

Katie's nails bit into her palm as she realized she had interrupted Dori in the middle of a sentence about a totally different subject. "I'm sorry, Dori, I'm tired, and my mind wandered. If you'll excuse me, I think I'll have an early night." She glanced at Judd, and his face held a half smile as if he divined her thoughts. "I'll see you in the morning," she said to them both, leaving the table, her dignity in shambles.

"Is Katie all right?" she heard Dori ask Judd as she left the room.

'I'm sure she's fine," he responded, and then lower, "very fine."

His *double entendre* was not lost on her. She only felt a modicum of relief after locking the cabin door.

Katie sat at the piano deep in thought, her fingers automatically running through her practice routine. Judd had not shown up at the cabin last night or any other night of the week. Why did she feel dejected, disappointed? *I should be grateful.* The tension built until Katie wanted to scream. She took out the sheet music and began to play one of Chopin's Nocturnes, trying to clear her mind of thoughts about Judd.

The ploy wasn't working. Judd remained the center of her thoughts. He seemed to be everywhere she turned. She found herself watching him, her eyes moving over the masculine planes of his body, enjoying his rugged appearance, especially after he returned from riding over the ranch. His tousled hair when he removed his cowboy hat, begged to be combed by her fingers, and his mouth ... *Stop torturing yourself.*

Katie covered her face with her hands as she leaned over the piano keys. Chopin's Nocturnes soothed, but they inevitably led her, as now, to his Polonaise "Heroic". She began to play, and Chopin's passion soared as the flight of her hands swept over the keys. This piece, the most difficult of all the arrangements she had learned, moved her to tears.

A hand covered Katie's shoulder, startling her into jumping up and almost overturning the piano bench.

Judd looked down on her, his eyes intense, smoldering. "God, Katie," and his mouth covered hers as he pulled her to him in a crushing embrace. Words vanished as the tremors of passion swamped them. Judd's hands and mouth moved over her as he molded her to his hard body.

She responded, the powerful chords still coursing through her, a wanton flame hot enough to consume. Katie had no doubt their passion would have been consummated had the phone not rung shrilly in the kitchen.

"Miss Katie," Zita called. "The phone for you."

They heard Zita enter the butler pantry as she came looking for her with the information. Katie sat down abruptly on the bench, her hands falling on the keys, making a discordant sound as she tried to calm her breathing and her galloping heart.

Zita came into the parlor. "Miss Katie, you have ..."

Judd stood in front of Katie and managed to rein in his passion faster. He said. "We heard you, Zita. Please tell whoever it is, Katie will call them back shortly. Thank you."

When Zita left, Judd grasped Katie under her elbow, pulled her up from the bench, and lifted her chin with his hand. His thumbs brushed aside the tears trailing down her face. "You're killing me," he said, "slowly ... or is it softly? I'm not sure how much more of this I can stand."

Katie nodded and swallowed, unable to look him in the eyes. She understood what he was saying, but she didn't know how to handle her raw emotions. She wanted to fling herself into his arms with wild abandon and let the pieces of her fall where they may. She could stay on at Corazon after the year was up as his lover, but for how long? Her conscience was not only screaming, "Don't give in," but goading her with, "You'll never know if he loves you or Corazon more." She knew this was not what J.D. envisioned, nor had she. Even God had intervened, using the phone call.

"I need time." *Time to talk myself out of giving in.*

Judd watched the inner conflict play over Katie's face and knew he was losing her. He brought his lips down again to rebrand, but she moved back, pulling away from his kiss and metaphorically, his hold over her.

Her golden eyes opened, and another facet of Katie was revealed. "I need time. I can't take my feelings, my beliefs lightly." She maneuvered around the bench away from him as she heard him gently lower the lid to cover the keys.

~

Katie walked to the kitchen in a daze and released a pent-up breath. *Thank you, God.* She was thankful for the timely intervention. *What am I doing?* Then more to the point, *What can I do?*

Zita looked at her curiously as she entered the room.

What is she reading on my face? Automatically, her hand went to her cheek and smoothed her hair, circling her neck in agitation. She wanted to hide. Emotional bouts left visible marks on her skin.

"Miss Merit call you and leave her number. She say very important you call."

"Thank you Zita. I'll call her from the cabin." Katie left the house, thinking about Merit's saving call. *What does Merit want that is so important?*

Merit answered on the first ring. "Hope I didn't catch you at a bad moment," she said, "but I thought you ought to be warned. Adrienne and Max just left here, and they're on their way to Corazon.'

CHAPTER FORTY-THREE

Katie knew when Max and Adrienne arrived because Dori ran to the cabin after school to let her know.

"My grandfather and grandmother are here," Dori told her while catching her breath. "Daddy gave them your room, but my grandfather is going to stay in Aunt Helene's room. He said he snored, and later he whispered the real reason. My grandmother snores real loud, and he can't sleep with her." Dori giggled. "He's funny. I didn't know girls snored. Did you?"

Katie smiled at Dori's pronouncement and nodded. "Everyone does sometimes, even me."

Dori looked at her momentarily shocked. She continued, "Daddy wants you to eat dinner with us tonight. I'll sit next to you. My grandmother is sca … ry."

Katie decided not to encourage this discussion. "Tell your daddy I'll come to dinner tonight." This was her night to cook in the cabin, and she took the chicken breast from the sink and returned the partially frozen meat to the refrigerator.

"My grandmother doesn't like me," Dori stated as she traced the arm of the recliner with her fingers.

Join the club, Katie thought. *Not prudent. Don't go there.* She needed to address Dori's comment. "Why do think she doesn't like you, Dori? You're her only granddaughter; so, you must be her favorite."

Dori cocked her head, eyes wide, and questioning her with a look that said, *Are you nuts?* She walked to the door, shaking her head in disbelief. "I can tell. She looks at me funny, and it's not nice. She looks like she's mad at me. I can just tell."

Katie followed and pulled Dori to her chest in a hug. "Maybe your grandmother hasn't had a chance to get to know you, and she's afraid *you* don't like *her*. She needs your love, and I know for a fact, you are very lovable. You have to show her that love. Be nice to her. She won't be able to resist. I promise." Katie hugged the little girl and prayed Adrienne would respond the right way.

Dori hugged her back. "I'll try. But I like my grandfather better. He's nice to me."

~

Dinner felt like a formal affair. Adrienne and Max dressed like they were having dinner at the Yacht Club while the rest of them wore casual wear.

Max was quiet and smiled at everyone. Adrienne looked constipated, and Judd looked amused by something.

"You look pretty." Dori said to her grandmother. "I wish my hair was that color."

Adrienne turned to her and smiled for the first time. "Thank you. What a dear you are!"

Dori wiggled in her seat, a pleased expression on her face.

Katie was proud of Dori for making the effort. Her compliment was rewarded. *Thank you, God.*

Judd appeared pleased that Dori broke the ice. He took over and asked his parents their future plans.

"We're going to spend some time at Mossy Cove."

Katie remembered this was the property J.D. left Max in his Will.

"We need a rest, and then we have plans to tour the Far East. Max isn't too excited about the trip, but he said I'm not going by myself," Adrienne replied and looked at him gratified by her hold on him.

"It's true," Max said. "I'm not looking forward to being jostled and robbed by the hordes we'll encounter." He gestured dramatically, using both hands and voice. "Heaven forbid we get sick over there. I mean, we could die in unsanitary conditions."

"I don't want you to go," Dori said. "I don't want you to die."

"That is the nicest thing I've ever had said to me," Max said, smiling big at Dori.

"Nonsense," Adrienne countered. "We'll be staying in the finest hotels, and our tour guides will see to our safety. We know how to watch what we eat."

"I think we should stay here a while and get to know our granddaughter. She's obviously bright, and I like her," Max said, nodding his head in her direction.

Dori beamed. "I can show you alligators and cowboys. Daddy gave me a calf named Snowball because she's white.

"Really," Max said, like she had told him something extraordinary. "That settles it. We'll stay a while and let you show us around."

Adrienne leaned forward, not ready to give in to his proposal. "Not so fast. We've let the staff know to get the house ready for us. Remember?"

"A week won't make a difference. They'll understand. I'm sure everything will be fine for a week."

"And I have a new puppy named Scooby. You'll really like him," Dori piped as if that would be the deciding factor.

Adrienne sat back in her chair, lips pursed, and huffed her displeasure. She turned to Katie. "What about you? Are you climbing the walls yet? You must be bored out of your mind."

"I love Corazon. I'm having a wonderful time, and Dori makes life interesting. You'll enjoy getting to know her."

"What are your plans when you leave here?" Adrienne asked.

Judd said, "Maybe she won't be leaving. Dori and I like having Katie here." His blue eyes captured hers, and the timbre of his voice proclaimed victory as if the matter were settled.

Dori clapped her hands, grinning. "Yesss, she can stay." She turned to Katie excited. "Daddy said you can stay, Katie."

Adrienne and Max turned their full attention on Katie with varying degrees of interest. Max said, "Are you thinking marriage?" he asked his son.

"You, more than anyone, should know the answer to that one." Judd replied without hesitation.

Katie squirmed inside. Of course. She knew the answer, too. Judd had made his feelings all too clear at The Blue Adagio. "I appreciate the offer to stay," she said, plastering a smile on her face, "but I have a job I enjoy in Shreveport, and I miss my family." She refused to look embarrassed and held her head up. *I'm not looking at Judd. Don't you dare look!*

"We'll see," Judd said, his voice confident.

Adrienne stared at her as if she couldn't believe what she was hearing. For once, she didn't have anything to say.

Zita brought each course, cleared the remains, and stayed out of sight as much as possible. She had become nervous when told Max and Adrienne were coming to Corazon. "Dios Mio, what do I do?" Katie had never seen her so flustered.

"Don't worry about it. I'll help you. Things won't be that bad. We won't let them upset us. Right?" she said looking into Zita's eyes until her words registered.

"You a good woman, Miss Katie," she said and cheered up.

The rest of the meal passed quietly as if they were all lost in their own thoughts.

Dori finally broke the silence. "I can play the piano. Katie is teaching me. We can play for you. Do you want to hear us play?"

"Of course we do," Max said. "I always wanted to play the piano, but my left hand wouldn't cooperate." He held his hand up and wiggled his fingers. "These little *piggies* just wouldn't do what I wanted them to do, much to my mother's chagrin."

Dorie giggled and lifted her hand, wiggling her fingers. "I thought *piggies* were toes."

"You might be right," Max said. "Just shows you I don't know everything."

Katie was beginning to like Max. Adele was Max's mother. Katie could picture her trying to help Max play the piano and smiled at the image in her mind.

"Dori's talented," Katie told them, "and she's learned several songs."

"Katie plays like a concert pianist," said Judd. "I haven't heard the instrument used so passionately since Del left." He smiled at Katie. "You'll have to play for us."

Katie felt her face warming and excused herself from the table. "I'm turning in early tonight. Maybe I'll see you tomorrow. Goodnight.

Dori came home from school in a bad mood. She plunked her backpack on the kitchen floor without speaking and went to the refrigerator. Rosita wasn't around to help.

Katie had made lemonade that morning and had come to get another glass. *And maybe get a glimpse of Judd. Now you're acting like a teenager.* "How was school?" she asked as Judd entered the kitchen door.

Dori pulled out the heavy pitcher and spilled some of the drink on the floor.

Judd reached to help her before she dropped the container, and Katie mopped the liquid with a paper towel.

"Suzie's not my friend anymore," Dori said.

Judd added to this statement. "She and Suzie got into an argument after school, and I'm glad I arrived before fists flew.

Dori frowned at him. "As if..." she responded with disgust.

"An argument about what?"

Dori glanced at Katie, a mulish look on her face. She said, "You're a little rich girl", and I said, I'm not". She kept saying,'rich girl, rich girl' to me."

Max entered the kitchen. He had made a point to see Dori after school. "Just ignore her, Dori. She'll stop saying it when she sees it doesn't rile you."

Katie listened to Max amazed by his wise comment. Judd also took notice.

"I'm not rich!" Dori exclaimed, and stomped her foot.

Katie bent to Dori's level. "Yes, you are rich, and I don't want you to ever forget it."

Dori looked at her wide-eyed.

Without turning, Katie knew she had Judd and Max's undivided attention. "You're rich because you have a daddy who loves you very much and family and other people who love you. But most of all, God loves you. The Bible tells us that God owns everything. Because God is your Heavenly Father, that makes you a child of the King. You can't get any richer than that."

Dori snuffled and threw herself into Katie's arms almost toppling her. "I love you, Katie. You're rich too."

"I know," Katie said, her face buried in Dori's hair.

"I'll be," Max said, slapping his thigh. "I don't think I've ever heard that explanation. Dori, if you love me, I'm rich, too."

Dori ran to Max and hugged him. "I do love you, Gramps."

Max's eyes teared, and Katie believed the cause might be Dori used her pet name for his father, J.D.

Max cleared his throat as Dori left him to hug her dad. "I love you too, Daddy, more than anyone in the whole world."

Judd looked at Katie over Dori's head, his appreciation shining in his eyes.

Embarrassed, Katie took a damp paper towel and mopped the sticky spot left by the spilled lemonade. She took her glass and started back to the cabin.

"Dori, I think Scooby is looking for you," she said as she closed the screen. Scooby and Jammer circled her by the steps, tails wagging and looking for attention

Dori came out and sat on the steps, letting the dogs lick her in welcome.

Katie smiled as she walked to the cabin. She would do some reading and let Dori get to know her grandparents.

~

Dinner became an animated affair as Dori regaled Katie and Adrienne about her daddy and Gramps taking her with them as they rode over the ranch. "We didn't see Snowball this time, but Gramps said he would see her before he left."

Dori turned to Adrienne. "We can show you, too. And I have an Indian Mound named after me. It's on Daddy's map."

"That's nice," Adrienne replied, smiling a bit. "I don't have anything named after me." Her voice had a plaintive sound.

Judd regarded his mother, considering his words before speaking. "You know, Mother, Stetson's should rename its exclusive department after you. Adrienne has a certain European flair that will appeal to our most discerning customers."

Adrienne's mouth dropped open as she stared at Judd.

Max started to say something but held the words back. He looked at Judd, eyebrows raised.

"I don't know what to say," Adrienne said when she was able to speak. "You'd do that for me?"

"Yes," Judd said decisively. "I only have one mother," he began, paused, and added, "You always look beautiful and chic for any occasion."

"Here, here," Max said, raising his wine glass to Adrienne. "Well said. I agree."

Dori, not to be left out, said, "You are beautiful. Now Daddy's named something for you."

"Ahem." Max caught their attention. "I don't have anything named for me."

"Now, that will take a lot more thought," Judd said dryly, tongue in cheek.

"And Katie, too." Dori said.

Katie's face flushed. "You can name your next doll after me," Katie said, hoping to take the attention off of her.

"Yes," Dori said, excited. "I'll have to get a doll with black hair," she said to Judd.

"I'm sure we can find one," Judd told his daughter.

Rosita brought out her chocolate cake, and Max groaned. "Zita, you'll be the death of me." He grinned. "But I'll die happy. Make it a big piece."

Adrienne grimaced. "Max, let's not overdo it."

Max's grin widened. "Sounds like you want me to stay around."

Adrienne's expression smoothed, and she looked younger.

"Do you want to hear me play the piano?" Dori asked.

"Of course, we do," Max replied.

They finished dessert, and moved to the parlor. Dori took out the hymnal and turned to "Amazing Grace."

Katie smiled as Dori made it look like she read the music instead of playing by ear. She saw Max and Adrienne's reaction when she played the final chord. Everyone clapped, but Max stood and gave her a standing ovation. "That was fantastic! I'm truly impressed."

Dori preened with the attention, and Judd smiled his pride. "I think Katie should play. She's the one who brought the instrument out of retirement. And had it tuned.

Katie took out some of Adele's music to play. She played *Clair De*

Lune and *Rhapsody in Blue*, ending with one of Chopin's Etudes.

Everyone clapped and Judd stood. "It's my turn."

Max and Adrienne looked perplexed until after a playful warm-up of his hands and fingers, he sat at the bench and launched into a passionate rendition of "Chopsticks."

Dori jumped up and down. "Let me do it, too." She joined him in a duet, ending with deep bows. The evening finished on a good note.

Katie escaped to the cabin after saying good night. She was uncomfortable in the limelight, especially when Max and Adrienne had her in their sights.

~

Ten minutes later, a knock sounded on the door. Katie opened it cautiously and faced Judd through the cracked space.

"Don't look so worried. I'm not coming inside. I wanted to catch you before you turned in, to thank you for today."

"You're welcome," Katie said looking down, anything to keep her attraction to him under wraps. She started to close the door.

"I mean it," Judd said. His booted foot kept the door from closing.

He sounded so sincere; she opened the door a little more.

"I've spoken with my parents more this visit than I have in years, and Dori ... you must know you have played a crucial role in her relationship with her grandparents. Max melted when she called him, Gramps. I did, too."

Katie looked up. "I'm glad," Katie managed to say and looked down again. "I'll see you tomorrow." *That sounded lame.*

"Good night, Katie, Sweet dreams."

Katie stared at him surprised. She always said that to Dori at night, and it appeared he adopted the expression.

Judd's knowing amusement wreathed his face. His crooked smile, white teeth, and the intensity of his eyes flashing in the shadow, made her want to run.

He can't help looking like a wolf-in-waiting. That's your imagination.

Katie closed the door and leaned against the rough wood, her hand to her chest, which seemed to be pounding double time.

Judd's ploy to charm her was working. Her barricades were melting, and her trembling knees, an indication she stood on shaky ground. She pushed away from the door and checked to make sure all the curtains were closed. *What's the matter with you? Do you think he's still outside, foolish girl?*

She turned on the light, sat in the recliner, and reached for J.D.'s Bible.

~

The next day dawned with a heavy fog and a thirty per cent chance of rain.

Katie met Rosita in the kitchen and poured herself a cup of coffee. "We might get some rain today."

"Si," Zita said. "We need it. Mr. Judd, he in the office early. He say to get him when Dori eats and ready for school."

"Hmmm," Katie responded. She refilled her cup, picked up a banana, and put a couple of pieces of bread in the toaster. "Have you seen Max and Adrienne this morning?"

"No, Miss Katie, they sleep mornings." She put half a dozen eggs in a kettle of water to boil.

Curious, Katie asked if she saw much of the couple during the day.

"Mr. Max, he spend a lot of time with Mr. Judd. Ms. Adrienne watch television and read magazines a lot." She looked at Katie, her lips pursed in thought. "You know they different than usual." She looked beyond Katie. "They different." She stopped talking as if she felt she had said too much.

Dori came into the kitchen dressed for school. Her attitude was chipper, yesterday forgotten. Not quite. "I hope Suzie says I'm rich today, so I can tell her I am." She beamed at Katie.

"Just don't forget to tell her why you're rich."

"I won't."

"What you want for breakfast?" Zita asked in Spanish

Dori responded, "Eggs scrambled, toast, and orange juice" in kind and in sentence form.

"You Spanish good, Miss Dori," Zita said.

"I'm always amazed how fast children pick up a new language," Katie said. "I'm still trying to learn the names of things."

"You doing okay," Zita said.

Katie finished her breakfast and told Dori to have a good day at school.

Dori hugged her.

"Tell Mr. Judd, Dori ready to go," Zita said as Katie walked to the door.

"Okay, Dori, get your book bag, and I'll walk out with you," Katie said, feeling like a ninny for avoiding Judd.

Dori picked up her backpack and followed her out. "What are you doing today?" she asked, hugging Scooby and Jammer in turn.

"I don't have plans, yet. It might rain, so I'll probably practice on the piano and read. I have a dentist appointment tomorrow. I wish it were today."

"I don't like to go to the dentist," Dori said.

"Me neither, but I go, so my teeth won't fall out or need to be pulled. Thankfully, I'm just getting them cleaned."

Dori knocked and entered the office after Katie waved goodbye.

CHAPTER FORTY-FOUR

Katie ate lunch in the cabin and sat down after cleaning up to write notes to her family.

A knock sounded on the door, and Katie looked up to see Adrienne standing on the porch.

"Come in," she called as she put her writing in a neat pile. Dread seeped into her bones. *What now?*

Adrienne came inside and looked around, her curiosity obvious. "I had a hard time believing you moved out here," Adrienne said.

"Why is that?"

Adrienne walked around, her fingers skimming over the recliner, table, and books. "I guess my opinion of you was off base."

Katie remained silent as she watched her circle the space. She stopped at the corner post to look at Dori's mosaic of her family. Having Adrienne in the cabin with her was like having all the air sucked out of the room, leaving Katie breathless.

Adrienne traced her finger over the etched lines, reading them aloud. "J. loves A.," and "Del loves you more."

She turned and studied Katie. "You know J.D. and Del's marriage … such a tragedy. They never liked me, you know. I was the bitch who stole their precious son and ruined him." She inhaled deeply before continuing. "You'll find this hard to believe, but I felt sorry for them, especially Del."

Katie found her voice. "I know what you mean. I'm glad they each found a measure of happiness in the end, one way or another."

"Yes, you're right; they managed." She looked Katie in the eyes and followed that with, "How did you manage to get rid of Helene?"

Katie's back stiffened. "Helene left of her own accord, not because I wanted her gone."

Adrienne looked at her, the intensity of her eyes so like Judd's.

"Why did she leave?" she pressed.

"She gave up. Helene believed Judd would never get past her being Rita's sister. She had a business to run, and Dori no longer needed her."

"Helene didn't strike me as a quitter. She would have fought tooth and nail for Judd if there was a glimmer of a chance. We're alike in that respect, so your explanations don't fly." She walked purposefully toward her and Katie stepped back, her hip bumping the table.

Adrienne stopped a foot from Katie, and perused her face. "Don't be afraid. You'll find my bark is worse than my bite."

Katie smiled at this trite cliché dropping from Adrienne's perfectly painted red mouth. She felt like Alice when she fell down the rabbit hole and later confronted the Queen of Hearts.

"You surprised me at the Christmas Gala ... no, you floored me. I couldn't believe the transformation. When you stood up to me, I knew you had a backbone. I admired your pluck, not to mention your stunning ensemble. I've spoken with Bob and Meredith. They reported changes taking place, and Merit speaks highly of you, too, a coup in itself."

Adrienne walked by Katie and peeked into the second room.

Katie was glad she had made up the bed. Her relief was short-lived.

"I'm guessing Judd hasn't slept with you, yet." She pivoted and watched amused as Katie's face flooded with color.

"Yes," she said as she placed a stray lock of hennaed hair behind her ear, "I believe Helene left, my dear, because she couldn't compete with you. How delicious!" She walked to the recliner and sat, a pleased expression on her face.

Katie slid down on the nearest chair, not knowing what to say or even how to react.

Adrienne continued, "I knew Judd was enamored with you when he made that over-the-top bid on the little tree. Judd Stetson isn't a frivolous spender." She folded her hands under her chin and looked over Katie, one arched eyebrow raised.

Katie squirmed inside, her discomfort probably written on her face.

"Yes, I know it was a good cause, and Judd certainly believes in donating to charity, but you must admit, you were as stunned as everyone else in the room.

"Is that Luke person also a contender?" his mother asked. "Helene was livid … no, humiliated. She was so confident.

"I was pleased and proud when Judd asked me to dance. Then he warned me to tread lightly and not to insult you specifically."

Adrienne sounded like she saw her in a different light, and Katie was at a loss for words.

"Well, am I right? Helene *knew* she had lost him to you."

"Not quite," Katie responded. "I believe her words were to the effect J.D.'s Will and his leaving me half of Corazon gave me the advantage."

Adrienne leaned forward. "Do you believe that?"

Katie dropped her eyes, not wanting to reveal her true feelings.

Adrienne saw through her at once. "You do. You have feelings for Judd, but you aren't sure where you stand with him." She leaned back, chewing her lips as she mulled these new revelations.

Her regard shifted to Katie. "It's no secret, I hated Rita. She ruined Judd, left him with a small child, opening the door to Helene. He became bitter and cynical, a carbon copy of J.D."

Katie remembered Aaron Pickering saying Rita was a lot like Adrienne. Maybe so, but Katie saw something more. She was sure Adrienne cared for Judd, as a mother.

"I want to apologize for what I said at the reading of the Will. It's inexcusable, I know. Max is forever telling me to think before I speak, but for some reason, I can't."

Now Adrienne looked down, not sure of Katie's response.

Adrienne was beginning to thaw, and Katie saw an opportunity.

"I've been known to do the same. Tensions ran high that day, and I do understand why everyone was left with an unsavory impression. I told Judd when he accused me of using his grandfather, that I wanted no part of the estate. He challenged me to tell Mr. Pickering, and I did." Katie stood and paced the floor. "You know why I was silent and why J. D. wanted Dori and me at Corazon for a year. Everyone knew, including Judd. You saw his reaction."

Adrienne stood and touched her shoulder, stopping her. "I'm sorry. Within a couple of weeks, Judd let us all know we were wrong about you, and that you never saw J.D. after you saved his life."

Katie returned to her seat, mainly because her legs threatened to buckle, and Adrienne also sat.

"I see now J.D. was right to bring Dori back to Judd. She really is a delightful child, nothing like her mother. And she's away from that scheming woman's influence," Adrienne declared.

"Helene did a commendable job while they were together. Dori learned manners and was exposed to educational and creative opportunities. I believe Helene genuinely loves Dori." Katie knew Helene deserved credit, and Adrienne needed to know.

"You can say something nice about that woman, after she gave you hell for months? Don't' bother to deny it. I know she did."

"Helene wasn't so bad. We got along because I didn't try to compete with her. Besides, I knew I couldn't. Sometimes, you have to let nature take its course."

"So, you are wise, as well as, strong. Max gloried in telling me word for word what you told Dori about being rich. He was impressed. And for all the rumors about him not being bright, Max is not easily impressed."

"I like Max. I hope he and Judd reconnect. Dori has certainly become fond of him."

"I know, and he's overjoyed at the prospect of having a beautiful, smart, and talented granddaughter." She smiled, and Katie knew she meant it when she said, "I am, too. How on earth did you manage to teach Dori to play the piano in so short a time?"

"I taught her some chords. She plays by ear and doesn't really read music. Learning the notes frustrates her. She'll play well if she continues to practice."

"That little squirt. She certainly had us fooled, looking at the book." Her voice was playful, soft, that drew her mouth into a half-smile.

"I'm sorry, I haven't offered you anything to drink. I have water and apple juice if you're interested."

"No, thank you. I just wanted to find out what was going on and to apologize for my rude behavior. Are you really planning on leaving in May?"

Katie let that pass. She wouldn't be pressured.

"I've seen you present at our virtual Board Meetings, but you look disinterested and haven't said a word, like now. Do you truly not want a Stetson share?"

Katie guessed Adrienne wouldn't believe her, whatever she said. *What difference does it make whether or not she knows my plans?* "I'm going back to Shreveport. I have a job waiting for me, and my family lives nearby. We're close, and I miss them."

Adrienne's eyelids closed, and Katie wondered if she thought of her own fractured family. Katie saw Adrienne's hands twisting in her lap.

"Max and I have noticed a change in Judd, a change for the better. He appears more relaxed and accepting of things he once ignored, like his feelings for J.D., his acceptance of our presence. I think you are the key to that change." Adrienne's eyes bored into her.

Katie remained silent.

"I'm sure you've wondered why Max and I sent Judd to boarding schools."

When Katie didn't respond, Adrienne pressed, "Haven't you wondered?"

"It's none of my business how other people raise their children. I'd make it my business only if I knew a child was being abused."

Adrienne appeared taken aback and melted back in the chair as if she wanted to disappear into the upholstery. Her voice quavered. "Some would say sending a child away was abuse." She faced away, and Katie waited until she turned back to catch her reaction.

Katie looked her in the eyes. "I'm sure you had your reasons."

The floor seemed to fall away at Adrienne's response. "I was an abused child." She squeezed her eyes closed, her shoulders slumped, her posture one of abject humiliation.

Katie was stunned by this unforeseen revelation.

Saying the words was more than Adrienne could take. She put her face in her hands and wept, her cries heart-wrenching.

Katie took napkins from the table, went to her and knelt at her feet, pulling her into an embrace she hoped would comfort.

Adrienne stiffened then caved, leaning on her.

"I shouldn't have said that," she sobbed. "Why did I say that?" When her crying subsided, she spoke earnestly. "I was afraid my uncontrolled outbursts would hurt Judd. I feared disciplining him. It would have killed me to hurt him physically or verbally. He was and still is my whole world, but you *know* what he thinks of me, of us."

Katie heard the pain in Adrienne's words and handed her the napkins.

"Max knows, of course, and he's stayed with me." She blew her nose. "Sending Judd away was the most difficult decision of our marriage." She shook her head as if to negate the thought. "You saw me at my worst. I had gone off my medication, believing I was better. When I slapped Max, he was so humiliated. God, I wished I had died on the spot."

Katie knew the feeling. She searched for words to say as she held her. "Have you sought counseling?"

She nodded. "Twice. The second time, Max was brought in to hear all the sordid details." She sniffed and a tremor wracked her body. "Talking helped, but the damage was done. We can't go back. Max should have left me years ago. Why didn't he?"

"I think he must love you very much," Katie told her.

"Some people confuse love with need. Max needs me. He was never the man J.D. wanted him to be. I gave him fidelity and the strength to turn from a life he didn't want." She blew her nose. "We gave the Stetsons, Judd, but until several years ago, do you think J.D. had one kind word for us?" She turned her head away. "Max was hurt because J.D. never treated him like a son, only a nuisance he had to deal with. He tried to get his father's attention, but he was only noticed when he was in trouble. Business was all J.D. cared about. Even Del left him in the end."

She glanced at Katie. "I'm sure you don't know what it's like to be treated like a pariah, or how hard it is to hold up your head and act like it doesn't hurt." Tears rolled down her face.

Katie felt an unexpected compassion for this woman. She shook her head. "No," she said quietly, "I always knew I was loved." Hesitantly, she continued, "I'm so sorry I misjudged you. Please forgive me."

Adrienne waved her hand dismissively. "I don't want your pity." She blew her nose again. "You and Max are the only ones I've told. I'm so ashamed. I can't believe I told you." She shook her head, distraught.

"Adrienne, you were a victim. You sought help. You did what you could to save Judd. You *must* tell him."

Adrienne pulled away, her eyes wide with shock. "No! Judd must never know. You can't tell him. I'll kill myself. I will." She grasped Katie's arms. With mascara running down her cheeks, her lipstick smeared, and panic in her voice, she looked deranged.

"I'm not going to tell him." Katie's words seemed to calm her. "As an outsider, I see things differently. Is your pride so great, you'll let Judd believe you rejected him? He wasn't loved?"

"I can't. It's too late. He will never understand."

Footsteps crossed the porch, and a knock sounded. "Katie, I need your help."

It was Judd. Katie went to the door.

"Max and I are in the middle of something important. Would you pick up Dori for me?"

"Of course," Katie said, starting to close the door.

"What's wrong?" Judd studied her face

She tried to look nonchalant. "Nothing."

"I'm not buying that." He pushed the door open and walked inside. When he saw his mother, he said, "What's going on?"

Adrienne sat like a statue, her face turned away.

"Mother," Judd warned, starting toward her.

Katie stepped in front of him. "Please leave, Judd. Please," she implored. "We're talking, and you need to leave."

Judd started to push her aside, and Katie blurted, "Your mother came to apologize. Please leave."

The words stopped him, and incredulity masked his face. He backed toward the door, his disbelief clamping his jaw to keep from saying more.

"I'll get Dori, Judd, don't worry."

When Katie closed the door and walked back to Adrienne, she stood.

"I should leave. I've imposed on you enough."

Katie closed the space and once again embraced her. "You're not an imposition."

"Thank you for that," Adrienne said, and Katie knew it was because she sent Judd away.

Katie backed up and looked her in the eyes. "Pride is a terrible thing. I won't say anything to anyone. But please think about how much better all of you will feel by giving up this burden you have carried for so long. I mean, can things get any worse than they are now? Think about it."

Adrienne nodded, wiped her face, and said, "I hope I can depend on your discretion."

She nodded, and Adrienne left without another word.

Katie slumped into the recliner, her thoughts tumbling in her head. *Did the last thirty minutes really happen?* She looked at her watch. Dori would be out of school in an hour.

Dinner was quiet. Max said Adrienne had a headache, and he'd carry her some dinner later.

"Suzie told me I was rich again today," Dori said. "She didn't like it when I said I knew it already." She looked at Gramps.

Max harrumphed.

"Then I told her she was rich, too, and she said she wasn't, so I told her why."

Katie said, "Tell them the rest of the story." She looked at Max and Judd. "She told me on the way home from school."

"She started crying. I didn't know her mother died before Christmas, so I told her mine died, too. Now we're buddies because we both don't have mothers, and we know we are loved. She likes being rich, too."

Judd rose from the table and hugged Dori. "I'm so proud of you. How did I get so lucky to have you as a daughter?" He looked at Katie and mouthed, "Thank you."

Katie saw Max studying her, and instantly she knew Adrienne told him about their talk.

As if to confirm it, Max nodded, and Katie flushed.

She picked up her fork and attempted to eat. *What a day!*

CHAPTER FORTY-FIVE

Katie sat in the old recliner with the book, *Priceless Florida,* open in her lap. The book contained beautiful photos of natural Florida, but her mind was distracted.

Judd's comment about her passionately playing the piano brought back the physical passion and how close she had come to succumbing to Judd's sexual magnetism. She remembered Helene's comment. "I'd settle for Judd in a heartbeat, with or without love or commitment."

Katie's favorite composer was Chopin. She remembered from her music appreciation class, the story of his lover, the novelist, Auore Dupin, better known as George Sand. Auore's George Sand persona was an unconventional enigma and muse for Chopin during their stay together on the isle of Majorca.

Sand adopted the wearing of men's clothing and smoked, giving her access to places women of her time were forbidden. She moved comfortably in the company of the literary elite and took lovers at whim. Her boldness and freedom to express herself piqued Katie's imagination, and the story fed her romanticism. Katie didn't know why she was drawn to the life of a woman whose views were diametrically opposed to her own. Maybe because George Sand was not afraid to be herself, uncaring about what others thought of her. *Sometimes, I wish I could be like her, uninhibited, free to follow my passions without remorse.*

Katie knew the consequences of indiscriminate behavior could be devastating. She didn't want Dori to believe she condoned living with her father without marriage. Surely, Judd wouldn't want that either.

"He'll marry you to keep Corazon intact." Helene had said as a parting shot. *That's why I have to hold out. Lord, I need help.*

~

Max and Adrienne stayed at Corazon a week. Katie spent most of her time in the cabin, reading or driving around to look at new territory. She enjoyed exploring rural roads and finding new, interesting places. Katie had driven around the big lake several times and found sugar cane fields and sod farms, profitable industries in Florida. She discovered dairies and cattle ranches, orange groves, field crops, and even a horse farm, Good Ride Stables.

On one trip, she stopped at the stable office and asked about learning to ride a horse. The owner, Patty Rushing, told her she would be happy to give her lessons. The horsewoman, a large woman with steel gray hair and piercing, black eyes had a state-of-the-art facility where she boarded horses "for city folks from Palm Beach." She boarded a couple of polo ponies locals used for practice. They walked around the stable looking at the horses and learning which were an easy ride and the ones ridden by the most competent. Patty set up a schedule with Katie to begin her lessons the following week.

Katie decided to keep the lessons a secret. She didn't want Dori to get excited about learning to ride, unless Judd was comfortable with the idea. Maybe, he would want to teach her himself. Since the week they worked the cows, he had taken Dori for a ride on his horse a couple of times. Judd kept his promises, and Katie marked his dedicated commitments to Dori as one of his most endearing qualities.

~

Several times Judd's parents brought up her living in the cabin instead of the house.

Katie told them, "I enjoy the freedom to be independent and make my own decisions. Besides, Judd doesn't want me underfoot, which I'm sure you can appreciate."

Adrienne didn't seek her out again or act like she had shared a life-changing confidence. As the week progressed, Adrienne remained aloof but didn't show her mean or sarcastic persona. Katie thought the time they talked in the cabin was an embarrassment Adrienne wished she hadn't shared, and she didn't refer to it.

Max enjoyed a second childhood. Katie watched Dori and him walk to the shed hand-in-hand followed by Jammer and Scooby. They carried bamboo fishing poles Pliny had loaned them and returned from their trip on the cart with a bucket of small fish. Dori hoped she could keep them alive in the bucket. They were caught using rolled up pieces of bread and were too small to cook. Judd told her the fish would die, and Katie drove her back to the ditch to release the ones that were still alive.

"Gramps said he would read to me. I need to get some of my books."

Katie enjoyed seeing Max and Dori bond. "Come by anytime to get them. I'm glad you're enjoying your gramps. How are things going with your grandmother?"

Dori was silent a few seconds. "She's okay, I guess. I don't like it when she pats me on the head and tells me what a good girl I am."

"Think of it as a compliment. She isn't around children much, and she has probably never said those words to another child."

"Doesn't she like children?" Dori asked.

"I'm sure she likes you. She called you a squirt for fooling them about playing the piano. She was impressed and told me so."

"She did?"

"Yep. My dad always told me if someone calls you a name or teases you, it's because they like you and are trying to get your attention."

"Billy Diaz calls me Dori-Cat-ori and pulls my hair. That means he likes me? Ick."

Katie laughed. "I'm glad boys aren't your main concern now."

After their talk, Dori tried to include her grandmother. She took Adrienne a favorite doll and asked her if she would help her with the doll's hair. Adrienne looked pleased. She took the brush and parted the long, bushy tangles. After she smoothed the hair, she showed Dori how to plait it. Dori was fascinated, and she practiced until she did a credible job.

"Would you plait my hair?' Dori asked her.

"I'll need a bigger brush and a couple of bands to hold the braids," Adrienne replied. After that, Dori let her fix her hair several times. Adrienne asked her questions about the ranch and her life in Connecticut.

Katie saw she was less stiff with Dori and silently applauded her show of interest.

Before Max and Adrienne left Corazon for Louisiana, they each hugged Dori and promised to keep in touch.

Dori held her father's hand as she waved goodbye.

Judd watched their car drive away, his mind trying to demystify their desire to visit Corazon and their interest in Dori for the first time.

He remembered the day at the cabin when Katie said his mother had come to apologize and her insistence that he leave. His mother apologizing didn't fit the mold in which he had placed her.

Then seeing the unmasked incredulity on her face when he told her they should rename a department of Stetson's after her was revealing. For the first time, Judd saw his mother as a needy person. *My mother*. He had begun to think of her as his mother, not just Adrienne, Max's screwed up wife, and the woman who banished him to boarding schools during his formative years.

They had not been a traditional family. His friends in school shared many of the same problems, and he wasn't alone in exile. He had made significant business contacts over those years and Stetson Enterprises benefitted. Only now, having Dori and Katie at Corazon, did he realize the enormity of the responsibility fatherhood required.

CHAPTER FORTY-SIX

Dr. Jan Mazore called Judd, and they arranged to meet the following Saturday morning at nine-thirty to check Dori's Mound.

Bobbie Jean was invited to join the group, and the swamp buggy was used to return to the site. The ride was exciting for the girls and Katie loved the ride also. The seats were high because of the oversized tires which could maneuver through tall grass, over palmettos, and navigate in swampy areas.

Dr. Mazor, a professor of anthropology at Florida Atlantic University said, "Little is known about the Indians living in the area around Okeechobee and the interior of South Florida before the Seminoles. The pottery sherds you showed me in your office were categorized as Belle Glade Plain. This type of pottery was first found and typed in Belle Glade, a small town near the big lake, and the culture that produced it carried the town's name.

"When the drought brought the lake surface down, new sites were revealed and are presently being studied. Belle Glade type pottery is mostly found in Glades, Hendry, Highlands, and Palm Beach counties." Dr. Mazor told them about Ft. Center, an important site in Glades County. "The Spanish wrote accounts of Indians living in the interior, using information given by captured and rescued Spanish slaves. These slaves also provided priests with the beliefs and traditions of the people."

"Dr. Mazor, do you have any interest in studying the sites on the ranch?" Judd asked.

"Please call me Jan. I don't have time to do an archaeological survey of the ranch this summer, but a few of the graduate students might want some work."

The party walked over the mound and searched the perimeters for exposed artifacts brought to the surface by rain and erosion. Dr. Mazor encouraged them to leave their finds in place. She picked up artifacts, studied and recorded them on her paperwork. She photographed them, and they were replaced.

"Archaeology is an exacting science, and the story of a people can be lost if artifacts are removed or the site is disturbed by digging without a plan. Looting is a problem."

Judd explained looting meant removing artifacts from a site illegally and without documentation. "Unfortunately, some land owners can legally dig on their properties for artifacts to trade or sell to collectors."

Dr. Mazore talked to them about how some people viewed archaeology as a romantic adventure or treasure hunt. "My students learn in field school that digging and sifting are dirty work and the paperwork, if finished correctly, can be tedious. The discipline isn't for everyone, and only the dedicated continue the course."

Bobbie Jean said, "I want to be an archaeologist."

"Me, too," Dori said.

Dr. Mazor smiled at their enthusiasm. She carried paperwork attached to a clipboard and entered information for the Florida Master Site File. She showed Dori where Dori's Mound was recorded and given a site number. "Your dad can make a copy for you when we get back to his office."

She took out the government USGS Map and circled the general area Judd pointed out on the map. A GPS gave her the coordinates.

"The coral pieces are from coastal areas, and the chert or fossilized limestone are from quarries found near the surface. The pink or orange pieces were heat-treated."

"Would this be a burial mound?" Judd asked.

"Without an investigation, it's hard to tell. This might be a midden, or living area built up to be a dry place during times of high water. The surface pottery and lithic material indicate this is the most likely use. I'm intrigued by the ridged areas, radiating outward." She made a rough sketch of them on her paperwork.

"Some mounds are built up for a special event and left. No artifacts are found. A burial mound is usually away from a village site." She looked around. "This mound is too small to be a village site, but it was ideal for hunters who moved to different areas seasonally."

Judd drove them to several other sites, and Dr. Mazor recorded each. She looked at Dori and said, "You did the right thing by not picking up everything."

Dori's shoulders came up as she hugged the compliment, a big smile on her face.

"You are so lucky to have your name on a map," Bobbie Jean said.

"I think we have another area we can name for you," Judd told her.

Bobbie Jean squealed, her excitement contagious. She hugged Dori, and they jumped up and down, laughing.

After the archaeologist finished the forms, they headed back to the office, and Judd made copies for his files.

~

Katie's riding lessons progressed until she felt comfortable enough to ask Slim if he had a horse she could ride.

"How much ya know 'bout horses, Miss Katie? Ya ever rode one?"

"I'm taking lessons at Good Ride Stables, and Patty Rushing said I'm a natural."

"How many lessons ya had?"

"Six. I haven't fallen off," Katie informed him.

"I doan know," Slim said as he scratched his head. "Let me ask the boss. Our horses are purty frisky. Can't think ah one to put a beginner on ta."

When Judd came to the kitchen later for lunch, he spoke to Katie. "Slim said you were asking about a horse to ride."

"Yes. I've been taking lessons," and she told him about the stables.

"All our horses are cow horses used to move and sort cattle. We also hire cowboys who bring their own. Six lessons don't make you a proficient rider."

Katie straightened her back. "Then I guess I'll have to buy one."

Judd shook his head in a negative response, pressing his lips in a flat line. "Why haven't I heard you were taking lessons?" he asked.

"Do I have to tell you everything I'm doing?" His questioning annoyed her, and her voice held a caustic tone.

Judd moved and stood over her, his hands on her shoulders and his eyes intense, holding her own. "I need to know your whereabouts and any involvement you have with the outside community."

Katie shook off his hands, stepping back. "You're not my father or my master. I don't have to report anything I do to you."

Judd pulled her to him, lifting her chin with one hand. "I need to know," he ground out, "because I care about you, and I don't want you to get hurt."

"Hurt how? I'm taking lessons from an award-winning rider with a good reputation."

"As a member of my household, you're vulnerable. You're so naïve, you believe everyone is good, their intentions toward you honorable."

"And you, of course, are one of those people I'm supposed to believe has honorable intentions." She tried to move away, but he held her fast.

"I would never hurt you, Katie." His voice softened and held enough care, tears swelled in her eyes.

"There are people in this world who would enjoy hurting you, for no other reason than to make me pay for my position or any slights they have cobbled into a vendetta. I have enemies, Katie, not of my own choosing or because I've earned their enmity."

Katie looked at him, a tear rolling down one cheek. "I feel sorry for you, Judd. I can't live my life believing someone is plotting to hurt me." She swallowed her reluctance to boldly speak. "I believe in God, Judd. I believe He is in control, and He will equip me to handle any situation. I refuse to live my life in fear."

Judd's mouth covered her own, but this time, she didn't respond, and Judd let her go.

"I'll find you a horse," he said to her departing back.

Katie felt whipped as she walked to the cabin. "Maybe I was wrong, God," she said aloud. "This is not what You want for me ... is it?" she added hopefully. "No, better to know it now, Katie girl" as her daddy often said when things went awry. Gunnar was a case in point.

Judd stared at the screen door that snapped shut behind her. Katie had a will of her own. She had the fortitude to deny him what he knew they both wanted. She even questioned and scoffed at his authority. Grown men, powerful men were cautious in his presence. Katie walked a dangerous path supported by her faith, and Judd's strength took a hit. *She feels sorry for me. God, what am I doing wrong?* he thought before he realized he had appealed to the Almighty. *What's happening to me?* Judd wondered if J. D. had any idea how this year would turn out. Katie had called him on his honorable intentions. She placed him in the category of people he warned her against.

Judd was glad Dori had come home, but this woman, this enigma J. D. had saddled him with for a year shouldn't be here. The thought that J. D. deeded twenty-four thousand acres of Corazon and ten percent of Stetson Enterprises' stock to Katie, galled him. What if she decided to sell her half? The possibility didn't bear thinking about. *Luke is no longer a threat. He and Pam are engaged and planning to marry in April.*

Katie is running from my advances. What will she do with her inheritance when she leaves in May? He believed now, she would leave, and there were other men out there to woo her into marriage.

She would stay at Corazon to the bitter end, not for him, but for Dori. He knew she loved Dori. *She loves me. I know she does.* His thoughts about his place in Katie's life also took a hit. He was having a more difficult time convincing himself of the fact.

Judd would try to find a horse suitable for Katie to ride. Dori needed to learn, too. He took out the phone book and called Good Ride Stables.

~

Judd surprised Katie when his truck pulled up with the horse trailer attached.

Dori ran out excited to see a horse inside.

Jammer and Scooby barked, and Judd shooed them away from the trailer. The cacophony of sounds brought Katie out of the cabin to see what was happening. She put her hands over her mouth when she saw Judd leading Firefly, the Paint horse she had been riding, from the trailer. She was saddled and ready to be ridden.

Dori picked up Scooby, and Judd commanded Jammer to sit and stay. The dogs howled, but other than rolling her eyes, Firefly did not appear perturbed by the animals.

"Oh Judd," Katie cried. She moved forward to run her hand down

Firefly's neck. "How did you talk Patty into letting you borrow her horse?"

"I bought her," Judd said, his voice crisp and decisive.

Katie looked at him, but he didn't appear to be bothered by the astronomical price tag Patty Rushing probably charged him. She had told Katie just last week, Firefly wasn't for sale.

Dori peppered her dad with pleas to let her ride, and he told her she must have lessons first. "I'll teach you to ride," he said.

Katie hugged Judd and thanked him profusely for his magnanimous gift. This was not the first time he had splurged to get her something she wanted. The Christmas tree came to mind.

Judd handed Katie the lead and entered the trailer to bring out currying tools and the rest of Firefly's accoutrements.

Dori moved forward to pat the horse. "What's its name?"

"Firefly. I've been riding her at Good Ride Stables while taking lessons."

"She's so pretty. Where will she live?" Dori asked her dad.

"I'll have to put her in the pen behind Slim's cabin until we build a stable for her. The wood and building materials will arrive later today."

"Can I ride her?" Dori pleaded.

"May I?" Katie corrected without thinking.

"May I ride her?"

"You heard what your daddy said, but maybe he'll let me lead you around for a bit." She looked at Judd.

He nodded and gave Dori a boost onto the saddle. "Hang on to the saddle horn."

Katie led Firefly around the yard, and Dori loved the ride.

"When can I learn, Daddy?"

"Soon, sweetheart, soon." Dori needed to learn since she was staying at Corazon, and she was old enough. Patty Rushing had told him Firefly was gentle and the horse she used for beginners. Judd unholstered his phone and made a call. "Slim, saddle Rico for me, and bring him to the house." He listened for a moment and said, "That's okay. We'll get him," and replaced the phone on his belt. "He's not in the vicinity. We'll ride over and get him."

"I want to go," Dori said as Judd lifted her out of the saddle.

"Not this time, pumpkin. Firefly can only carry two of us."

Katie understood Judd was going to ride with her. The realization they would share one horse filled her with trepidation.

"Up you go," he said to Katie. She put her foot in the stirrup and pulled herself up on the saddle. Judd checked the stirrup length, and took her foot out of one. He swung up behind her in one easy motion. Judd put his arms around her waist. "Okay, take us to Slim's cabin."

Katie had trouble breathing as she adjusted the reins and moved Firefly forward. Having Judd hugging her back, with his arms around her, was disconcerting. Her excitement at his proximity was hard to contain.

They were walking down the dirt road when Judd prompted her to 'move it.' "Can't you go any faster?"

"Hold on," she hollered and gave Firefly the go-ahead. They raced down the road, and Judd held her tightly to him.

As they entered Slim's yard, Judd said, "Okay, you've made your point, now slow down and take her around to the pens." Slim's dogs barked an alarm from the kennels, but Firefly ignored them.

Good Ride Stables had a number of noisy dogs. Jammer raced up as Judd walked in the building to get his horse's tack, and the dogs howled. Judd entered the pen and separated Rico from the other horses.

Katie watched how efficiently and expertly Judd readied his horse. He led Rico out of the pen and closed the gate. Judd swung into the saddle, and they trotted down the dirt horse path through the hammock and avoided the graveled areas.

Judd saw how well Katie handled Firefly and admired her control. Thinking about Patty Rushing's assessment, Judd saw Katie's confidence and poise. She was a natural. Katie had surprised him when she gave Firefly her head and raced to Slim's cabin. He had to hang on to keep from falling off. Katie felt good in his arms, too good. He had to think of the work piling up in the office to stay in physical control.

Judd opened the gates when they rode through the pastures.

Katie noticed cows began to move in their direction.

Her exhilaration as they galloped down a trail through a large hammock showed on her face.

Judd stopped at a cistern with a windmill, and they dismounted. The large, round concrete container held water for the cattle.

Cows began to show up in groups. They mooed and pressed in until Katie backed into Judd's arms.

"They won't hurt you. They're curious and want you to see if you have something to eat." He pointed out one of the mineral blocks they put out around the ranch and told her they also put out molasses to encourage the cattle to eat the dry, native grasses and roughage during the winter months.

The poles with covered ropes strung between them had a repellant to keep flies away. The cows walked under the rope and let it roll over their backs.

Judd turned Katie in his arms and brought her face up where he could enjoy her eyes bright with excitement and the flags of color in her cheeks. He covered her mouth with his and she leaned in, a willing participant. Judd took advantage of her compliance and deepened the kiss. His hand came up to mold her breast, and he pulled her closer.

Katie backed away embarrassed, her step reluctant.

Judd laughed. "You know what I think?"

Katie shook her head, her eyes wide and waited for him to make fun of her.

"I think we should get naked and go skinny dipping."

"What?" Katie said, backing up in disbelief. She tripped over a palm boot and landed on her fanny with one hand in a fresh cow plop. The cows had moved away. She laughed as she drew her hand from the steaming mass. "Ick! It's still warm."

Judd doubled over laughing. He stooped to pull her up by her other hand, unable to stifle his mirth. He then headed to nearby trees and picked up some moss. Judd wiped off most of the pungent mess and led her back to the cistern. He used his wet handkerchief to wash her hand. He discarded the cloth and scooped out water for another rinse. Judd wiped her hand on his jeans.

Katie took the incident in stride, without castigation or grumbling. The laughter they shared lightened Judd's spirit.

"You know you belong on Corazon, Katie," he stated with conviction. His reassessment and the realization he needed her to stay settled deep in his bones.

Katie leaned over the cistern, looking at her reflection in the dark water. *Two more months, too much time, and too little willpower left.* "Were you serious about getting in here?" she asked, trying to change the subject.

Judd laughed again. "Yep, but it's too cold now. Cowboys have been known to shuck down and take a dip on hot days." He looked at her with a grin and smoldering eyes. "I have to admit, I need a cold bath right now," and when he began unbuttoning his shirt, Katie gulped and fled to her horse.

Judd laughed again. "I'm teasing you, silly goose." He re-buttoned his shirt and sauntered to Rico for the ride back home. *Home.*

CHAPTER FORTY-SEVEN

March arrived with a downpour. Judd told them it rained four inches during the night, and he called Melvin to help him pull boards. He explained to Katie and Dori, "The water filling the ditches has to be lowered or the pastures and groves will flood. Slim, Sam and a few of the men have to move the cattle to higher ground."

Judd slipped on a yellow slicker and put a fitted plastic covering over his hat. He handed Dori her red raincoat, boots, and cap. "Put your backpack in a plastic bag."

Zita went to the pantry for a small garbage bag.

"Katie, will you take Dori to school this morning?"

"Not a problem," she responded as she picked up the umbrella by the door. "Dori, I'm going to the cabin for my purse, and I'll pick you up around front. Wait on the porch for me."

Judd kissed Dori on the forehead. "Have a good day at school. I'll pick you up."

Dori was waiting on the front porch when Katie drove around. Water sluiced off the roof in a waterfall, and she put up her umbrella and brought Dori to the car. Katie was soaked, and water dripped down her legs onto the floor. She checked to see if Dori was dry.

"Did your daddy say if the rain would continue much longer?" she asked.

"He said the rain wasn't moving fast, so it wouldn't stop until later. Do you think Snowball is all right?"

"I'm sure she's fine. Her mother will stay with her."

"What about Scooby."

"I'm sure he's in one of the sheds out of the rain with Jammer."

Katie wished she had the Expedition. Her Pathfinder was lower to the ground, and the water was collecting in the ruts, making her wary of crossing where the water covered the road.

She managed to get Dori to school and noticed they weren't the only ones late because of the rain.

Driving back to the cabin was slower. Some of the pastures were already underwater and looked like lakes. Water washed across the road leaving ruts that were deeper than when she left the house. She stopped in time when she saw part of the road had washed away, and the area was widening as the water rushed through from a higher to lower area.

Katie backed her car away from the washout and searched her purse for the phone to warn Judd.

His phone rang four or five times and went to voicemail. "There's a washout on the road coming in, so be careful if you're driving out. It's hidden around a curve on your side. I'm backing up and going around to the other entrance."

Backing a car had never been easy for Katie, and the rain on the back windshield blocked her view. The side mirrors were little help, and ten minutes later, her back wheel went off the road and mired down.

She tried to regain the road, but her vehicle didn't have 4-Wheel Drive.

Taking her umbrella, Katie got out of the car to see how badly the car was stuck. One wheel was almost completely covered, and the other wheel had slipped off the elevated road, tilting the car. Katie hoped it wouldn't sink any lower. Her Pathfinder would have to be towed out, and she was reluctant to call Judd. He had a lot of work to do, and Katie didn't want to distract him.

Wet and cold she climbed back into the car and waited. The vehicle finally settled. Judd would notice she hadn't returned and call her when he wasn't busy.

Her body began to shiver. She didn't have an overcoat to cover her wet body, so Katie started the car and turned on the heater.

Time passed and Katie became sleepy and nauseated. She needed air. Her phone rang, but she didn't have the energy to pick it up. She felt strange and tried to open the door, but Katie didn't have the strength to push the door out.

Suddenly, cold wind and water hit her face, but her eyes refused to open.

"Katie! Katie!" a frantic voice called. The words sounded distant.

Judd. What's wrong? I'm here. Her lips moved, but no words came out. Strong arms held her close, rain soaking her.

Judd carried her to his truck, calling her name over and over. "Katie! Katie! Wake up! Open your eyes!" His heart pounded a loud drumming in his ears. *She has to be all right.* Fear heightened his senses.

She tried to answer, but her tongue wouldn't work.

"Katie Mulholland, if you die on me, I'll never forgive you," he hollered at her.

Die? Her muddled mind tried to process the word. *Why would I die?* She gurgled a laugh, her throat sore. "Wha …"

"Katie, Katie, wake up and breathe!" He shook her, and she gulped air as instructed.

Her eyes opened to slits. Judd looked distraught. "Wha … happened?" She finally got out the words which sounded like a long string of syllables.

Feeling returned slowly, and Judd kissed her mouth, face, and neck. "Thank you, God."

She tried to think. *Why? What?* Judd had tears on his face, or no, must be dripping water, not tears. Katie laughed, and it sounded pathetic to her ears. The more she tried to stop, the more the horrible sound came out.

"You're going to be all right, Katie. Take deep breaths." Judd patted her cheeks with cold, wet hands.

Her eyes focused on Judd. He was standing in the open door of the truck with water pouring off the roof and over him. His yellow slicker covered her body. "Why don't you get out of the rain?" she asked, the words forming slowly. *What's wrong with me?*

Judd pushed her farther into the truck and closed the door. When he moved to the other side of the truck, Katie saw her car. The back passenger side was underwater.

Judd started his truck and leaned over the console. "How do you feel?" he asked, concern written on his face.

Katie shook her head, trying to clear her thoughts. "I'm tired," she said and turned her head back against the seat, closing her eyes.

Judd shook her shoulder, and he wasn't gentle about it. "Open your eyes, Katie," he commanded.

"Stop it," she said, her head pounding.

"Wake up, you infernal hussy and stop scaring me!"

Katie heard the phone as he punched in the numbers. "Nine-one-one," she heard and mumbled, "Nine-one-one?"

Judd called an ambulance, giving his location. "I'll meet you on the road. She needs oxygen. Carbon monoxide poisoning."

Katie struggled to sit up. "Me?" she said, her voice squeaking.

"Yes, you," he replied. "Your exhaust pipe is underwater. If I hadn't found you when I did, you might have died," he said and thought, *or be a vegetable for the rest of your life.* "Thank you, God." he said again.

Katie looked at him as she tried to push herself up in the seat. *Is he talking to God?* She looked around for Him.

Judd backed down the road and checked to be sure she was breathing. "Don't close your eyes," he ordered.

Katie's hands came up, and her fingers pried her eyes open. "They're open."

Judd loosed a nervous laugh. "Keep them open."

"Not easy," she replied.

The ambulance pulled in behind the truck, and Judd carried her to the open back doors. He filled the EMTs in on the situation. They put an oxygen mask over her face, covered her with blankets, and began to take her vitals.

"I'll see you at the hospital," Judd said, before the doors closed.

Katie was still in the emergency room when Judd arrived. One of the nurses took pity on him and allowed him into Katie's cubicle. She was hooked to an IV and had an oxygen tent over her head. Her wet clothing had been removed, and she wore a hospital gown.

Katie opened her eyes when he scraped a chair close to the bed. "Did you call me a hussy?"

"Is that what you dreamed?" he replied.

Katie moved restlessly, her forehead furrowing in thought. "It seemed so real. You didn't?"

"Maybe I said it when I wasn't thinking straight." Judd admitted. "What else do you remember?"

"Why did you call me a hussy?"

"I hoped it would make you mad, and you'd wake up. You did. I'm sorry if I offended you."

"The doctor said you saved my life. Thank you."

Judd brushed her thanks aside. "Why didn't you call me when you got stuck? I was frantic when I returned to the house, and Zita said you hadn't come back." He remembered the fear that consumed him when he thought she might have been hurt. "I called a dozen times while driving around to look for you and you didn't answer the phone."

"I didn't want to take you from your work," she said haltingly. "Did you pick up Dori?"

Judd looked at his watch. "It's only 11:10 in the morning." *Always thinking of others.*

"Oh, it seems like a long time. When can I leave here?"

"I don't know. You'll stay as long as necessary. The doctor has the last word. Don't worry about Dori. I'll pick her up."

"I'm sorry for all the trouble. Driving in reverse has always been a problem for me."

"I'm giving you lessons, and that's the end of the subject."

CHAPTER FORTY-EIGHT

Easter would come early this year, and Katie was anxious to go home for Spring Break. Dori's eighth birthday was a little over a week away and her mother's fiftieth, two weeks from now. Birthdays in Katie's family were celebrated. Katie became twenty-five last July, two months after coming to Corazon. She hadn't told anyone she had a birthday because she didn't want anyone to feel the need to get her a present. Her family sent cards, books, and gift certificates. She had no idea when Judd had a birthday, and she hadn't asked. She would be twenty-six in four months.

Merit and Katie had forged a friendship since Christmas. Katie's trips to Palm Beach became a weekly respite from Judd's effort to coerce her into a relationship which would keep her at Corazon. Merit had helped her cobble together a casual wardrobe for various occasions. The older woman took her under her wing, and they enjoyed one another's company.

Katie called Merit. "I need to find Dori a snowsuit for her birthday. She and Judd are going skiing in Colorado during Spring Break. The trip is Dori's birthday present."

"I remember him getting the trip at the gala. What a great idea!" Merit said. "I want to help."

A trip to Palm Beach was planned. Merit checked with her buyers and found a site on the Internet to order children's snowsuits. Katie ordered a turquoise ski pants and jacket set, and Merit bought her a turquoise and pink snow cap with gloves to match.

Katie filled Merit in on the carbon monoxide incident and about Judd saving her life. "He called me a hussy to make me mad and to wake me up. It worked."

Merit was appalled at how close they had come to losing Katie.

"Judd must have been 'crazy worried' about you. I know he has feelings for you, Katie."

"I know. He's conflicted." Then laughing, Katie told her about riding lessons, the cistern story, and landing in cow poop.

Merit laughed until tears rolled down her cheeks. "You have been so good for Judd. He's really loosened up, and he's regained his sense of humor." She reached over and touched Katie's hand. "J.D. would be pleased. I'm sorry you're planning to leave Corazon. We will all miss you."

Katie nodded as her eyes misted. "I know, and I'll miss all of you."

"You're in love with Judd, aren't you?"

Katie nodded and swallowed her pride. "He won't marry for love. At first, I believed his unfortunate marriage to Rita was the reason. From things he's said, I now believe he won't bend to J.D.'s expectations for him, and I don't blame him." She picked up the napkin, folded it, and then twisted it in her hands. "J.D.'s Will was a bitter pill for Judd to swallow. Having Dori at Corazon has tempered some of his ire, but she's his daughter. Dori belongs there. I'm not only an interloper, I hold a half-interest in Corazon, the one thing he loves most next to Dori."

"What are you going to do with your inheritance?" Merit asked. "Will you sell your half of Corazon and your shares?"

Katie looked at Merit, surprised she would ask so personal a question. She didn't want to share her plans. "No, I won't sell. Judd can handle the business side without my interference."

"Judd must be frantic, wondering what you'll do."

"That's his problem. Only one of many, I might add." Katie told Merit about her conversation with Judd and about his paranoia. "He thinks I'm vulnerable, and someone might use me to get to him."

"That's partly J.D.'s influence. Each Board Member was required to take rigorous self-defense classes and aggressive driving instructions to elude capture. The most important thing we learned was to keep our eyes open and to know what is going on around us. J.D. personally knew some corporate ransom victims, and he made it a policy that ransom would never be paid for him."

Katie remembered J.D. telling her that when he thought he was being kidnapped.

"Until the last few years of his life, J.D. had security people with him for meetings and trips. He left most of his business in the hands of competent managers. His remote cabin in the backwoods of Louisiana only had perimeter security." She smiled at Katie. "We never did find out what wild notion made him leave the cabin in a storm, by himself, in so much of a hurry, he ended up in a canal."

"I refuse to live my life in fear, and I told Judd I felt sorry for him."

"Oh my! You're fearless. I can just imagine how he took that." Merit sat back in her chair and regarded the young woman she had grown to like and respect. "You cut him off at the knees and live to tell about it. My lips are sealed. We certainly don't want to bandy about that my dear cousin has a weakness."

"Judd isn't weak. He just doesn't know how to lose."

"I believe J.D. knew exactly what he was doing, placing you and Dori on the ranch with Judd for a year." Merit nodded her head as she thought about the situation. "J.D. also had an aversion to losing. I'm betting he won't lose this time either."

"That remains to be seen. I can say without a doubt, you and Judd share the same trait ... confidence in an outcome."

Merit smiled.

CHAPTER FORTY-NINE

Homecoming at Corazon after Spring Break filled Katie with a new sense of dread. She would be leaving in five weeks. The days would go fast, and she didn't want her time at Corazon to end.

Dori followed her to the cabin, chattering about the ski trip and being able to ski without poles. "Daddy had to have poles to ski. He looked so funny when he fell down. I fell down, too, but it didn't hurt. We got to ski together when the lessons stopped."

"I'm glad you enjoyed your trip. Snow skiing looks like fun."

"You have to do it, too. Daddy can teach you, and he can pick you up when you fall."

Katie tried to smile and look happy, but she knew that scenario wasn't likely.

Judd joined them in the cabin after Katie brought in her luggage. Dori pulled on Katie's shirt to get her attention. "You know what?"

"That's what," Katie said without thinking. It was her mother's response to all of her questions spoken with these words.

Dori looked at her, trying to figure out Katie's meaning, but she didn't stop for long. "We went dog-sledding, and it was sooo much fun," she recounted excitedly. "Daddy got to run the sled by himself, and I sat in it, under the covers. The dogs went on trails and through the woods. And it snowed on us." Dori didn't slow down, and only stopped to catch her breath. "The dogs are beautiful, and I got to hug them afterwards. Daddy said we can do it again. You'll love it!" Judd sat on the Bentley rocker and listened to his daughter's stories.

Katie looked at Judd. He smiled his satisfaction, and his eyebrows rose, challenging her to disagree.

She turned from his confident face. "Maybe someday. We'll see."

Katie turned down the air conditioner as the temperature outside had reached ninety degrees. The cabin seemed warmer, smaller, and more intimate with Judd inside.

"How was your trip?" Judd asked. "Did everyone come to your mother's birthday party?"

"Yes," Katie responded. "Everyone showed up. We all chipped in and gave Mom a combined Birthday and Mother's Day present." This had been the highlight of the vacation. "We gave Mom and Dad a trip to Ireland this summer. Dad helped, and we had the brochures, tickets, and itinerary in a flight bag for her. She was overwhelmed and cried."

Katie remembered her mother's surprised reaction to what she called, "the best gift ever." "She's always wanted to make the trip, especially after doing some genealogy on our Irish roots.

"Karen and Hank sent their love. They hope you'll be able to get together again."

"Yesss," Dori said, and pumped her arm in her familiar expression of joy.

Katie unpacked without looking at Judd.

He finally rose from the chair and asked her if she would have dinner with them.

"Not tonight," she said. "I've been on the road since two this morning. I had a sandwich earlier. I'm going to get some sleep."

They left, and Katie sat down on the bed, the unfamiliar loneliness, a new companion.

~

April brought showers, and the zinnias and pinks Zita planted made a colorful display in the garden. Katie regarded zinnias as old-fashioned. She kept fresh, cut flowers in a Mason jar on the table.

Katie walked to the stable as she did each morning. Judd had it built behind the cabin, and he helped with its construction. She groomed Firefly and fed her every day. Most mornings when Dori was in school and the weather permitting, she saddled Firefly and rode over the ranch. She waited until Judd went to the office and tried to get away before he noticed. Katie thought the less she saw of Judd, the easier leaving would be.

Judd had Rico saddled and waited for her at the stable.

Katie stopped in her tracks, unsure how to handle the situation.

"I thought I'd ride with you this morning. You've been avoiding me and sneaking off to ride." His voice was low as he chided her. "I never thought you a coward."

Katie's eyes came up to meet his own.

Judd regarded her intently, his eyes challenging her to respond to his plain speaking.

Katie turned and began to ready Firefly for the ride. "I call it self-preservation, not cowardice. I'm leaving in two weeks. I don't need reminders of what I'll miss."

"You don't have to leave or miss a thing," he added in a velvet voice, ripe with meaning.

Katie ducked under Firefly's neck and mounted.

My sole consolation is knowing I won't be the only one missing something, but she didn't voice the thought. The less she said the better.

Katie moved Firefly around Rico and took a trail through the hammock, skirting the grove. She didn't look back but knew Judd followed. When she got to the long road bordering the pastures, she let Firefly run.

Judd watched Katie leave him without saying more. He mounted Rico and rode after her, his emotions in turmoil. *She's committed to leave Corazon and me. How could she leave Dori?*

Firefly was fast, but Judd caught up with Katie when she stopped to open a gate. She moved Firefly through and left Judd to close the gate.

Katie was running from him, and it didn't sit well with Judd that she had the temerity to leave all he could offer her if she stayed.

Katie rode cautiously across the pasture. She didn't want Firefly to get hurt.

Judd caught up with her when she entered a hammock of large oaks. Most of the underbrush had been shaded out, leaving cleared areas under the outstretched limbs. "Hold up", he said and caught her reins when she refused to stop. "We need to talk,"

"I don't think so," Katie countered.

"Stop being stubborn, woman," he said, lifting her off her horse.

When he set her on the ground, she started to remount, and he caught her as he swung down from his ride. "Don't run away. Talk to me."

"I have nothing to say to you."

"Say you want to stay at Corazon. Tell me you don't want to leave me, leave Dori. I want you Katie, and I know you want me, too."

"I can't. I won't. Talking isn't going to change the outcome."

"Talking is overrated." He drew her close and kissed her, possession paramount.

She was in the arms of a fully aroused male, and her knees buckled. Tears fell and she leaned in, drying them on his shirt. Her hands clutched his shoulders, wanting him with every fiber of her being.

His fingers opened the first two buttons of her shirt before she put her hands over his and stopped him.

"Please, Judd. Don't do this. You know you can, and I won't resist, but I'll never forgive you."

"God, Katie," he rasped, frustrated, trying to regain physical control.

"Please let me go, Judd. Please."

He loosed her and backed away, his expression of disbelief revealing the hurt of her rejection.

Katie remounted and headed home before she gave in to temptation.

Judd watched Katie ride away, a storm gathering within. *She can't leave me.* This certainty, like his early dreams, slipped away like the sands at low tide. *Yes she can.*

~

Katie paced the cabin, wiping tears. She put her wants behind her and concentrated on what needed to be done. Talking to Dori headed her list.

Luke and Pam had invited them to their wedding in a few days. If they went together, she would have to deal with Judd. His look of hurt at her rejection wore her down. *I can't feel sorry for him. I can't. He's responsible for his feelings, his obstinance.*

Dori knocked on the door, and Katie gave her permission to enter.

"Why are you crying?" she asked as soon as she saw Katie's face.

Now was as good a time as any to speak to Dori. She sat on the bed. "I'm sad that I'll be leaving Corazon soon. I'm really going to miss our time together."

"Oh," Dori said and wrapped her arms around Katie's shoulders as if to comfort her.

"I'm going to miss you, too. Why won't you stay? Daddy said you could stay."

"I know, sweetheart, but I have to get back to my work, and I have a family, too. They miss me."

"Oh." She sat next to Katie on the bed. "Are you coming back?"

"I may come back, but it will probably be a while. Maybe your daddy can bring you to Louisiana when he has business there. Karen and Hank want to see you again."

Dori leaned into her shoulder, and Katie was glad to see she seemed to accept her leaving without the tears she had shed at the pizza parlor. "I was hoping you would take care of Firefly for me. Will you feed her and take care of her?"

"I'll take good care of Firefly," she promised. "Daddy says he's going to teach me to ride."

"I'm glad. You'll make a good cowgirl."

Dori stood, her face downcast, her mouth pursed in thought. She looked at Katie, her gaze unwavering. "Do you like my daddy?"

"Of course, I do. Why would you ask me that?"

"You don't come to the house anymore, and daddy and me are sad." Dori sounded older than her eight years. "I want to hear you play the piano."

"It's hard to say goodbye to people you love. Sometimes, it's easier to stay away."

"If you love them, you should want to see them a lot before you go." Dori's lower lip began to quiver, and her eyes welled.

Katie hugged Dori. "You're right, Dori. I'm such a wimp."

"Will you come to dinner?"

"Yes, I want to spend time with you," Katie said. Dori put her to shame. She was growing up fast. Dori, no longer the displaced child, spoke with confidence and clarity.

~

Katie entered the kitchen and Zita bustled over to welcome her. "I so glad to see you." Her eyes sparkled, and impulsively she hugged Katie, then stepped back, a look of surprise on her face.

Judd stood and seated Katie when she walked to the table. His smile reached his eyes, and they registered hope.

Dori grinned big. She jumped up and hugged Katie. "I told you she was coming to dinner," she said to her father.

Katie had to smile at the little girl's enthusiasm.

Dori wiggled in her chair, assured she had accomplished something big.

"Thank you for joining us tonight," Judd said, warmth in his voice. "We've missed you at our meals."

"I appreciate Dori's invitation," she said, and Dori patted her shoulder and took her hand.

Before anything else was said, Dori bowed her head and prayed. "Thank you, God, for Katie coming to dinner, and thank you for our food, and thank you for Daddy. Amen."

"Amen." Judd said softly, and Katie looked at him again. He looked subdued, and Zita entered with the night's fare.

"What you want for drink, Miss Katie? Sweet? Unsweet?"

"Sweet," Katie said, deciding to splurge. *Is Judd rethinking commitment?*

"I have a great thought," Dori said. She looked at Katie and then her daddy. "Why don't we plan to go dog-sledding next year, and Karen and Hank can have fun, too. Katie can learn to ski."

Katie bowed her head and raised her napkin to hide a smile. Dori took on the role of matchmaker.

"Sounds like a good plan to me," Judd said, looking at Katie.

This line of thinking needed to stop. "I'm not sure if I'll be able to get off work next year. I've been gone a long time."

Dori's face fell, and she chewed her lips thinking. She brightened. "If you worked for my daddy, he'd let you have a vacation."

Katie patted Dori's hand. "My work is not something your daddy can use. Maybe Hank and Karen's family will want to go sometime. They can meet you there."

Dori frowned. Her ploy wasn't working.

Judd said, "Stetson's can always use a good ad agency. You can have your own business."

Dori perked up, and her eyes lit with hope.

Katie looked at Judd. *Is he serious? Yes, he'd make it possible.* "I'm sorry, Judd," she said. "That won't work for me. Thank you for the offer." She took a roll out of the basket, asked Dori to pass the butter, and changed the subject. "When will you finish harvesting Valencias?"

"Probably in late May."

They engaged in small talk until Judd said, "I'll drive you to the wedding."

Katie froze. "Maybe we should take two vehicles."

"Why would we?" Judd countered.

"I'd like to go to the reception at the Albritton's afterward. You won't want to go."

"Why not?" He smiled his amusement, knowing she was looking for an excuse.

Dori's head swiveled back and forth following the conversation.

"I thought you weren't interested in large social affairs," Katie answered.

"I think I can manage a few hours. We'll take the Expedition."

CHAPTER FIFTY

Saturday's weather didn't disappoint. The sun came out for Luke and Pam's wedding day. The reception at the Albritton's home would be beautiful.

Judd and Katie sat in the same pew with Dori between them.

Luke looked handsome in his tux, and Katie watched him as Pam walked down the aisle. She saw love and pride shining on his face.

Judd also watched Luke. He thought about how time changed everything. A few months ago, he thought Katie would be the bride walking down the aisle instead of Pam. A sigh of relief escaped, and Katie noticed. Judd smiled and thought. *You didn't marry the man who epitomized the perfect husband. You love me, Katie, and in the end, you'll stay.* He tried to banish any other outcome.

Pam looked radiant. Her gown had a vintage look with a pleated empire bust line and antique lace covering her shoulders and arms. The veil was trimmed in the same lace, and it was attached on the top of her head with cream orchids and pearls. Her shiny, blond hair curled unbound down her back.

Katie wondered if the dress had belonged to Pam's grandmother. She had seen her own grandmother's wedding picture but didn't know if the gown she wore had been preserved.

Reverend Tom Dickon conducted the service. He spoke to the couple about commitment, fidelity, integrity, and the importance of communication in a marriage. "Marriage is a covenant you make with God and with each other. Keep Christ as the head of your home, and He will provide for your needs."

Judd glanced at Katie and saw her wiping tears. *Is she sorry? No, I know she's genuinely happy for them.* The tears made Judd uncomfortable, and his confidence was shaken.

The service lasted under thirty minutes, and Judd drove them to the Albritton's home while the couple and the wedding party stayed behind for pictures.

Numerous people arrived before them, and Judd realized many of those attending had not been at the service. The Albrittons must have made other arrangements.

When the wedding party arrived, Luke's sister walked to Katie and hugged her. "I want you to know we are praying for your happiness and the man you will one day marry."

Katie's lip quivered as she said, "Thank you, Janet. I covet your prayers, and I appreciate your family's friendship more than you know."

Pam and Luke made the rounds and came over to her when Judd took Dori to get some dinner. "What are your plans, Katie?" Luke asked.

"I'll be going home in a week." She took a deep breath, not wanting to get emotional. "This year has been a fairy tale. Thank you for your friendship and help making the cabin comfortable. I'll never forget the laughter and Florida history we've shared. I know you'll both be happy, and I'm happy for you."

Pam moved forward and hugged Katie. "Thank you," she whispered in her ear.

Katie thought she understood, but she decided not to dwell on the comment. "I hope if you come to Louisiana, you'll look me up, and I'll give you the grand tour."

Luke hugged her and whispered, "Be happy, Katie."

She nodded, and they walked to another group of friends. Katie spotted Judd, and noticed he kept his eyes on her as she moved in the crowd.

Bobbie Jean and Dori sat together eating. Jan and Joel Madsen sat with them.

Katie would miss her new friends.

Judd came to Katie's side. "Would you like to get something to eat?"

"Not right now. I'm not really hungry. You go ahead."

"Let me know when you're ready to leave," he said before walking back to the food table.

Katie found the Raulersons and thanked them for their friendship and asked about Pam's gown. She was right. The dress had been worn by Sandra Raulerson's mother.

"Pam is a beautiful bride, and the gown makes the wedding even more special," Katie told them.

"Thank you for coming today," John said, and he put his arm around Sandra's shoulders, hugging her to his side. "We've been married forty-two years. We believe Luke and Pam will also have a lifelong marriage."

"I'm sure you're right," Katie said before going to the refreshment table for punch.

She would wait until Judd and Dori finished eating before asking to go home and put Judd out of his misery. She noted he ate with some of the men from the church, and he looked comfortable. Maybe she was wrong in her assumptions.

~

Judd carried the Bentley rocker out of the cabin and placed it in the back of Katie's Pathfinder.

Katie tucked her luggage and personal items around the chair. She had to put the box of Christmas ornaments and tree skirt on the front seat. Katie debated about leaving them, but figured they would end up in another box, forgotten. The angels would bring to mind the memories of a special evening when she felt like a princess and danced with her prince.

Dori would be home from school soon, and Katie wanted to be sure and tell her goodbye.

Judd placed his hands on Katie's shoulders. "I'm not comfortable with you driving by yourself so early in the morning."

"I've found early morning is the best time to travel. The lights are mostly green, no traffic to speak of, and I'll be on I-10 before rush hour. Don't worry. I stop at rest areas with security and at businesses with people."

"Katie, I want you to keep in touch. Dori's already asking me when we can see you again."

"I know. She's growing up so fast, and I'll miss seeing her every day."

"Then don't go." Judd took a deep breath, pulled Katie into his arms, and put his chin on the top of her head. "I don't want you to leave, Katie."

She heard his heart beating in her ear and savored the moment.

"You're part of Corazon now. Please stay. I need you to stay, for me."

Katie moved her face against his shirt, smelling his masculine scent, and enjoying the safe harbor of his arms. "I know." She stepped back, a wan smile on her face. "This has been the most incredible year of my life. Thank you for finally accepting me."

She returned to the cabin, and Judd followed her inside.

"I meant what I said about setting up an ad agency for you."

"I know, but leaving now is best for me. I need to get back to the real world, to my job, and my family."

Judd kissed her forehead and cradling her face moved down to kiss her lips.

Katie backed away. "Please, Judd, don't make this any harder on either of us. I'll see you at dinner and tell Dori and Zita goodbye."

When she turned away, he asked, "What are your plans for Corazon, your inheritance?"

Katie closed her eyes, and a crushing pain stabbed her in the chest. *Of course, he has to know.*

She faced him and looked into his eyes. "Don't worry, Judd, I'll never sell Corazon."

He nodded. "If you ever change your mind, I'll give you top dollar."

"I never doubted that."

The screen door snapped behind her, and the sound echoed in her mind like a death knell.

CHAPTER FIFTY-ONE

The New Orleans streets, slick with rain, reflected the lights and colors of the city in the puddles of Canal Street. Katie drove along the old trolley tracks toward the French Quarter. She had a reservation at The Royal Orleans, and she had left Corazon at four in the morning. The drive had been exhausting. Katie was glad her appointment with Aaron was at ten the next morning. She needed a good night's sleep.

The Royal Orleans, the hotel where she had stayed last year, brought back memories of Judd, the drive to Aaron's office, and the reading of J.D.'s Will. She couldn't deny the changes she had seen in the past year.

She and Merit Stetson had become good friends. Merit helped Katie with a simple wardrobe that fit her lifestyle, and they had met for lunch several times over the last few months. Merit's sister, Meredith, and her husband Bob were less antagonistic, and when Max and Adrienne left Corazon, they told her they looked forward to another visit and wanted Katie to come to see them at Mossy Cove.

Dori and Judd were inseparable. Judd took more time to be present in Dori's life, and she bloomed with his attention. The precocious eight-year-old softened Judd's heart.

Judd was never far from her thoughts. Katie's heart ached thinking about him, and her body ached for his touch, his kisses. The year had been a fairy tale, and she was now awake to reality. She seemed destined to love the wrong men, first Gunnar and then Judd. No, Gunnar didn't count because she hadn't really loved him; she only thought she did. *There are worse things than being single. I won't give my heart to another man. What man could ever measure up to Judd?*

She pulled up to Valet Parking and took her overnight case from the trunk. The car was jammed full of her belongings.

The time was close to ten when she entered the room. She had stopped at rest areas to walk when she felt tired and taken a half -hour lunch break. Her dinner had been peanut butter crackers, chips, an apple, and a bottle of water. No wonder her stomach rumbled. Afraid she might fall asleep if she sat down, she headed straight for the bathroom and a refreshing shower.

As she readied for bed, Katie thought of her visit with Aaron Pickering. She had peace she was doing the right thing, but reviewing her year at Corazon kept her awake for a good hour.

Aaron Pickering didn't age. He remained the same distinguished, courtly gentleman as he came and took her hand in both of his. "You're looking well, Katie."

She knew Merit's help with her wardrobe made a statement, and Aaron's discerning eye, noticed.

"How was the trip? I hope you didn't try to do it in one day."

"I did, but I wanted to get everything settled, so I could get home and see my family."

"You haven't changed your mind?" The timbre of his voice lowered and contained a grain of hope.

"No, it wouldn't be right." She sat on one of the large, maroon leather chairs, and Aaron sat on its twin. "I've had an incredible year, an experience few have the opportunity to enjoy."

"You've made a difference in a number of lives. What are your feelings for Judd?"

Katie looked at her hands folded in her lap. She felt calm and in control. She knew Aaron cared about her answer, so she told him. "I love him more than I will ever be able to love another man."

"I see." Aaron leaned toward her, his eyes intent upon her own, his voice sincere. "Have you thought about keeping your half of Corazon as a reason to see him? I know he can't be immune to your charm. Maybe he needs more time. A year is fleeting in the scheme of things."

"No, this is best. I don't want Corazon to be held hostage or as a reason to have me stay. If Judd can't commit, it's better for me to get on with my life. He'll have Dori now and the ranch. He's free to get on with his own life, without regrets. I believe he's changed for the better. J.D. would be happy."

"I'm sure J.D. would be happy, but I think he had a merger of sorts in mind for you."

"Judd will be glad his grandfather didn't have the last say in his personal life." Speaking the words brought with them anxious feelings, and she leaned toward the attorney wanting to get the process finished. "Do you have the paperwork ready for me to sign?"

"I do, but I wish you would reconsider. You will be giving up all rights to the inheritance J.D. wanted you to have."

Katie looked at him steadily. "I know. If Judd has any feelings for me, it won't be because I have a hold over him."

"I must say, I admire your integrity and your fortitude. If your generosity doesn't get Judd's attention, I'm going to have to believe he's gotten dull."

Katie smiled. "I don't want him to be grateful, but I hope to know how he feels sooner rather than later."

The attorney rose and gathered the paperwork for Katie to sign. "I hope you will keep in touch and always consider me a friend. I'll be around for a few years if you need me."

~

At Centaur International, the secretary, Lynn Watkins, showed Katie into Hershal Cleeland's office. Her former boss was the same bear of a man with his full, black beard. She noticed threads of gray on his chin and more at his temples. Hershal stood and walked around the desk. When she took his extended hand, he pulled her into a hug.

"We've missed you, girl." He set her back and looked her over. "You look better than ever. A year's vacation does wonders."

Katie chuckled and said, "I've missed you, too. I noticed my cubicle is being used by Chuck Hamrick."

"You know I couldn't leave such a valuable space empty for a year. It was a business decision, you understand. Your job is still here, and you'll get the next space that comes available."

"I won't be taking someone else's place," Katie said.

"Nah, you know me better than that, Katie girl."

"People change."

"Ah, you've become a cynic? What have the Stetsons done to you?"

It didn't bode well that Katie had to think about his observation.

He motioned her to a chair and sat behind his desk.

"The Stetsons are not so bad. Everyone has flaws," Katie told him.

"Speak for yourself, young lady."

Katie laughed. "Same old Hershal."

"I take offense at that. I'm a mere fifty-two, not even close to old. And thank you for the Christmas card. We thought you'd forgotten us." He leaned back in his chair and studied her. "Okeechobee, huh? You may as well have been on the other side of the world. I called that attorney fellow, Pickering, to ask about you. He was not forthcoming. In fact, he was downright mysterious. Said you were on a year-long sabbatical."

Hershal's look was one of speculation. "That Judd Stetson is a good looking devil. You didn't get mixed up with him, I hope."

When Katie didn't answer, he said, "He came by here the day you left, and he was quite intimidating. I gave him what for, if you know what I mean?"

Katie smiled at Hershal's attempt to get information. She remembered Judd's take on that visit and remained silent.

He caved. "Well, you're here now, and we have one or two projects you might find interesting. Let's see if we can find a space for you."

Walking around her former place of employment felt strange. Her secretary, Mrs. DuPuis, welcomed her back, but others she knew and greeted as they toured the facility regarded her curiously. Even Evan Collins, her superior, seemed remote.

One year had passed, and it might as well have been ten. She was another year older and wiser. Katie tried to bypass self-pity, but the hole created by the loss of seeing Dori and Judd every day left her doomed to a lonely place.

The sights and smells of printing ink and reams of paper brought back memories. She felt far removed from her old life. Katie missed the fresh air, the lowing of the cattle, and the early morning mist rising over the savannas of grass and the hammocks.

She missed Judd, and the ache of it flagged her spirit. Katie was glad to get away from Centaur and return to the home where she grew up. Right now, she needed the reassurance of her family's love. Her father would help her unpack the car later at her apartment.

CHAPTER FIFTY-TWO

Judd looked at the cabin wall and remembering, touched his lip. The physical evidence had healed long ago. The emotional fall-out, however .... Judd sighed and picked up the Bible. It fell open to the folded note from J.D. to Del.

"Del, my love, I'm so sorry for the years we wasted. No, I wasted. I'd give everything I own to go back and start over. You were right. I was a greedy SOB and too full of myself to accept your love and forgiveness. I can't tell you this now because you're gone. They say to a better place. You might be surprised to see me there one day. Sandy was a good man. Today, I mourn the loss of my friend. So, my dearest Del, I've been set free, and have been trying to make right everything I can.

If you have any influence up there, I could use some help. Your repentant husband, Judson"

The note had been written after his grandmother's death. Sandy died last year, which dated the note. He wondered if Katie had seen it. Judd read the words several times, refolded the unsent plea, and returned it to its former resting place in the book of Ephesians.

J.D. had indeed changed in the last five years. Judd thought about J.D. and the conviction and forgiveness he had read between the lines. The note touched him beyond understanding. His grandfather's words made evident the void in his own life.

He replaced the book on the table, relocked the door, and walked to his office.

The pride that always accompanied a new store opening or acquiring another investment asset now failed to give Judd the same satisfaction. He had noticed the lack but attributed the failure to his dysfunctional upbringing and reliving his past disappointments. *Does my happiness hinge on taking business risks or successfully accumulating things? Katie's right. I'm becoming my grandfather.*

⁂

The next day, Judd sat in his grandfather's recliner brooding over Katie's departure. She was trying to force his hand. Like the Rock of Gibraltar, he wasn't moving.

The memory of the day he pulled Katie from the car half-dead from carbon monoxide poisoning took him back to the overwhelming fear he might lose her. The close call brought him to the realization life has an expiration date, and life without Katie a puzzle with a key piece missing. He was thinking about Katie's contributions to Corazon without expecting or taking anything for herself when the screen door opened and Dori appeared. She walked to Judd and settled on one leg. They sat not speaking for a minute.

"Do you hurt?" Dori asked as she tapped his chest. "Katie said when you hate someone, it hurts you inside, and you get sick."

"I don't hate Katie, Dori."

"I know," Dori said in a small, plaintive voice. "You hate my mother."

Judd looked into his daughter's large, luminous eyes, and he saw Rita looking back, not bitter or angry, just sad. He hugged Dori to his chest and swallowed hard to get the words out. "How could I hate your mother when she gave me you." Saying the words released the tightness in his chest, a burden lifted.

Dori put her arms around his neck, and he tightened his hold. *God must give parents hugs like this as rewards,* Judd thought. An old Jimmy Stewart movie came to mind. *I just thought about you, God. Your angels and J.D. must be ringing bells in heaven.*

"Your mother was a beautiful woman. You look a lot like her. She made mistakes. We both did. I believed her biggest mistake was leaving you behind." Judd loosened his daughter's arms and pushed the hair back from Dori's face until he could see her eyes. He wanted her to know the truth as he now saw it.

"I'm the reason your mother left, not you. She didn't like living here, and Corazon became a prison to her. Your mother ran away to a life she thought she wanted ... needed to be happy. I think she left you here to help me, and I failed her and failed you." *That had to be the reason Rita left Dori behind. He had assumed she didn't want to be hampered by a child. Maybe I was wrong.* "Your mother didn't want me to be sad or angry."

Dori tightened her arms around his neck.

Judd sighed. "I made a mistake when I let your Aunt Helene persuade me you needed more than I could give you here at Corazon."

"I love it here, Daddy."

"I know you do, sweetheart, and I'm not going to let you go away from me again." They belonged together. *Thank you, J.D.* Judd was genuinely thankful. *You were right to bring Dori home.*

"Do you feel better now?" Dori asked.

"Feel better?"

"You know. Because you don't hate my mother anymore."

How simple were the answers children found to solve problems over which adults pondered and agonized. "Yes, Dori, I do feel better." And he did for several minutes.

Then Dori said, "I miss Katie." She buried her face in Judd's chest crying, "I love her. Can we go see her soon?"

Judd squeezed his eyes shut, sharing his daughter's pain of being left behind. The hurt drilled deep into his bones, leaving him weakened, his confidence shaken. He struggled internally to revive what had been lost. *She'll be back. I know Katie loves us. She'll be back.*

CHAPTER FIFTY-THREE

Shreveport

Judd filled the doorway of Katie's apartment clad in a casual navy sport's jacket and khaki pants, a perfect fit on his physique. His eyes spoke his intent more than words. She read determination and desire, a refusal to accept anything less than her capitulation. Katie's knees wobbled, and she clutched the edge of the door for support.

Self-consciously, Katie smoothed her hair, embarrassed he would catch her in her running shorts and looking like she felt, sweaty and exhausted after her three-mile run. She had started running as a way to relieve stress and to stay in shape. Katie had been in the process of undressing for a shower when the doorbell rang. "Judd, I ...," and she couldn't finish her words.

Judd looked at her, amused by her discomfort. She looked worn out, and he wanted to hold her in his arms and erase the lines of worry and exhaustion from her face.

"Come back to Corazon with me." Judd's voice deepened. "I need you, Katie," and he added the decisive argument, "Dori needs you. She loves you, and ...," his voice lowered and caught. Insecurity, unfamiliar and unwelcome, swamped him. *She has to know how much I need her peace, her laughter, her love in my life.* The words he said, "We miss you," did not convey the depth of his feelings.

Adrienne's words came back to her. "Some people confuse love with need. Max needs me." *Yes, Judd and Dori need me. Will that be enough? I knew the answer to that before I left.* Katie turned from him, away from the magnetic pull of his compelling blue eyes, pleading, demanding a response she wasn't prepared to give.

Judd felt his stomach clench. She couldn't reject them. *No. I won't accept her denial of what she wants as much as I do.*

"Katie," he said, putting his hand on her shoulder. "I need you like I need my next breath."

Katie stopped. The words sounded like a declaration. *Did his words speak love, or was she grasping for any reason to return to Corazon with him?* Her chin dropped to her chest.

Judd's hand massaged her shoulder as he held her in place. "I love you, Katie Mulholland, and I never thought I'd say those words to another soul, except Dori."

Katie sighed, her eyes closed, her breath leaving her. *I never thought I'd hear you say them.* She turned back to him and searched his eyes. "You don't have to say you love me, now, Judd. I've deeded my half of Corazon back to you and returned the stocks and money. I never wanted them in the first place. You already have what you want."

"I know." he said, not taking his eyes from her own. "Aaron gleefully informed me this afternoon when I met with him. He also told me how you tore up the first check and set J.D. on a different path."

Katie swallowed. "He did?"

"Um humm, and he gave me a piece of his mind when he let me know. I think he's half way in love with you himself."

"I like him, too. He's been lenient with my time away from the ranch, and he's the one who encouraged me to honor my commitment. You haven't made that easy."

Judd took her in his arms, holding her sweaty body close. "I know, but you're wrong about me having everything I want."

"I'm ruining your jacket." She tried to pull away, but he didn't loosen his hold.

Judd was not going to be distracted. "J.D. knew what I needed before I knew it myself. I didn't want him to be right, Katie. I've fought my feelings for you since the first day you arrived at Corazon, *Mi Corazon.*" His hands bracketed her face and he took her mouth in a kiss that lingered. "I want you. Come home with me, Katie. You are my heart. I need you to make me whole." His breath fanned her face, and his lips returned in a searing kiss meant to ignite passion and demand surrender.

Katie pulled away, her flesh weak, her mind wanting to rationalize. "I love you, Judd, but I can't come back without commitment. Loving is the easy part. We come from two different worlds. Maybe you should give that some thought."

Judd grinned. "I've thought of nothing else. Your world is the only one I need. Will you marry me, Katie, have my children, and give me hell when I step out of line? I find myself wanting a family."

Katie threw her arms around his neck. Her heart pumped as if it would beat out of her chest. "When you give a girl an option like that, it can't be ignored. Yes, I'll marry you. Yes, yes, yes." She kissed him to seal the promise.

Judd took a velvet box out of his pocket. When he opened it, a cluster of diamonds winked at her from an engagement ring. "This was my grandmother's ring. I believe it represents a great love interrupted by circumstances. I would like for it to complete its mission, but you may want to choose your own. I'll be happy, whatever you decide."

"Oh, Judd," Katie said, removing the ring from the box. "It's beautiful. Your grandmother would be so proud of you today. The ring is perfect."

Judd took the ring and slipped it on her finger. He raised her hand and kissed it. "Thank you, Katie. Thank you for loving me, loving Dori, and most of all, for choosing me, the one with baggage. I'll make it up to you."

Katie hugged Judd. "I love you, Judd. None of us is perfect, least of all me." J.D.'s Will had brought her full circle from The Blue Adagio to a proposal she didn't see coming. God had been merciful, and she silently promised Him, she wouldn't disappoint. "You know, I think Mrs. Judd Stetson has a nice sound."

Judd laughed. "I won't feel safe until you say, 'I do.'" He pulled her to his chest, savoring the feel of her in his arms, not wanting to let her go. "Thank you, God, for this woman," and he murmured in her ear, "I don't deserve her, but I'll do everything I can to make her happy." He tightened his embrace and lifted his head. "Did you hear that J.D.? I'm going to marry this woman without your bribe or coercion."

Katie pulled back and looked up laughing. "I'm sure J.D.'s happy. I know I am."

"That reminds me," he said, lifting her chin. "I read a note in J.D.'s Bible; a note J.D. wrote to my grandmother. He found his real love, too late. I won't make the same mistake. We need to travel, get away from the ranch, live somewhere else if you want. I'm giving my family more responsibility in managing Stetson Enterprises, to have more time with our family."

Katie ran her fingers across his cheek and through his hair, looking into the face that haunted her dreams. She brought his head down for a kiss, and her prince didn't disappoint. She pulled back to catch her breath and consider his words.

"I'm happy at Corazon, Judd, but travel is something I've always wanted to do. Dori will also enjoy exploring new places." Katie liked the sound of Judd saying, "our family." *We're going to be a family.* "Maybe we should let Dori and my parents know our plans."

"I've already spoken to your father and let him know my intentions. He gave me his blessing and a bit of a scare when he told me I'd have to meet your qualifications which wouldn't be easy."

"That's my dad. What about your parents? How will they feel about me as your wife?"

"They'll both be happy. Max already thinks you're wonderful, and Adrienne has accepted you enough to trust you with her secret. Yes, I know. After you left us to come here, she and Max showed up at Corazon. They had hoped for a different ending. I was stunned.

"My mother shared what she had told you that day in the cabin when you were so insistent I leave. She also told me not to give you a hard time for keeping her secret to yourself. I'm glad you encouraged her to tell me." He remembered his surprise to find his parents at Corazon and theirs to find Katie gone. "She's embarrassed, but we've made peace, and I've seen signs she's mellowing. Max promises to see she stays on her medication."

"I'm so glad she mustered the courage to speak to you. She's carried the burden far too long, and so have you."

"Max helped her get through the confession, but you were the catalyst. I have you to thank for a number of changes in my life. My parents are just the latest. I love you, Katie, and I meant what I said about you completing my life."

Katie hugged him and lifted her mouth for another kiss.

"Go on, get your shower, woman, and get dressed. Dori's waiting at your mom's." As Katie hurried down the hall, Judd said, "Call me if you need help or you want your back scrubbed."

CHAPTER FIFTY-FOUR

Max and Adrienne hosted the Rehearsal Dinner at The Blue Adagio, where Katie and Judd began their journey a little over a year ago.

After the toasts, dinner, and festivities, Judd took Katie outside on the patio enclosed by the parking lot and dock. The manager, by special request, piped Julie London's, "Sentimental Journey," outside.

Judd pulled Katie into his arms and began to dance. "Yes," he said as he kissed her on the tip of her nose, "I remember every moment of that first night. You took my breath away, and I knew you were different from every other woman I'd ever met."

Katie put her arms around Judd's neck. "I thought you were arrogant, handsome, and sad."

"Sad?" Judd stopped and looked at her.

"Yes, your daughter didn't live with you, and I thought how tragic and how much you were missing."

Judd resumed dancing, pulling Katie closer. "Only you would be thinking something like that while I was trying to seduce you. I left so frustrated that night, Little Red Riding Hood, I couldn't sleep."

Katie remembered him calling her that before kissing her senseless. She had felt relief to escape the wolf's plans for her that first night and cried for the loss.

"I was scared, Judd. I was drawn to you, feeling things I hadn't felt before, and I knew whatever happened, the night would end. I didn't want to be just another plaything to a playboy, and you made your thoughts plain enough."

"I can't tell you how many times I've regretted saying those words."

Katie laughed softly. "Had I given in to passion, how would the story have ended, Judd?"

"You would have probably been just another woman in my life, but" and he hesitated, "after the reading of J.D.'s Will, the fun might have continued without having to bring Helene home to get your attention. Instead, quite literally, love had to bite me to get *my* attention." He pulled her close and kissed her forehead when she stepped back, looking appalled. "I'd like to think our ending would be the same, and your love and character would overcome my cynicism in the end."

Katie punched his shoulder. "Am I going to have to worry when beautiful women throw themselves at you?"

Judd was amazed how Katie winnowed out the chaff and homed in on a point. "No. Definitely no. You're all the woman I want or need, and I wouldn't jeopardize what I have now for any number of beauties. As some critic pointed out, 'they're a dime a dozen.' You're one of a kind, Katie, the woman I love."

Katie thought she would never tire of Judd saying he loved her. "Mr. Stetson, I think I'll keep you around for the next half century."

He kissed her, and his passion gave her other nights to think about.

~

Judson Alexander Stetson married Kathryn Kerr Mulholland in September. The church, too small to hold all in attendance, set up a virtual feed to the Fellowship Hall, where the overflow of guests could watch the ceremony. The wedding was on a smaller scale for Society Nuptials. Katie didn't want the event to be a drain on her parent's resources, and they were too proud to accept help. Judd let Katie and her family make the arrangements they wanted.

Because the marriage had international interest, people flew in from around the world. The press ringed the perimeter of the church eager for pictures and any tidbit of information.

Myra was Katie's Matron of Honor. Dori and Karen were giggling flower girls, and Hank looked dignified in his role as ring bearer. Aaron Pickering stood as Judd's Best Man. He winked when she looked at him, and Katie had to squelch the desire to laugh aloud. *This is the happiest day of my life. Thank you, Lord, for Your blessings.*

Judd couldn't stop smiling as he watched his bride approach on her father's arm. Katie glowed, and in a few minutes, she would be his forever wife. *Lord, please help me be the husband Katie needs. Thank you, J.D. Thank you.*

The ceremony took less than forty minutes. Katie's eyes sought Judd's as he slid the diamond and platinum wedding band on her ring finger.

His eyes never left hers as he slipped the ring on and mouthed, "Forever," causing her eyes to mist.

When the minister introduced them as Mr. and Mrs. Judson Stetson, Judd kissed his bride. He caressed her face with his hands and eyes, and he smiled. *Lord, I love this woman.* The unexpected depth of his feelings for Katie humbled him.

They turned as newlyweds and faced their well-wishers. Katie saw some of the people who had contributed to her life: family members, friends, Hershal Cleeland, Merit Stetson, Luke and Pam Albritton.

So many came, even Helene. She had surprised Katie in the dressing room where Katie's mother was arranging her veil. "I'm happy for you, Katie. Judd's a lucky man. I hope he knows it." Her smile appeared forced, but her words and eyes conveyed sincerity.

"Thank you, Helene. I believe you, and I appreciate your kind words."

"I'm hoping we won't be strangers in the future. I love Dori, and I want to be a part of her life. She's all I have left of family." Helene's lips trembled as she said the words and tried to keep her composure.

Katie felt Helene's pain and knew the effort she made to repair the past. Compassion welled up for this successful woman, who had lost so much. "I'm sure Dori will want to spend time with you. We'll make arrangements for future visits."

Max and Adrienne sat in front, with Adrienne weeping into a handkerchief. Katie hoped they were tears of joy. She hugged Judd's parents, and Judd hugged hers before the trip down the aisle. Judd's arm held Katie close as they walked outside into an exploding fuselage of blinding lights.

CPSIA information can be obtained at www.ICGtesting.com
Printed in the USA
LVOW10*2233250315

432054LV00002B/6/P